Danielle,

Rumpelstiltzchen was a mise...
than you would have given him. I...
enough to repent his crimes.

Evil as the filthy creature was, how much worse was his partner? A human betraying his own kind to the fairies. Very much like your stepsisters once did, no?

In gratitude for helping to rid the world of this foul creature and the human traitor, I've decided to offer you a gift. I've freed your stepsister Charlotte from her fairy mistress. Come alone to Stone Grove tomorrow at sunset and I'll return her to you, to deal with as you see fit. Or if you're too weak to see justice done, I'll finish her myself.

Yours,
R

The handwriting was beautiful, every loop and whorl drawn precisely in brown ink. Danielle read the note a second time before passing it to Beatrice.

"What is it, Your Highness?" Andrew—the royal page—whispered.

Talia grabbed Danielle's arm. "From this moment, you go nowhere alone. I want you armed at all times." She turned to Andrew. "Go straight to King Theodore. Tell him to double the guards at the gates and on the walls."

"You know who sent this," Danielle said, staring at the severed toe.

Beatrice folded the note and returned it to the box. "Roudette has entered the palace once before. She would have killed me if not for Talia's aid."

"She's known as the Lady of the Red Hood," said Talia. "Having failed to kill Beatrice, it looks like she's coming for you."

Danielle stared. "You're telling me *Little Red Riding Hood* wants to kill me?"

RED HOOD'S REVENGE

Jim C. Hines

DAW BOOKS, INC.
DONALD A. WOLLHEIM, FOUNDER
375 Hudson Street, New York, NY 10014
ELIZABETH R. WOLLHEIM
SHEILA E. GILBERT
PUBLISHERS
http://www.dawbooks.com

First Printing, July 2010
1 2 3 4 5 6 7 8 9

DAW TRADEMARK REGISTERED
U.S. PAT. AND TM. OFF. AND FOREIGN COUNTRIES
—MARCA REGISTRADA
HECHO EN U.S.A.

PRINTED IN THE U.S.A.

To my parents,
who continue to support and believe in me to this day.

Acknowledgments

You hold in your hands my sixth novel for DAW. According to Wikipedia, six is the number that follows five, but precedes seven. Which you probably knew already, but I've spent the last two days buried in revisions, so my brain is mush and it's helpful to double-check these things. Anyway, like my previous five books, this one wouldn't exist without the help of a great many people:

My wife and children, first and foremost, who continue to put up with me and my bizarre writing habits; my editor, Sheila Gilbert, and everyone else at DAW—Debra, Josh, Marsha, and the whole family; my agent, Joshua Bilmes; my cover artist, Mel Grant—at the time I wrote this, the cover wasn't actually done yet, but based on Mel's previous work for my goblin books, I have no doubt this cover is going to rock.

Thanks also to fellow DAW author Seanan McGuire, fastest beta reader in the West. (Seanan is the author of the Toby Daye books, starting with *Rosemary and Rue*—check 'em out!)

Though she passed away in 2008, I also want to thank Janet Kagan, author of *Uhura's Song* and *Hellspark*. Janet was one of the nicest people in the world, and her support and encouragement were invaluable to me as I was trying to figure out this crazy business.

Huge thanks to my online network of writers, fans, and fellow SF/F readers. The community and friends I've found online at places like Facebook, LiveJournal, my own site at www.jimchines.com, and yes, even Twitter, have been absolutely wonderful. Thank you for your support, your friendship, and just for being there to geek out with.

Finally, thank you the reader. I hope you enjoy this latest adventure of Talia, Snow, and Danielle.

LORINDAR
and surrounding nations

N
E W
S

NORTHLANDS

M. ALLESANDRIA

MOROVA

KAGAN SEA

LYSKAR

HILAD

NAJARIN

CARIFORNE SEA

LORINDAR

ARANTINE OCEAN

ARATHEA

Chapter I

IF QUEEN BEATRICE'S PREDICTION WAS correct, this night would end in death. Unfortunately, Bea had been rather vague about whose.

Danielle pulled her cloak tighter against the chill of the autumn air as she crossed the courtyard. The walls of Whiteshore Palace broke the worst of the wind from the sea, but after sneaking from her bedroom, where the embers of the fireplace warmed the room and Prince Armand warmed the bed, even a gentle breeze was enough to make her shiver.

Leaves rustled against the base of the walls. The flowers on the ivy vines were shut tight against the cold, as were the wooden shutters on the windows. Atop the walls, the guards stayed close to their towers. If anyone did happen to glance into the courtyard, they wouldn't see anything unusual in a lone servant girl hurrying to the storeroom by the stables on some unnamed errand. They certainly wouldn't expect the Princess of Lorindar to be up and about at such an hour, or dressed in such a plain wool cloak and simple gown.

Danielle's sword bounced against her left thigh as she joined her two closest friends. She hoped the sword would be unnecessary, but Queen Beatrice was rarely wrong about such things.

"Is everything prepared?" she asked as she reached the storeroom.

"I'm hurt you even have to ask." Snow White's voice was light and musical, almost childlike in her merriment. She had thrown back her own hood, allowing the breeze to play through her hair. Snow was younger than Danielle, though strands of white mixed with her night-black locks, the price of magic spells cast years ago. The moonlight accentuated the paleness of her face. Beneath her cloak she wore a white scarf and a fitted gown of blue linen that accentuated the curves of her body.

"We've been waiting nearly an hour. I was tempted to do this without you." Dressed in a heavy cape over a rust-colored wool tunic, Talia Malak-el-Dahshat appeared to be the very model of a proper lady-in-waiting. She stood beside the storeroom wall, blending into the shadows. "They're inside, where it's warmer." ·

"Don't mind Talia," Snow said. "You know how cranky she gets when she hasn't pummeled anyone in a while."

"I had to wait for Armand to fall asleep," Danielle said. If the prince had known what she had been doing these past two nights, he never would have agreed to let her risk herself. Especially after Queen Beatrice's warning of blood and death.

Snow grinned. "There are ways of helping a man sleep."

"I don't think the queen would let you cast a sleeping spell on her son," Danielle said.

Snow blinked innocently. "Who said anything about spellcasting? Some magic even you can perform, Princess."

Two years ago, such comments would have left Danielle red-faced and stammering. Now she simply raised an eyebrow. "What makes you think I didn't?" She turned to Talia, ignoring Snow's choked laughter. "Please tell them I'm ready."

"Yes, Your Highness." Talia moved with the grace of a hunting cat as she strode to the door. She made no sound, despite the arsenal she kept on her person. Even on a normal day, Talia carried at least three knives, a set of darts, a small whip, and several more exotic weapons. Tonight she could probably arm an entire squadron of the king's guards.

The storeroom door opened without a sound, thanks to a liberal coating of oil Talia had applied three nights past. The smell of dust and straw wafted from within.

Talia was first through the door, searching the corners before stepping to the right. Snow followed, taking a position on the opposite side. Piles of straw filled the storeroom, rising nearly to the roof and leaving only a narrow pathway down the center. An old spinning wheel sat at the very back of the room. A small, covered lamp hung from the far wall, the blue flame dancing in the draft. The fairy-spelled light would burn nothing but oil, unlike a regular lantern, which could have set the entire room ablaze.

Standing near the back of the storeroom were a middle-aged man and a young girl. A fringe of unkempt brown hair circled the man's otherwise bald scalp. He wore an oft-patched jacket and stained trousers tucked into old boots. He smelled of sweat and mud. The sole of one boot flopped loosely as he stepped forward and dropped to one knee. "Your Highness."

The girl did her best to imitate the movement. Her brown dress was little better than sackcloth, and her limbs were like sticks. She looked no more than five years old, though Danielle knew she should have celebrated her seventh birthday two months earlier.

Danielle slipped a hand beneath her cloak, touching the hilt of her sword. The weapon was glass, the hilt inlaid with hazelwood. This weapon was the last gift she had received from her mother's spirit. Like her slippers, the glass was all but unbreakable, and the hilt fit Danielle's hand as if cast to her flesh. The touch of that gift helped to ease Danielle's anger, and she even managed a smile as she greeted Lang Miller. She crouched before the girl, and this time her smile was genuine. "Hello again, Heather."

Heather ducked her head, hiding behind tangled hair. "Hello."

From a pocket of her gown, Danielle pulled a small, paper-wrapped pastry. She peeled back the paper, revealing a honey-glazed cake made with figs and almond milk. "I saved this from dinner. Prince Jakob likes them, and I thought you might too."

Heather pounced, snatching the cake from Danielle's hand. Lang cleared his throat, and Heather froze.

"My apologies, Your Highness," said Lang. "We've gone too long without proper meals, and I'm afraid my daughter's manners—"

"I understand." Danielle nodded to Heather, who needed no further encouragement to stuff the cake into her mouth as though she feared someone would try to steal it. "She looks like she's not had a proper meal in months."

"Her powers take a great deal out of her, I'm afraid." Lang rubbed a dirty hand through Heather's hair.

"Given those powers, I have to ask why . . ." Danielle gestured at their ragged appearance.

Lang chuckled. "Forgive my boldness, but you were once a commoner yourself, were you not? Locked away in the attic to serve your stepsisters and stepmother. Your father was doubtless a good man, but he couldn't shield you from—"

"Your point, Master Miller?" Danielle hadn't meant to speak quite so sharply. Talia glanced back, eyes narrowed in warning.

"I can't protect her from such people," Lang said. "Nor can I buy her safety. For a poor miller to start flashing gold about would be a siren song to every thief and kidnapper in Lorindar. I'm a simple man, Your Highness. All I want is for my girl to be safe and happy. I can't give her that, but you could."

"You have my word I will do everything in my power to protect her." Danielle forced a lighter tone. "Heather will be well cared for."

"So we have a deal?" asked Lang. Behind him, Heather's tongue darted out to lick the last few crumbs from her lips. She stared up at Danielle, brown eyes wide.

Danielle grabbed a handful of straw and squeezed, feeling the stalks crunch and break in her hands. "The first night I suspected trickery. The second, I began to believe." She gestured to Snow and Talia. "My servants have inspected every corner of this room. If your child can work her magic a third time, then we have an agreement."

"You hear that, Heather?" Lang knelt and squeezed the girl's shoulders. "Spin straw into gold again tonight, and you'll never go hungry again. Princess Cinderella here will take care of you, and when you're old enough, you'll marry her son, Prince Jakob. You'll grow up to be Queen of Lorindar!"

Heather's expression didn't change. Her gaze was empty, almost bored. Either she didn't understand or else she didn't care. She sucked her fingers and trudged toward the spinning wheel.

"We'll hold a public betrothal tomorrow," Danielle said. "When Jakob reaches thirteen years of age, they shall be wed."

"Thank you, Your Highness." Lang took Heather by the hand and whispered into her ear, then backed away. "Come morning, my darling girl will have filled this room with gold. Lorindar will soon be the richest nation in the Arantine Ocean."

Danielle said nothing as she led Lang and the others from the storeroom. Talia pulled the door shut behind them, leaving Heather to her work.

"Snow will find you a place to sleep," Danielle said.

"Thank you." Lang rubbed his throat. "I don't suppose I could trouble one of you ladies for something to drink? All that straw and dust is murderous harsh on the throat."

"Of course." Danielle was still watching Snow, whose brow was slightly furrowed.

Snow studied the storeroom, almost as if she could see through the wooden walls. Slowly, she smiled. With one hand she tugged her scarf free, revealing the shine of silvered glass from her choker.

At that signal, Danielle spun so abruptly that Lang almost walked into her. Forcing herself to relax, she said, "Before we retire, I would like to watch your daughter work, to observe this miracle for myself."

Lang flashed crooked teeth. "I wish you could, but to view such magic is to rob it of its power. I stole a peek myself the first time she told me of her gifts. The gold vanished in an instant, swept away like sweets before a glutton. The shock of Heather's broken magic left the poor girl abed for days. Don't you worry, though. How she does it matters less than the results, eh? Those results will fill your treasury for years to come."

Talia's stance changed so subtly most people wouldn't have noticed. Knees bent, one foot slightly forward, her eyes never leaving Lang Miller. Her hands remained tucked into her sleeves, where Heaven only knew what weaponry awaited.

Snow finished unwrapping her scarf. A choker of oval mirrors and gold wire circled her throat. Lang's smile faltered slightly at the sight. He might not recognize the power of Snow's mirrors, but he knew such decoration was unusual for a simple palace servant.

"Years, you say?" Snow tossed the scarf to the ground and reached into a pouch at her belt, pulling out a piece of straw. "Strange. Most fairy glamours fade within a week at most." She snapped the straw between her fingers and flicked it to the ground.

"Glamour, you say?" Lang's grin tightened as he watched the straw fall. So intent was his gaze that he failed to notice Talia slipping up behind him until her arm snaked around his neck, pressing the tip of a curved Arathean dagger to his throat. His eyes went round, and a faint squeak escaped his lips.

Danielle winced as a thread of blood welled and dripped down Lang's neck. Despite Queen Beatrice's warnings, Danielle intended to do this without bloodshed if she could. "Easy, Talia. We want them alive."

Talia snorted. "Alive and unharmed are two very different things."

"If it's fairy magic, I'm as much the victim as yourself," Lang stammered. "Perhaps the fair folk left a changeling in my daughter's bed. She *has* been behaving most strangely of late, not talking to anyone, refusing food until she starts to waste away—"

"If that's true, then you've nothing to fear." Danielle pushed her cloak back from her shoulders, revealing the sword at her side. The blade slid soundlessly from the leather sheath.

"What's this?" Lang raised his hands. "You're not trying to rob me of my prize, are you?"

"Your *prize*?" Danielle turned, her voice soft. It was a tone that would have sent her son fleeing in fear, but Lang didn't know her well enough to recognize the signs of her fury. He would learn soon enough. "I wonder what her parents would say to hear her described so. Shall we ask them, Lang Miller?"

"My daughter—" Lang's voice turned to a squeak as Talia jerked him around to face the door. He turned his head, trying to pull away from the knife. "What magic—"

"Snow's spells won't harm Heather," Danielle said.

"Her magic will simply ensure that nobody can leave this room by magical means."

"I spent half a day preparing," Snow said cheerfully, moving toward the door. "You're right about the straw, by the way. Nasty stuff."

"Remain silent." Danielle readied her sword and nodded.

Snow yanked open the door.

Inside, Heather sat playing in the straw. Behind her, a tiny man dressed in red sat at the spinning wheel. Had he been standing, his feathered cap would have barely reached Danielle's midsection. Gold straw tangled the white mane of his hair.

He cried out, jumped to the ground, and clapped his hands together.

Nothing happened.

"That won't work." Snow beamed. "The wards are similar to those on the palace wall, the ones that prevent anyone from using magic to enter the grounds. I removed those three nights ago, just for you."

"Rumpelstilzchen?" Danielle rested the tip of her sword on the dirt floor. "Also known as Tom Tit Tot, Whuppity Stoori—"

Rumpelstilzchen covered his ears. "Stop it! What demons whispered those names in your ear, lady?" Spying Lang beyond the door, he hopped up and down, fists clenched. "Lang Miller, you ungrateful traitor!"

"Actually, I'm the demon who learned what you really are," Snow said brightly. "With some help from Ambassador Trittibar of Fairytown."

"Don't blame me for this mess, you miserable dwarf!" Lang shouted. "You're the one who said Lorindar would be an easy target! I told you we shouldn't have come here!" With those words, Lang seized Talia's wrist with both hands, forcing her knife back. He twisted free of her hold and swung a fist at her.

Danielle winced as Talia ducked easily beneath

Lang's punch. In the same movement, Talia stepped close and drove an elbow into his stomach. Danielle winced again.

Shortly after Talia's birth, the fairies of Arathea had blessed her with various "gifts," including superhuman grace and the ability to dance like an angel. Such skill and grace had helped her to become the deadliest warrior Danielle had ever known.

"Never tell the prisoner you want him alive," Talia said, following up with a kick to Lang's knee. "It makes them overconfident."

"Sorry." Danielle rested both hands on her sword. "Tell me, Rumpelstilzchen, how many children have you stolen over the years?"

He watched Snow and Danielle warily. "The boy's right. I should have known better than to set foot on this isle. Your people and your damned treaty, shackling fairykind like dogs."

"*We* shackle *you?*" Danielle looked pointedly at Heather, who continued to play in the straw, oblivious to everything going on around her.

"She's happy," he insisted. "Free of worry or woe."

"With no memory of who she was." Danielle raised her sword. "Victim of the same spell you meant to cast upon *my son*, robbing him of his memories before you stole him away."

"I rescue them from lives of mortal drudgery!" He clapped his hands again, then scowled at the walls.

"A gnomish friend taught me how to block summoning magic," Snow said. "He was much better at it than you. Better looking, too, with a much longer beard."

Outside, Lang shouted, "Get out of my way before I rip you apart, wench!" His voice carried clearly through the open doorway. A moment later, the wall trembled, and a shower of dirt and dust rained down from the roof. Danielle could hear Lang groaning.

Snow shook her head. To Talia, she called out, "Remember, Beatrice is going to make me patch him up when you're through!"

Shouts carried through the courtyard. The guards must have heard the commotion. Even now they would be racing down the stairs.

"Why?" Danielle whispered to Rumpelstilzchen. "Why do you take them?"

"Can't help myself, really." He edged closer. Snow folded her arms, and moonlight flashed from her choker. Rumpelstilzchen raised his hands in surrender. "It started with just the one. Is a single unborn child so much to ask in exchange for turning a peasant girl into a queen? But after the first, I wanted more. Your people will trade anything for the promise of wealth and power. I've collected royal children from lands you've never dreamed of, Princess."

"And now you'll turn them over to me." Danielle was amazed she could still speak with such calmness. This wretched creature had come here to take Jakob, to rip away her son's mind and turn him into another pet prince for his collection.

"You want them back?" Rumpelstilzchen smiled. "Then it seems we've a bargain to arrange. You can keep the girl, of course. I'll throw in a bouncing lad in exchange for your witch lowering her wards. Keep Lang, too. The boy's long since outlived his usefulness."

Danielle's sword hissed through the air. Rumpelstilzchen yelped and dove behind the spinning wheel. The severed feather from his cap drifted down to land in front of his chin.

"You misunderstand me," Danielle said slowly. "You will release *every* child you've stolen, and you will give us their names so that we can restore them to who they were. When I'm satisfied, you will be turned over to Lyskar to face whatever punishment they see fit."

Rumpelstilzchen picked up the feather. "Forgive me, but that doesn't seem like much of a bargain, Highness."

"I'm. Not. Bargaining." Danielle jabbed her sword into the dirt. For three nights she had swallowed her anger, watching helplessly as Lang Miller whisked Heather away each morning. Three nights working to confirm Heather's identity while Snow prepared her spells. Tonight this ended. "Refuse, and I'll give you to Fairytown. I'm told human justice pales at the torments the fairy lords can inflict."

"You've no idea, my lady." Rumpelstilzchen gestured with one hand, and Heather stood. "Very well. Take her. Assuming she *wants* to be returned." He shouted a word in a language Danielle didn't recognize.

Snow yelled a warning as Heather screamed and threw herself at Danielle. Heather's face was feral. She kicked and bit, her nails clawing at Danielle's skin.

Danielle shoved her away, holding her sword high to keep Heather from impaling herself. Rumpelstilzchen ran past, but she trusted Snow to deal with him. As Heather attacked again, Danielle said, "Hevanna V'alynn Presnovich!"

The girl collapsed to the floor. Danielle's throat tightened. She had practiced for hours to make sure she could pronounce Heather's true name, but neither Snow nor Trittibar had known exactly what would happen when Rumpelstilzchen's spell was broken. Was Hevanna's the death Beatrice had seen? The girl had come so close to killing herself on Danielle's blade.

Snow blocked the doorway, but as Danielle watched, Rumpelstilzchen clapped his hands and Snow vanished, reappearing behind him. Snow's wards kept him from escaping, but he could still use his powers within the confines of those wards.

Now, Danielle said silently.

Rats burst from the straw, swarming over Rumpelstilzchen. He screamed and fell, rolling about as their teeth pierced clothes and skin.

Danielle winced at his cries. She hadn't asked the

rats to be quite so bloody, but this wouldn't be the first time animals had responded to the rage in her heart. She turned to check on Hevanna. The girl's eyes were closed, and her breathing came in quick gasps.

"She's all right," Snow said. "She needs rest and real food."

Danielle sagged in relief. She turned to see Talia standing in the doorway. "What about Lang?"

Talia glanced to one side. "He'll live."

She could hear the guards approaching. "Tell them to be careful with Lang. We don't know what tricks he might have learned from a lifetime with Rumpelstilzchen."

Talia nodded and disappeared out the door. Danielle stepped toward Rumpelstilzchen and ordered the rats back.

"Lyskar will kill me!" he gasped.

"They might show mercy once their daughter is returned." Danielle nudged one recalcitrant rat with her toe, pushing him away. "Five years they've hunted for her."

"It's a sickness," Rumpelstilzchen said. "I've tried to stop, but every time I looked upon those sweet, succulent faces, those helpless lads and lasses—"

"You should probably stop talking now," Snow suggested, fiddling with her choker.

"Return every last child," Danielle said, fighting to keep her voice even. "Give us their names. I will ask Lyskar to spare your life."

"You won't leave me even one to—" Something in Danielle's expression made him swallow. "All of them. My word as a fairy."

Snow removed one of the mirrors from her choker and reached toward him.

"No need for magic," He protested, squirming away. "Fairy vows are unbreakable."

"We know," said Talia. Danielle hadn't even noticed

her return. "Just as we know how easily that word can be twisted. You'll free them, but when? Where? In what condition?"

Snow pressed the mirror to Rumpelstilzchen's forehead and whispered an enchantment. When she pulled back, a silver oval marked his skin. "It's not a true fairy mark, but it should bind him just the same."

Danielle sheathed her sword and scooped Hevanna into her arms. "Take care of him while I find a bed for our young princess. I'll contact Lyskar and let them know we have their daughter." She started toward the door, then hesitated. "Thank you both."

"It was fun," Snow said brightly. "I've wanted to try that binding spell ever since Trittibar showed it to me."

Talia was staring at Rumpelstilzchen. "You should have let the rats finish him."

Danielle didn't trust herself to answer. She stepped into the night air and breathed deeply. Two guards were carrying a moaning Lang Miller away. The rest drew to attention.

"Is everything all right, Your Highness?" asked one, obviously uncertain how to react to the sight of his princess and her servants having beaten two strangers into submission.

"It is now." Danielle smiled. Charles was new to service, and, like many, he probably assumed Danielle's glass sword to be a ceremonial weapon meant only for show. "Thank you for your quick response."

"And Queen Bea thought this would be hard," Snow said, brushing straw from her dress.

Danielle said nothing. Beatrice had predicted blood and death. True, the rats had left Rumpelstilzchen bleeding from dozens of wounds, but none of his injuries were serious. Talia had also held back, as far as Danielle could see. Perhaps Beatrice had been mistaken. Or perhaps the danger hadn't yet passed. "Snow, could you—"

"I'll make sure our guests don't try anything," Snow said.

Danielle hugged Hevanna to her chest. "Well done, both of you."

"You too, Princess." Talia gave her a wry smile. "I think you're finally starting to get the hang of this."

CHAPTER 2

DANIELLE AWOKE THE NEXT MORNING to
the sensation of a two-year-old prince plopping his
knee squarely into the middle of her stomach. "Mama,
up!"

She groaned and tousled Jakob's blond hair. "I'm
awake."

Jakob grabbed her hand and tugged her toward the
edge of the bed. "Up!"

Prince Armand stood in the doorway, smiling as he
watched them. Tall and lean, wearing a jacket of dark
green velvet that brought out his eyes, he looked so different than he had when Danielle first danced with him
at the ball. That night he had been polite and formal, a
prince even as he flirted. This morning, he was simply a
father and husband, content to watch his son maul his
wife. "I let you sleep as long as I could, but he was getting upset."

Stifling a yawn, Danielle stood and scooped Jakob
into her arms. She hadn't bothered to change clothes
before crawling into bed, and her gown was a wrinkled
mess.

"Long night?" Armand asked. A neatly trimmed beard
couldn't hide his mischievous smile. "I'm told there was
a commotion in the courtyard near the stables."

"We found Princess Hevanna," said Danielle.

"Hevanna of Lyskar?" Armand stared. "That's wonderful! How—"

"A foreign fairy named Rumpelstilzchen. Beatrice asked that we not announce Hevanna's rescue until she's safely home." Danielle squeezed Jakob until he squirmed, then reluctantly set him down. "Hevanna was the first of twenty-three children he returned to us."

Danielle had been up most of the night finding room for them all and people to look after them. She hadn't gotten to bed until nearly sunrise.

"Oh, no." she said, staring at the window. The sunbeam was nearly vertical. She started for the door, then spun back around. "Where did I leave my sword?"

Armand opened the wardrobe and retrieved her sword from between her skirts. "You left it beside the bed. When I woke up, Jakob was dragging it toward the door. No doubt planning to threaten Nicolette into giving him more sweets."

"Thank you, love." Danielle kissed him, bent to kiss her son, and raced into the hallway toward the stairs. "I'll be back soon!"

Low-floating clouds drifted overhead as she crossed the courtyard, heading for the chapel. Talia was already waiting. She looked alert as ever despite spending the entire night helping Snow and Danielle with the children.

Danielle stifled her envy. Talia hadn't slept a single night since awakening from her cursed slumber. On those nights when she wasn't fighting fairy kidnappers, she passed the hours roaming the palace or practicing her fighting skills or, more recently, checking to make sure Prince Jakob hadn't woken up and snuck out to explore.

"You're late." Talia smirked as she took in Danielle's appearance. "Are you barefoot?"

"Hush!" Danielle glanced behind, half afraid she would see her handmaidens chasing after her. Sandra and Aimee would be outraged at the thought of their princess running about in such a state, straw tangled in her hair, rat fur clinging to her gown. "Is Snow here yet?"

"Still sleeping." Talia stepped aside and pulled open the door. "Magic takes a lot out of her lately. The binding spell wasn't too bad, but then she stayed up using her mirror to try to break Rumpelstilzchen's charms. The little beast didn't even know the true names of half of his stolen children."

The smell of incense greeted Danielle as she entered the chapel. In the past, she and the others would have reported to Queen Beatrice in the secret chambers beneath the palace, but everything had changed after a mermaid attacked Beatrice more than a year before.

A knife to the chest would have killed most people. It would have killed Beatrice if not for Snow's quick intervention. Today the queen's spirit was strong as ever, but her body was so frail she could barely manage stairs without assistance.

Beatrice sat with Ambassador Trittibar of Fairytown near the front of the chapel, heads close together as they spoke.

Danielle hurried to join them. The stone tiles were cool beneath her feet. As she walked, she could feel herself relaxing. She glanced at the stained glass windows in the upper walls, the colored panes laying spells of peace and protection over all who entered. Father Isaac's magic was subtler than Snow's, but it was still powerful.

"I'm so sorry," Danielle said as she reached the queen. "I asked Aimee to wake me, but—"

"I told her I'd have her shoveling stables if she dared." Beatrice gripped a gnarled oak staff in both hands for support as she rose to her feet. "You've earned a night's rest, Danielle."

Danielle kissed the queen's cheek. She smiled to hide her grief at Beatrice's appearance. Everything about

Beatrice was *thin*. Her hands, her hair, even her voice was weaker than before. She wore a heavy cloak lined with rabbit fur for warmth, though the day was relatively mild.

Beatrice was dying. Almost everyone in the palace recognized this, though none spoke of it. Every day she faded a little more.

Danielle blinked and turned to Trittibar. She put one hand to her mouth as she took in the monstrosity of the fairy's wardrobe. Enormous blue feathers sprang from his cap. His doublet was dyed the same shade of blue, though the inside of his slashed sleeves were lined in red silk. His trousers were the green of spring pines, trimmed with white ribbon. Worn leather sandals revealed blue lacquer on his toenails. A rainbow of glass beads braided into his white beard topped everything off.

"That's awful," Danielle said, laughing. "Even for you."

Trittibar glanced down at himself. "The toenails are too much, aren't they?"

"Can your people even *see* color?" Danielle asked.

"Better than yours, in most cases." He brushed his beard, clinking the beads. "Why you humans insist on dressing so blandly I'll never know."

He spread his arms to embrace Danielle. The fairy had a pleasantly earthen smell. He backed away and switched to a more formal tone. "On behalf of my lord and lady, I thank you."

"Thank *you*," Danielle said. "You were the one to spread the rumors of our financial need, and to make sure word of Prince Jakob reached Rumpelstilzchen."

Talia sniffed. "If your lord and lady truly wanted to help, why didn't they hunt the bastard down themselves? How many years has he been running this con? How many more children would he have stolen if Beatrice and Danielle hadn't planned this trap?"

"A trap that would have failed without our assistance," Trittibar pointed out.

"What assistance?" asked Talia. "I didn't see you there last night."

"Rumpelstilzchen is not of Fairytown. We have no responsibility or authority to—"

"Stop this," Beatrice said mildly. She stepped over to embrace Talia, cutting off the debate. "You know as well as I that Rumpelstilzchen might have sensed another fairy. His presence could have undone all of our efforts."

Talia grunted but didn't press the matter.

Though Beatrice tried to hide it, a gasp of pain escaped her lips as she lowered herself back to the bench. "Rumpelstilzchen and his partner are on their way to the docks. Lyskar is sending an escort for Hevanna."

"What about Lang?" Danielle asked. "Did Snow ever learn his true name?"

Beatrice bowed her head. "Lang Miller *was* his true name. He was under no spell. He helped Rumpelstilzchen of his own free will."

"Lang was stolen from his parents," Danielle protested. "How could he help to take other children—"

"Lang was stolen as a babe," said Beatrice. "Rumpelstilzchen was the only family he ever knew."

"He still had a choice," Talia snapped. "Look at Snow. Raised by a woman so evil she hired a man to cut out her own daughter's heart. Snow turned out all right. More or less."

"Don't underestimate the allure of fairy magic," Beatrice said, gazing into the distance. "They can tempt even the most chaste."

Trittibar cleared his throat. "For that reason, perhaps it would be best if Rumpelstilzchen were turned over to my people. I was telling your queen how he's been a blight upon our honor, and I can give you my word he would never again trouble another mortal."

Beatrice shook her head, though she was smiling. "And I was telling Trittibar that if Fairytown wanted

Rumpelstilzchen for themselves, they would need to negotiate with Lyskar." She turned back to Danielle. "You're certain you retrieved all of the children? None of them were harmed?"

"He gave his word." Danielle's fists dug into the folds of her gown. "Some spoke languages even Snow didn't recognize. I've asked Nicolette to see to their needs."

"They've been away from this realm a long time," Trittibar said. "Mortal food will help, as will the passage of time, though the older ones may never fully adjust."

The queen frowned. "When Rumpelstilzchen and Lang were taken alive, I thought perhaps the death I had dreamed was one of the children."

Danielle sat down on the bench in front of Beatrice. "For some of them, death might have been kinder." There had been a Hiladi boy, older than most, who had done nothing but hold his knees and rock, mumbling in a simple singsong. Another girl had screamed herself hoarse, ripping the clothes from her body and gouging her skin until Snow finally cast a spell to make her sleep.

Beatrice took Danielle's hand. "We'll do everything we can for them. You did well, Princess."

For a moment, Beatrice's praise made Danielle feel like a child again, basking in her mother's smile.

The chapel door swung inward and Snow rushed inside, stuffing the last of a muffin into her mouth as she hurried toward them.

"I'm glad you're here," said Beatrice. "I spoke to Lyskar this morning by crystal. The queen asked me to pass along their gratitude to each of you." She smiled. "Once she finally accepted I was telling her the truth, that is. This should strengthen ties between our nations for many years to come. More importantly, Alynn and Francon will have their little girl back."

"Has Heather—Hevanna—woken yet?" Danielle asked. "I'm sure her parents will want to speak with her."

"Not yet," said Snow. "A few of the children have been running wild, but most were exhausted."

"She's slept a long time." Danielle, glanced at the open door. She hadn't checked on the children since last night. "Are you sure the spell hasn't—"

"I checked in on them myself earlier this morning," said Trittibar. "I promise you Hevanna will recover. In time, most of her experiences will fade like a bad dream."

Danielle's response went unspoken as a boy in the green cap and jacket of a royal page burst into the chapel. His footsteps echoed against the stone as he ran, a small wooden box clutched in his hands. Beatrice stood, her face tight with pain and something more.

"What's wrong, Andrew?" Danielle asked.

"The carriage . . . the prisoners." Andrew tucked the box under one arm and used his sleeve to blot sweat from his young face. His cheeks were flushed, and he struggled to catch his breath. "They were attacked. Less than an hour ago."

Talia was already moving toward the door. There should be no danger here, but Talia wasn't one for taking chances. She checked outside, then pulled the door closed.

"How did it happen?" asked Beatrice. Her voice was calm and commanding. She sounded almost like her old self.

"Nobody saw who did it," said Andrew.

"Impossible." Talia stopped behind Andrew, arms crossed. "The road switchbacks down the hillside, in plain view of the docks."

Andrew backed away. "Whoever it was, he must have been hiding in the bushes beside the road. The dock-workers heard the screams, but by the time they arrived, it was over."

"Did anyone survive?" Danielle asked.

"I'm sorry, Highness."

Danielle fought to keep her face composed. She knew everyone in the palace by name, but the carriage had left while she was still asleep. Who had been driving, and which of the guards had accompanied them? Which of her friends had died today?

Beatrice closed her eyes. "They died violently." It wasn't a question.

"They found this with . . . with the bodies." Andrew held out the box.

Carved in crude letters on the lid was the name *Danielle de Glas*. Danielle's name from before she married Armand. She reached out, but Talia was faster, snatching it from Andrew's hand. She held the box to the light, examining the hinges, then turning it about to study the latch, a simple iron hook through a small loop.

The box appeared plain enough, made of unfinished wood and hammered iron. It was no wider than Danielle's hand.

Snow's choker brightened slightly. "I don't see any magical traps."

Talia set the box on a bench and dropped to one knee. A knife appeared in her hand, and she used the blade to unfasten the catch. The tip of the knife slowly raised the lid to reveal a folded note sealed with red wax. Talia opened the lid, scooped out the note with her knife, then swore.

"What's wrong?" Danielle asked.

Talia turned the box so they could see the severed toe, barely larger than a cashew, sitting on a velvet cushion. She cracked the seal and unfolded the note, then passed it to Danielle. Brown bloodstains marred the corner of the page.

Danielle,
*   Rumpelstilzchen was a miserable wretch who deserved far worse than you would have given him. I promise in his final moments, he lived long enough to repent his crimes.*

Evil as the filthy creature was, how much worse was his partner? A human betraying his own kind to the fairies. Very much as your stepsisters once did, no?

In gratitude for helping to rid the world of this foul creature and the human traitor, I've decided to offer you a gift. I've freed your stepsister Charlotte from her fairy mistress. Come alone to Stone Grove tomorrow at sunset and I'll return her to you, to deal with as you see fit. Or if you're too weak to see justice done, I'll finish her myself.

Yours,

R

The handwriting was beautiful, every loop and whorl drawn precisely in brown ink. Danielle read the note a second time before passing it to Beatrice.

"What is it, Your Highness?" Andrew whispered.

Danielle barely heard. It was more than two years since she had left Charlotte behind in Fairytown. She still prayed for her stepsister some nights, but for the most part she had tried to push those memories from her mind. It was a part of her life she preferred not to think about.

She remembered the cooing of the doves at her wedding. The birds had lined the eaves of the palace, while the rats watched hidden in the grass. Her only friends, come to celebrate as she and Armand were presented to the crowd.

The doves had swooped down, attacking her stepmother and stepsisters. They blinded her stepmother, who eventually died from her injuries. Charlotte and Stacia survived, but the attack left them both scarred.

Danielle grimaced as she examined the toe. The skin was wrinkled, the nail ragged and yellow.

Her stepsisters had conspired to kidnap Armand and kill Danielle. Closing her eyes, she could still see the despair and hatred on Charlotte's face as she prepared to murder Danielle and her unborn son.

Talia grabbed Danielle's arm, yanking her back to the present. "From this moment, you go nowhere alone. I want you armed at all times." She turned to Andrew. "Go straight to King Theodore. Tell him to double the guards at the gates and on the walls."

To Andrew's credit, he waited for Beatrice's nod before rushing off.

"You know who sent this," Danielle said, staring at the severed toe.

Beatrice folded the note and returned it to the box. "Roudette has entered the palace once before. She would have killed me if not for Talia's aid."

"She's known as the Lady of the Red Hood," said Talia. "Having failed to kill Beatrice, it looks as though she's coming for you."

Danielle stared. "You're telling me *Little Red Riding Hood* wants to kill me?"

"Asked Cinderella of Sleeping Beauty," Snow added with a smile. She plucked the toe from the box. "Interesting choice of bait. It was a clean cut, for whatever that's worth. Look at the bone, where—"

"I'd rather not," said Danielle.

Talia pushed back one sleeve, revealing a pale scar that cut across her forearm. "Roudette gave me this the last time she was here. She's stronger than she looks. Faster, too. Some say she's every bit as fierce as the wolf from her story."

Danielle wanted to laugh, but she knew Talia wouldn't take a lesser threat so seriously. "How much of her story is true? There was a wolf and a hunter both."

"Nobody knows." Trittibar looked more somber than Danielle had ever seen him. "Roudette is the hunter now."

Danielle sank onto the bench beside the queen. "Why would she want to kill me?"

"A better question is who hired her to kill you," said Talia. "Roudette isn't cheap, but for the right price, she'll murder any target you choose. King or newborn, it makes no difference."

Trittibar tugged the braids of his beard. "When she attempted to kill your queen, she carried a fairy-forged blade, hoping to frame my people for the murder. Had she succeeded, it could have ended the treaty and renewed the war between our people."

"She seems to prefer fairy targets," Talia added. "Fairies and their human allies."

"Allies like us." Danielle felt strangely calm, like an actress playing a role. None of it felt real. Who could possibly hate her so much that they would pay an assassin to kill her? Charlotte and Stacia were different. Their hatred had been personal. Roudette was a stranger. "You're sure this is a trap? We *did* capture Rumpelstilzchen. Maybe this is her twisted way of thanking us."

"She sent you a *toe*," said Snow. "That's not the sort of thing you give your new best friend. Except maybe among goblins. I hear they prepare the toes of their enemies as snacks, smoking the meat and—"

"Roudette doesn't do favors," Talia said. "She means to lure you out and kill you."

The flat certainty in Talia's words broke through any remaining doubt. "So why not sneak into my room and cut my throat as I sleep?"

Snow beamed. "Roudette can't get within a hundred paces of the palace without me knowing. Talia gave as good as she got in that last fight. There was more than enough blood for me to be able to key the wards in the wall directly to Roudette. She won't come here a second time. You're safe here."

"There's no such thing as safe," Talia said. "Snow's right, though. Any two-penny fortune-teller could have warned Roudette what would happen if she tried to enter the palace."

"So why bother with Charlotte?" Danielle asked. "Roudette had no problem ambushing Rumpelstilzchen on the road. Why not wait until the next time I leave and do the same with me?"

"You'd be under guard," said Snow. "And Roudette might have a time limit. If she was paid to make sure you died by a certain day, she might have no choice but to lure you out."

Talia turned to Snow. "Use the toe to scry on Charlotte. If you're lucky, you'll get a glimpse of Roudette as well. From Roudette's note, we have until tomorrow night before she tries again. I'll talk to Father Isaac about strengthening the wards."

"What about . . ." Danielle's voice trailed off. They had already decided to let Roudette kill Charlotte. She looked toward the altar at the front of the church. Charlotte's crimes had certainly earned death, and yet—

"Danielle?" Beatrice's brown eyes, so similar to Armand's, never left Danielle. Those eyes were gentle, even compassionate, as though she knew exactly what was going through Danielle's mind.

Talia looked from Beatrice to Danielle. "You've got to be joking."

"You think I should let Roudette kill my stepsister?" Danielle asked.

"I think I should have killed her myself when I had the chance," Talia shot back.

"You're probably right." Danielle watched the queen, trying to read her expression. How could she explain her conflict to Talia when she didn't understand it herself? All she had to do was sit back and do nothing, and her stepsister would die. Danielle wouldn't even have to be the one to order Charlotte's death. Danielle's hands would be clean.

Beatrice nodded ever so slightly.

"We left Charlotte in Fairytown," Danielle said. "Alone, bound to a fairy master. It's possible the years have changed her."

Snow glanced up. "It's also possible beanstalks will start growing out of my—"

"Roudette took Charlotte, but if I do nothing, then I share the responsibility for Charlotte's death."

"So where's the problem?" asked Talia. "For all we know, Charlotte was the one who hired Roudette to kill you!"

"Hired her with what? Even if she wanted me dead, she'd never cut off her own toe to do it."

"*If* she wanted you dead?" Talia repeated. "Were you paying attention the last time she tried to kill you? If she were in your position, she'd let you die in a heartbeat."

"I know," Danielle whispered, thinking of her mother. "That's why I have to be better than she is."

Talia turned to the queen. "She's mad."

"So we do it your way," Danielle said. "We let her die. What then? You think Roudette will simply give up and go home? If threatening Charlotte doesn't lure me into the open, Roudette will keep killing until she finds someone who will. At least this way we know where she'll be."

"Never let the enemy define the battle," Talia said. "Choose your own battlefield. Make her come to you, on your terms."

"Talia is right." Beatrice pushed herself to her feet, leaning heavily on her staff. "You cannot go. Roudette would likely kill you if you tried to save your stepsister. You're Princess of Lorindar. Think of your people. Think of your husband and child. You know what it's like to lose a mother. Would you do that to Jakob?"

"That's not fair," Danielle whispered.

"I know." Beatrice took her hand. "Snow and Talia will go to Stone Grove. They will save Charlotte if they can." That last was spoken with a stern look at Talia. "However, their first priority will be to protect you by stopping Roudette."

Trittibar cleared his throat. "I would like to accompany them, Your Majesty. Assuming Talia will allow it. The Lady of the Red Hood has tormented my people for many years. Those I serve would be pleased to see her punished for her actions."

Talia looked as though she had eaten something sour, but she said nothing.

"So my friends risk their lives while I stay safely hidden behind these walls?" Danielle knew Beatrice was right, and she hated it. Snow had magic enough to protect herself, and Talia had fought Roudette before and lived. What could Danielle do? Summon a mob of squirrels to pelt Roudette with nuts?

"I understand how you feel," said Beatrice. "What do you think it's like for me each time I send you out? But this is what must be done." To Snow and Talia she said, "Stone Grove is less than a day's ride. You leave tonight."

Snow groaned. "We have until sunset tomorrow. Wouldn't it be better to leave *after* a good night's sleep? Maybe midmorning, after a nice warm breakfast?"

"Giving Roudette time to rest while she waits for us?" asked Talia. "I'd rather face a groggy murderer, myself."

Beatrice smiled. "Go and prepare for your journey. And be safe."

CHAPTER 3

TALIA UNSTRAPPED TWO FLAT KNIVES from her right thigh, where the hem of her tunic had hidden them from casual view. She handed both weapons to Danielle. They were simple single-edged blades. Not great for throwing, but with Danielle's aim, that hardly mattered. Talia had sharpened both knives herself less than a week ago, and they should serve Danielle well if she was attacked in close quarters. "Your sword is good, but you'll be safer with a few extra blades hidden away."

"Assuming Jakob doesn't get his hands on them." Danielle examined the sheathed knives. "Snow's wards should keep Roudette away from the palace."

"Do you want to trust your life to magic?" Talia opened the chapel doors and checked the courtyard. "Do you want to trust Jakob's? Better to be safe, Princess."

Danielle nodded and hiked up her gown so she could strap one of the knives to her right leg, below the knee. Talia helped her attach the other to her forearm.

"Stay in the palace until we return," said Talia. "If you sneak after us, thinking you can help, I swear I'll kill you myself."

Danielle pulled the sleeve of her gown over the knife. "I won't. I don't like the idea of letting a killer confine me to my home, but—"

"Roudette is no ordinary killer." Talia tugged Danielle's sleeve down, then studied her to make sure the weapons weren't noticeable. "Do you remember what I told you when your stepsister tried to kill you in your room?"

"Forget dignity and scream like a frightened child," Danielle recited, smiling slightly. "I'll be fine, Talia. I'm more worried about you and Snow and Trittibar."

"Don't be." Talia escorted Danielle back to the northwest tower, making sure the extra guardsmen were at their posts. She grabbed the closest by the sleeve. "Princess Danielle is to go nowhere without armed escort, by order of Queen Beatrice."

He gave a quick bow. Unlike Danielle, Talia had never been friends with most of the palace staff, but they knew who she was and that she served Queen Beatrice directly.

Danielle sighed. "Talia—"

"Remember, if you evade your bodyguard, he's the one who gets disciplined for losing you." Talia hurried away, heading for the royal quarters and the hidden stairway within the fireplace.

The room shared by the king and queen was empty. Talia jabbed a hidden stone in the fireplace to open the passage, then descended through the darkness until she reached the bottom of the stairs. There, oil lamps flickered beside an arched doorway. In the armory beyond, weapons of all shapes and sizes hung on whitewashed walls. Most were bladed, ranging from a tiny razor hidden within a gold ring to a sword as tall as Talia herself. There were also staves, clubs, and various missile weapons. Talia had bought or commissioned many of them herself.

A mosaic map of Lorindar covered the ceiling. Slate ships moved through lapis lazuli seas, each tile magically bound to an actual ship of Lorindar.

Talia studied the walls as carefully as a master chef

selecting the ingredients for a banquet. She picked out several throwing knives, as well as two curved Arathean daggers long enough for hand-to-hand fighting. A single-edged short sword went onto the back of her belt. She also retrieved her zaraq whip, a spindle-shaped weapon with a thin line of troll hair connected to a sharp lead weight.

Rubbing the scar on her forearm, Talia moved to the far side of the wall where several sets of armor hung from wooden pegs. She grabbed a pair of black leather bracers and tried them on, making sure they wouldn't prevent her from drawing the knives on her arms.

From there, she passed through the far doorway into the library and laboratory where Snow was working. Shelves lined the walls, bowing under the weight of collected scrolls, tomes, and other oddities. Old barnacle-encrusted jars filled one shelf. Another held a small, horned skull with a crack down the center. A troll-hair weaving sat in a discarded lump in the corner.

Snow didn't appear to have noticed Talia's presence. She sat on a stool in front of her famous mirror. Beside her was a scarred and heavily stained wooden table, currently bare save for Roudette's box and an untouched mug of tea.

The magic mirror was as tall as Snow herself, liquid smooth and framed in platinum. At the moment, it showed only Snow's reflection as she grimaced and leaned closer, examining her appearance. She touched the corner of her eye, stretching the skin as if to hide the faint wrinkles there.

"You're beautiful," said Talia. "Get over it."

"I know." Snow spoke without conceit or pride, but she didn't pull away. "I doubt I'd be the fairest in the land anymore, though."

"Depends on which land." Anything more Talia might say would only make them both uncomfortable. Instead, she fell back on familiar banter. "Are you going to spend the whole day admiring yourself? We *do* have a killer to catch, remember?"

Snow brushed her fingers through her hair, picked at a few white strands, and grimaced.

"If it bothers you so much, there are dyes—"

"That's cheating." Snow tossed her hair back and flashed a carefree smile. "My mother used them all as she got older. It's not the same." She reached over to take Roudette's note from the box.

Talia moved closer, hopping up to sit on the edge of the table where she would have a better view.

Snow touched the note to the glass. "Mirror, mirror, hear my plea. Show the killer Red to me."

"Not bad," said Talia. "The second part was a little forced, but it's better than some of your other rhymes."

"Hush." Snow stuck out her tongue. Her reflection rippled and faded. Red smoke filled the glass, swirling like bloody fog and obscuring all but a shadow that might have been a woman.

"Didn't this happen last time, too?" Talia asked.

"It's her cape." Snow picked up the cup of tea and sipped absently. Her face wrinkled. She whispered a quick spell, and steam began to rise from the mug. "It's enchanted to deflect magic."

"A useful quality for an assassin."

Snow took another drink, still frowning at the mirror. The smoke thinned briefly, and for a moment Talia spotted hard-packed earth and pale tree roots. A blur of brown passed through the image.

"What was that?" Talia asked.

"I'm not sure." Snow pressed her fingers to the glass, but the smoke had already obscured whatever it was. "Could have been her shoes, or it could have been a frightened chipmunk."

"How close is she to Stone Grove?" Talia grimaced. "Trittibar's fairy falcon is fast enough to make the trip in an hour. If we had to, we could—"

"She's already there." Snow stared at the mirror. "I can't see her, but those roots were definitely from Stone Grove."

"That's impossible. Even at a full gallop, she couldn't have killed Rumpelstilzchen and made it back so quickly." Talia squinted at the red smoke. "Are you sure your magic is working right?"

Snow set down the mug and the note and turned to face Talia. "You're welcome to take a turn if you think you can do better. My mother didn't exactly leave a book of instructions for this thing. I could spend the rest of my life trying to unravel its secrets."

"So if Roudette's hidden, what about Charlotte?"

Snow plucked Charlotte's toe from the box and held it to the mirror. "Mirror tell us what you know. Find the bitch without a toe."

"I like that one," said Talia.

The red smoke thinned enough to make out Danielle's stepsister. Tree roots as thick as Talia's leg snaked past Charlotte's body. Her arms were bound at the wrists and elbows, and had been secured to the tree roots. Her legs were stretched out, tied at the ankles. A blood-soaked bandage circled her right foot.

"There's your proof." Snow pointed to the smoke that continued to dance and curl at the edge of the image. "Roudette's with Charlotte, close enough that her cape is interfering with my mirror." Almost as an afterthought, she added, "She looks awful."

"It's a good look for her." Charlotte's pale face was filthy, save where tears had streaked the dirt. The brown curls of her hair were short and knotted. Old scars around her eyes marred her once-smooth beauty. She wore only a torn, filthy gown which hung loosely from her shoulders. Talia leaned closer. "What's wrong with those trees?"

Snow massaged the back of her skull. "You really need to spend more time in the library. One of the earliest battles between humans and fairies was fought at Stone Grove. The dryads slaughtered more than a hundred men before our wizards managed to petrify the first of the trees. As the battle shifted in our favor, the dryads changed tactics, toppling their trees onto the attackers. They say the last dryad gathered up the seeds of her companions and disappeared. One day, when their new trees mature, they'll return to seek vengeance against us."

Talia shrugged. "Let me know when they're all grown up, and I'll deal with them too."

Charlotte's eyes were round with fear, her focus jumping constantly from one point to the next. She reminded Talia of a frightened animal.

"She's been dragged from Fairytown, maimed, and tied up in a fairy graveyard," Snow said. "I think it's safe to say she's not working with Roudette."

Talia turned away in disgust. Charlotte was a cruel, selfish fool who had latched onto anyone she believed could bring her power. Her stepmother, her sister Stacia, the Duchess in Fairytown. If Roudette had asked, Charlotte almost certainly would have helped her of her own free will.

"How could Roudette make it back so quickly?" Talia asked. She toyed with the idea that Roudette had hired a partner. Roudette could have sent someone else to dispatch Lang and Rumpelstilzchen. But the Lady of the Red Hood worked alone, and the butchery had been too quick, too thorough.

"Magic." Snow guessed. "It helps to explain why nobody's ever managed to capture her."

Talia hopped from the table. "Get your things ready. I think I'm going to pack a few more knives."

When Snow was a child, she used to stay up half the night, reading by light that she captured from the moon and stored in smooth stones from the river. These days her body demanded more rest. She had managed a quick nap before dinner, but it wasn't enough. Within an hour of leaving the palace, she found herself nodding off, jerking awake when her body tilted too far in the saddle.

The tiny snores coming from her belt pouch only made her grumpier. In order to stay inconspicuous, Ambassador Trittibar had shrunk down to his natural size, no larger than a rag doll. Most of the time, the fairy ambassador used magic to make himself appear more or less human, presumably so nobody would step on him by mistake. Not to mention what could have happened to the poor fairy when Prince Jakob was teething.

The fog had begun to roll in from the east. Taking the coastal highway meant Snow could see the Arantine Ocean through gaps in the woods to her left. It was a nice change from her previous view of the trees and the backside of Talia's horse.

Talia glanced over her shoulder. "How are you feeling?"

Snow covered a yawn. Before she could speak, Talia pulled her horse to a halt, blocking the road.

"You're falling asleep in the saddle," Talia said.

"I just need to stretch." She climbed down from the horse and tossed back the hood of her riding cloak, rubbing the back of her neck with one hand. She dug through her saddlebag until she found a small parcel of willow bark. Normally she would have brewed a tea with the bark, but in a pinch, it could be used raw. She popped a strip into her mouth and grimaced at the bitter taste.

"You're eating trees!"

"Only the bark," Snow said. "To keep my back from tightening up. We don't all have fairy magic coursing through our bodies to keep us graceful and limber, you know."

"Your back," Talia repeated. "Right." Concern made

her words unusually awkward. "You've used a lot of magic this week. Preparing the storeroom for Rumpelstilzchen, breaking the spells on the children, then tracking Charlotte and Roudette. Are you sure you're ready for this? Your injury—"

"Is fine. Tymalous said so himself." Snow threw the rest of the bark back into the saddlebag and yanked it shut. In truth, her head had been throbbing for most of the day. "If the king's healer says my skull is healed, who are you to argue?"

"I'm the one who sees you every day, who sees the way your eyes tear up when you overexert yourself magically and notices the way you rub the back of your head when you think nobody's watching. I'm the one who saw you crumpled on the steps after being slammed against a wall by a mermaid's angry air spirits."

Snow said nothing. Tymalous *had* pronounced her skull healed from the fracture she had received during that fight. He had also warned her that some damage yet lingered beneath the bone and that the effects of such injuries could last for years. All of which Snow already knew. Just as she knew she wasn't going to spend the rest of her days as an invalid.

"You need me," Snow said. "You need my magic to help sneak up on Roudette and counter whatever tricks she might have prepared."

Talia slid from her horse. She lowered her eyes, her words momentarily losing their edge. "Not if it's going to hurt you. Trittibar can be my magical backup."

"Trittibar?" Snow laughed, nearly spitting out her bark. "You two would kill each other before you even reached Roudette." She sighed and rubbed her eyes. "I promise to rest once this is over. Will that satisfy you, Mother? I swear you're as bad as Danielle."

"Rest now. We can ride double."

Snow stiffened. "I have some medicines in here that

will wake me up. Give me a moment to find them, and I'll be—"

"How many times have you lectured me about those medicines?" Talia demanded. "How each one takes its toll, and how most of the time the best thing for a body is rest, not drugs?"

"When did you start listening to me?" Snow muttered.

There was a time she would have joined Talia without hesitation. They had ridden together countless times on missions for Queen Bea. Snow had grown up without brothers or sisters, but she couldn't imagine a sister being as close as she and Talia had become over the years. Two princesses, both exiled from their lands, both given a new home by Beatrice.

Sometimes she wondered if that wasn't why Beatrice had sought them out, to unite each of them with the one person who might understand what the other had lost. Talia had become her closest friend, but things had changed last year when Snow learned Talia's feelings for her went beyond friendship. Neither of them had spoken of it, and most days Snow did her best to pretend she didn't know, but—

"Stop wasting time," said Talia. "Even if you make it to Stone Grove without falling off your horse, the last thing I want is an exhausted sorceress flinging magic around while I'm trying to fight a killer."

Snow stuck out her tongue, but Talia had a point. She finished buckling the saddlebag and surrendered to logic, walking over to join Talia.

Talia's grip was strong and calloused. She hauled Snow up with ease, settling her in the front of the saddle. Mumbled protests erupted from Snow's belt pouch. She settled the pouch into her lap with a quick apology to Trittibar for nearly sitting on him. She tucked her cloak around her body, then pulled her hair over one shoulder, tucking it into the cloak so it wouldn't blow in Talia's face.

"Relax," said Talia. "I told you I wasn't going to drop you."

Snow leaned back. "How am I supposed to relax? It's like trying to sleep on a weapons rack."

Talia snorted, but she adjusted her belt, sliding several knives around past her hips and removing a pair of hooked throwing blades from the leather vest she wore over her shirt. "Better?"

Snow didn't move as Talia reached around her to take the reins. Talia's body was more tense than usual, her arms stiff against Snow's sides. The saddle wasn't built for two, and the curve of the leather pressed their bodies together.

"Try not to drool in your sleep." Talia squeezed her knees, urging the horse forward. A cluck of her tongue brought Snow's mount following behind.

"Aren't you going to sing me a lullaby?" Snow asked, falling back on familiar teasing to hide her discomfort.

"Sorry. The kind of songs you like never sound as good sober."

Snow settled her body, leaning her head on Talia's shoulder. What was she worried about? Whatever feelings Talia might have for Snow, Talia was also the last person who would ever take advantage of someone in their sleep. Or awake, for that matter. Snow had known priests who flirted more than Talia.

"You smell like oil," Snow whispered.

"From the knives. Go to sleep."

Snow closed her eyes. "Wake me when it's time to kill Red Riding Hood."

CHAPTER 4

~~~~~~⊹~~~~~~

SNOW DIDN'T EXPECT TO GET MUCH SLEEP, but between the rhythm of the horse's hooves and the warmth of Talia's body, she drifted off almost immediately. Talia woke her twice during the night to switch mounts.

The third time she woke, they were coming up on a small farmhouse. Snow's head lay in the crook of Talia's neck, and Talia's arm circled Snow's waist, holding her in place. The skies were dark, but only for two or three hours longer, judging from the position of the moon.

Ambassador Trittibar had crawled from her pouch at some point during the night. He now sat comfortably between the horse's ears, his arms twined in the mane for support.

Snow grimaced and spat. Bits of willow bark crusted her lips. She wiped her mouth on the corner of her cloak.

"I made you spit that stuff out last night," Talia said. "I was afraid you'd choke."

"Thank you." She sat up and tried to rub the stiffness from her neck. Her head felt better, but she needed a real night's sleep before she'd be fully recovered. She touched her choker, whispering a quick spell to try to locate Roudette.

"Anything?" asked Trittibar.

Snow shook her head. "It's that cape of hers again. I was lucky to see anything at all yesterday. Who wears such a garish thing, anyway?"

Talia jumped down. "Eastpointe is just ahead, which means Stone Grove should be west of here. We'll have a better chance of catching Roudette off guard if we go on foot. Try to see Charlotte while I talk to these people about watching the horses."

Snow gripped the saddle with both hands and lowered herself to the ground. Spying on Charlotte would have to wait for more urgent matters. Leaving Trittibar to watch the horses, she disappeared into the woods. Much as she enjoyed these outings for the queen, there were times she preferred to stay at the castle where she could enjoy cooked meals, a real bed, and most importantly, a proper privy.

By the time Talia returned, Snow was digging through the saddlebags for something to eat. She grinned when she saw what Talia had packed. "You remembered!"

"Always," Talia said.

Snow pulled out the small basket and yanked back the top. Her mouth watered at the smell of finely ground figs, saffron, and a touch of nadif spice, all fried in dough and glazed with caramel. She pulled off a few crumbs for Trittibar, then took an enormous bite for herself.

"Charlotte?" Talia asked.

"Sleeping, as far as I can tell," Snow said around a mouthful of food. "Roudette's cape shields Charlotte, but the toe gives me enough of a connection to pierce the smoke. That interference means they're still together. Did you bring anything to drink?"

Talia was already transferring some of their belongings to her person. She grabbed a small leather bottle, took a drink then handed it to Snow.

"How can you drink this stuff?" Snow's nose wrinkled at the burned, bitter smell of cold coffee. She gulped it down, rinsing her mouth the best she could. If nothing else, the coffee helped shove the last of the fatigue from her mind.

She tossed the bottle back to Talia. Gripping one of the smaller mirrors on her choker, she whispered a command. Gold wire unwound from the glass, releasing the mirror into her hand. The edge was rimmed in gold leaf, protecting her fingers from the sharp edges.

"What are you doing?" Talia asked.

"Roudette's expecting Danielle. If we can sneak up on her, great. If not, I thought disguises might help us get close enough to take care of her." She stared into the mirror, summoning an image of Danielle from the day before. Holding that image in her mind, she returned the mirror to her choker.

She watched her hands change, losing the pale perfection of her own skin and taking on the light tan of Danielle's. She raised her left hand, admiring the gold band on the fourth finger. "If Danielle polished this thing any more often, it could blind you."

Talia pursed her lips. "Not bad. Your voice sounds the same, but you don't talk like Danielle does. You definitely don't move like her, but Roudette shouldn't know the difference. So what makes you think Roudette won't simply sneak up and kill you?"

"As if you'd let that happen." Snow tapped her choker. "Besides, she can't come within ten paces without my knowing. Remember the wards on the castle walls? I've got the same spell in my mirrors."

"And if she decides to shoot you from a distance?"

Snow shrugged. "Roudette prefers to kill up close. She likes to be sure."

"Be careful," said Talia. "Don't overdo it with the magic before we've even found her."

"I'm fine," Snow said lightly. "The mirror does most of the work."

"What about my disguise?" asked Talia. "There's no way Roudette will have forgotten what I look like."

Snow grinned and touched another of her mirrors.
"You're going to love it."

"I can't decide how I'm going to kill you," Talia said as
she made her way through the woods. The trees were
older here, the canopy thick with leaves whose colors
were just beginning to change. The ground was soft
earth, bare of all save mushrooms, rotting branches, and
fallen leaves. "I thought about beating you with this
walking stick, but there's also something to be said for
using your bare hands."

"It's a great disguise." Snow's insistence would have
been more convincing without the smirk. "Can you
think of any way to make you look *less* like Talia Malak-
el-Dahshat?"

She had a point. This was about as different as Talia
could get while remaining human. She grabbed the mirror pinned to her cloak, turning it to study her reflection.
A thick gray beard covered a pale, wrinkled face. Her
scalp was bald, spotted by age. One milky eye stared off
at an odd angle. The other was pale blue. Talia reached
up to touch an oversized nose. "Where did you come up
with this?"

"The library," said Snow. "That's Gregor Vindamar, a
very important wizard. He discovered the four laws of
binding. If not for him, I'd never have been able to make
this choker."

"What about the staff?" Talia asked. Her voice was
different as well. Deep and raspy.

"You couldn't be clumsy if you tried. Your grace gives
you away." Snow reached over to rap the staff, which she
had shaped from a sapling near the edge of the woods.
"Hard to be graceful with a limp."

"I suppose." Talia gave the staff a quick spin. The
wood was solid enough to make a serviceable weapon.
This could work.

"If anyone asks," Snow added, "you're my personal chef and eunuch Gregory."

Talia jabbed the staff into the dirt. "Bare hands it is."

Snow ignored her. She raised a hand for silence, peering into the darkness. "We're getting close," she whispered.

Talia moved ahead, making as little noise as possible, nothing anyone should be able to hear over the sounds of the forest.

A branch cracked overhead. Talia leaped back, staff raised, but the branch fell harmlessly to the ground a short distance to her right. A woodpecker attacked a tree in the distance. The wind brushed through the leaves. She searched the trees, but saw nothing unusual.

"Relax." Snow's features were Danielle's, but the amused smile was all Snow. "The dryads are long gone. Without them, these trees are nothing but wood." She glanced upward. "To be safe, I wouldn't go waving an ax around or starting any fires, though."

"How much farther?" Talia asked.

"We crossed the outer boundary of the grove just now. Didn't you feel it? Like stepping through wet cobwebs. Centuries ago, they were strong enough to warn even the most magically blind away from this place."

Talia turned around, trying to make the motion as casual as possible. There had been a flicker of motion in the distance. The darkness turned every shape into a potential threat. A clump of leaves overhead could be a killer waiting in ambush. A fat stump could be Roudette herself, crouching with weapons drawn.

"Malindar fought here," Snow whispered. "He was young then, but already powerful."

Talia stepped over a fallen tree. "I care about that why?"

"Talia, some say this is where the war between men and fairies started! Without Malindar, this whole isle might belong to the fairies. Malindar's Treaty—"

"Has nothing to do with finding Roudette. History lessons later." Talia spun, searching the blackness behind them. A shadow the size of a large dog trotted through the trees. Talia switched her staff to her left hand and reached for a knife, but whatever it was didn't appear interested.

"Check on Charlotte again," Talia whispered. "Make sure Roudette's still with her."

"I'm sure." Snow tapped her mirror. "It's the old fairy magic making you jumpy."

"I am *not* jumpy." Talia scowled at the darkness, jammed her knife back into the sheath, and moved on.

The ground beneath her feet soon changed, taking on the feel of crushed stone. They reached another fallen tree, this one as wide as her outstretched arms. Talia crouched to pick up an acorn. She never would have known it to be stone without touching it. She pressed a hand to the tree, feeling the cold, heavy bark beneath her palm.

"Even the insects within the wood," Snow whispered, plucking a tiny stone ant from a hole in the side of the trunk. "Amazing."

Talia peered past the tree. She could make out a clearing ahead. She grabbed Snow's sleeve, pulling her attention back to the task at hand. "Up there. Tell Trittibar."

Snow untied her pouch, leaving it open so Trittibar would be able to act. While Snow whispered to the fairy, Talia reached into her left boot and pulled out a flat leather sheath containing a pair of Hiladi throwing knives. The weapons were deadly, but they were a pain to carry. Not only were the blades razor sharp, but a second, smaller, blade jutted from the pommel. The crossguard was pointed as well, long enough to penetrate almost the length of Talia's thumb. She untied the sheath and unfolded the flaps that protected the secondary points.

She took one knife and held it against her staff with

her left hand. The other she gripped with her right, pressing the blade to her wrist and tugging her sleeve forward to conceal it. Wordlessly, she and Snow approached the clearing, using the other trees for cover.

Enormous stumps covered the earth ahead, the roots so thick they wove together, forming dark pits and caves. Charlotte sat in one such cave, bound and helpless as Snow had described her. Her head hung low, in either sleep or despair, Talia couldn't tell.

Behind her, perched atop the stone roots of a fallen oak, waited the Lady of the Red Hood. She held a short horn-tipped recurve bow, already drawn. So much for catching her off guard.

"Princess Whiteshore?" Roudette moved the bow toward Talia. "I told you to come alone."

"I brought no guards," said Snow, keeping to the safety of an old pine tree.

Charlotte jerked awake. "Who's there? Danielle?" There was no haughtiness in her words, only fear. Perhaps two years in Fairytown had broken her pride.

Snow's magic gave her Danielle's voice but not her intonation or her patterns of speech. It wouldn't take long for Charlotte to realize this wasn't her stepsister.

Snow ran a hand over the branches, snapping stone needles into her palm. "This is my servant and personal chef, Gregory. I came as you requested, but I refuse to go back to eating peasant food."

Charlotte's eyes narrowed, but she said nothing. Talia limped forward, making sure she presented more of a target than Snow. Not even Talia could dodge an arrow at this range, but her chances were better than Snow's, and she could probably twist enough to keep it from killing her.

Roudette was much as Talia remembered. She was older, probably in her early forties. Her blonde curls had lost much of their color, and her complexion was cracked leather. Black fur lined the inside of her famous

cape. Golden characters in a language Talia didn't recognize bordered the edges.

"I didn't expect you to come," Roudette said. "I know
what Charlotte and her sister tried to do to you."

Snow didn't move. "Are you all right, Charlotte?"

"Am I all right? She *cut off my toe!* I haven't eaten in
three days!"

This was definitely Danielle's stepsister. Talia adjusted her grip on her knives. If she could kill Roudette
with the first knife, that left the other for Charlotte. The
idea was tempting . . . but Danielle would hound her
about it for years.

Talia stepped to the right, trying to get a better angle.
Roudette had positioned herself where Charlotte's body
would help shield her. That left the eyes and the throat
as the best targets.

"Give Charlotte to me," said Snow.

"You're welcome to her." Roudette's mouth twisted.
"I'll thank you for taking her off my hands. How you
lived with the bitch for so long without gutting her I'll
never understand."

"I wonder the same thing sometimes," Snow admitted.

A wolf howled in the distance, and Charlotte whimpered. Roudette smiled at the sound. "The Duchess was
right about you, Princess. She assured me you'd never
leave your stepsister to die, despite everything she did to
you. Just as she told me you would bring help."

"The Duchess hired you?" Talia asked. The Lady of
the Red Hood working with a would-be fairy ruler?

Roudette laughed, a sound of genuine merriment.
Her bow never moved from Talia. "The Duchess has
nothing that would persuade me to work for her. She
merely provided me with the tool to finish the job."

Charlotte shook her head. She was even paler than
before, her face sweaty. "I won't," she whispered.

"Bravely spoken," Roudette said. "But you speak as
though you had a choice."

"Why do you need Charlotte to kill me?" Snow asked.

"Not you. Your companion."

"You can't have Gregory," Snow said firmly. "He's my favorite eunuch!"

Talia scowled but said nothing. She still couldn't get a clear line on Roudette.

Another wolf called out, this one from the opposite side of the grove. Roudette's smile grew. "Don't bother using your tricks on them, Princess Whiteshore. You may be able to influence rodents, but my wolves won't dare disobey their pack leader."

Talia took another step forward. "What do you want from me?"

"Your disguise is marvelous, Talia," said Roudette. "But you've done nothing to change your scent."

"My *scent*?" Talia threw her first knife. At the same time, Roudette loosed her arrow and leaped away. The arrow buzzed past Talia's ear just as Talia's knife sparked against the stone stump.

"You could have killed me, you stupid cow!" Charlotte yelled.

Talia was already diving for cover as Roudette's next arrow flew past. Snow had ducked behind a tree, where she was muttering a quick spell. She raised her hands to her mouth and blew.

Stone needles flew like tiny darts. Roudette dropped her bow and raised her cape. Most of the needles buried themselves in the cape, but a few struck Roudette's hand and face. Roudette cursed and pulled a spiked war hammer from her belt.

Talia started forward when she heard something crashing after her. She turned her next step into a roll, tumbling to the side as a wolf landed in the dirt beside her. Still prone, Talia flung her second knife at the wolf. It was an awkward throw, resulting in a shallow wound to the wolf's chest, but it slowed the animal long enough for Talia to rise and draw her sword.

By now, Trittibar had freed himself from Snow's pouch and stood human-sized once more. In his hand he held a slender sword with a gold blade and a basket hilt.

Roudette was already disappearing through the trees. Talia jumped over Charlotte, only to turn back as the wolf charged after her. The wolf was no longer alone. Talia counted six closing in around them. The smallest was half again as large as any wolf Talia had ever seen.

"I thought Roudette worked alone," Snow shouted.

Trittibar sliced through the ropes holding Charlotte's arm, then spun to face one of the wolves. Charlotte stretched to grab Talia's fallen knife and started cutting herself free.

Talia plucked the knife from Charlotte's hand and threw it left-handed at another wolf. "Where's Roudette? If we kill her, will it break her control over the wolves?"

"I'm not sure," said Snow. "She's got them pretty riled."

"They're fairy beasts." Trittibar jabbed his sword at one.

"You're a fairy," Talia snapped. "Stop them!"

"Kill Roudette, and I'll do my best."

Talia glanced to the side, searching for Roudette. She spotted a glimpse of red moving through the trees, but before she could act, another wolf jumped onto the top of a stump and crouched to pounce.

"Snow!" Talia lunged forward, jabbing her blade at the wolf. An instant later, one of Snow's steel snowflakes spun through the air and stabbed the wolf's nose.

"I got him!" Snow beamed and grabbed another snowflake.

The wolf on the stump pounced, crashing into Trittibar. It grabbed Trittibar's arm in its jaws even as the fairy thrust his gold blade into the wolf's side. Talia tried to help, but had to turn away to fend off another wolf.

Trittibar yelled as he was ripped off his feet, but he kept his grip on his sword, twisting the blade in the wolf's side. The wolf cried out and tried to back away, but Trittibar followed, ramming the blade home until the hilt struck fur. Only then did he yank his weapon free. His other arm hung limp and bloody at his side.

In the distance, Talia saw Roudette unfasten her cape and flip it about so the wolfskin was on the outside. As the cape settled over Roudette's body, she snarled as if in pain. The wolfskin tightened around her, crushing her into a new form. Even over the sound of battle, Talia could hear bones and joints popping and shifting. Roudette rose on all fours and shook like a wet dog.

"Did you know she could change into a wolf?" Snow asked.

"There have been rumors." Trittibar's face was pale, his mouth tight from pain. "We can't fight them all. These creatures were raised by the fairy queen herself."

"Stay close to me." Snow flung another handful of stone needles, magic turning them into tiny darts. When the wolves jumped away, she dropped to her knees and cast a new spell. Dirt swirled around her. The wind grew, flinging dirt and stone around them all.

Talia lowered her sword and backed toward the others. Dirt and grit abraded her face, but it was nothing compared to the wall of stone and wind passing in front of her. "What are you doing?"

Snow didn't answer. Her choker shone, each mirror burning like a tiny sun as she worked her magic. Stronger and stronger the wind blew, breaking stone branches from fallen trees and tossing them like missiles. The wolves backed away.

Roudette had joined the wolves by now. She was smaller than the others, her fur black as shadow save where it whitened near the muzzle. Golden eyes watched Talia through the maelstrom.

Charlotte was clawing frantically at her ropes. "You

have to get me away from her! I don't want to die like this, torn apart by wolves."

"I could kill you myself," Talia offered.

"You wouldn't dare!" She turned to Trittibar. "You can't let her."

Trittibar shrugged with his good arm. "Legally speaking, there's little I can do to stop her. You're human. They're human. The treaty prohibits me from intervening."

Charlotte sagged. "Just do it quickly."

"I would," said Talia. "But your stepsister is a kinder woman than I am." Talia slashed the ropes holding Charlotte's other wrist. She handed Charlotte a knife. "Cut your legs free and make yourself useful. Snow, any chance you can get us out of here?"

"I'm a little busy right now," Snow said, the words coming in gasps.

"What about your summoner friend, Arlorran?" asked Talia. "Can he pull us into Fairytown?"

"Don't take me back there!" Charlotte said.

"Arlorran can't pull us through Fairytown's borders. His magic isn't—" Snow cried out. Pebbles and sticks fell to the ground. The wolves surged closer. Snow clutched the back of her head with one hand. Slowly, the wind regained its strength.

Talia switched her sword to her left hand. In her right she drew her last knife. No matter how many weapons she packed, it never seemed to be enough. "On my signal, drop the spell. We throw everything we've got at Roudette. She's not walking away either. Not this time."

"There is another way," Trittibar said slowly.

"So do it," Talia shouted.

"Fairies have always moved beyond the boundaries of this world," Trittibar continued. "Cloud striders, for example. They don't actually fly. They've simply learned to climb mountains that don't exist in this world."

"You're as bad as Snow," Talia snapped. "If you can help—"

"Legally, I can't," Trittibar said. "Malindar's Treaty specifically prohibits the use of fairy rings."

Talia dropped her sword and grabbed his arm, spinning him about. "You'd let them eat us because of a thousand-year-old treaty?"

"He has no choice," Snow said. "He's a fairy, remember? They're bound by the terms of the treaty. The only way he could break those terms—" She turned to face him. "Oh, Trittibar."

"What is it?" Talia demanded.

Snow closed her eyes. "Malindar's Treaty applies only to the fairies of Lorindar. It has no hold over exiles who have been cut off from the fairy hill."

"Or those who choose to sever that connection of their own free will," Trittibar added. "I was hoping you might have another option."

"I'm sorry," said Snow.

Whatever else Talia might think of Trittibar, once the fairy made a decision, he wasted no further time. Trittibar pressed the tip of his sword into the ground. He turned, and the blade gouged the stone, leaving behind a golden arc. He stepped past Charlotte, tracing the circle through roots and earth alike. "You might want to close your eyes. Humans find this . . . disconcerting."

Talia watched the wolves moving closer. Through Snow's failing spell, she saw Roudette staring back at her. Talia grabbed her sword, and then she was falling into the earth.

CHAPTER 5

⚔

ROUDETTE DRAGGED A BOOT THROUGH THE LINE of ash that marked the fairy's ring. Fairy magic smelled like burned bones, turning her stomach as nothing else could. The ring was empty, her prey stolen away.

"Snow." The Duchess had warned her. Danielle had come to Fairytown with two companions, Talia and the witch Snow White. Roudette had been so intent upon Talia, she had dismissed Snow as a possible threat.

Roudette smiled, remembering the last time she had faced Talia. Roudette was no stranger to narrow escapes, but Talia had come closer than anyone to actually killing the Lady of the Red Hood. She would have taken this job just for the chance to face Talia again.

Not even the power of her cape could postpone the effects of age, and today was the first time in years that Roudette had been uncertain how a battle would play out. She couldn't remember the last time she had felt so alive. But Snow and her fairy had stolen Roudette's victory.

She picked up the ruined remains of her bow. She had dropped it when she dodged Snow's attack, and it had been burned by the magic of the fairy ring. The blackened wood splintered in her fist. She flung the pieces away.

Her wolves couldn't pierce illusion, nor could they have known of the fairy wizard Snow carried in her pouch. The failure was Roudette's alone, for trusting a tool provided by a fairy. "Duchess. Duchess. Duchess."

Her wolves jumped back as the earth at Roudette's feet crumbled, opening a round pit into darkness. A pale, round face framed in wisps of white hair looked up at her. A jade and platinum circlet sat on the Duchess' brow.

"Roudette," said the Duchess. "I didn't expect to hear from you so soon."

"You could be hearing from me again very soon indeed," Roudette said. "You lied to me, lady. Talia was here, and Charlotte did *nothing*."

One slender eyebrow rose ever so slightly. "Interesting. I take it from your impotent fury they escaped?"

"For the moment," Roudette said. "You promised—"

"I have no bargain with you, human." The Duchess smiled. "I agreed to help you as a favor. I did precisely as I said I would, loosing Charlotte into Fairytown for you, carrying the spell I was given."

"A spell that failed."

The Duchess shook her head. "Charlotte was never as skilled in the arts of magic as her dearly departed sister, but desperation can be a powerful teacher. Perhaps she's finally begun to learn the use of power."

"A pitiful wreck of a human, yet she can overcome your fairy magic." Roudette realized she was smiling. She nudged a stone into the pit, watching as it passed through the Duchess' image. "How delightful."

"Hope." The Duchess waved a hand, and the stone shot back upward.

Roudette dodged it with ease. "What do you mean?"

"Princess Danielle came to save her, did she not?" She smiled. "They rescued her from your grasp. Hope brings strength, even to one such as Charlotte. Strength enough to fight. At least for a while."

Roudette froze. "How long?"

The Duchess took her time in responding, her enjoyment obvious. "For a skilled witch, a day. Perhaps two. In Charlotte's case, I imagine her strength will fail before the sun sets."

Roudette circled the pit. She never would have worked with fairies had there been any other way, but some prizes were worth the price. "If I lose Talia because of your failed magic, I will come for you next."

The Duchess feigned a yawn. "Shouldn't you be off chasing after your quarry, little wolfling?"

Roudette's smile grew. Perhaps she would return to Fairytown regardless. She preferred not to kill without a contract, but there were exceptions to every rule.

Unfortunately, the Duchess was right. Roudette spun away, reversing her cape and allowing the magic of the wolfskin to flow through her flesh. She couldn't track the fairy's magic, but there was only one place they would have gone.

If hope had given Charlotte the strength to fight, then Roudette would have to remove that hope.

Moments later, she was bounding through the woods toward Whiteshore Palace.

Danielle stood with Armand in the courtyard beneath the shade of a cherry tree. A short distance away, Jakob was playing with some of the younger children they had rescued from Rumpelstilzchen. She counted fourteen, most of them gathered around the fountain. Three of the biggest children had climbed into the wide bowl of the fountain. They linked hands around the central pedestal, giggling madly as the water sprayed down on them.

Jakob stood clutching the edge of the fountain with both hands, jumping in place as fast as his stubby legs allowed and squealing with delight every time the water splashed his face. Even from here Danielle could see how badly her son wanted to join the others.

Nicolette and four other nursemaids were doing their best to keep the children under control. Nicolette was trying to herd the group inside for breakfast. A few of the nursemaids had other, more pressing concerns. One was having an earnest debate with a little boy about why he really should put his pants back on. Another lectured a red-haired girl on what was and was not a privy.

"Trittibar was right," said Armand, squeezing Danielle's hand. "The children seem to be doing well."

"The younger ones, at least." Danielle winced as Jakob lost his grip and fell, landing hard on his backside. He sat stunned for a moment, then climbed to his feet and hurried toward Danielle and Armand. His movement was clumsy, as much a waddle as a run.

"Mama!"

Danielle smiled and scooped him up. Water dripped from his hair and shirt.

"They went in fountain." Jakob's round face was serious. "*I* stayed on grass."

"Yes, you did." Danielle rubbed a hand through his hair.

"Mama, where Aunt Tala?" Jakob asked.

Danielle hugged him, heedless of the water dampening her own clothes. "She'll be back soon. Go play." She waited until he was away before turning to Armand. "They should have reached Stone Grove by now."

"If anyone can handle Roudette, it's Snow White and Sleeping Beauty."

Danielle stared. "What did you say?"

Armand looked thoroughly pleased with himself. "You thought I'd never figure it out?"

There was no point in denying it. "When did you know?"

"I guessed the truth about Snow shortly after the mermaid incident." He lifted Danielle's hand and pushed back her sleeve, revealing a copper bracelet with a small mirror in the center. "She gave me a magic mirror too, remember? Magic mirror, white skin, not to mention she goes by the name 'Snow.'"

"Most people assume it's a nickname, because she looks like Snow White." Danielle glanced at the mirror, willing it to show her Snow and Talia, but nothing happened. "What about Talia?"

"I heard her singing to Jakob last month." He chuckled. "I've heard many gifted singers in my time, both human and fairy. Talia is something in between. Her voice, that was one of the gifts the fairies gave her? Like her grace? I've long suspected a magical element to her skill in battle. Hearing her song gave me the final piece I needed."

"And now that you know the truth?" Danielle asked.

"If they wished their identities known, they wouldn't be working as servants to my mother." He shrugged. "I've heard the stories of Snow White and Sleeping Beauty. Who hasn't? The fact that they're here in Lorindar, alone, tells me those stories didn't have as happy an ending as the bards would have us believe."

"They're *not* alone," Danielle said firmly.

"You know what I mean." He squeezed her hand. "You could have told me."

"It wasn't my secret to share."

"I know." He winced as one of the children let out a particularly piercing scream. He started to say more, and then his expression hardened.

Danielle followed his gaze to see guards racing toward the main gate. "Nicolette, get the children inside."

"You too." Armand took Danielle's arm.

One of the guards turned back, shouting for Tymalous. Danielle's heart pounded, and she pulled free of Armand's grip. "If this were an attack, they'd be calling for reinforcements, not the king's healer."

By now most of the palace staff had stopped to see what was happening. Father Isaac emerged from the chapel, faded black robe flapping behind him as he ran. Tymalous moved more slowly as he followed.

Snow was the first through the gate, half-carrying the exhausted and battered Trittibar. His arm was a bloody mess, the sleeve and skin shredded. Talia followed, pushing Charlotte ahead of her.

"Roudette got away." Danielle could see it in Talia's expression. Nothing enraged Talia more than her own failure, and whatever had happened, she blamed herself.

Danielle put a hand on Armand's shoulder. His entire body was tense as he watched Talia hand Charlotte over to the guards. The last time he had seen Charlotte, she and Stacia had used magic to enslave him.

Snow and Trittibar sat down right there in the grass. They had obviously come straight from battle, without taking time even to bandage Trittibar's wounds. Tymalous and Isaac shooed Snow away as they inspected the damage to Trittibar's arm.

Snow swayed and might have fallen if Talia hadn't caught her. Danielle was already running toward them, Armand close behind.

"What happened?" Danielle asked. "Are you both all right?"

"I'll be fine," said Snow. "It's Trittibar's fault, whisking us away so suddenly. He broke my wind spell, and the backlash was worse than I expected." She gave Talia a wan smile. "It's embarrassing, really. Breaking wind in the middle of a fight."

"That's terrible." Talia punched her lightly on the shoulder. "Roudette—"

"I know," said Danielle. "She escaped. Which means she'll be coming after me again."

"Not you." Talia glanced over her shoulder, as if she expected to see Roudette charging through the gate behind her. "Me."

The throne room was Danielle's least favorite part of Whiteshore Palace. Standing here surrounded by such wealth and opulence still made her feel like an imposter.

Marble pillars framed a circular dais. Twin thrones sat at the top, each one carved of dark-stained oak and inlaid with gold and ivory. The back of the king's throne was shaped to resemble a griffon. The queen's was carved with a swan motif, the wings folded forward as though to embrace Beatrice.

From Danielle's place beside the queen, she could make out every line in the swan's feathers, each one carved with inhumanly fine detail. The queen sat stiffly, her back not quite touching the back of the chair. Beside her, King Theodore was whispering something to Chancellor Crombie, a sour old man with a wrinkled face and permanently ink-stained fingers. Crombie sat to the right of the dais, parchment and ink laid out on a wooden desk before him.

Armored guards stood to either side of the double doors at the far end of the throne room, their mail polished until it shone almost as brightly as Snow's mirrors. Father Isaac waited to the left of the dais, silver crucifix clutched in both hands, his head bowed in magical prayer.

The room was otherwise abandoned. Imposing as the throne room could be, the emptiness made it worse. There would be no audience for this hearing. Only Chancellor Crombie was in attendance to document Charlotte's sentencing.

Danielle straightened her belt, adjusting her sword. "Have we heard anything about Ambassador Trittibar?" she whispered.

"Tymalous will take care of him," Beatrice assured her.

"I meant from Fairytown," Danielle said. "Will they really exile him for saving Snow and Talia?"

"He violated the treaty." Beatrice made no effort to hide her sadness. "Fairies are not known for ignoring the rules. Twisting them to meet their needs, yes. Something like this . . . no matter the circumstances, I'm afraid they've no choice."

Theodore turned to Danielle. "Ambassador or no, Trittibar will always be welcome in this palace."

"None of this is your fault," Beatrice assured her.

"No?" Danielle glanced at the doors. "I'm the one who insisted we save Charlotte."

"You made the right decision," said Beatrice. "This was our best chance to stop Roudette." The guards straightened, and Beatrice's expression grew stern. "They're here."

Talia and Snow entered together, Charlotte hobbling between them. Two more guards followed close behind.

Charlotte's wrists were shackled. Iron chain clinked loudly as she brushed her gown and picked at her hair, a halfhearted attempt at primping. She kept her head low, refusing to look at anyone.

Her appearance filled Danielle with sadness. Charlotte was a withered shadow of the woman she had once been. She was skinny enough to pass for a fairy, and unlike Talia and Snow, she had been given no time to prepare herself for court. Grime covered her face, almost hiding the scars by her eyes. The bandage on her foot was black with dirt and blood. Her gown was in tatters. An iron bracelet circled her wrist.

"She wasn't wearing that bracelet when she first arrived," Danielle whispered.

"It was made by Father Isaac to prevent her from trying to use magic." Beatrice took Danielle's hand. "Whatever happens, remember that your stepsister chose her own path. Her fate is her responsibility, not yours."

King Theodore waited for Charlotte to reach the base of the dais. Charlotte knelt, as did her escort. Theodore beckoned them to rise. "How is Trittibar?"

"Resting," said Snow. "The wolf's teeth tore deep into

the arm. He shouldn't lose the limb, but it may never regain its full strength."

Beatrice leaned forward. "What of your own injuries?"

"I'm fine." Snow was paler than usual, even the color in her lips faded to a light pink. Judging from Beatrice's frown, she could see through Snow's facade as easily as Danielle did.

"Charlotte Moors." King Theodore's voice filled the throne room.

Charlotte cringed. "Your Majesty."

She appeared . . . broken. Submissive, even. Whether from her years trapped in Fairytown or the knowledge that she was alone, Danielle couldn't guess.

Theodore stood. "Two years ago, you conspired with your stepsister Stacia to kidnap Prince Armand of Lorindar. My son. You then attempted to murder Princess Whiteshore. Later, you tried again to kill the princess and her unborn child both."

Charlotte began to cry, but said nothing.

"While in Fairytown, Princess Whiteshore spared your life, showing you mercy." The king's voice was stone, his face as hard as Danielle had ever seen. "She overstepped her bounds."

Danielle bit back a protest. Even Snow and Talia looked surprised at his pronouncement.

"You committed treason against Lorindar," Theodore said. "You entered my home, attacked my family, and stole my son. Do you deny these acts?"

"No." Her voice was barely audible.

"In other circumstances, you would be put to death. After consideration, we have decided to give you one chance to save yourself, to earn exile rather than the gallows." He glanced at Beatrice, making Danielle suspect the queen had been influential in that choice.

Charlotte looked up, hope and wariness on her face. "Anything, Your Majesty."

Beatrice leaned forward. "Help us find Roudette. Tell us what happened to you and what role you were to play in her attempt to kill Talia."

Charlotte sagged. "After Cinder— After Danielle and her friends freed Armand, I was left in the Duchess' service. She kept me on as a slave. I was nothing, lower even than her goblins, given scraps for food, forced to sleep in—"

"In other words, you were treated as you once treated your stepsister," Beatrice said.

"Yes." Charlotte glanced at Danielle, then looked away, but not before Danielle saw something she had never imagined from her stepsister: shame.

"Go on."

"A short time ago, the Duchess grew bored with me. She cast me out. One of her creatures led me as far as the queen's labyrinth in exchange for—" Charlotte shook her head. "Please don't make me tell you."

Danielle imagined the greed of the fairies from her last journey to Fairytown, demanding her unborn child and worse. What had they taken from Charlotte? "We only care about Roudette."

"Thank you." Charlotte's face twisted as though the words burned her mouth. "The little beast said if I could make my way through the labyrinth before sunrise, I would reach the hedge that borders Fairytown and be able to escape."

"You survived the fairy queen's labyrinth?" Snow asked.

Charlotte shook her head. "I ran until my legs lost their strength. Turns doubled back on themselves. Pathways ended without warning. I collapsed, unable to move another step, or so I thought. Then I heard the howling of the queen's wolves. I dragged myself onward, eventually finding a passage that opened onto the chasm. Not the escape I had hoped for, but a quick leap to my death was better than facing the wolves. I tried to make myself jump, but in the end my fear was too great. I couldn't do it. That was when Roudette found me.

"At first I thought she was the fairy queen herself, come to watch my death. Instead, Roudette dragged me from the edge, then turned to await the wolves. She . . . quieted them somehow, almost as if she were talking to them. Like my stepsister used to do with her vermin."

Charlotte touched the scars on her face. "The wolves allowed us to pass. Roudette led us from the maze, the wolves following her. We soon reached the goblin encampment at the hedge. It was the goblins who recognized her, calling her by name. Until that moment I had no idea who she was. The goblins tried to flee. Some escaped. The rest fell to Roudette and the wolves. She left only one alive, forcing him to guide us through the hedge."

Danielle closed her eyes, remembering her own journey through that hedge and the goblin who had helped them, though she had never been able to recall his name. She prayed he had been among those who escaped.

"Roudette's cape is magical," Snow said. "She used it to transform herself into a wolf. That must be how she controlled the queen's animals."

"I've already sent word to the guards to watch for wolves," Talia added.

"Good." Beatrice studied Charlotte for a long time before asking, "You and Roudette traveled together from Fairytown to Stone Grove. What can you tell us of her? How did she behave? What did she say to you?"

Charlotte's chains clanked as she massaged her shoulder. "She wanted to know about Danielle. How she and her friends rescued Armand from the Duchess. Whether Danielle would truly want to save me, and if I thought she would bring her friends. After that, she barely spoke to me."

Snow cleared her throat. "With Your Majesties' permission?" She waited for the king's nod, then said,

"Roudette expected you to perform some task to help her. What was it?"

"I was supposed to identify Talia."

"You're lying." Danielle studied her stepsister. Charlotte had never been one for subtlety or hiding her emotions, but two years in Fairytown had changed her. Growing up, Danielle had learned quickly to read her stepsisters' moods, knowing when to carry out her chores in silence and when to avoid them at all costs.

This was different. Charlotte was scared but also resigned. The woman Danielle remembered would have been weeping or begging, or ranting against the injustice of it all. "Roudette fought Talia once before," Danielle said. "She wouldn't need your help in recognizing her."

She stepped down from the dais, crossing the throne room to stand before her stepsister. Charlotte's eyes were red and shadowed. She appeared ready to pass out from exhaustion, but her expression was *pleading*.

"What did they do to you?" Danielle whispered. Charlotte said nothing, not even watching as Danielle circled her. "Let us help you."

"You can't." Charlotte wiped her nose on her sleeve, then hastily tugged the shoulder of her gown back into place.

If Danielle hadn't been watching her stepsister so closely, she would have missed it. She reached out, and Charlotte tensed. Danielle grabbed Charlotte's torn collar and pulled, exposing a faded strawberry mark on the skin. "Two years ago Stacia and the Duchess gave you this mark to prevent you from betraying them."

"Yes," said Charlotte.

"I remember that mark being smaller."

Charlotte shivered, but said nothing more. If she had been bound by a fairy mark, she wouldn't be able to speak of it. The penalties for breaking such a bond were limited only by the creativity of the one who cast it, and fairies were unmatched when it came to inventing cruel new torments.

"Isn't that clever," Snow said, moving closer to study the mark. She pressed her fingernail to the edge. "A second curse placed over the first to conceal it. I wonder if the first retains its magic."

"Can you remove it?" asked Beatrice.

"The mark or the shoulder?"

Charlotte whimpered and backed away, keeping Danielle between herself and Snow.

"Relax," said Snow. "Even if we cut off the shoulder, it wouldn't solve anything. That mark is only the external sign of the curse flowing through your blood." She beckoned for Father Isaac to approach. "What do you think? I'd want Trittibar's help, of course."

For the first time, Charlotte appeared hopeful. She reached for Danielle's arm.

Talia's heel slammed into Charlotte's chest, knocking her to the floor.

"She wasn't trying to hurt me." Danielle crouched beside Charlotte, who was gasping for breath.

"Would you gamble your life on that?" Talia's expression made it clear she would happily pound Charlotte into the floor if she so much as twitched.

The king rose. "Do what you can to remove the mark. If she's cursed, we can trust nothing she says until that curse is broken."

· "Did Roudette ever say who hired her to kill me?" Talia hadn't asked for leave to speak, but it was clear King Theodore tolerated such outbursts from Beatrice's closest servants and companions. Chancellor Crombie's scowl was the only apparent sign of disapproval.

Charlotte swallowed. "Yesterday afternoon. Roudette had just returned. There was fresh blood on her cape, and she was in a good mood. She even offered me food." She turned away, hiding her face. "I offered to pay her whatever she wanted if she'd free me."

"Pay her with what?" Danielle asked. She had to strain to hear Charlotte's reply.

"I told her *you* would pay." Charlotte steeled herself. "I told her you were soft, that you lacked the spine to turn your back on your stepsister, no matter what I had done."

Snow coughed and turned away, but not before Danielle saw her smirk.

Queen Beatrice jabbed her staff against the floor. "Tell us what you learned from Roudette."

"She was leaning over a hollowed stump," said Charlotte. "She sprinkled something yellow inside. I can't cast spells, but I can feel them sometimes. This felt like she was making a potion. She started speaking to the stump."

Father Isaac turned to the king and queen. "It rained two nights ago. A hollow stump of stone would still hold water. She could have been using it as a scrying pool."

Charlotte nodded eagerly. "I couldn't understand the language. She kept saying 'tav.'"

Talia moved closer. "Tiav?" she asked, stretching out the vowels.

"Yes." Charlotte looked from Talia to Danielle. "What does it mean?"

"It's Arathean," said Talia. "It means 'soon.' What else did she say?"

Charlotte shook her head miserably. "How would I know?"

"Talia?" Danielle reached out, but Talia slapped her hand away.

The guards started forward, looking uncertain. Talia didn't even appear to realize what she had done.

"No," said Danielle, waving them back. "It's all right."

Talia punched a hand to her palm and took a deep breath. "Did Roudette ever say the name Lakhim?"

"I don't think so."

Talia relaxed slightly. "What about Mutal or Mahatal?"

Charlotte nodded eagerly. "Yes! I remember, near the end!"

Beatrice inhaled sharply. Even Snow appeared sober. They were both staring at Talia, whose face had gone pale.

"Mutal and Mahatal ela'Ghelib," said Beatrice.

"Oh, Talia." Danielle recognized the names now, though Talia had never spoken them in her presence. Mutal and Mahatal were the twin princes of Arathea. The sons of Sleeping Beauty.

"They're the men who hired Roudette?" asked Charlotte.

"Not men, but boys." Beatrice pushed herself to her feet. "Arathea has sent an assassin against our household."

For the first time, Chancellor Crombie rose to speak. "We have no proof," he said hesitantly. "The word of a condemned criminal is hardly adequate grounds for such an accusation."

"I'm telling the truth," Charlotte shouted. She flushed and lowered her head. "Believe me or don't. I don't care. Just get this damned mark off of me."

"I believe you," Danielle said softly. She glanced at the king, who nodded. To Father Isaac, she said, "Would you and Snow please do what you can to remove the curse?"

"What then?" asked Charlotte warily, showing hints of her old self.

Danielle watched the king, but he held his silence, allowing her to answer. "Once they've removed the curse and you've told us everything you know, I want you gone from Lorindar. Forever."

Charlotte's face reddened. For a moment, Danielle thought she might actually start shouting as she had done in the past. Instead, she whispered, "Thank you."

She spun toward Snow. "You heard her. Remove this thing at once!"

Danielle spotted Talia disappearing out the doors. Danielle bowed hastily to the king and queen before hurrying after.

"Where are you going?" Snow asked.

"To stop Talia from doing something foolish."

Danielle hated visiting Talia's room in the palace. Most of the senior servants shared quarters in the base of the northwest tower. Talia and Snow were among the few to have their own rooms, courtesy of Beatrice. Snow's room was a carefully cultivated masterpiece of clutter, with a few small magical traps scattered throughout to turn away anyone who got too nosey.

Talia's room was the opposite. Small but tidy, with a folded cot that never saw use, it was little better than a closet. She deserved so much more, but every time Danielle raised the subject, Talia brushed her off.

Danielle found Talia removing her clothes from a small trunk, laying each garment into one of three piles on the floor. Talia didn't bother looking up. "You make too much noise when you walk, Princess. That scabbard slaps your leg with every step. Remind me to adjust the straps before I go."

"You're not leaving," said Danielle.

"Roudette got away. She'll keep coming for me."

"You fought her before," Danielle pointed out.

"It doesn't matter." There was no fight left in Talia's words. "Queen Lakhim knows where I am. If not Roudette, she'll send someone else. She'll keep trying, and she won't care who gets caught in the bloodshed."

Danielle pulled the door shut behind her. Sunlight squeezed through a narrow window on the far wall. "They're your sons. Surely we can talk to Arathea, explain—"

"Mutal and Mahatal are seven . . . no, eight years of

age. Roudette might have been hired on their authority, promised their gold, but the order came from their grandmother. Lakhim won't stop until I've paid for the murder of her son."

Danielle sat down beside her. "It wasn't murder. What he did to you—"

"You think she cares? Prince Jihab was her only son." She stumbled ever so slightly over the name. "I cut his throat while he slept. I thought it poetic, considering what he did to me during mine. With him gone, his mother rules as haishak—as regent—until her grandsons come of age." Talia tossed a sash onto the closest pile. She stared at the pile, looking lost. "My own sons, and I can't even remember what they looked like."

Danielle picked up the sash and began refolding it. Talia might be fairy-blessed, but her gifts didn't extend to laundry.

"I remember their crying," Talia said. "Sometimes I think that's what woke me from the curse. Not the pain of childbirth, but the crying." She pushed back the mattress on the cot, and dust wafted through the air. She snatched a long dagger from beneath the mattress and tucked it beside her clothes. "I can't tell you what they looked like, but I remember their father. I remember his triumph when he returned to claim me. His prize, Princess Talia Malak-el-Dahshat. His family's key to the throne of Arathea. I killed him, Danielle. No treaty gives Lorindar the right to shelter a prince's killer."

"So we'll write a new treaty," Danielle said.

That earned a weak smile. Talia reached into the trunk and pulled out a long-stemmed pipe. She held it to the light, inspecting the carved ivory bowl and the curved wooden stem before returning it to its case. "In Arathea, family comes before all. I'm only surprised it took them so long to find me."

"What about Snow?"

"We both know there's no happy ending to that tale.

It's past time for me to move on." The tightness in Talia's shoulders belied her casual tone. "She's been uncomfortable with me for a while now."

"I never told her how you felt about her," Danielle said.

"I know." Talia pulled a makeshift stiletto from the bottom of the trunk. Made of a thick metal spike with frayed twine covering the lower half, it was far from intimidating. "I made this in Arathea from a stolen tent peg. Three times it saved my life."

Danielle stood, trying to ignore the emptiness in her chest. Talia was one of her closest friends. One of her only friends, really. The life of a princess didn't lend itself to trusting relationships. "You can't leave. You swore an oath to serve Beatrice, remember?"

"Beatrice is dying," Talia said flatly. "I serve her best by eliminating Roudette and by making sure nobody else is drawn into my feud with Arathea."

"What do I tell Jakob?" Danielle asked. "How do I answer when he asks why Aunt Tala had to go away?"

"Low blow, Princess."

"You're the one who taught me to fight." Danielle forced a smile. "Talia, please give us a chance. Let Theodore and Beatrice talk to Arathea."

Talia looked past her, toward the door. Footsteps hurried through the hallway, stopping outside. Talia rose, tent stake knife clutched behind her back.

"Princess Danielle?"

"Nicolette?" Danielle rose to open the door.

"The queen said I'd find you here." Nicolette was out of breath, her hair a sweaty mess. Bloody scratches marked her neck, and her lip was swollen. "Jakob's run off, Highness."

"What happened to you?" Danielle asked.

Nicolette touched her face. "Jakob was playing some sort of hiding game, but I'm afraid it frightened the others, and that scared him in turn. All of a sudden they were screaming and running every which way. I scooped him up, and he hammered me good with his forehead." She licked her swollen lip. "I handed him off to Marguerite so I could try to contain the rest, but he managed to slip away from her."

"Talia, will you help us look?" Danielle asked innocently. "Jakob might come out for his Aunt Tala."

Talia narrowed her eyes. "You don't need me. There are only so many nooks and corners a boy his age could get to."

"What was the game?" If Danielle knew what Jakob was playing, it might help her figure out where he'd gone.

"I'm not sure," said Nicolette. "Something about hiding from the wolves."

Danielle grabbed Nicolette's arm. She tried to keep her voice calm, though her heart was pounding. "How was Jakob acting? Was he laughing, or did he appear serious?"

"He wasn't laughing." Nicolette stared, alarm in her eyes as she took in Danielle's reaction. "What is it, Princess?"

"He's Beatrice's grandson. This wouldn't be the first time he's shown signs of her gifts." Danielle started to run. "Get the children inside. All of them."

Talia was already keeping pace beside her. "It makes no sense for Roudette to come here. She knows she can't enter the palace without being caught."

Danielle hurried up the steps. "How long would it take Roudette to reach the palace from Stone Grove?"

They froze as they entered the courtyard. The howls were faint, but the sound raised goose bumps on Danielle's skin.

Talia swore. "Not long at all."

Chapter 6

IF ANYTHING COULD HAVE HELPED to clear Talia's mind, it was the arrival of an enemy to fight. She was almost grateful to Roudette for the distraction.

She stepped in front of Danielle and searched the courtyard. The wolves sounded as though they were running through the city streets. She heard screams as well. The palace staff were looking about in confusion.

"Get inside," Talia shouted, pushing the closest toward the door. She waved to get the attention of the guards atop the wall. When that failed, she scooped a piece of stone from the ground beside the wall and threw. It clanged from the closest man's helm.

"What in God's name—" The guard straightened, spotting Danielle.

"Bar the gates," Talia shouted. "Make sure the king and queen are safe!"

He started to argue, took another look at Danielle's expression, and made for the gates.

"You too, Princess," said Talia.

"Jakob is out here." Danielle didn't even bother to stare her down. She simply shoved past Talia and shouted for her son.

"Talia!" Snow was running from the chapel. "Roudette is on her way."

"We know." Talia jabbed a finger at Danielle. "Her son already warned us."

"Unfair!" Snow stopped. "I spent hours working on those wards, and *Jakob* spots her before I do?"

"Jakob's hiding," said Danielle, running toward the storeroom. She was keeping her fear under control, but Talia could hear the panic in her voice. "Can you find him?"

"Maybe," said Snow. "But he knows where my mirrors are placed. Remember the last time he hid from us, after he threw your husband's shoes into the well? The kid's too smart for his own good."

Talia moved into the center of the courtyard. She turned slowly, listening as she tried to understand what Roudette was doing. After all of her work to lure Talia out into the open, why risk everything by attacking the palace directly?

Screams and snarls broke out closer to the gate. A dog's barks changed to whimpers, then fell silent. The wolves were almost here.

What then? The wolves couldn't get inside, though that wouldn't stop Roudette. The north and east walls of the palace rose directly from the white cliffs, meaning Roudette would need to enter through the south or west.

Talia waited, mentally tracking the sound of the wolves. Atop the walls, guards rushed toward the south gates, where the wolves were loudest. Talia turned to face the western wall. "Danielle! The wolves are a distraction. Roudette's coming from the west. We have to get you out of here *now*!"

"Not without Jakob!" Danielle slammed the storeroom door and turned around, her eyes wide. "The bakehouse. Derrick was making honey cakes this morning."

"Go!" Talia followed at a distance, still watching the walls. That damned red cape should have been like a banner. Where was she?

"Jakob Theodore Whiteshore!" Danielle ran to the low brick building on the eastern wall and threw open the door. Inside, Talia could see the young prince sitting on the floor, his clothes caked in flour. Danielle scooped him into her arms. "What have I told you about running from Nicolette?"

"No to do it." Jakob clung to his mother. "There are monsters and a scary lady."

Monsters. Talia turned. "Jakob, where is the scary lady now?"

Jakob started to shake. He buried his face in Danielle's shoulder, but pointed toward the chapel.

"Impossible," said Snow. "I was just there. Roudette couldn't have gotten past us."

Jakob shook his head. Talia moved closer, straining to hear his words. "No Roudette," Jakob mumbled. "Charlotte. She hurted Papa Isaac."

"Damn her," Talia said. "I should have killed the bitch when I had the chance."

"Kill the bitch!" Jakob yelled.

"Thank you, Talia." Danielle switched Jakob to her other side. "Snow, get back there and—"

"Too late." Talia pointed a knife at the chapel, where Charlotte had emerged. Yellow fire burned along her skin. She stumbled as though drunk. Smoke swirled around her legs like a miniature dust devil. She was still wearing the iron bracelet Father Isaac had made. The bracelet glowed orange as though fresh from the forge. "I thought Charlotte couldn't do witchcraft."

"It's not her." Snow's hands traced a spell. "It's a fire sprite. A fairy creature."

"I hate magic." Talia glanced at Snow. "No offense. How the hell did that thing get through the walls?"

Snow's eyes were wide. "Charlotte must have been carrying it."

Danielle set Jakob on the ground and pushed him toward the bakehouse. "Get back inside and stay very quiet. I want you to hide in the flour chest until we come to get you. Do you understand?"

Jakob nodded. "Bye, Mama."

"Go with him, Danielle," said Talia. She threw a knife, but the flames knocked it aside.

Snow finished her spell. The flames flickered and shrank as though buffeted by a gale, dying enough for Talia to make out Charlotte's expression. Her eyes were round with terror, her mouth wide.

"Help!" she mouthed, but only smoke emerged. The smoke curled into a black knot and streaked toward Snow.

A wave of Snow's hand deflected the smoke skyward. Charlotte dropped to her knees, igniting a small fire where she touched the ground.

"Will killing her stop that thing?" Talia shouted, readying another knife.

"No!" Snow thrust her hands forward, sending another gust toward Charlotte. "She's *fighting* that thing. Kill her and you free it to do whatever it pleases."

"Talia!" Danielle kicked the bakehouse door shut and drew her sword. "Behind you!"

Talia spun, knife held high. The moment she spotted the streak of red racing across the courtyard, she threw. Roudette dodged, which slowed her enough for a pair of guards to close in.

They died before Talia could warn them. Roudette's hammer struck the first guard in the throat. The second thrust his sword, which Roudette deflected with her cape before flinging him to the ground and slamming the hammer into the center of his back.

Danielle screamed, the sound cutting through the chaos like an ax. Throughout the courtyard, faces turned and guards raced to protect their princess. Danielle raised her glass blade in both hands and flashed a smile at Talia. "You were right. Screaming works."

Talia ran at Roudette, only to leap back as Charlotte

sent another bolt of fire through the air. The flames seared her face as they crackled toward Roudette, who ducked behind her cape. The fire sparked and spread but appeared unable to penetrate the cape. That didn't stop Charlotte, who continued to pour fire at Roudette. Grass blackened and burned. The air rippled as Roudette continued forward.

"Where can I get one of those?" Talia muttered. She kept low, trying to watch Roudette and Charlotte both. Roudette seemed more interested in Talia than Charlotte, despite the flames crackling against her cape. Talia waited until Roudette was nearly upon her, then flung her knife straight up at Roudette's face.

The blade tore Roudette's cheek and ear. Talia jumped forward and grabbed Roudette's wrist. She slammed a knee into Roudette's forearm, trying to break her grip on her weapon.

Roudette swung her other arm, clubbing Talia in the back. It was like being struck with a tree. Talia dropped and rolled away, trying to stay clear of that hammer.

Snow was busy fighting Charlotte's magic. Danielle readied her sword and stepped forward to guard Snow's back. Her stance was good, but if Roudette reached her, she would rip Danielle apart as easily as she had the guards.

Sweeping her cape back with one hand, Roudette pulled a small red dart from her belt and threw. She turned back just in time to meet Talia's charge. They crashed to the ground together, each grabbing the other's wrist.

From the edge of her vision, Talia saw Charlotte drop to her knees. A spot of red protruded from her throat. "Snow! That dart will be poisoned!"

Roudette's grip squeezed the knife from Talia's hand. Her strength was far beyond human. Talia brought her forehead down to bloody Roudette's nose, but Roudette simply tossed her aside.

Roudette rose slowly, glancing about to take in the guards who had spread out to surround them. Not even the Lady of the Red Hood could dodge a dozen crossbow bolts fired at such close range.

"Charlotte!" Danielle tried to approach her stepsister, but the flames burst outward, pushing her back.

"You're too late," Roudette whispered. "Already she feels the poison burning through her veins, her heart hardening, her lungs collapsing. Her vision constricts, and her hope dies."

Fire leaped from Charlotte's arms, tearing through the grass to encircle them. The guards jumped back. Roudette smiled, her face bloody but triumphant.

Snow turned around, looking at the fire. "This is not good."

The flames grew higher, obscuring everything beyond. Black smoke rose overhead, blocking out the sun. Talia could hear shouts from the other side of the fire, guards warning everyone to stand clear and calling for water, Prince Jakob yelling for his mother. They sounded far away, their words becoming fainter with every passing heartbeat.

The world lurched, and for the second time that day, Talia felt herself falling into the earth.

Snow might have admired the artistry of the fairy ring if not for the fact that she had no idea where it was taking them. Beside her, Danielle was doubled over, clutching her stomach with one hand. Talia and Roudette were still fighting, though far less effectively than before. Even Talia had a hard time keeping her balance while plummeting between worlds.

"Stay back from the edge," Snow warned. She sensed powerful magic, the waves buffeting her as strongly as the heat of the fire, but no life. The sprite must have destroyed itself to create this ring. "Be still and let me work!"

Snow closed her eyes, using her mirrors to see the fire all around her. In theory, the ring should function the same as the one Trittibar had created earlier in the day. But Trittibar's ring had brought them to the outer gates of the palace, unable to pierce the wards of the walls. This one was strong enough to tear through those same wards as though they weren't even there.

Magic was magic. This thing might be powerful, but at its heart, it obeyed the same rules. A fairy ring was nothing but a hole in reality. In this case, a particularly big and deep hole, but a hole nonetheless. Snow reached out, using the connection between her choker and her mirror back at the palace to slow their fall. The ring of flames wobbled like a spinning coin. Smoke began to fill the circle.

"What did you do?" Talia shouted.

"Tossed an anchor over the side." Snow coughed and dropped low. "I don't know where this thing is sending us, but I didn't feel like going there."

Roudette raised her war hammer. "You can't!"

Talia crouched to strike, but Snow merely smiled and said, "Go ahead. Kill us all. I hope you enjoy spending the rest of your existence trapped in a hole to nowhere."

"Can you take us back to the palace?" Danielle asked.

"We're still traveling, just slower than before." Snow gestured to the fire. "I'm not strong enough to pull us back. Even if I could, I don't know what would happen if I brought us out too close to the original ring. It could create a loop, a portal that leads only to itself. It would be an interesting experiment, but I'd rather not try it with us inside."

An unfelt breeze carried a new scent into the circle. A sweet, organic smell, like resin and sand and dried grasses.

"Then take us somewhere else in Lorindar," Talia said. "Somewhere far enough from the palace—"

"Anywhere in Lorindar would still be too close." Snow wiped her eyes and squinted at the flames. Was it her imagination, or had the ring contracted?

"So what do we do?" Danielle asked.

Snow waved at Roudette. "How about we start by taking away her hammer? She won't fight you now. Not unless she wants me to drop her through the ring."

Roudette gripped her hammer more tightly. "You're lying. Your power isn't—"

"I wonder where you'll end up," Snow said. "A hundred leagues above the ocean? The middle of the icy northlands? Or maybe you'll just fall into the fairy realm and be trapped there."

Roudette tossed her weapon onto the grass.

"Very good." Snow waited for Talia to retrieve the hammer. "Now tell me where this thing was supposed to take us."

"Arathea." It was Talia who answered. "Charlotte was supposed to help you bring me to Queen Lakhim. Alive, if possible, so she could be the one to carry out my sentence."

Snow pursed her lips. "This could be a problem."

"What's wrong?" asked Danielle.

"I've never been to Arathea! I don't know what the silly place looks like." She crawled toward Talia. The circle was definitely shrinking, and the smoke was growing worse. Snow grabbed Talia's hand. "Congratulations, you've just become my apprentice."

Talia tugged away. "What are you talking about?"

"A fairy ring is a hole in our world. At one end is the fairy ring we fell through. At the other side is a second ring. Unless you want to show up on Lakhim's doorstep, I have to shift that second ring, but the farther I push, the more likely I am to destroy the whole thing." Snow tapped her choker. "Stare into the mirrors and think of Arathea. Help me find a safe place to bring us out. Quickly, if you don't mind?"

"You're mad."

"We can argue about that later," Snow said.

Talia bit her lip and stared into Snow's choker. Snow closed her eyes, looking through the mirrors. For a moment she saw only Talia, her face sweaty and full of uncertainty. Talia's image vanished, and Snow saw instead a path of crushed red stone leading to a covered well, a small room with a crumpled sleeping mat and worn blanket, a copper pot full of steaming rice and meat.

With the memories came fragments of emotion. Fear, mixed with budding trust. Love and regret. Grief so sharp it brought tears to Snow's vision.

"Got it," Snow whispered. She grabbed a mirror from the side of her choker, keeping the memories in her own mind. The mirror slipped free in her hand. She reached out to take Roudette's war hammer. The weapon was heavier than it looked. The head felt like iron—perfect. Gripping the head of the hammer, she tapped the point against the mirror in her other hand.

The glass shattered into powder. Snow dropped the hammer, cupping the powder in her hands. She blew a glittering stream of dust into the flames. The glass spread out, merging with the fire.

"Will this work?" Roudette whispered.

Snow shrugged and scooted back. The flames brightened, heat pushing them to the very center of the circle.

Between one breath and the next, the fire vanished. Smoke wafted away, revealing a field of grain.

Talia and Roudette moved at the same instant. Roudette's fingers closed around the handle of her hammer. Before Roudette could rise, Talia's heel slammed into her temple. Roudette fell back, groaning.

Talia struck twice more, keeping Roudette off-balance. Roudette raised her hammer, and Talia slammed a vicious punch into Roudette's fingers, crushing them against the handle of her own weapon. The hammer dropped.

Danielle thrust her sword through the bottom of Roudette's cape, pinning her in place long enough for Talia to land another punch to the side of Roudette's head. Roudette reached up to grab Talia's wrist, so Talia dropped a knee into her stomach.

That was enough. Roudette doubled over, and Talia pressed a knife to her throat. Danielle yanked her sword free, keeping it pointed at Roudette. The whole fight was over before Snow could even decide which spell to cast.

"Care to try that again?" Talia kicked the hammer away.

Roudette flexed her fingers. "Striking the hand that holds the weapon. That's an unusual tactic."

"First rule of sik h'adan," said Talia. "Attack whatever target your enemy presents."

Roudette laughed. "Risky. Miss by even a tiny distance, and you break your hand against my hammer."

Talia's breathing was fast but steady. "I don't miss."

Danielle turned around. "Where are we?"

"Arathea," said Talia. "Outside the city of Jahrasima."

Snow started to stand, and the world shifted as though she were still in the fairy ring. She sat back, fingers digging into the dry earth as she blinked to clear her vision.

Jahrasima sat upon an island in the middle of a perfectly circular lake. Snow remembered reading about this city. Jahrasima and its eight sister cities were gifts from fairykind, meant to atone for the curse of Sleeping Beauty. They said the water in the lake never dropped, even in the hottest part of the dry season.

Trees ringed the water, tall and broad-leafed. A stone path, somewhere between a dam and a bridge, offered a road into the city proper. Orange sunlight rippled on the dark water. Snow cupped her eyes and looked to the sky. Arathea was far enough west of Lorindar that the sun appeared to have jumped backward.

They had arrived a short distance beyond the lake's

edge, in a farmer's field. Small gullies ran in parallel lines from the shore, diverting water to irrigate the crops.

"I thought we were supposed to arrive in the city itself," Talia said.

Snow pointed to the water. "Do you know how much magic it takes to sustain that lake? Bringing us into that city would be like trying to throw a stick into a whirlwind. You're lucky we got this close."

Danielle still held her sword. Beads of sweat covered her forehead, and she looked queasy. Given how seasick Danielle got while sailing, Snow could imagine how the fairy ring must have affected her.

Despite her nausea, Danielle's voice was firm as she faced Roudette. "What did you do to my stepsister?"

"I needed someone to carry the sprite." Roudette didn't try to move. She was far calmer than anyone in her position should have been. "To bring Talia here alive, if possible. Charlotte was supposed to release the sprite at Stone Grove. I didn't think she had it in her to fight."

"But she did," said Danielle. "So you killed her."

"The Duchess killed her," said Roudette. "Your stepsister was dead the moment the Duchess gave her that gown with the fire sprite hidden within it."

"Snow could have saved her."

"Maybe." Snow rubbed her fingers against the base of her skull. "The gown carried the sprite's essence. Trying to remove it could have freed the sprite."

"Charlotte died well," Roudette said. "She died fighting them."

"Shut up." Danielle pushed back her sleeve, exposing her bracelet. "Fairytown will be told exactly what the Duchess did today. If Trittibar earned exile for saving your lives, the Duchess has earned far worse."

"What about Roudette?" Snow asked.

Danielle swallowed, her uncertainty clear to anyone who knew her. She glanced at Talia, who nodded and adjusted her grip on her knife. Danielle straightened.

"Would you like a moment to pray and prepare yourself, Roudette?"

Roudette kept perfectly still. "Kill me, and the three of you will never see another sunrise."

Talia dug the edge of her knife into Roudette's throat. "Not even the Lady of the Red Hood can kill us after she's dead."

"You think it's me you need to fear?" Roudette smiled. "I've lived with death as long as I can remember. It holds no terror for me anymore. But kill me, and before morning comes, you'll wish I'd turned you over to Queen Lakhim."

"I'm willing to take that chance," said Talia.

"Do you believe that final fairy spared your life out of kindness, all those years ago?" Roudette asked.

Danielle lowered her sword slightly. "What are you saying?"

"She's saying whatever it takes to stay alive," Talia snapped.

"Poor Sleeping Beauty," Roudette said, smiling up at Talia. "Cursed to die upon your sixteenth birthday, until that curse was altered by the final fairy's wish. Instead of death, you would merely sleep. Only you weren't the only one to fall into that enchanted sleep, were you?"

Snow's breath caught. She leaned closer, pain forgotten in her excitement. Why had she never seen it before? "The fairy lied. That last wish wasn't supposed to break the curse. It *dispersed* it!"

Roudette's lips pulled back in a grimace. "Instead of killing you, the curse blanketed the palace. Everyone within the fairy hedge slept for a hundred years, all triggered by the prick of a spindle."

"By a zaraq whip," Talia corrected her. "An assassin's weapon. The tip was poisoned."

"Who made that poison?" Roudette asked. "What mortal toxin could plunge an entire palace into a century of cursed sleep?"

"You're saying the fairies planned this," Snow breathed, awestruck by the elegance of the plan. "The final two fairies worked together to prepare their curse."

"The assassin was human," Talia protested. "He was—"

"He was a fairy slave." Roudette rose, ignoring the weapons pointed at her. "They wouldn't have sent one of their own, knowing what was to come. Why condemn even the lowest fairy to such a curse when a human would do the same for mere gold?"

"Why?" asked Danielle. "What would they gain from such a spell?"

"Chaos." Talia stepped back. She kept her knife ready, but her gaze was elsewhere. "In a single day, they removed the entire ruling line of Arathea."

"One hundred years of war and rebellion and death," Snow whispered, thinking back to the history of Arathea. "Leaving fairykind free to do whatever they wished."

"It's worse," said Talia. Her knuckles were white where she gripped the knife. "For the next hundred years, every family with a drop of royal blood sent their sons and brothers to try to penetrate the hedge. All died, impaled upon the thorns. They eliminated my family, and then they removed every male heir who might have taken the throne and reunited Arathea."

"And who helped to save your land from that century of darkness?" Roudette asked. There was no mockery or cruelty in her tone. She appeared almost as pained by the revelation as Talia. "Who spread throughout Arathea to help the poor humans, to build new cities, to advise the tribes and factions?"

"The fairies," Talia whispered.

Snow turned toward Jahrasima. History described the lake cities of Arathea as gifts, but few fairy gifts were truly free. More than half of Arathea's population lived in these nine fairy-built cities. Within each one, fairy advisors stood behind every ruler, guiding their path.

"Do you remember what it was like when you awoke?" Roudette pressed. "How deeply they had infiltrated your culture? Today the lowest fairy is higher than any human. But it's not enough. Despise your mother-in-law if you'd like, but she's managed to unify this country under human rule again. For that alone, the fairies would see her dead. Her and all her kin. Or if not dead, at least removed from power. Eliminated just as your own family was."

"The curse." Talia stared at her hands.

"The fairies mean to use you against Lakhim," Roudette said. "To trigger your curse a second time. I was to bring you to Lakhim. Alive if possible, so her sages could study your curse. Dead if necessary."

"Why kill Talia?" Danielle asked. "If Lakhim discovered this plot, why not kill the fairies behind it?"

"They've tried," said Roudette. "A century ago, such a plan might have worked. The fairy who cursed Talia was hunted by the people and burned to death. But today, Lakhim wouldn't dare move openly against the 'saviors of Arathea.'"

"So why not cast a new curse?" Snow asked.

"That has been tried as well," said Roudette. "Time and again, without success. With one of the original fairies dead and Talia gone, they've been unable to duplicate the exact spells used in her curse. They will do anything to claim her."

Snow shook her head. "The Duchess prepared the fairy sprite you meant to use. Why would she work against her own kind?"

"Fairies are no more united than humans." Roudette spat. "In this land, they say fairies are creatures of fire who betrayed the gods and were banished from Heaven. They were *born* of treachery. Don't ask me to understand their twisted alliances and betrayals. I was told the Duchess would help. I didn't question what she would receive in return."

Talia was staring toward the city. She didn't appear to be listening, but when Roudette fell silent, Talia whispered, "Who leads the fairies in Arathea?"

Roudette pushed Danielle's sword away. "The one you want is called Zestan-e-Jheg. Spare my life, and I'll help you kill her."

CHAPTER 7

ROUDETTE SAT BOUND BY THE THIN LINE of Talia's zaraq whip. Testing the whip had done nothing but cut her wrists, so now she waited in silence as they debated her fate. She might have been able to break the whip, but Talia was watching her. By the time Roudette freed herself, Talia would have planted one knife in Roudette's chest and would be throwing the second.

So she waited. Waited and listened, using the wolf's senses.

"Roudette is a murderer," Danielle was saying. "How many people has she killed today alone?"

Snow chuckled. "When Danielle Whiteshore says you can't trust someone, it's time to listen."

"She's telling the truth about what the fairies did to me. What they did to Arathea." Talia's eyes narrowed as she watched Roudette. Did she suspect Roudette could hear them? Talia lowered her voice further. "I can't let it happen again."

If Roudette were in their place, she knew what her answer would be. Faith and trust got you killed, and Talia knew exactly how dangerous Roudette could be.

Death didn't bother her. Roudette had accepted the possibility of death the first time she donned the wolfskin, the same day she killed for the first time. What frightened her was the idea of dying without being able to finish this final task. Talia held the key to everything Roudette had worked for these past thirty years, but if she fell into Zestan's hands, all Arathea would suffer.

"What about a binding?" asked Danielle. "The spell Snow used on Rumpelstilzchen kept him under control."

The hair on Roudette's neck and arms rose. Not since she was a child had she allowed magic to be used upon her.

"Even with a binding, I don't trust her," said Snow.

"Neither do I." Talia was watching Roudette's face. "But you saw the way she spoke of the fairies. I trust her hate."

That seemed to settle the matter. Talia held her sword ready as Danielle approached to say, "You have a choice. Accept Snow's spell, which will bind you to your word. Or refuse and accept the punishment for your actions."

In other circumstances, Roudette might have chosen death. Instead, she stood and pushed back the shoulders of her cape, exposing herself to Snow's magic.

Snow placed a thumb in the hollow of Roudette's collarbone. Roudette's skin grew cold, then numb. A thread of smoke rose from beneath Snow's thumb, smelling of new-forged metal.

"By this mark, I charge you to protect the three of us with your life," Snow said. "You will not raise a hand against us, nor will you allow us to come to harm. Your contract with Queen Lakhim is broken. When Zestan is dealt with, you will surrender yourself to Lorindar. At no time will you stray more than fifty paces from either myself, Danielle, or Talia. Should you break this bond, your blood shall boil within your body."

Danielle grimaced. "That's a little gruesome, don't you think?"

"It's a standard fairy clause," Snow said. To Roudette, she asked, "Do you accept this mark?"

The tip of Talia's sword pressing against her neck left little choice. "Yes."

The skin of her collarbone burned to life, but even as Roudette yanked away, the pain was dying. Roudette used her bound hands to pull back her shirt, examining the mark.

A spot of silver the size of Snow's thumb marred her skin. Roudette dug a fingernail into the mark, and was rewarded by a dark crescent of blood. Gouging the skin wouldn't remove the spell beneath. Wordlessly, she extended her hands. Talia untied the whip.

"You didn't ask for how long," Danielle said softly.

Roudette tilted her head. "Excuse me?"

"Most people, upon being given such a curse, would want to know how long it would last. How many years you would remain our prisoner, and whether you would ever be given your freedom."

Danielle was more perceptive than Roudette had realized. "Most people spend too much time thinking about what is to come. I trust my path will lead me where I'm meant to go."

They didn't return her hammer, but Roudette hadn't expected them to. It made little difference. Roudette could kill almost as effectively with her bare hands. She pulled her cape back into place. The runes on the cape protected her from external magic, but the fairy mark was within her now. The cape couldn't remove it.

But it might slow the effects. Not for very long, but perhaps it would be enough to do what she must.

She watched Snow and Danielle closely. She knew Talia, but these two were new. Danielle appeared soft, yet she hadn't hesitated to join the battle back at Whiteshore Palace, even though Roudette could have killed her as swiftly as a thought. As for Snow, her magic had held off fairy wolves and diverted a fairy ring, two things Roudette had thought impossible.

They were an impressive team. It was a shame she would have to destroy them.

Danielle sat with her back to a tree as she waited for the mirror on her bracelet to respond to her kiss. Talia had left them at the edge of the lake, where the thicker trees and grasses provided cover from the dust and wind, not to mention concealing them from the city.

"Danielle?" Prince Armand looked up at her from the tiny mirror. "Are you all right? What happened? Where did you—"

"We're safe," Danielle said. "We're in Arathea, outside the city of Jahrasima. Talia has gone ahead to find us a place to stay. Is Jakob—"

"He's here with me," said Armand, tilting the mirror so Danielle could see her son. "He wants to know when you're coming home."

"As soon as I can. I promise." Danielle braced herself. "Armand, what of Charlotte?"

"Dead." Armand's voice was cold. "According to witnesses, it was a quick death."

Tears filled her eyes. Roudette had said as much, but still Danielle had hoped that somehow Charlotte might have survived. Even though Charlotte had always hated Danielle, she had also been the last survivor of Danielle's childhood, the only piece of her former life. "Before the fairy ring took us, Jakob said Father Isaac had been hurt."

"Burned, but he'll survive." He was choosing his words carefully, trying not to upset Jakob. "The protective spells in the chapel saved his life. The sprite couldn't attack him, but its mere presence was enough to set his robe afire. Tymalous is seeing to his care."

"It wasn't Charlotte's fault," Danielle said. "She controlled it as long as she could."

Armand didn't answer.

Danielle watched Roudette pacing through the trees. "How many others were killed?"

Her anger grew as Armand recited the list of the dead. Eight guardsmen had died today, not including those killed earlier when Roudette attacked Rumpelstilzchen. Melvyn the rathunter and three of his dogs had also fallen to Roudette's hammer. A young woman and her mother were killed by Roudette's wolves at the southern gate. Eleven others had been injured and brought into the palace, where Tymalous was doing the best he could to keep them alive. "Father Isaac is helping as well, against Tymalous' orders."

This wasn't the first time Danielle had faced death, but rarely had it felt so *casual*. Roudette killed without a thought, disposing of anyone with the ill fortune to get between her and her target. "Roudette is bound by Snow's magic. She'll return with us to Lorindar, and she will pay for what she's done."

"When?" asked Armand. "I can send Captain Hephyra and the *Phillipa* to wait for you. If you're in Jahrasima, that puts you in the central region of northern Arathea. You'll have to make your way to—"

"There's more." Danielle told him what they had learned about Zestan-e-Jheg and Talia's fairy curse.

Armand's image grew as he brought his mirror closer. "Your friend Talia is under sentence of death. By Arathean law, anyone who aids a murderer shares in that person's guilt. If Talia is caught, you could all be executed." He spoke in a whisper, trying to keep Jakob from overhearing.

"What would you have me do?" Danielle asked. "Turn my back on my friend and flee to Lorindar?"

"Yes!" He sighed. "And I know you won't. Promise me you'll be careful, love. Arathea sent an assassin to Lorindar. They want Talia badly enough to risk war. They won't hesitate to kill you as well."

"I promise," Danielle said.

"Remember who you are. If anyone learns the Princess of Lorindar has directly involved herself in this conflict, the consequences could be far-reaching, and not just from Arathea."

Danielle smiled. "I wasn't planning to wander about in my crown and glass slippers."

"Thus far, Arathea refuses to admit any knowledge of Roudette or her mission," said Armand. "We will continue to press them. For now, please try not to start any wars while you're there."

"I'll do my best. And I'll be home as soon as I can." She smiled as Armand handed his mirror to Jakob, and planted a loud kiss on the glass.

"I love you both," she said, returning the kiss. When she pulled away, the glass showed only her reflection.

Under different circumstances, Talia might have felt guilty as she lowered the farmhand's body into the mud. He would have a nasty headache when he awoke.

She crouched beside him, hiding behind the grain and counting slowly to herself as she waited to make sure nobody had heard. When she reached a count of twenty, she began stripping the man of his clothes. They were a little large, but that would work to her advantage. She pulled the trousers on over her own garments. The shirt followed, though she had to hack off the ends of the sleeves to keep her hands free. Smears of dirt and mud finished the job, turning her from a palace servant of Lorindar into another filthy peasant. It wouldn't pass a close inspection, but hopefully nobody would pay that much attention.

She froze as one of the man's companions passed by, whistling as he dredged the irrigation ditch a short distance away. Talia waited for him to pass, then dragged the body deeper into the field. She whispered into her bracelet, a twin to the one Danielle wore. "Snow, I've got a body for you to take care of."

"Already?"

"I could dump him in the lake to drown, but Danielle would probably complain." She yanked her sleeve down and made her way toward the road, easily avoiding the other farmhands.

Her entire body felt tight, braced against old memories as she stepped into the open. The damp earth changed to stone beneath her feet. The air was deliciously dry in her nostrils, carrying the sweet scent of freshly tilled earth. The crops wouldn't be ready for months, but somehow the air smelled green and alive.

The roads into the city were built like wide stone walls cutting through the lake. Archways far below were said to allow the water to flow freely, but few humans were mad enough to dive in to find out for certain. Some said strange creatures inhabited the deeper water of the lake.

Like a fisherman's hook, the smallest things drew remembrances from her past. The reeds growing along the edges of the path as she crossed the lake. The same swordlike fronds had grown in the pools back at her palace. As a child she had liked to play in the water, picking the waxy red teacup flowers for her mother.

The lake lapped the stones on either side of the road, reminding her of the last time she had walked this path. That had been at night, the starlight reflecting off the canals behind her.

She hadn't planned to kill Prince Jihab. From the time she staggered out through the hedge, it had been as though some part of her still slept under the fairy curse. She stumbled through the following days in shock, not knowing from one day to the next whether this was real or a nightmare. Her family was gone, her sons' cries echoed in her ears, and then Jihab and Lakhim had arrived to take them back to their palace.

How long would she have remained in that trance if Jihab hadn't come to her bed that night, meaning to claim her once again? In a way, the stories were true. Prince Jihab *had* awakened her. Not with a kiss but by shocking her into action.

She remembered sneaking from the palace, climbing out the window, and making her way along the walls. She made it to the edge of town before the alarm bells began to ring. There she found a farmer preparing to transport cattle to Jahrasima, four days south. All the gold she had taken when she fled went to pay for her safe passage.

They were stopped three times on the way to Jahrasima, but nobody discovered her. Even with their prince dead, few soldiers were loyal enough to dig through a wagon full of cow dung to discover the girl huddled beneath, protected by a heavy canvas tarp and breathing through the cracks at the bottom of the wagon.

Talia shuddered. The putrid scent had lingered in her hair and skin for days, no matter how hard she scrubbed.

Blue light blossomed in the water beside her. Talia glanced down to see a glowing serpent swimming through the reeds. A jaan, a fairy creature who lived in the water. They were said to bring good fortune to those who fed them, but Talia had nothing to give.

She had never believed that superstition. More likely, feeding the jaan was a way to keep them trained. These creatures guarded the city gates as much as the uniformed men on the far side of the road. Anyone trying to swim across the lake would find himself surrounded by eager jaan, their glowing bodies illuminating the intruder for all to see.

Not that many people worried about the south road. This was the least traveled of the four roads, leading to the poorest part of Jahrasima. The gatehouse was in poor repair, as were most of the buildings beyond. Even from here Talia could see where one home had crumbled to the onslaught of time and overgrown grapevines.

Two men stepped out to meet her as she approached the gatehouse. Their armor was lighter than that worn by their counterparts in Lorindar. Arathean warriors valued speed and skill over protection, not to mention the toll heavy mail could take in the desert heat. One carried a short spear. The other held a war club, a short, slender weapon with a knobbed end. This was a northern design that could double as a spearthrower, carried by all those in service to Queen Lakhim.

Both wore green sashes marked with the royal crest. The white tiger was the symbol of Lakhim's family. The small huma bird flying above the tiger had been the symbol of the crown for more than three hundred years. Lakhim hadn't eliminated the huma bird from her crest, but she had diminished it to little more than an afterthought. The green mountains in the background represented the fairy race.

"What happened to you?" asked the one with the spear.

Talia licked her lip, still swollen from her fight with Roudette. "Wolf attack."

The other moved closer. "Are you all right?"

"I will be." Talia did her best to feign fear. "I need to get to the temple. My friends were hurt. One was mauled too badly to move."

She shifted her balance, one hand ready to snatch a knife from her sleeve. Few had ever seen Sleeping Beauty in the flesh, but it never hurt to be prepared.

"What about the wolf?" asked the one with the war club. He sounded almost eager. Probably looking for something to break the tedium of guarding the poor quarter.

Talia shook her head. "It won't bother anyone else."

Her body remembered the route to the temple. She left the main road, taking a shortcut through an alleyway and around an old warehouse, finally emerging onto a road of broken stone. Weeds and vines pricked her legs, catching her trousers as she walked toward the low, nine-sided building at the end of the road.

A waist-high stone wall surrounded the temple grounds. The wall was in poor repair, little more than a symbolic barrier. Even from here Talia could smell the urine and decay of the sick and the dying.

Her heart drummed in her chest as she approached, following a dirt path through the open gate. Inside, the grounds were better tended. Red stone crunched beneath her feet. Fig trees grew to either side, straggly but alive. Smaller flowers and herbs grew at the base of the temple walls. Three younger girls in the black robes of the temple were tending the gardens. Talia smiled as she watched them, remembering a time when she had done the same.

An old woman with only one leg lay sleeping in the shade of a fig tree. A man with a splinted arm walked through the yard. He tilted his head in greeting, then coughed politely, drawing the attention of the gardeners to Talia.

One of the girls jumped to her feet. She hurried to the path, where she stopped to offer a half bow. "Welcome to the Temple of the Hedge. May you find peace and health within our walls."

Both her words and her movements were careful and precise, as though she had to remind herself of the proper greeting. She couldn't have been here more than a month.

"Thank you." Talia's mouth went dry as she looked about. She had tried not to think about what she might find when she arrived, but now that she was here, her palms were damp, and her heart was beating painfully hard. She swallowed and asked, "Is Sister Faziya available?"

The girl's shoulders tensed. "I'm sorry. Faziya left the temple more than a month ago."

Talia stared. Fairies could have razed Jahrasima to

the ground, and it wouldn't have struck Talia so hard. "I don't understand. This was her home."

"You were a friend of hers?" The girl cocked her head at Talia. "Your accent is strange. Where have you come from?"

From the entrance of the temple, an aged voice said, "Escort our visitor inside, Wijaq."

Talia straightened at the sound. Mother Khardija's voice was every bit as regal and commanding as a queen's.

Mother Khardija stood in the wide rectangular entryway into the temple proper, her arms folded over her chest. She appeared unchanged, still dressed in the same faded robe Talia remembered, more gray than black now. Wrinkles covered her old face like cracked glazing, almost hiding the small blue thorn tattooed on her left cheek. Two ivory rods pinned her thin gray hair in a tight knot.

"She doesn't appear sick, Mother," said Wijaq.

"Are all ailments visible to your eye? After so little time in our company, can you diagnose the sick with a single glance?" The rasping voice sounded more amused than upset, though Wijaq was likely too new to recognize the difference. "Let the temple rejoice, for none have ever before come to us with such a gift. From this day forward, let this place be known as the Temple of Wijaq."

Wijaq bowed low, her face dark. Two other girls giggled behind her, the sound cut short by a glare from Mother Khardija.

"Forgive me," said Wijaq.

"Don't worry," Talia whispered, trying not to smile. "Mother Khardija used to say far worse to me when I wore the black robe."

"Not that you ever listened." Khardija beckoned Talia closer.

Talia hurried up the path. She had forgotten Mother

Khardija's preternatural hearing. The woman could hear a patient coughing—or an acolyte gossiping—from the other side of the temple.

Khardija put her hands on Talia's shoulders and pulled her close. "You should not have come here," she said softly. "Jahrasima isn't safe."

"This wasn't a planned visit, Mother Khardija." Talia awkwardly returned the embrace. "The girl out front told me Faziya left the temple. I don't understand. Why—"

"Arathea has been troubled in recent times." Khardija kissed her forehead, then stepped back. "Faziya . . . she believed she could best serve elsewhere."

"Faziya was the most devoted sister I ever met."

"We can talk of this later. You need food and rest."

"Thank you," said Talia. "We'll be away as soon as we can. My friends—"

"Nonsense. You and your friends will stay as long as you need, and we will keep you safe, as before." Khardija stepped back, glancing around to make sure nobody was nearby. "I knew you would return to us, but I wondered if I would live long enough to see it. Your time is soon, Princess."

Talia pulled away. "My time?"

"To overthrow Queen Lakhim and reclaim your family's throne," said Khardija. "To take your place as ruler of Arathea."

CHAPTER 8

ROUDETTE'S SNARL YANKED SNOW INTO alertness. She sat up too quickly, groaned, and clutched her head. Beside her, Danielle was reaching for her sword.

"It's only Talia," Snow said.

"How can you tell?"

Snow turned toward the distant figure crossing the lake. The sun was setting, and Talia was little more than a shadow. Snow tapped her choker. "I lost track of her when she passed into the city, but that's her."

"I hope she's brought food," Roudette said.

Talia was dressed in a black robe. A matching scarf covered her head and face, exposing only a narrow stripe of skin and eyes. She carried a rolled bundle over one shoulder. She glanced about as she hurried through the field, but most of the workers had already retired for the night.

"You look bleak," Snow said, studying Talia's robe.

"All of the sisters wear black." Talia tugged her scarf down past her chin. "Anyone may join the temple, rich or poor. No matter what clothes you wear when you take your vows, it's simple enough to dye them black."

Snow made a face. "Black makes me look too pale."

"You're not going to be sisters." Talia grinned and

tossed the bundle to Snow. "You're farmhands. Poor, injured farmhands."

Snow pulled out a loose tunic with long sleeves. A wide scarf followed. "Magic would be easier."

"Have you ever seen Arathean peasant wear?" Talia grabbed a second tunic and held it to the moonlight. "Could you mimic the red and yellow tribal patterns on the collar? The goat horn buttons? Don't forget the linen undertunic. Get one detail wrong and you could find yourself hauled before the raikh."

"The raikh?" Danielle asked.

"The city ruler." Snow held the clothes to her body. They were heavier than she had expected. "The equivalent of a lord back home."

"The raikh of Jahrasima is named Rajil." Talia spat the name. "A devout worshiper of the fairies, and a spoiled brat. She's ruled Jahrasima for more than ten years. Her family backed Lakhim's claim to the throne, and Lakhim gave her Jahrasima in exchange for that support. If it were up to Rajil, all of Arathea would follow church law above all else."

"So be careful, witch," said Roudette. "Siqlah law is unforgiving of those who practice human magic."

Danielle was already changing into the disguise Talia had brought. She glanced at Snow "Siqlah?"

"The law of God, set forth by the fairy church," said Snow. "Legally, the church holds only advisory powers, but these days the distinction is a thin one. Human law, enforced by Queen Lakhim, is called Siqkhab. The fairies are bound to a 'higher' law, known as Siqjab."

Danielle held up one of the head scarves. "Even wearing these, anyone who looks closely enough will see we're not Arathean."

"I can take care of that," said Snow. "An illusion to darken the skin and eyes."

Roudette sniffed as she picked up one of the scarves. "My cape won't allow your illusions."

"I assumed as much," said Talia, grabbing a handful of long rags. "You were all injured tonight. I'm taking you back to the temple for healing. Roudette, your face was mauled." She tossed the rags to Roudette. "Let me know if you need any assistance making it believable."

Roudette touched her cheek where Talia's knife had cut her. The wound still oozed blood. She spat, but began wrapping the rags around her face.

"Don't do that again," Talia said without looking up. "Obscenity won't help you blend in here."

"Obscenity?" Danielle asked.

Snow pretended to spit. "Wasting the body's water." To Talia, she asked, "Where is this place you're taking us?"

"The Temple of the Hedge." Talia jabbed a finger at the clothes in Snow's hands. "Assuming you ever get ready."

Snow stuck out her tongue, then stepped away to change. When she returned, Talia was helping Danielle to adjust her head scarf.

Snow whispered a quick spell, and Danielle's skin darkened to match Talia's own. Danielle's hair turned a shining black, even as Talia twisted the hair into a knot and pulled it into the scarf.

"Does everyone wear these things?" Danielle asked.

"In the city, most people use the sheffeyah as a hood, keeping the faces exposed." Talia tugged the scarf tight over Danielle's nose and mouth. "The more ardent followers of Siqlah also cover their faces as a sign of modesty before God. In the old days, they were used to keep the sand out of your ears, mouth, and nose."

"It smells like old sweat," Snow complained.

Talia yanked the scarf from her hands and pulled it taut like a garrote. "Either you wrap this around your neck or I will."

Snow sniffed and plucked the scarf from Talia's hands. Snow did her best, but Talia had to show her how to properly pull the ends tight to keep the scarf's edges from tugging loose. She fussed over Danielle the same way, then waited impatiently for Roudette to pull an oversized shirt and skirt over her cape.

Snow cocked her head to the side. "You look … bulky." Rags covered all of Roudette's head save the left eye, which peeked out through a thin layer of gauzy cloth. "Can't you carry that old cape instead of wearing it?"

"You can take my cape once I'm dead," Roudette said.

"We should get moving," Danielle said quickly, probably trying to stop Talia from commenting.

Frogs croaked as they neared the lake. Snow stopped to crouch at the shore, studying the animals. The frogs preyed on the insects, and the glowing jaan hunted any frog foolish enough to stray from the damp rocks into the deeper water.

"Get up and stop gawking," Talia whispered. "You're wounded, remember?"

Snow paid little attention to the guards, allowing Talia to deal with them. Instead, Snow peered through lidded eyes as she tried to see the enchantments cast over the city. She had entered Fairytown upon several occasions, as well as spending time in Trittibar's apartment in the palace, studying fairy magic. The power of this place was more muted than in Fairytown, but the magic was almost as strong. It would have to be, to maintain such a lake in the middle of the desert.

Snow looked about as they walked through the city streets, trying to pinpoint the source of that power. If Jahrasima were built upon a fairy hill, every fairy with magical abilities would be able to draw upon that magic. Yet she couldn't sense any source to the city's magic. There was no ebb or flow, no currents of power.

It reminded her of the fairy ring Charlotte's sprite had created. The wards of the palace *should* have cut that sprite off from its magic, yet it had built the most powerful fairy spell Snow had ever witnessed, and it had done so with no obvious source of power. It was as though the sprite and Jahrasima both used an entirely new kind of fairy magic.

She needed to talk to Trittibar or, better yet, to raid his library. Even if most of his books were doll-sized, there were lenses she could use to read them, and Trittibar's collection included the most detailed histories she had ever encountered of ancient fairy magic going back to the days of the peri and the deev.

Snow nearly bumped into Danielle when they finally reached the temple. She blinked and looked about as Talia led them inside. She spotted several women in black robes tending to patients in the yard, murmuring reassurances as they doled out medicine.

The temple itself was built of mud bricks and cut stone, a style Snow had read about but never seen. Brown stone formed square support pillars set about ten paces apart. Between them, darker bricks filled in the walls.

An older woman in a faded robe greeted them in the temple doorway, introducing herself as Mother Khardija.

Danielle leaned toward Snow. "What's she saying?"

"Haven't you been studying Arathean?" Snow whispered.

"Which dialect?" Danielle made a sour face. "I'm doing the best I can, but between Arathean and Morovan and Sylan and Hiladi . . . I can introduce myself and ask for a translator, but not much more."

Khardija was already leading them down a wide hallway with no ceiling. Cats trotted along the tops of the walls. A lanky tom with spotted fur and long ears jumped down to rub against Danielle's legs.

"You see?" said Snow. "At least something here understands you."

Danielle scooped the cat into her arms. "What are they saying?"

"Khardija is taking us to the back of the temple," Snow translated. "She wants us hidden from casual visitors."

Khardija led them through a doorway in the inner wall. Oil lamps hung on the inside, illuminating a wide circular garden. Budding vegetables poked through fresh-tilled earth. Fruit trees bordered several paths, all leading to a small pool at the center. A pair of white ducks floated on the water, apparently asleep.

Khardija hurried them along the path, but Talia stepped away, moving toward a small vineyard near the back wall. She spun, hands shaking. "I told you to burn these."

"I know," Khardija said gently. "When you are queen, I'll obey your commands. Until then, I lead this temple."

Snow studied the vines more closely. They were a deep green, mottled with brown. The thorns had a liquid sheen, purple in color. They reminded her of the hedge at Fairytown.

"Why?" Talia demanded.

"You know why." Khardija put a hand on Talia's shoulder. "Every temple has such a vineyard, to remind us of our beginnings. I know the sight brings you pain, my dear Talia. Just as you know some pain is natural. Pain alerts us to injury, reminds us to take the time to heal. Ignore the pain, and the wound festers."

"Your lectures haven't changed," Talia said.

Khardija smiled. "Neither has your stubbornness."

Snow knelt to study the vines. The plants hummed with fairy magic. "These are from the hedge that surrounded Talia's palace. I thought they died with her curse."

"The land around Princess Talia's palace could no longer sustain them," Khardija said. "We saved cuttings from the dying hedge. Replanted here, they would over-grow the temple if not carefully tended." Laugh lines deepened in her cheeks. "When kept under control, the vines produce a small, potent fruit, like tiny yellow grapes. Sales of fairy wine help to support our work here, allowing us to help those who cannot afford the services of the larger temples."

"Do you know how many people died on these thorns?" Talia demanded.

Khardija straightened, her expression hardening. "Remember whom you address, Talia. I served at the first temple for sixteen years before coming here. I know their names. While you slept, I listened to their cries. It's for them that I tend this plant. For them and for yourself, to make certain nobody ever forgets."

While Khardija's attention was elsewhere, Snow slipped her knife free and cut a small length of vine. She wrapped it in the folds of her gown, careful to avoid the thorns. The hedge at Fairytown was a mere imitation of Talia's hedge; this was a chance to study the real thing.

"I apologize."

Snow whirled, trying to remember the last time she had heard those words from Talia. From the expression on Danielle's face, she was as surprised as Snow.

Mother Khardija embraced Talia again. "Your anger is healthy. I prefer it to the silent stone you were when I first met you." She gestured toward the far side of the garden. "Come, all of you. You need food and rest." To Talia, she added, "My rules still hold, Princess."

Talia actually blushed. "Yes, Mother."

"What rules?" Snow demanded.

Talia shrugged. "No wandering the tops of the walls or sneaking into the city. No stealing from the patients." She glanced at the vines. "No ripping those accursed things from the ground and burning them."

Khardija chuckled as she led them into another hall-way. They passed several other women in black robes before stopping at an arched doorway. Khardija pushed a curtain of goat wool to the side, waiting as they passed into an unfurnished room. Heavy carpets covered the ground. Several sleeping mats were rolled in one corner. A single lamp sat in a round window.

The ceiling was a heavy woven mat of undyed wool, stretched taut over the brick walls. Wooden pegs protruded from the walls just beneath the ceiling. Six black robes hung on the left wall.

Khardija gripped Talia's arms, an odd expression of pride and anticipation on her face. "Welcome back, Princess."

Snow waited for her to leave before asking, "What next?"

Talia paced slowly through the room, brushing her fingers over the wall. "There's little more we can do tonight. You're safe here, for now. Eat, rest. Tomorrow we hunt Zestan."

Talia's bare feet made no sound as she finished her walk. She kept the hood of her robe pulled low, hiding her face. Khardija wasn't the only one who might remember her, but she was the only one Talia truly trusted.

The temple hadn't changed in her years away. The same dusty air, the same cracking walls, the same bland food. Even the temple cats were familiar.

She watched a lean young cat disappear into the garden, stalking prey Talia couldn't see. One of the tuft-tailed mice that were always nibbling the shoots in the garden, no doubt. Talia could see the kitten's resemblance to its mother, a pitiful old thing named Akhar'ba who had the same mottled fur, at least where that fur wasn't falling out in clumps. Danielle would have liked her. The sisters had tended to Akhar'ba with the same care they provided their human patients.

Talia checked to make sure the hallway was empty before pushing back her hood and looking upward. The skies of Lorindar were rarely so clear. She searched until she found the faint band of light that stretched across the sky. The River of the Dead, the old priests used to call it. Guarded by Halaka'ar the dragon, who made sure each soul found its proper destination.

A cry of pain made her flinch. The sounds of the injured were familiar as well, though that was one thing Talia hadn't missed. Without conscious thought, she found herself hurrying to the front of the temple to help. She smiled, remembering Mother Khardija's voice. *If you're to stay with us, you can make yourself useful, princess or no.*

Talia spent the next hour holding a young boy in place while another sister attempted to remove splinters of glass from his hands. She had fought grown men who struggled with less ferocity, but eventually the last of the glass was removed, and the boy's father was able to rock him to sleep.

Talia ignored the thanks of the sister and returned to her room before anyone else could try to talk to her. She found Snow sleeping against one wall, her mirrors still maintaining the illusion of her brown skin. Roudette was curled tightly in the corner, twitching as she dreamed.

Danielle sat beneath the window, holding her bracelet in her hands. Talia had no doubt that if she looked, she would see Prince Jakob's sleeping form in the glass. One of the temple cats was curled in Danielle's lap. Talia remembered this one: Haut el'Faum, the fish thief. Haut had lost part of his tail as a kitten, making him easy to recognize.

"Hello Talia," Danielle said softly. "I tried to sleep, but—"

"You're not her." Talia glanced at Snow. "Falling through fairy rings or traveling across an ocean doesn't bother her in the slightest. You're different. You worry."

Danielle pressed her lips to the mirror, then returned the bracelet to her wrist. "I never understood how hard it must have been for you when you first arrived in Lorindar. Everything is so different. The language, the clothes, the smells—"

"Anything was preferable to staying here to be beheaded for murder." Talia sat down beside her. "When I first awoke, Arathea was almost as alien to me as it is to you. You wouldn't believe how much can change in a hundred years. I nearly pissed myself the first time I heard a cannon fired. Everything was strange, with just enough similarity to remind me of what I had lost."

Danielle smiled. "It's still your home. You're more relaxed here, even with fairies and nobles hunting you. Especially here in the temple . . . you trust these people."

"They saved my life."

Her smile grew. "One of the first things you ever told me was that I was too trusting."

"You are." Talia rested her head against the familiar bricks of the wall. "Khardija risked the lives of everyone here to protect me."

Danielle scratched Haut's neck. "Snow told me some of what Khardija said in the gardens. About the vines from your hedge."

Talia rubbed her right hand, remembering the night an assassin had given her the teardrop-shaped scar in the meat of her palm. He had come upon her in the afternoon. Dressed in black with a simple ribbon of red round his brow, he had attacked the instant he spied her.

Talia could still remember the zaraq whip lashing out like a snake. She had dodged the first attack without thinking. The weighted tip of the whip shattered the window behind her head. Talia tried to flee. He followed her into the hallway and attacked again.

Fairy-blessed reflexes allowed her to block the second strike with her palm. A stupid move, looking back. A direct blow would have shattered her hand. Even deflecting the weight had broken one of the bones.

The barbs of the weight tore her flesh. Blood welled from the wound. Talia fell, and with her, so did three hundred years of her family's rule.

She glanced at Roudette to make sure she was asleep before saying, "Once my family fell under my curse, the rumors spread quickly. Only a true prince, the rightful ruler of Arathea, could awaken Princess Talia from her slumber. Soon every man and child with any trace of royal blood was traveling to the palace to try his luck."

"The hedge killed them?" Danielle guessed.

Talia allowed herself a small, bitter laugh. "Not directly. That would be a violation of Siqlah and Siqjab both. The fairy church teaches that their race was sent to protect us, even from ourselves. The hedge was simply meant to shelter me from the unworthy. So my would-be rescuers lived. Impaled by thorns, trapped within the hedge, they survived for weeks or months. Sometimes even longer. Every effort was made to free them. Nothing succeeded. No blade could cut the vines, no shovel penetrated the earth. Not even fire would burn the hedge. Those who tried to fight the hedge often ended up impaled as well.

"The first temple arose to care for those trapped princes. The sisters used bowls attached to long poles to deliver food and drink. They used those same poles to send medicines to ease the pain. For those who asked, they would send other medicines to end it all.

"One prince survived for three years, five months, and eleven days. That was the longest, though he was mad at the end, his mind destroyed by his imprisonment and the heat of the desert sun. Others died when their wounds festered or disease took them or they simply gave up, refusing food or drink until they withered away.

"The temple did everything they could to turn princes away. They asked any prospective rescuer to spend a week working in the temple, tending the poor fools stuck in the hedge. It was enough to save a few souls, those smart enough to recognize what awaited them, but most were too headstrong to be dissuaded. They were royalty. You know how they can be."

"I've learned," Danielle said dryly.

"Each one was certain *he* was worthy to pass through the hedge and save the sleeping princess trapped beyond. Each one failed, and with every death, Arathea fragmented further. By the time Prince Jihab arrived, Arathea had spent most of a century at war, and the Temple of the Hedge had spread across the country, offering their services to all in need. Most of the royal bloodlines donated generously to the temple for the care of their sons. By the end, the temple's coffers rivaled those of the fairy church."

Danielle glanced at Snow. "How are they at treating injuries to the head?"

"I doubt there's much Khardija could do for her that Tymalous hasn't already tried."

"I'd still like to ask, if there's time."

"If there's time." Talia pursed her lips. "Snow won't be happy."

"I'll deal with Snow." Danielle looked around at the plain walls, the frayed panels overhead. "I take it the temple's fortunes changed?"

Talia massaged her scarred hand. She rarely spoke of what came next, not even to Snow. "Prince Jihab and his family brought enchanted axes against the hedge. The hedge had claimed Jihab's father years before. By the time Jihab arrived, the curse was dying. For weeks they hacked their way through, until finally they reached the palace. Jihab entered alone. When he was unable to waken me, he returned through the hedge, the first prince ever to emerge alive. He declared me dead and ordered the palace sealed from the outside. Rumors spread that the temple had known, that they had lured princes to the hedge in order to fund their growth. Jihab was a hero for discovering the truth, and the temple was nearly ruined.

"Nine months later, I awoke." She flexed her hand, remembering the pain of bone still broken after a hundred years. "Everyone I had ever known lay dead. Jihab's family murdered them in their sleep, to prevent them from ever awakening to challenge their rule. I've no doubt he would have done the same to me, if not for his uncertainty as to what my death would do to the curse. He left twenty men to guard the hedge, and the temple remained to help care for the handful of surviving princes. Jihab refused to let his axes be used to free them."

She shook her head. "When I awoke, childbirth had left me torn and weak. I staggered from the ruins of my home and made my way through the path Jihab's men had carved. The hedge was dying, but retained enough evil to bloody me as I escaped. Its final act of hate. My awakening had broken the remains of the curse, and the hedge died soon after.

"One of Jihab's soldiers nearly killed me that day, thinking me a demon escaped from the thorns. When they realized who that bloody, whimpering creature was, they brought me to the temple. The sisters did what they could to tend my wounds. They sent someone to retrieve my children from the castle—"

"You left them behind?" Danielle asked. Talia simply looked at her until she turned away, saying, "I'm sorry, Talia. I don't mean to judge."

"I didn't know who they were. Even if I had, I couldn't have carried them with a broken hand." Only deep down, she *had* known. The pain and blood from her loins had been proof enough. She simply hadn't wanted to believe. "Jihab's men sent word, and he came for us soon after. He and his mother had already seized power, but I was the key to sealing their rule. He had awakened Sleeping Beauty. Surely he was destined to be king.

"We were married the day we returned to his palace." She closed her eyes, knowing better than to fight the memories that followed. If she resisted, they would only grow worse. Their wedding had been a hastily arranged farce at the palace, officiated by a fairy priest with a beard so thick it had creatures living within it.

"After I killed him, I fled and made my way to Jahrasima." She remembered the warmth of his blood on her hands, the way it stuck between her fingers as it dried. He was the first man she had ever killed. "I came to this temple, not knowing where else to go. They protected me, even after they learned I had murdered the 'rightful' ruler of Arathea. If I was discovered, this temple and everyone in it would have been burned to the ground. Instead, Khardija and the rest did what they could to help me."

Few had known the true identity of their patient. Talia smiled, remembering the day Sister Faziya learned the truth. She had erupted with a string of profanity to make even Talia blush.

Her muscles, already tense, tightened further at the thought of Faziya. What could have been so important as to make her leave? Talia glanced toward the doorway, wondering if she should have pressed Mother Khardija about Faziya's whereabouts. Not that it would have made any difference. In all her time here, Talia had never once won an argument with Mother Khardija.

She rubbed her eyes, pushing back the old emotions until she regained her composure. "You should try to sleep, Princess."

Before Danielle could answer, the cat in her lap hissed and leaped to the floor, fur raised. He ran to the doorway, then raced back to nip Danielle's palm. He hissed again, tail lashing.

"What's wrong?" Danielle asked.

Talia was already on her feet. Far in the distance, she could hear the barking of hounds.

"They're coming." Roudette stood and pulled her cape tight. She strode toward the doorway. "I'll need a weapon."

"Who's coming?" asked Talia.

Roudette yanked back the curtain and peered into the hallway. "I warned you this would be your last night as a free woman without my help. Zestan has been hunting for you, Princess."

The baying of the dogs had grown loud enough to wake even Snow. She yawned and looked around, the magic of her choker brightening the room. "Arathea is too noisy." She frowned. "Those dogs aren't natural, are they?"

"The hounds signal the arrival of the Wild Hunt," said Roudette. "They've come for Talia."

CHAPTER 9

R OUDETTE STOOD, EYES CLOSED as she listened to the Wild Hunt: the howling of the dogs, the hoofbeats pounding over the streets, and the screams of those caught in their path. The sounds taunted her, and her limbs twitched with eagerness.

"This isn't the full hunt." She knew too well the sounds of the Wild Hunt and their victims. "Zestan must know you're in Arathea, but she doesn't know where. This scene is playing itself out in towns throughout the country. Talia, come with me. The rest of you stay hidden."

Talia blocked her way. "You don't give the orders here."

"Have you ever faced one of the fairy hunters?" When nobody responded, she pulled her hood up over her face. "If you want to protect your friends, you'll do as I say. Who knows, with both of us fighting together, we might even survive the night."

Talia looked to the others. "My spell binds her," Snow said. "She has no choice but to protect us."

Talia's expression was easy to read. *I don't need her protection.* But she said nothing.

Danielle retrieved Roudette's hammer, pressing it into her hand.

Talia and Roudette slipped into the hallway. Talia

twitched at every cry from the street, her tension visible even through the robe.

"You knew about this," Talia said.

"I knew they would come for you," Roudette agreed. "If not tonight, then soon."

"You should have—"

"It would have made no difference." For a moment, Roudette was a child again, running through the woods, branches tearing at her cape and hair. "The Wild Hunt ride wherever they choose, or they did until recently. They've been sighted more and more often in Arathea, though they rarely enter the cities."

"Zestan?" Talia asked.

Roudette twirled her hammer. "Had you asked me a year ago, I'd have told you no one, human or fairy, could command the Wild Hunt."

Two sisters ran down the hall toward them. Roudette recognized the old woman who had brought them in, Khardija. The other was unfamiliar. Both smelled of fear, though the older one hid it better.

"Do you know what's happening?" the old one asked.

"Keep everyone in their rooms," said Roudette. "Remain calm. If you flee, the Hunt *will* ride you down."

The sister looked to Talia for confirmation.

"Do it," said Talia.

"The Wild Hunt rides from midnight until an hour before dawn." Roudette moved into the garden, assessing its value as a place of ambush. "They'd be upon you already if my cape hadn't obscured our trail."

"Since you're the one who dragged me back here to begin with, I'm having a hard time feeling grateful."

"You will once you face a hunter." Roudette pointed to the far side of the garden. "That doorway is closest to the main entrance."

"I'll lure him into the garden," said Talia.

Roudette shook her head. "You're his prey. When

he spots you, he might summon the rest. Wait by the wall. I'll keep his attention on me. Strike quickly, and the Hunt won't realize they've lost one of their number until they depart before dawn."

Talia moved to the right of the doorway, crouching against the wall where a row of olive trees would help conceal her from view. She waited with a short curved sword in one hand, a knife in the other.

Roudette moved into the middle of the garden, making sure the moonlight shone upon her red cape. She gripped her hammer in both hands as she paced around the pool.

Even a single hunter was enough to rouse the wolf's hunger. She fought the urge to don the skin and charge into the night, chasing down the hunters and ripping them from their mounts. Tearing into their throats until every last one of them lay dead before her.

The next howl was closer, eliciting cries of fear from within the temple. Roudette heard the sisters rushing through the hallway, doing what they could to calm their patients.

She smelled the hunter before she saw him. The sulfurous stink of a fairy curse mixed with the bloody musk of the hounds. Two hounds, but only a single huntsman. The leather-wrapped handle of her hammer creaked in her grip. She could remember her first glimpse of a fairy hunter, though she hadn't known what he was at the time. Fool that she was, she had believed him to be a rescuer, come to save her from the wolf that had consumed her grandmother.

Shouts broke out from the yard. Footsteps pounded through the hallway as the more able-bodied patients fled, ignoring the pleas of the sisters. The hounds' barks grew louder in response.

"In here," Roudette shouted. The first one through the doorway was a young man with a splinted arm. Roudette pointed to the back. "Keep running."

He vanished through the rear doorway. Four others tore through the gardens, and then the hunter appeared.

Flanked by his hounds, he could have passed for human. A bronze helm fringed with black horsehair masked his face. He held a spear with a leaf-shaped point in one hand. Fresh blood darkened the tip.

Swirls of blue, either painted or tattooed, decorated his bare chest. His loose blue trousers were bound at the knees. A bone-handled knife hung on one hip, a bronze-rimmed horn on the other.

The dogs wore neither collars nor leashes, though they appeared to strain at invisible bonds. Long-legged and lean, their ears flat, they growled at Roudette. Their eyes had a faint blue-green glow, barely visible in the moonlight.

Joy surged through Roudette's heart as she charged the hunter. His dogs raced to intercept her. She saw Talia launching herself from the shadows, silent as the darkness.

Roudette swung at the dog on her right, the iron weight of her hammer crushing the animal's shoulder. The other dog slammed into her. She fell, releasing her weapon and digging both hands into the dog's throat. She kicked her legs into its ribs and hurled it through the air to land in the pond behind her.

The hunter had dodged Talia's first attack. He pushed her back with his spear, then grabbed the horn from his belt. As he raised it to his lips, Talia knocked his spear aside and kicked high. Her foot cracked the horn and knocked several teeth from his mouth.

"Try blowing that thing now," Talia said, breathing hard.

Roudette grinned and turned her attention back to the dogs. She finished off the wounded one first, stomping his skull. She picked up the body and tossed it at the second dog, knocking it to the ground.

Talia was on the defensive now. Her speed and reflexes were fairy-blessed, but this was a fairy hunter. She parried every attack, but the man was impossibly fast. Each time she tried to strike, the spear lashed out like a serpent. Talia shifted her weight, and the spearpoint cut her thigh. A second thrust tore the sleeve of her robe.

"I'll deal with the hound. You help Talia!" The voice came from Danielle, who stood on the far side of the garden, glass sword in her hands. Danielle stared at the remaining dog, her forehead wrinkled in concentration. "Come to me."

The idiot! This was no common mutt. The dog was already charging toward Danielle. Even if she tried to flee, the animal was too fast. It leaped, jaws bared.

Snow stepped from the shadows, one hand to her lips. She blew, and dark splinters flew out to strike the dog.

Danielle twisted aside as the animal crumpled to the ground, whimpering in pain.

Roudette laughed and picked up her hammer. "Forget the princess and face me, you fairy-cursed bastard."

The fight ended quickly after that. Roudette wasn't certain who landed the final blow. Talia was the one who cut the hunter's hand and wrested the spear from his grip, but it was Roudette who smashed his knee, knocking him to the ground. She thought her hammer struck an instant before Talia's sword, but she couldn't be certain.

Talia kicked the fallen spear away.

"He's dead," said Roudette. "I can smell it." She scratched her arm, then flinched. Pushing back her sleeve exposed bloody gouges from one of the dogs. She hadn't even noticed.

Talia was pressing a hand over the cut on her thigh. "Will there be more?"

"I hope so." Roudette licked her lips. The magic of the wolfskin was more intoxicating than any drink. Having tasted blood, she wanted more. She stepped toward the doorway, the cries from beyond the temple walls tugging her forward. With her strength and Talia's speed, how many more hunters could they destroy before the sun returned? The wolf cared nothing for her plans, wanting only to punish those who had hurt them.

"Soon," she whispered, forcing herself to turn away from the screams.

Talia hurried through the garden toward Danielle. "What were you thinking? What would you have done if Snow's little darts hadn't stopped that thing?"

Danielle ignored her. Her attention was on the hound, still writhing from whatever Snow had done to it. "What's happening to him?"

Roudette wiped gore from her hammer, then walked over to join the others. The dog was whimpering and biting his side. Foam dripped from his jowls. He tried to stand, only to collapse again.

"What did you do?" Talia asked.

"The spell is the same one I used on Roudette's wolves," Snow said. "This country doesn't have a lot of pines, so I used a handful of thorns from the vineyard instead."

The vines which had come from the fairy hedge. Without a word, Roudette swung her hammer, ending the dog's torment.

"Are you all right?" Khardija stood in the doorway. She appeared shaken, but her voice was firm.

Talia jabbed a sword at the hound. "*This* is why you should destroy that thing. The thorns retain their curse. They kept the animal alive, tormenting it but refusing to let it die, just as they did to the princes."

Khardija turned to face the other sisters who had gathered behind her in the hallway, as though Khardija could shield them from the horrors that had invaded Jahrasima. "See if anyone else was hurt, and do what you can to calm our guests. Reassure them the danger has passed for now." She waited until they had left before addressing Talia. "The danger *has* passed?"

"For tonight," said Roudette. She cocked her head, listening as the howls echoed through the city. "They'll return tomorrow night, and it won't take them long to discover where this one fell. I'd make sure this place was empty by then."

"We can't," said Khardija. "Some of our patients are too ill to move."

Roudette shrugged. "Then they'll die."

"Mind your tone," Talia snapped.

Roudette bared her teeth. One hand went to her hammer before she caught herself. With the wolf's rage still upon her, it was all she could do to pry her hand free. She wanted to *fight*, and to hell with Snow's curse.

"I'm sorry, Mother." Talia's voice dripped anger and guilt. "They came for me. I didn't realize—"

"The temple will survive," Khardija said firmly. "If not this one, then the others throughout Arathea. We will move those patients we can and do our best to protect the rest."

"You can't," Roudette whispered. "You can't stop the Hunt. None of you can."

But Roudette could. With Talia's help. Very soon now, she would.

Once the initial panic passed, the sisters dealt with the aftermath of the attack as calmly and efficiently as Talia expected. By the time you had worked here a month, dealing with crises of every variety, you learned to push your immediate reactions aside in order to treat the injuries before you. Talia remembered the first time she learned that lesson, the night a man had walked up the path with a carving knife protruding from his skull.

Faziya had led the man into the temple as if she saw such wounds every day. She packed bandages around the blade and sent Talia to fetch one of the senior sisters. It was only later that day, after the man had died

and Faziya was alone with Talia, that Faziya had allowed
herself the luxury of fear and grief.

Emotion could wait. For now, the sisters tended the
injuries left by the hunter and did their best to calm
the temple's guests. The hunter's body was brought to
the back of the temple, where it would be stripped and
burned tomorrow along with the three people he had
killed, including one of the sisters.

Talia knew they were right. Nothing could be done
tonight, not with hunters still roaming the city. She did
her best to imitate Mother Khardija's steadiness as she
returned to her room.

Talia raised an eyebrow at the sight of three temple
cats outside the door. As she approached, one of the cats
darted inside. Talia peeked through the curtains to see
Danielle scratching the cat's neck. "Our guardians are
your doing, I assume?"

Danielle whispered to the cat, who arched his back,
then sauntered out to join his fellows. "The others are
atop the walls. If another hunter approaches the temple,
they'll let us know."

Talia drew her sword, sat with her back to the wall,
and began to inspect the blade. The edge had chipped
where she struck the hunter's spear. She dug a small
whetstone from her pocket and set to work. Without
looking up, she said, "How do you know about the Wild
Hunt?"

Roudette cocked her head, listening as a hound
howled in the distance. "It was a fairy hunter who found
my grandmother. He cut this wolfskin from her body
while I watched, hidden in the closet."

Talia flipped the sword and began to work the other
side of the blade. "Has anyone ever fought them and
lived?"

"Individual hunters like tonight, yes." Roudette's
upper lip pulled back. "It makes no difference. They'll
replace the man we killed. They always do. If you're

thinking of trying to defend the temple, you'd be better off falling on that sword of yours."

Danielle leaned forward. "How do they replace their fallen companions?"

"The fairy church believes a man's death is ordained from the moment of his birth. Decreed by God himself." Roudette leaned back, resting her eyes. This was the calmest Talia had ever seen her, as though killing the hunter had allowed her to truly relax. "Most of those struck by a hunter's blade fall dead as you'd expect, but a few live on, joining the Hunt. Those are the ones whose time hasn't yet come. They accompany the Wild Hunt until they reach the end of their allotted days."

"The man we fought tonight?" Snow asked.

Roudette smiled. "The church would tell you it was God's will his life ended on this day. We were merely instruments of God."

Talia didn't dignify that with a response.

"Where did they come from?" asked Snow. "The stories I've heard say the Wild Hunt was cursed to ride for all time, but every curse can be broken."

"Not this one," said Roudette. "Some say the leader of the Hunt is one of the old gods, fallen from power. Others believe him to be a mortal king who insulted a fairy lord and was cursed for his rudeness. The church describes them as servants of God, sent forth to harvest the souls of the damned. They say Arathea has fallen into sin, and the Hunt is God's punishment. Until tonight, the Hunt has mostly been attacking the Kha'iida tribes, avoiding the cities."

"Kha'iida?" asked Danielle.

"Nomads," said Talia, thinking of Faziya. Few Kha'iida ever left their tribes. Faziya had never spoken of her reasons for turning her back on her people.

Snow pulled a mirror from her choker and concentrated. Her face brightened. "Beatrice! Is Trittibar around? The Wild Hunt is after Talia, and we could use some help figuring out how to fight them."

"You've been gone less than a day," Beatrice protested. "How in the name of—no, I don't want to know. Is everyone all right?"

While Snow consulted with Beatrice, Talia turned back to Roudette. "I won't let the Hunt destroy this place."

"You speak as though you have a choice," Roudette said, her expression distant. "My cape will hide you for the moment, but now that the Wild Hunt has marked you as their prey, they *will* find you, and they will destroy everything in their path until they do."

"If Zestan has the power to set the Hunt on my trail, she can also turn them away." Talia held her sword to the lamp's light, studying the edge. "All we have to do is find her and persuade her."

CHAPTER 10

*T*HE CAPE NEVER WORKED IN HER DREAMS.
    Roudette stood at the edge of the woods. Three steps would take her beyond the trees to the road, but she couldn't bring herself to move.

Fire had torn open the sky, and the riders thundered forth like the vanguard of Hell. Their dogs howled as they raced ahead. Their cries never wavered; the beasts of the Wild Hunt never drew breath. Roudette covered her ears, trying in vain to block the sound. Urine spread down her thighs.

Windows and doors swung open. A few brave souls stepped outside to see what was happening.

"Don't run." Her voice wouldn't carry. She tried again, but fear had stolen her voice. She could only watch as they turned to flee, only to be run down.

The first to fall was Vaughan, an older man and a hunter in his own right. He raised a short wooden bow, but before he could draw the string, an arrow punched through his mouth.

His death spread panic through the village. Roudette's friends and neighbors poured from their homes like rats fleeing a fire. One by one, the Hunt chased them down.

Roudette pulled the wolfskin over her shoulders, but nothing happened. She had to reach her family. She had

*to save Jaun. The rest would die, but she could still save
her brother. She could see herself dragging him into
the woodpile, protecting him with her body as she deliberately pulled the firewood down about their heads.
Somehow she had sensed that the Wild Hunt lived for
the chase, that if they tried to run, the Hunt would chase
them down.*

*Only the wolfskin had no power in her dreams, and
her body wouldn't obey.*

*And then she was in a different town, close to the bor-
der. She and Jaun cowered in the chapel, listening to the
howling that had never really stopped since that night a
month before when the Wild Hunt destroyed their home.*

*"They're after me," Roudette whispered, pulling the
skin around her body. She had finished sewing the fur to
her cape that very afternoon, combining the power of her
grandmother's gift with the protections woven into the
cape. "I'll lead them away."*

"Don't go." Jaun's filthy hand clamped around hers.

"No matter what happens, don't try to flee."

*"Don't leave him!" Her dreamself heard nothing but
the hounds as she set out into the night.*

Gentle shaking jolted her awake. She gasped and
slapped Danielle's hand away.

"You cried out in your sleep."

Roudette dug her fingers into the cape, feeling the
wolf's strength, letting its anger and hunger wash over
her. She closed her eyes, listening to the howls from the
street. The sound never stopped. "I thought they had
come for me."

For a month the Wild Hunt had pursued them. Roudette had killed one of their number, and she believed
they meant to avenge that death, but revenge was human. They cared only for finishing the hunt, and that
night they had come for Jaun. "They never tire. They
never stop, and they will kill anyone who comes between
them and their prey."

"So how do you survive?" asked Danielle.

Roudette bared her teeth. "Become the hunter, not the prey."

Talia found Mother Khardija in the garden, working by the light of the moon to pinch undersized blooms from a row of fire lilies.

"Everything we grow serves one of two purposes," she said as Talia entered. "Food or medicine. Food we can buy in the market if we must, but medicine . . ." She turned in a slow circle. "Should anything happen to this garden, it would take months to regrow. Do we harvest everything tonight, though many of the plants are too young, or do we leave them alone and hope no harm comes to them?"

Talia crouched by a small flower with long orange leaves. "How many people have you treated for addiction to ruquq leaf? Leave those plants unguarded, and every flower will be stolen before nightfall." She stood. "Harvest the plants that would do harm in the wrong hands. As for the rest, take enough to see you through four days. That gives you time to contact the other temples, and they can send what medicines you need."

"A wise solution, Princess." Mother Khardija's smile made Talia suspect she had already decided to do exactly as Talia suggested. "Arathea has need of such wisdom."

"What wisdom is there in waiting here to die?" Talia asked. "The Wild Hunt will kill you if you stay."

Khardija sighed. "Jenx el-Barhud is four years old. He was burned in a fire three nights ago. Here we can use salves and potions to keep him asleep, but the slightest movement cracks open the wounds." She turned, peering at the wall of the garden as though she could see through the bricks to the people beyond. "In room three a Kha'iida woman named Risha lies motionless, her back broken in two places. The journey here left her paralyzed. To move her again risks her death. There are others in similar conditions. Would you have me abandon them to the Hunt?"

"You can't protect them all," Talia protested.

"Perhaps. There are stories in which the Hunt spares those with the courage to face them."

"No." Talia stood, fighting the urge to shake her. "You can't trust your life to a story."

Mother Khardija brushed her hands together, signaling the end of a conversation. "How is your leg?"

"I'm fine. Snow stitched the cut."

"And your friend, the one who was bitten?"

Talia sighed. "She's not my friend, and she tended her own wound."

"Animal bites are particularly dangerous," Khardija said. "Ask one of the sisters for a poultice of—"

"Why did Faziya leave the temple, Mother?"

She turned away. "You know the temple requires no oaths. Anyone is free to leave at any time. Your friend is Kha'iida. It's in her nature to wander."

It stung to think Mother Khardija would lie to her. "Faziya spent eight years of her life in this temple. This was her home. The only time she left was to attend church."

"There are aspects of fairy beliefs that always appealed to her."

"I know." How many times had they fought over Faziya's loyalty to the fairy church? "She saved my life, Mother. You healed my body, but she's the one who helped me to find myself."

"By turning you into a criminal," snapped Mother Khardija. "Pranks in the kitchen are one thing, but Faziya and her rebel friends nearly got you killed."

"I was already dead," Talia answered. "Those people gave me a reason to live."

"So Faziya explained each time she brought you back to me," said Khardija. "Each time I had to bind your wounds and set your bones. For what? Burning down one of the raikh's warehouses? Robbing a royal caravan? You are a princess of Arathea, but you behaved like the petty nobles who snarled and fought over the bones of our land for the past hundred years, lashing out in anger and destruction with no larger goal until that anger threatened to consume you."

"These people were the closest thing I had to a family," Talia protested.

Mother Khardija brought one hand to her neck, massaging the pressure points to either side. "They were thieves and murderers."

"We fought Lakhim—"

"Your petty crimes were nothing more than the bite of a fly. Do you know why Queen Lakhim fears you? It's more than your curse. More than her need to avenge her son. She fears your power." Rarely had Talia heard such urgency in Mother Khardija's voice. She used this tone only when fighting to save a life. "She fears what will happen when Sleeping Beauty returns to Arathea. Her family has ruled but a handful of years. Yours ruled for three centuries. The people would rally to you, Talia. They would follow you."

Talia swallowed. "I didn't come here to take back my throne, Khardija. Queen Lakhim isn't the threat. Zestan and the Wild Hunt are."

Screams and hoofbeats from the street interrupted them. Talia drew her knife without thinking, but the rider was already thundering past the temple.

"Faziya believed, as you, that Zestan and the Hunt were the greater danger."

"That's why she left, isn't it?" Faziya was no warrior, but she was clever. "She went to the church, didn't she? To ask for their help to protect her people from the Hunt." No one knew more of fairy history than the priests of the church.

Mother Khardija sighed. "I might have been wrong when I tried to stop Faziya from helping you."

Both the unexpected admission and the change in subject threw Talia off-balance. "I don't understand."

"Even as I tended your body's wounds, I could see your soul growing stronger." She knelt and began cutting the ruquq flowers. "I worried what the company of criminals would do to you. Looking at you now, seeing the woman you have become, I admit Faziya might have known your needs better than I."

Talia bent down to help, gathering the round flowers into a single pile. "What happened to her, Mother?"

"When Sister Faziya failed to return, I went to the church myself. Father Uf'uyan was unavailable, but Father Yasar told me Sister Faziya had come to see them. He said Faziya was upset and had most likely returned to the desert."

Talia shook her head. "She wouldn't leave without speaking to you."

"I agree." She raised a dirt-smeared hand to Talia's face. "I know you, child. Even now you think to smash down the doors of the church and beat the truth from the priests."

Talia was already rising. "Something like that, yes."

"Faziya may be beyond your help."

The words were like a sword sliding through her chest. "If so, the priests will need more than prayers to protect them."

The temple storeroom was as busy as Talia had ever seen, with sisters bustling past to pack everything they would need to care for their patients. Talia dodged to one side as a young girl emerged carrying a stack of blankets.

Inside the storeroom, Talia helped herself to a dark gray silk shirt and a pair of black trousers. She chose clothes for the others and hurried back to her room, stopping only to grab food and drink from the kitchen.

The cats still patrolled the entrance, but apparently they had accepted her as safe, as they allowed her to pass without waking Danielle.

Talia changed in silence, leaving her sleeves open and loose to allow her to reach the knives on her forearms. The pants she tied off at the ankles. A black sash circled her waist, knotted on the left hip. She hoped fashion hadn't changed too much in the time she had been away.

She tucked a longer knife through the sash. Her zaraq whip balanced things out on the other side, hidden by the knot. Her sword went through the back where she could reach it with either hand. She draped a white cape over her shoulders, buttoning the top. Black tassels at the hem weighted the cape enough to hide her weapons from casual view.

The sounds of the Wild Hunt had vanished. She glanced at her companions, reluctant to wake them. Snow in particular needed sleep after working so much magic the day before.

The noise of the temple saved her that choice. With the Hunt gone, the sisters redoubled their efforts to evacuate the grounds. Footsteps hurried past, and the groans and cries of the patients soon filled the temple as people hobbled from their rooms on injuries not yet fully healed.

Roudette was first to wake, bolting upright and staring at Talia for a moment before relaxing. Danielle followed, and finally Snow pulled her blanket over her head and mumbled, "It's still dark!"

Talia grabbed the edge of the blanket and yanked it away. "The Hunt is gone. If you won't get up on your own, I'll find something to help you. The desert is full of snakes and lizards that love to curl up with a nice warm body."

Snow glared. "Try it and I'll turn you into one."

Roudette was already helping herself to the breakfast Talia had brought. Steam rose from a torn loaf of black-crusted bread. Several bunches of grapes sat nested between the loaves. On the back of the tray were two clay jugs, warm goat milk in one and beer in the other.

Snow sniffed the jugs. "Beer for breakfast?"

Talia grinned. "Welcome to Arathea."

Roudette snatched the beer and drank several huge gulps directly from the jug, following it with a huge bite of bread. "This bread tastes like gravel. Isn't there any meat in this place?"

Talia grabbed a handful of grapes, her mouth already watering. The sour taste made her smile. Lorindar's grapes were too sweet. She helped herself to the milk next. Warm and thick, with a sweet aftertaste. It was far too long since she had eaten a proper breakfast.

"Snow, are you strong enough for spellcasting?" she asked. Snow's illusions had vanished after the fight with the hunter. "Foreigners are rare this deep in Arathea."

Still chewing, Snow gestured with one hand, restoring her disguises to Danielle and herself. "What about Roudette?"

"Her skin is light, but she might pass for a northerner." Talia circled Roudette. "That blonde hair will draw attention before we're two steps out of the temple, and the cape has to go. Only the fairy folk wear such vivid colors."

"I wear this cape until the day I die," Roudette said.

Snow wrinkled her nose. "That would explain the smell. I didn't want to say anything, but—"

"Wait here." Talia jogged through the hallway to the kitchen. She squeezed past two young girls who were busy packing food. Ignoring their protests, Talia snatched a pot and filled it with water from the cistern. She crushed several handfuls of tea leaves into the water and returned to the room.

By now, Snow and Danielle had changed clothes, donning the plain shifts and capes Talia had brought. The sleeveless shifts would have been unseemly back home. Though the material covered both women from throat to ankle, the thin white linen left little to the imagination. Danielle was already buttoning her cape.

The material was a dark green, almost brown in color. Large horn buttons ran from neck to waist, providing a bit of modesty.

"I want clothes like yours," Snow complained.

Talia snorted. "Servant's garb is the closest thing to invisibility you have. Unless you can lose your accent and change the way you move? You stand too far from people, and you look away too quickly. Even with your illusions, it wouldn't take long for someone to notice there's something not quite right about you."

Danielle smiled. "I notice that about her too."

Snow threw a grape at her.

"Fix your hair," Talia said. "You'll want it braided or knotted back, unless you want to be mistaken for prostitutes. Keep the sheffeyah wrapped about your faces. Your skin might be the right color, but your features might give you away." She set the tea on the floor. "Snow, can you heat that for me?"

"Beer and milk weren't enough?" Snow adjusted her choker. Sunlight shone from one of the mirrors. Moments later, the water began to boil, and the smell of tea filled the room.

Talia shoved the pot at Roudette. "The tea should darken your hair enough to let you pass for Arathean." That left only the cape. Fortunately, the temple had just the thing to go with it.

The sun was rising as Danielle and the others made their way through the temple. Roudette followed a short distance behind, wearing an all-encompassing robe Talia called a hiqab.

The robe was a filthy tan thing of camel hair. According to Talia, the hiqab marked Roudette as a leper. It had no sleeves, fitting over Roudette like an oversized sack with only a single ragged hole for her head. A deep hood hid her face, and the lack of sleeves prevented her from touching anyone, not that anyone approached that closely. Even the sisters moved to the side as Roudette passed.

Mother Khardija stopped them at the main entrance. She kissed Talia's forehead, then pressed a beaded purse into her hands. Snow translated her words for Danielle. "The church will expect a donation."

"I can't take this." Talia tried to give the purse back, but Khardija refused. Talia lowered her voice. "Even if the Wild Hunt spares the temple, you'll need every scrap of gold to help those who were hurt in last night's attack."

"I know you." A smile eased Khardija's words. "If I give you this, you'll use it well. If I don't, you'll simply take what you need from random passersby on the streets."

Talia blushed, but she tucked the purse into the sash at her waist. "I don't know when I'll be able to repay you."

"Repay me by staying alive." Khardija made shooing motions with her hands. "Be safe."

They joined the exodus leaving the temple, sisters escorting patients into the streets. Others in the black robes stood outside the gates, gently turning away those who had come for help.

Talia shook her head. "I brought the Wild Hunt into her home, and she repays me in gold."

"She loves you," said Danielle.

"I know." Talia looked back at the temple. "I just hope that love doesn't get her killed."

As they departed the Temple of the Hedge, Danielle got her first real view of Jahrasima. In the darkness the night before, she had seen little more than shadows. This morning, with the sun already baking the air, she could make out every detail. Including the destruction left by the Wild Hunt.

The rooftops were flat, thatched with straw that had turned brown from dust and sand. The windows were larger than those in Lorindar, covered only by shutters or heavy curtains. Stones were laid out on the borders of paths and property. Many of the homes had been in poor repair already. Mud bricks crumbled from the walls. Rats disappeared into the cracks and holes.

The Hunt hadn't bothered with subtlety. Stones were kicked aside, showing where riders had moved from house to house. Doors were smashed, shutters ripped from the windows, even whole walls had been knocked down.

At one house, a little boy sat crying in a patch of dirt darkened by blood while an older girl tried to comfort him. "What happened there?" Danielle whispered.

Snow tilted her head to listen as they passed. "The boy's dog tried to protect him from a hunter."

"It will be worse tonight," Roudette said. "This was but a fraction of the Wild Hunt's power."

Danielle turned to look at Roudette. The hiqab's hood shadowed her face, but it couldn't hide the hatred in her voice. Roudette hadn't hesitated to murder innocent people back in Lorindar, and she had delighted in the death of the hunter. But the aftermath of the Hunt had clearly shaken her.

Roudette stopped to look at a larger house, one that had obviously been expanded over the years. The Hunt had trampled straight through the walls, and a group of men now worked to keep the rest of the building from collapsing.

Their passage drew stares. Small, dirty faces watched from shadows and windows. The adults' expressions were warier. Their glances lingered on Danielle's sword. They spoke in low voices, if at all, as though they were afraid the sound might bring the Wild Hunt back to their city.

"They're all human," Danielle said softly. "I thought fairies and humans lived together in Arathea."

"The fairies live in the northern part of town." Talia

slashed a hand through the air for silence as a young girl approached with a basket of dried figs. Talia took three, offering a pair of copper coins in return.

The girl bowed and said something in Arathean. Talia grimaced, but repeated the words.

"What did she say?" Danielle asked.

Snow made a face. "Blessings of the peri be upon you."

"The peri?"

"The first fairies," said Snow, taking one of the figs. "They say the peri are the ancestors of all that's good in fairykind, whereas the evil deev gave rise to the trolls and ogres, the goblins and giants. They fought for centuries—"

"Using humans as their pawns." Roudette's voice was huskier than usual. "The 'blessed' peri hid in their mountains, sending mortals out to die against the deev. Some say their war scoured the land, turned Arathea into a desert. Be grateful they never spread beyond this land."

The road widened, dust and dirt changing to paving stones. The homes here were taller, their lines straighter. Grain bins topped the flat roofs like giant beehives. Heavy canopies stretched from the front of the houses, sheltering merchants on the street and inviting potential buyers to take advantage of the shade. This morning, many of the merchants sat alone, their wares untouched. They called out to passersby, but their energy was muted.

Snow started toward one merchant who was showing off what looked like a baby dragon in a silver cage.

Talia caught her sleeve. "No."

"But he's—"

"No." Talia glanced at the dragon. "The scales are falling out, and he's yet to belch a single spark. Do you really want a diseased dragon?"

Snow pointed to another merchant, a woman surrounded by piles of brightly colored silk. "What about—"

"No."

Snow folded her arms. "Fine. But when we're finished here, I want a dragon."

"Who's going to clean up after it?" Talia asked.

"Enough!" Roudette swept past them. "Your prattling is worse than any fairy torment." She stopped a short distance beyond, looking at a collapsed building. The small garden behind was trampled and blackened as if scorched. A small group was digging through the rubble. Roudette sniffed the air. "Three people were crushed when the walls fell."

"The Hunt wanted us," Danielle protested. "Why would they hurt these people?"

"Don't look for reasons," said Roudette. "The Wild Hunt were once men, but they're more fairy than not now, reborn of chaos and whimsy and destruction. Place two identical children before them, and they'll leave one untouched while their dogs savage the other. This . . . is restrained, for the Hunt."

"What did they do to you?" Danielle asked, her voice gentle.

Roudette turned away, hiding within the darkness of her hood. "My grandmother tried to fight them. She failed. They killed everyone they could find. In a single night, they reduced my town to rubble and ash."

"I'm sorry," Danielle said. Wails of grief broke the stillness as they walked. Danielle could hear the pain in the distant cries, even if she couldn't understand the words. Men and women alike wept together.

"At least my grandmother tried to fight," Roudette said disgustedly. "Talia's people have surrendered their magic. Obeying Siqlah and trusting God to protect them. Even after last night, look how few bother to carry weapons."

Talia spun. "So they should have fought? The Hunt would have slaughtered them all, just as they did your people."

"Instead they surrender their souls to the fairies," Roudette said.

"That's enough." Danielle and Roudette stared at one another until Roudette snorted and turned away.

Talia moved on without answering, leading them another block to a stone bridge that crossed a canal. On the far side of the bridge, the streets were paved with white stone. Sandstone statues with horned helms and inhumanly narrow features bordered the road. Fig and olive trees grew behind the statues, shielding the homes and buildings beyond. Small whirlwinds blew through the street.

"Air dervishes," Snow said. "Fairy sprites, sweeping the dust from the roads."

Roudette snarled at one of the dervishes. When it approached too close, she jumped forward and stomped on it, moving too quickly for the sprite to dodge. It burst in a small explosion of dirt and dust. "Ha!"

Slowly the sprite re-formed, gathering the worst of the dirt back into itself. Roudette growled, and it raced away.

Danielle might not speak the language, but she could read the disapproval in the faces that turned to watch. "You probably shouldn't do that again."

The populace here seemed an equal mix of human and fairy. A wrinkled dwarf rode a white donkey through the street. A man whose body seemed made of black smoke drifted past, his feet leaving a faint trail of soot. A yellow-skinned woman walked by conversing with a hooded serpent draped around her neck. Everywhere the fairies traveled, humans moved aside to let them pass.

"Maybe Arathea deserves to fall to the fairies," Roudette said.

Talia stiffened but didn't break stride.

Before Roudette could say anything further, Danielle caught her arm and pulled her to the side of the road. "Snow's fairy mark prevents you from harming us. Which means there's little you can do to defend yourself when Talia decides she's had enough. So by all means, continue to insult her home and draw attention to us. See how much longer her patience lasts."

"Be grateful that mark protects you, Princess." Roudette pulled away. "Show me one fairy who suffered so much as a bruise last night. This is—" Her voice broke. "This is what my home was like. Few of the 'blessed race' lived among us, but the blind respect and worship was the same. Time and again my mother warned me not to stray from the path as my grandmother had done. We followed the path of the fairy church, and it destroyed us. I've no sympathy for those who embrace fairy lies."

People were stopping to stare, humans and fairies alike. Danielle lowered her voice, hoping Roudette would do the same. "We're going to a fairy church. Tell me now whether you can do this."

Roudette glanced around. "I will do whatever is needed."

Danielle took that as a yes. "I'm sorry about your mother. About your home."

Roudette said nothing.

The crowds grew as they neared a domed structure of green-painted stone. Two giant statues framed the entrance, where a wide stairway led down into darkness. The statue on the right sat with one hand extended in welcome. His other hand clutched a sword carved so that it appeared to be on fire. He wore a helm that shone like real gold. Spiral antlers rose from the sides of the helmet.

The other statue was a woman seated in a similar pose. Her extended hand overflowed with coins, mostly copper and silver, which spilled into a large bowl at her feet. As Danielle watched, a family stopped at the statue and placed a bracelet into her hand, dislodging several coins into the bowl below.

"The statues are enchanted," Snow said softly. "Someone is watching through their eyes."

"My cape will shield us," Roudette said. "It was made to avoid the eyes of the fey." She stood like an island in a stream, with people doing their best to avoid her and her disease. Her voice was calm once more, with no hint of the pain from moments before.

"We're here for information," Danielle reminded her. "To learn about Zestan. That's all."

Roudette shrugged. "Get me alone in a room with the priest, and I promise he'll tell us whatever we need to know."

CHAPTER II

TALIA TOSSED A HANDFUL OF COINS ONTO the statue's palm as she passed.

An acolyte in a green robe and matching sheffeyah bowed in gratitude. "May God reward your generosity."

"Where was God last night?" Talia muttered. The crowd pressed closer as they made their way down the staircase. If someone did recognize her, there was no way to flee through this many people. She lowered her head and shoved a path through the crowd, making sure the others stayed close.

Faziya had dragged Talia to this church six times for morning prayers before giving up. Never had Talia seen it so packed. She wondered if the fairy entrance on the far side was equally busy.

She followed the crowd into a familiar tunnel, remembering how Faziya had gone on and on about the symbolism. *"The tunnel represents our life in this world, a time of darkness until we emerge into God's light."*

Not that the tunnel was truly dark. Between the sunlight outside and the oil lamps burning within, Talia could see perfectly well as she entered the temple proper.

The first thing she noticed was the trickle of fountains. She had forgotten the sound of water spilling from the walls, pouring into the narrow stream that flowed around the inside of the church. Talia crossed a wooden bridge, peering down at the water as she passed. Glowing jaan swam in endless loops around the church. Many people pressed their way to the water's edge, cupping their hands to drink.

Faziya had once urged Talia to do the same, to drink of the blessings of God and the fairies. Talia had shied away in disgust, saying, *"You realize you're drinking jaan piss?"* Faziya had only laughed.

Higher up, a balcony of green stone circled the church. The upper level was reserved for the fairies and was less crowded than the main floor. Talia spotted trolls and goblins, sprites and spirits of every race. Sparks sprinkled down from a small group of pixies perched on the railing.

Talia moved to one side to remove her sandals, looping the laces over her neck. She waited for the others to do the same.

A round dais at the front of the church sat empty, save for thick beeswax candles mounted on either side, burning with green flames. The air was cool, almost chilly, though the stones were warm beneath her feet. She could feel the tension building as more people entered. They were afraid, and that fear could easily turn to anger. They came here seeking answers and reassurance after last night's attack. She hated to think what would happen if they failed to receive it.

Talia motioned Roudette toward a corner of the church where the river looped out from the wall, forming a small triangular island. "Roudette needs to wait with the sick and infirm. The water is supposed to protect the healthy from whatever diseases they might carry."

Roudette snorted, but crossed the water to join a handful of other worshipers too sick or demented to mingle with the rest.

Talia pushed her way toward the front of the church,

claiming a spot where one of the square pillars would
guard her back. She ran her fingers over the carving in
the column. It showed a sharp-eared fairy woman bringing a gift of meat and wine to a gathering of humans.
"Every gift carries a price," she whispered.

"What's that?" Snow asked, pointing to a painted
white stripe on the wall.

"The Path of Salvation," said Talia. The path circled
the entire church, looping higher and higher until it spi-
raled into the sun at the top of the dome. Paintings of
various obstacles blocked the path. In one, a beautiful
woman tried to lure a traveler into her home. A pile of
bones behind the house showed the fate of those who
gave in to lust.

She glanced at the other obstacles. The fairy church
hadn't been as strong in her parents' time. The rich man
crushed beneath the weight of his treasures, the murderer being cast to the dragon, these were the lessons
she remembered. She recognized many of the obstacles
from those stories, but they were tainted by the fairies'
influence.

A woman with blue skin guided an old man through
a crowd of unbelievers. A horned troll with a body like
wet sand chased away a desert wildcat to protect a pair
of children on a mountainside.

"I remember this story differently," Talia commented.
"My parents taught me the wildcat was a messenger
from God, warning the children away from danger. The
children ignored the warning, and the troll devoured
them both."

A woman shoved past Danielle, moving so close her
toes brushed Talia's. "Without the fairies, Jahrasima
would be nothing but a muddy pond in the sand."

"What of the riders who attacked last night?" demanded a man to Talia's left. "My uncle's cisterns were
smashed. His prized hunting falcon was torn apart by
those cursed hounds."

"God does nothing without reason," said the woman.

The man drew himself up. "What reason do you suggest he had for tormenting my family?"

Talia slipped a small knife from her sleeve. Keeping the blade cupped in her palm, she made two quick cuts, freeing the woman's purse from her belt. Talia tucked the purse into her shirt and returned the knife to its sheath.

"Forgive the interruption." Talia pointed toward the entrance. "I believe that beggar just made off with your purse."

The woman's hand slapped her belt. "In the church, no less!" She rushed off.

Snow clucked her tongue. "Shameless, these thieves."

A grinding sound drew Talia's attention to the front of the church. The air went still, and the arguing of the crowd died. The candle flames flickered as the wall behind the dais dissolved into sand.

Talia had seen it before, but the magic was impressive nonetheless. Falling sand changed to mist, and the mist thinned to reveal a doorway. Rain shrouded the pointed archway, framed by rainbow light.

"Show-offs," Snow muttered. "The rainbows are tacky, and they're overdoing the mist."

Talia elbowed her into silence.

The first to enter was a human boy in a blue wrap that left his upper body bare. He carried a polished onyx statue of a winged man. He set the statue into a small niche in the wall, then hurried to stand at one side of the dais.

A young girl emerged next, dressed in a more modest wrap of the same blue material. She carried a statue of jade, which she set in a second niche beside the onyx statue.

More children followed, until nine statues had been placed in their proper locations behind the dais. These were the nine messengers of God, but not as Talia had learned about them. The fairies had replaced the mortal messengers with their own kind.

It was a long time since Talia had believed in the lessons her father's priest had taught her, but seeing these mockeries made her want to smash them, preferably over the head of the nearest fairy.

The priest came forth next, head thrown back as he passed through the mist.

"Interesting fellow," Snow whispered.

"Father Uf'uyan," Talia said. "He's a naga."

From the chest up, Father Uf'uyan appeared to be a normal man in his forties. He wore a short emerald robe that left his muscular arms bare. When Talia was last here, Uf'uyan's hair had been more black than gray. The years had bleached most of the color from his chest-length braids.

Midway down his torso, his body became that of a snake. Thick as a man's waist, the long, serpentine tail was covered in horned brown scales that scraped across the stone as he moved.

He twisted around to face the statues, bowing so low his nose brushed the ground. He turned toward the crowd and bowed a second time. "Greetings, my children."

His words were clear, easily filling the church. Faziya had once told her it was a point of pride for Uf'uyan to speak as well as any human. He raised his voice, leading them in a hymn to praise the Path of Salvation and the promise of rebirth, as passed down by the peri themselves.

Talia mouthed the words, but refused to add her voice to the chorus. She waited impatiently while Uf'uyan led them through several formal prayers.

Danielle's hand touched her shoulder. "Try to relax. You look like you're preparing to fight the entire church."

"Faziya came here to learn the truth about Zestan

and the Hunt," Talia whispered, fists tight. "Uf'uyan has to know where—"

"We'll find Zestan and your friend both," Danielle promised.

Talia wasn't alone in her restlessness. All around her, people were beginning to stir and whisper.

Father Uf'uyan drew himself up taller than any human. He chewed his lower lip as he looked about, first at the fairies in the balcony, then at the humans gathered below. "So many new faces. Perhaps this is the first blessing of last night's events. Those who might have strayed have returned, while others have found the path for the first time.

"I know you're afraid. The deev are gone from our world, but their shadow remains. I've seen the streets of our city. I know you have lost friends and family. I've witnessed the destruction left in the wake of the Wild Hunt, and I grieve with you."

He glanced behind, looking through the doorway to the mist-blurred landscape beyond. Illusion, no doubt, meant to convey the impression of bountiful gardens and greenery.

Danielle leaned close. "He looks nervous."

"He's half snake," Snow said. "How can you tell?"

"He's also half human."

Talia studied Uf'uyan. She would have expected a man in his position to choose his words carefully. Yet there was none of the overly polished wordcraft she had heard so often from nobles.

"My friends. My children. I have failed you. For that, I beg your forgiveness."

Talia's eyebrows rose.

"Our kind were banished from Heaven for our pride," he said. "For untold years, we've worked to earn redemption by serving mankind. By guiding you along the path toward salvation, by protecting you from sin and evil. In that quest to be a source of good, we forget that fairykind can also be a source of darkness.

"When the first fairies fell, the peri chose the path of redemption. They fought to help mankind, hoping to earn forgiveness through their actions. Their brothers the deev chose the path of chaos. In their rage, the deev worked to destroy that which God had built. To punish mortal man, whom they resented. Those of us with fairy blood must never forget that we carry the potential for both the peri's wisdom and the deev's destruction."

Whispers spread through the church, not from the humans but from the fairies gathered above. Fairies could be hard to read, but to Talia's eye, they didn't appear happy.

"We walk this path together, sharing our strength as the trials grow ever greater. The Wild Hunt is but an obstacle to be overcome, a curse descended from the pride and evil of the deev. Do not surrender to fear. Seek neither to fight nor to flee. Find your strength in prayer and in the Path of Salvation."

"He knows," Talia whispered. Uf'uyan was warning his followers not to interfere, pacifying the humans for Zestan's servants. He knew the Hunt would return and that anyone who tried to fight would be slaughtered.

Another priest stepped through the mist. This one wore a mahogany helm carved in the shape of a jackal's head. As he stepped down from the dais, the mist drifted forward, dispersing into the crowd. Talia could feel the cold droplets on her skin.

Father Uf'uyan raised his arms. "May the waters of Heaven cleanse you of your sins and bring you strength. Guard yourselves from pride, and remember the word of the prophets. Cast sin first from your own heart and then from your home."

Talia watched closely. Father Uf'uyan started to say more, then appeared to change his mind. He lowered

himself and slid aside, allowing the other priest to lead
the church in closing prayers.

Afterward, humans and fairies began to make their
way from the church. Many of the humans appeared
genuinely comforted by Uf'uyan's words, and a number
of families gathered at the front to thank him.

Talia moved with them. She waited as Father Uf'uyan
sang a blessing to a boy roughly the age of Prince
Jakob.

"Treasure him and raise him well," said Uf'uyan, smiling. He stretched his tail back, lowering himself until he
was barely higher than the child. He pressed a hand to
the boy's forehead. "May God protect you and help you
find your way."

He spoke to several others before turning to Talia.
"Welcome, daughter. How may I serve?"

The traditional greeting of the church, reminding all
that the fairies had come to serve humans. Yet Uf'uyan
spoke the words as though he believed them.

"My friend is sick and hoped for your blessings." Talia beckoned for Roudette to join them. "She sought
healing elsewhere, but not even the Sisters of the Hedge
were able to help her. I hoped your prayers might give
her body strength."

"Of course." Uf'uyan brought his hands together,
then turned to look more closely at Talia. She forced
herself to relax. If he recognized her, they would be
hard-pressed to escape. She could kill both priests if
necessary, but the church was too crowded.

Uf'uyan's tongue flicked out briefly. "You have the
smell of one burdened by darkness."

"You could say that." Talia slipped her hands into her
sleeves and lowered her voice. "Father, I believe I know
where to find the Hunt's true prey."

Uf'uyan rose higher. His tail twitched against the
floor as he glanced about, as though making sure nobody else had heard. "Who are you, child?"

Talia loosened her knives in their sheaths. "One who can help you to find her."

Beside her, Snow reached to her choker. Danielle moved to one side, hand resting on her sword. Talia watched Uf'uyan. The naga carried his weight differently than a human, making it difficult to judge any shifts in balance. Talia ignored his body, concentrating instead on his tail. Any sudden movements would begin there.

Uf'uyan turned to the second priest. "Father Yasar, would you please tend to the others while I meet with this woman and her companions? Please see that we are not disturbed."

Yasar removed his helm, revealing a childlike face with a green pallor. He bowed to Uf'uyan before stepping down from the dais.

Uf'uyan beckoned them to follow as he slid toward the back of the church. Fog and illusion concealed whatever truly lay beyond the doorway. For all Talia knew, Zestan herself might wait for them. She glanced at Snow, who shrugged.

"I can't see through it," Snow said softly. "Not without using a lot more magic than I'd like."

So be it. Bracing herself, Talia followed Father Uf'uyan into the mist.

Roudette felt the glamours closing around her the instant she stepped through the doorway. On the other side, a glassy bridge stretched before her. Far beneath the bridge she could see mountains of green crystal, the fabled home of the peri. Iridescent clouds drifted above and below. Will-o'-the-wisps danced about like flaming mosquitoes. Roudette fought the urge to swat them all.

Instead, she dug beneath the hiqab robe, pulling up the hood of her cape. As she tugged the fur-lined hood over her head, the illusions faded, and she saw instead a wide hallway with walls of square-cut stone.

Sweat dripped down her face. Her cape was warm

enough, and with the added weight of the hiqab, she felt ready to melt. She found herself panting slightly as she walked. How easy it would be to throw off this ridiculous robe and slay the naga right here. Cut his throat and silence his damned lies.

Uf'uyan led them into a large room. Finely woven carpet, dyed deep blue and gold, covered the floor. Images of the nine prophets adorned the back wall. Caged rats scurried about in one corner. Snacks, Roudette guessed. Uf'uyan's face might appear human, but his appetite was fey.

A low desk sat against the opposite wall. Nooks in the stones held scrolls and small books. There were no windows, making the room feel cramped despite its size. Coals glowed in a hammered copper brazier in the center of the room, adding to the stuffy warmth. No doubt it was comfortable for a snake.

Uf'uyan shut a heavy wooden door behind them, then made his way to a circular basket padded with blankets. He curled his body into the basket, leaning his back against the wall as he studied Talia. A wave of his hand raised flames from the brazier. "You seem familiar to me."

Talia's sword seemed to leap into her hand. "I came here before, years ago, with Sister Faziya of the Temple of the Hedge."

"So we're not worrying about subtlety this time?" Snow asked.

Uf'uyan glanced at Snow. He didn't appear worried, but who could read the mind of a snake? "Your friends aren't from Arathea, are they?"

Roudette yanked the hiqab from her body so violently the material tore. She pushed back her hood and pulled out her own weapon, twirling the hammer through the air. The red cape earned a longer look from Uf'uyan. "No games, naga."

"I recognize you," he said. This time Roudette could

smell his fear. He inclined his head slightly. "Will you grant me time to pray, first?"

"I didn't come here to kill you," said Talia.

"Maybe *you* didn't." Roudette advanced toward the fairy priest. "Tell us where to find Zestan-e-Jheg."

"Or what?" Uf'uyan asked. "You'll kill me?" He laughed. "Strike then, Red Hood. Return me to Heaven."

Talia caught her arm. "Not yet." Stepping between Roudette and Uf'uyan, she said, "Faziya came here asking about the Wild Hunt. What happened to her?"

"Faziya was a kind woman," said Uf'uyan. "Until last night, few people cared about the Wild Hunt's raids on the Kha'iida. The settled people of the cities have turned their backs on their desert brothers. Many were secretly grateful to the Hunt. They hear rumors of Kha'iida raids, of children being stolen and caravans robbed, and they begin to believe Arathea would be better off without its 'savage' children of the sands."

"Lies," Talia said. "Kha'iida warriors used to raid neighboring tribes, but only to hone their skills and prove their superiority over their neighbors. Where's the challenge in raiding a caravan of soft, spoiled merchants?"

Uf'uyan studied Talia more closely. "Like all things, the place of the Kha'iida has changed, particularly in recent years. But you remember those times, don't you, Princess? I should have guessed your identity from your scent. The curse lingers in your blood."

Talia beckoned Snow closer. "Can anyone else hear us in this place?"

Snow pointed to the brazier. "Roudette's cape obscures it, but someone has been trying to eavesdrop."

Uf'uyan chuckled. "Father Yasar. Hoping to learn the hidden secrets of the church, that he might rise to the rank of bishop. He'll surpass me soon enough, I suspect. I'm afraid the church tends to reward ambition over faith these days."

"You said the place of the Kha'iida has changed," Talia said.

Uf'uyan lowered his body. "Our fault, at least in part. As more of Arathea turns to the church, there is less tolerance for those who reject it."

Roudette spat. "You mean they reject fairy rule, so you turn Arathea against them. Will Zestan send the Hunt against all who refuse to worship her, then?"

"What have we done to you?" Uf'uyan asked. "How have I earned such hatred?"

Roudette didn't answer. She remembered the screams of the dying, her own small hands digging through splintered boards and crushed stone. The cape fanned her rage, until it was all she could do to restrain herself from smashing Uf'uyan and this entire mockery of a church. "I've seen what your kind truly believe."

"All who judge must also face judgment, child." The calmness of his voice made Roudette want to strangle him. "The Wild Hunt kills because it is their nature. You kill because you enjoy it, targeting whomever you're paid to hunt."

"I enjoy some jobs more than others." Roudette clutched her hammer with both hands, the leather grip creaking beneath her fingers.

Uf'uyan leaned toward Talia. "I will try to help you, as I did Faziya."

"Then tell us where to find Zestan," Roudette demanded.

"She has never deigned to visit Jahrasima in person. She works through her servants, human and fairy alike."

Roudette spat. "Servants like you."

"Zestan's influence is strong, but not everyone believes as she does." Uf'uyan smiled. "I've even heard rumors that it was a priest of the church who warned Queen Lakhim of the fairy plot against her."

"What of Faziya?" asked Talia. "Where did you send her?"

"I told her to return to the temple," he said with no hesitation. "She refused. She spoke instead of the raikh."

"Rajil." Talia's expression was sour. "Will she know how to find Zestan?"

"I couldn't say." Uf'uyan sighed. "There are rumors she follows Zestan, seeing her as the savior of Arathea. If Faziya went to her . . ."

Roudette twisted her hammer in her hands, unable to stand another moment of that oily voice. "What do you gain from betraying your mistress, serpent?"

He actually laughed. "What could I possibly hope to gain for myself when you mean to kill me? I serve one master, and I help you because it's my duty to do so." He pointed to the desk. "Please bring me the scroll with the faded green ribbon."

Snow walked over to pick up the indicated scroll, studying it before handing it over.

Uf'uyan unrolled the parchment to show an image of green mountains beneath a cloudless blue sky. The paint appeared cracked, lines running through the mountains. "Do you know what this is?"

"I do." Roudette had seen similar illustrations growing up, though none had been as elaborately painted. "The church preaches that the fairy race fell to our world in Arathea, far to the south. The first fairy hill was no mound of earth ringed by toadstools, but a great mountain of green crystal containing all of your magic and power."

Snow studied the parchment. "They say the peri retreated to the mountain after banishing the deev, that they remain there to this day."

"Waiting to return to Heaven," Uf'uyan said. "Look more closely." He touched the cracks where the paint had flaked away. Instead of stained parchment, the missing paint revealed black shadows. "It's said that if the faith of Arathea should fail, the peri's home will crumble, and the deev will emerge from their underground prison."

"Your point?" Roudette asked.

Uf'uyan picked up the torn remains of the scroll. "I believe Zestan-e-Jheg is a deev."

CHAPTER 12

"IMPOSSIBLE." TALIA SEARCHED UF'UYAN'S face for any hint of deception. Deev were monsters from childhood stories, nightmares hiding in the dark rooms of the palace where Talia and her siblings dared one another to go. "The deev were imprisoned, guarded by fairy magic and mortals both."

"And what mortals were assigned that duty?" Uf'uyan asked.

Talia pressed her lips together. "The Kha'iida."

"I hope I'm wrong. For if one deev can escape, others could follow."

"Did you tell Faziya of your suspicions?" Talia asked.

"It was Faziya who planted the idea. We spoke of the Hunt's attacks on Kha'iida tribes. She grew emotional, denouncing the Hunt's cruelty, calling them no better than the deev. I asked if that might not be truer than we realized. She left shortly thereafter."

"If she believed Zestan to be deev, she had no choice." Talia glanced at the others. Snow's brow was wrinkled, and Danielle looked lost. Switching tongues, Talia did her best to explain. "The deev were always stronger than the peri. According to the stories, the only reason the peri won their war is because we helped them. Peri magic created champions. Each tribe sent forth their strongest warriors. The peri enchanted those men, making them strong enough to face even the most powerful fairy. Each fighter received a weapon crafted to slay the deev. Those weapons have been passed down to this day. The peri won, but they weren't able to destroy the deev. Instead, they trapped the deev deep in the earth. The peri retreated to the mountains, leaving the tribes to watch for the deev's return."

"The Kha'iida?" Snow asked.

Talia nodded. "In old Arathean, the word Kha'iida means oath keeper: those who swore to guard this world against the deev."

"That's why Zestan has been sending the Wild Hunt against them," Danielle said.

"Every Kha'iida is a threat to her." Including Faziya.

Uf'uyan coiled and uncoiled his tail, the naga version of pacing. "The raikh keeps a fairy garden atop her mansion, tended by magic and inhabited by creatures from every corner of this world. I've seen it many a time, back before Rajil renounced my teachings in favor of Zestan. Her menagerie . . . those are not the shapes they were born to."

Snow was whispering to Danielle, summarizing the conversation. She paused to ask, "You think Faziya was transformed?"

"Fairy magic," Uf'uyan said. "Performed by Rajil's adviser."

"And you did nothing." Talia was beginning to wish she had let Roudette finish off the priest.

"I'm not permitted to interfere with Siqkhab," Uf'uyan said. "Human law is Rajil's domain."

"Talia." Danielle's voice was gentle, the way it always was when she was about to say something infuriating. "You have to warn Queen Lakhim."

"Warn her of what?" Talia demanded. "That she should stop hunting me and search for a deev?" She whirled. "If Zestan is so damned powerful, why bother with me and my curse? Why not destroy Queen Lakhim herself?"

"The deev were strong," Uf'uyan said. "Perhaps too strong. Like the peri, they relied on force, never mastering the intricacies of magic. A deev's power could sink Lakhim's palace into the earth, but such power would also reveal Zestan. Can you imagine the response should Arathea learn of her presence? It would unite all Arathea against her."

"Which is precisely why you should warn Queen Lakhim," Danielle said. "She has to know the truth."

"Lakhim was never interested in truth." Talia grabbed the scroll. "We're going to the raikh's mansion."

Roudette straightened, raising her hammer in both hands. "What of him?"

Father Uf'uyan bowed. "I've told you all I can. My soul is ready."

"No," said Danielle.

"You can't afford to leave me alive," Uf'uyan said. "I understand, and you have my forgiveness."

"He's right." Talia raised her sword. "Even if I trusted him not to betray us, fairy magic could rip our secrets from his mind. The risk—"

"So we bring him with us." Danielle smiled as she studied the cage with Uf'uyan's mice. "He'll need to be smaller, of course."

Snow patted the mouse in her pouch. "Don't worry. The spell should wear off in a day or two." Hopefully they would be long gone from Jahrasima by then.

She barely noticed the fairy illusions as Talia led them back through the tunnel. The church was mostly empty, save for a handful of people lost in silent prayer. The children who had carried the statues earlier were now busy sweeping the floors.

"I hope Father Uf'uyan was able to comfort your

friend," said Yasar, eyeing Roudette. She had pulled her robe back over her cape, but she moved like a warrior, not a leper. He was already moving toward the tunnel, no doubt to find Uf'uyan and try to learn what had blocked his attempt to spy on their conversation.

"I'm afraid she's not one for comfort," said Talia.

Snow glanced at Talia, who nodded. Snow smiled and followed Yasar back through the doorway.

She returned a short time later, a second, slightly battered mouse resting in her pouch with Uf'uyan. Snow stopped at the entrance to dip her hands in the water and wash her face. Transformation was a complex spell. Casting it twice in such short time was enough to bring her headache back in full force. She noticed the others watching her and forced a smile. "So where exactly would we find the raikh's mansion?"

The heat made the pain even worse as she made her way out of the temple. She pulled her hood up to block the sun. The streets were noticeably less crowded than before.

"We'll want to sneak in soon, if we can," Talia said, leading them away. "Midday is the hottest part of the day. It's a time of quiet, a time to enjoy a meal and a cool drink."

The most obvious sign of wealth in the northern quarter was the abundance of water. The people here used water for decoration the way others used gold. Water fell past windows in tiny falls; it misted from grand fountains of black marble; it gleamed with reflected sunlight in long pools.

Humans and fairies alike hurried through the streets. A lamassu strode past, brown wings tucked back against her bull-shaped body. She barely seemed to notice the humans who backed aside, clearing a path for her.

"Do you think she'll mind if I run up and pluck a feather?" Snow asked. "I've never seen a lamassu in real life, and I'd—"

"No." Talia waited for the lamassu to pass, then pointed to a fresh pile in the street. "If you want a souvenir, you can take some of what she left behind."

Snow made a face. Already a human boy was rushing out with a shovel to take care of the mess.

The raikh's mansion sat on the end of its own road, surrounded by a stone wall. Men with curved swords stood unmoving at the gate, shaded only by the mulberry trees that grew alongside the road. Armor of overlapping metal rectangles, each the size of a playing card, covered the men from shoulder to mid-thigh.

The wall was little taller than the guards, topped by iron spikes. The mansion beyond was pure Arathean, with no sharp angles anywhere to be seen. The stone blocks fit together so cleanly the entire building appeared to have been cut from a single piece of orange sandstone.

The broad central structure was three stories, with a narrow tower in the back that rose twice as high. Secondary wings stretched forward from either side like arms reaching to encircle all who approached.

A small, circular balcony jutted out from the center of the building. Windows were thin but plentiful. Snow saw no glass, so it might have been possible to sneak in that way, if not for the difficulties of scaling the walls in the middle of the day.

"Rajil will have more men inside the doors," Talia said.

"Human guards are the least of your worries." Roudette pointed through the gate at the long, oval pool in front of the building. "Water nymphs. Three of them. They can't stray too far from their fountain, but if they catch you, they'll drag you under and drown you."

By now, the two guards at the front gate were starting to pay attention to them. Talia stepped to the side of the road, into the thin shade of what smelled like a bathhouse. "There will be guards around back as well, and the grounds don't offer much in the way of concealment."

"Where's the garden?" Snow asked.

"Atop the central roof." Talia cupped her eyes against the sun. "If you move back, you'll be able to see the green of the trees peeking out over the walls on the roof."

"Could Snow's magic get us in?" Danielle asked. "What if you transformed us into birds?"

Snow laughed. "Have you ever flown before, Princess? Even if Roudette takes off that filthy cape long enough for me to cast the spell, it takes a long time to master wings. One wrong move and you'll dash your brains against a wall." She peered at the mansion, squinting until she discerned the ripple of fairy magic. "There are magical protections as well."

"I was afraid of this." Talia started back down the street, away from the mansion.

"Afraid of *what*?" Snow demanded. "Don't tell me you're giving up."

Talia reached the intersection and glanced about, brows low. "When I was in Jahrasima, my . . . friends introduced me to other ways into various buildings. I was hoping to avoid them, but the sewers—"

"Arathea has sewers?" Danielle asked.

Talia made a face. "Another gift of the fairies. The lake circles Jahrasima, but there are a number of smaller reservoirs below the city. Hundreds of tunnels circulate clean water to the wells. Others carry waste to the edge of town, to be used as fertilizer on the farms."

"I'm *not* breaking into a mansion smelling like sewage," Snow said. "Can't we go in through the wells?"

"Most wells are public." Talia led them past a brown building that smelled like a bakery. "Even at midday, we'd never get in without being seen. The sewers are hidden away, out of sight. They'll attract less attention."

They ducked into an alley between the bakery and a butcher shop. Talia knelt beside a stone grate, the holes carved into the shape of a flower with oval petals around a central circle. The edges were stained a rusty brown.

Roudette wrinkled her nose. "Did I mention one of the gifts of the wolfskin is a strong sense of smell?"

Talia grabbed one side of the grate. "Roudette?"

Roudette growled deep in her chest, but she crouched to grab the other side. Together they wrenched the stone up and moved it to one side.

Snow tried one last time. "How do we know this will lead into the raikh's mansion? She wouldn't want a sewer grate within her own home."

"She'll have her own well," Talia said. "The sewers will lead us to the reservoir."

Snow blanched. "You mean the tunnels are all interconnected? Drinking water and sewage? What about the mist in the church? Please don't tell me we were being sprayed with—"

"The wells are clean," Talia assured her. "As pure as fairy magic can make them. The reservoir feeds the sewers, but the flow only goes in one direction. Come on, before someone finds us."

Snow scowled. "This is the last time I let you plan the break-in."

Talia stood with her feet braced on either side of the hole as she lowered Danielle into the darkness. She leaned forward, catching the edge of the hole with one hand. Danielle was heavier than she had been when she first escaped her stepmother, a result of better food, pregnancy, and the muscle she had gained from her training with Talia. "You should be able to see the bottom. It's a short drop. Keep your legs bent."

"I see it." Danielle released Talia's wrist, landing with a splash. Squishing footsteps followed.

Talia glanced around, but most people avoided these streets, especially at midday when the heat baked the sewers, filling the back alleys with scents even fairy magic couldn't suppress. Talia took Snow's wrist. "You're always saying you want to learn more about magic. Don't you want to see how the fairies built this place?"

"Some things I can learn from books."

Talia lowered Snow into the sewer. This time Danielle was able to help Snow from below, preventing any unnecessary splashing.

Roudette was next, and then Talia grabbed the edge of the hole and swung in. Her feet kicked the far wall. She steadied herself, then dropped, legs going wide to catch the narrow walkways on either side of the sewer.

"We need to pull the grate back into place." Talia grimaced and stepped into the flowing muck. Her sandals sank into what felt like a muddy stream, though mud had never smelled so foul. She laced her fingers together. "Roudette?"

Roudette put one foot in Talia's hands and the other on her shoulder. Talia fought for balance as Roudette reached up through the hole. The grate slammed into place, showering them with grit and sand. Roudette jumped back down, splashing them all and earning a curse from Snow.

The only light came from overhead, illuminating a thin slice of the tunnel. Dried mud and worse caked the lower part of the walls. The floor was sunken like an oversized gutter, with narrow ledges on either side. Talia stepped back onto a ledge and dipped a foot into the water, trying to rinse the worst of the slime away, but it was a losing battle.

Snow's choker brightened, the mirrors like tiny moons. Talia almost preferred the darkness. Patches of yellowed foam covered the water like fungus, broken only by unidentifiable lumps floating past.

"This way," said Talia. Within a few steps, the sounds from the surface quieted until she could hear nothing but her own breathing and the trickle of the water flowing past.

Roudette sniffed the air. "We're not alone down here."

"How can you smell *anything*?" Snow shuddered.

"Sewer goblins." Talia kept walking. "Most cities have an entire tribe. The goblins hunt rats and other vermin and keep the sewers from backing up. In exchange for this service, they get to keep whatever treasures might fall through the grates. They're unpleasant creatures, and very territorial, but I'm told they have an artistic side. One of the merchants yesterday was selling goblin-made sculptures."

"Made out of what?" Snow asked.

"You don't want to know."

Danielle wrinkled her nose. "Are they dangerous?"

"Individually, no." Talia paused, head cocked as she tried to shut out the sounds of her companions. The sewer lines split off like tree branches grown wild, spreading out to follow every street in Jahrasima. Those splits were the most likely points for an ambush. "Even you would be more than a match for a single sewer goblin."

"Thanks," Danielle said dryly.

"The real danger comes after the fight," Talia said. "Take a single scratch down here, and it's likely to turn septic. If you don't get to the sisterhood fast, you could end up losing a limb. The goblins also have the advantage of knowing these sewers better than anyone. Probably even better than the elementals who built them."

Talia drew a dagger. The sewers were too cramped for swords. The splash of water marked where two tunnels merged up ahead. She studied the darkness, searching for the telltale gold reflections of goblin eyes. The brighter light from Snow's choker would help her spot them, but it would also be a beacon to the goblins.

"Can't we talk to them?" Danielle asked. "We're the ones invading their homes."

"Exactly," said Talia. "They believe anything in the sewers belongs to them. Including us. Fortunately, they're cowards. They'll attack a lone target, but an armed group should send them running. Probably."

Roudette readied her hammer as an animal scream filled the tunnel. The cries of sewer goblins reminded Talia a little of cats in heat. Another scream answered far behind them.

"This place just keeps getting better," said Snow.

Talia hurried forward, but the goblin was gone by the time she reached the other tunnel. Fading splashes marked its retreat. Talia kept walking until she reached a square column of sunlight that marked another grate. She listened for a moment, trying to make sure she hadn't lost her bearings. Dark stains marked the walls, random lines and smears with no meaning to anyone except the goblins who had drawn them.

"At least they're running away," said Danielle.

"Maybe." Sewer goblins could move through the muck without a sound. The only reason to raise such a racket was to lure their prey after them. "Or else they're running to fetch reinforcements."

The mansion was only a short distance away, but movement was slower in the cramped tunnels. The stones of the ledges were slick and occasionally loose. One gave way beneath Talia's foot, splashing into the water. Without her gifts, she could have easily broken an ankle.

"Stay in the middle of the tunnel," Talia said, splashing forward. She wouldn't put it past the goblins to have loosened certain stones deliberately as traps. She paused at another junction, hesitating only a moment before choosing the upstream tunnel. The water flowed more strongly here, meaning she was getting closer to the raikh's personal reservoir.

Roudette's hammer scraped the wall as she turned. "More of them coming up behind us. This place is worse than the Fairy Queen's labyrinth."

The water was higher here but also cleaner, the smell

of human waste less overpowering. Sewer goblins continued to cry out, the sounds echoing all around them. More importantly, their screams blocked out the more subtle noises of their fellow goblins sneaking up the tunnels.

"Should we remind them we're armed?" Snow asked. "Someone once told me that should be enough to send them running."

"There are more than I remember." Talia peeked around another bend in the tunnel. "They've never been this bold before."

Roudette turned around and roared, the sound so unexpected Talia nearly planted a knife in her throat. It was enough to scare the goblins into silence.

"Don't do that again." Talia pressed herself against the wall. Up ahead, she heard a faint dripping sound, almost like rain. "The whole point of taking the sewers was to sneak in. The goblins are bad enough, but their cries shouldn't draw much attention. They shout and fuss every time they find something larger than a rat. But if anyone hears you, we'll find ourselves climbing right into a group of Rajil's guards."

She turned right, and the flow grew strong enough to wash most of the filth from her sandals. Beams of light from overhead marked another sewage grate, this one carved like a sun with nine wavy beams. That sun meant they had crossed beneath the wall and were within the boundaries of the raikh's home. "We're close."

The goblins still hadn't made a sound. Either Roudette had cowed them into silence, or else they had finished moving into position for their ambush. A sprinkling sound like a light rain came from directly ahead. That would be the reservoir.

Talia crept forward. The tunnel grew tighter, the ceiling lowering until she had to crouch. The archway into the reservoir was little more than a window, with water flowing into the tunnel as though pouring over a miniature waterfall. Roudette and her cape would be a tight fit.

Talia reached back to snag Snow, dragging her to the archway until her choker's light shone into the reservoir. Beyond was a wide, round cavern, filled with water. Were Talia to float on her back, she would be able to touch the cave roof without straightening her arm. Water dripped from thousands of tiny stalactites, like stone icicles covering the roof. There was no way to guess how far down the water went, though most of the reservoirs were at least twice as deep as the average home.

As she watched, a single goblin floated into view on the far side of the archway, clutching what might charitably be called a raft. Bits of wood and cloth were all snarled together, floating just well enough to keep the goblin's head above water as he clung to it. Talia made out a pale, wrinkled face with oversized pointed ears. Gold eyes glinted in the light.

"Where are the rest?" Snow asked.

Talia pointed, indicating the areas to either side of the window. One goblin to lure them in, while the rest waited in ambush.

Danielle readied her sword, holding it like a short staff. One hand gripped the hilt; the other clutched the blade a short distance from the tip. The enchanted glass wouldn't harm her, but using her sword that way should allow her to defend herself here in the cramped tunnels. Talia nodded her approval.

"We should find another way," said Danielle. "I don't want to fight if we don't have to."

Roudette merely grunted, but her expression made it clear what she thought of such an attitude.

The raft bobbed as the goblin shifted position. One skinny arm drew back. Talia shoved Danielle to the side as the goblin skimmed a flat stone along the surface of the water. The stone bounced twice and shot past, clattering against the wall.

"There *is* no other way," Talia said, dodging a second stone. This one struck Roudette on the shoulder, though her cape seemed to absorb the blow. Roudette flexed her arm and bared her teeth.

The goblin hooted, sounding more like an animal than an intelligent creature. As if this were a signal, the rest soon picked up the cry, until the laughter of a hundred goblins filled the sewers.

Talia wiped her face with the back of her hand. She glanced back down the tunnel, wondering how many goblins lurked behind in the darkness, waiting to flank them.

Danielle appeared to be thinking the same thing. "We can fight our way back through one of the tunnels until we reach another sewer grate. Maybe then—"

Talia pushed past Danielle, using her knife to deflect another stone. The impact jarred her wrist and chipped the edge of her blade. This one had come from behind. "Snow, give me one of your mirrors. Danielle, take the others into that side tunnel. Kill anything you find, then have Snow extinguish her light. I'll lead the rest of the goblins away. That should clear the reservoir. Once they follow, get up through the well and wait for me. If I don't return by—"

"No." All three women spoke at once, but to Talia's surprise, it was Roudette who was loudest. Roudette used her hammer to block another stone. She grinned. "If they wish to fight, who are we to argue? Goblins are cowards. Slaughter a handful, and the rest will flee."

Talia nodded. To Danielle, she said, "Roudette and I will go in first. If something happens, you and Snow get inside. The well will be capped, so you'll need to break through." She lowered her voice. "No matter what else happens, promise me you'll get Faziya out of there."

"Of course," said Danielle.

"Thank you."

Snow stared at her. "You care for her, don't you?" Her voice was strangely soft, almost childlike.

Talia couldn't meet her eyes. "Just be ready." She
glanced at Roudette, who raised her hammer. But before they could charge into the reservoir, Snow touched
their shoulders, pulling them away.

"Would you mind guarding my back?" Snow moved
toward the archway.

"What are you doing?" asked Danielle.

"These two barbarians did pretty well against that
hunter last night." Snow smiled. "I think it's time to remind them what a sorceress can do."

CHAPTER 13

SNOW STRETCHED A HAND INTO THE water spilling through the archway. It was cool and clean, carrying the tiniest hint of residual magic from the various enchantments that kept the wells and sewers flowing.

"This is wasting time," Roudette said.

Snow shook her head. "You're as bad as Talia. No subtlety at all. It's all fighting and stabbing and killing. Where's the artistry in that?"

"I'll show you some time."

Snow did her best to concentrate. Her pulse pounded in her skull, a precursor of the pain to come if she pushed too hard.

Fog rose from her fingers where the water passed over her skin. Tiny crystals of ice formed around her fingertips. At first the ice broke and washed away, but soon the crystals grew larger, touching the stones of the wall and spreading upward.

Goose bumps raced along Snow's arm. The rest of her body was sweating. Siphoning the heat from so much water could kill her if she wasn't careful.

"Goblins aren't known for their patience, Snow," Talia said.

"Then you and they have something in common."

Snow pressed her other hand to the water, pouring more magic into her spell and using her mirrors to try to dissipate some of the excess heat. The ice crept upward, creating a dam across the archway. The trickling of the water died. She flinched as another rock cracked against the wall. "Would you mind?"

Talia crouched, searching the water with one hand until she found one of the rocks. She sent it hurtling back down the tunnel. A goblin squealed in the darkness.

Perspiration dripped from Snow's forehead, tickling her cheeks as it fell. The ice cracked and refroze as it spread into the reservoir. The sound reminded her of damp firewood popping in the flames. Goblin howls changed to cries of shock, and Snow smiled.

The mice in her pouch chose that moment to squirm and struggle, making Snow jump. "Quiet in there," she said.

The crackling grew louder. The ice had reached the goblin's raft now, freezing it into place. The goblin's eyes widened. He reached out to scratch the ice with his claws. With a frightened squeal, he pulled himself onto the ice and tried to crawl away. He kept yanking his hands up as the cold tried to freeze his wet body to the surface.

"They live in the desert," Snow said smugly. "They've probably never seen ice before."

Panicked shouts and splashing signaled the goblins' retreat. The one from the raft scrambled across the ice, trying to catch up with the others. His hands and legs kept sliding out from under him until he finally flipped onto his back and grabbed the ceiling to pull himself along.

Snow broke her hands free of the ice. She couldn't feel her fingers, and her nails had a bluish tinge. She grabbed the side of the archway, but between the frost on the stones and her own dizziness, she nearly fell. Talia caught her arms and held her steady.

"What about the ones behind us?" Danielle asked.

Roudette snorted. "Frightened off by the screams of their companions. Cowards, as I said." She almost sounded disappointed.

"Wait here." Talia peeked through the archway. She grabbed the edges and pulled herself up. Snow could still hear two goblins screaming from within the reservoir. Those goblins' screams grew shriller as Talia moved onto the ice.

With Danielle's help, Snow followed Talia into the reservoir. There she found two goblins trapped in the ice. The closer goblin had only a single arm free. His claws dug long gouges as he tried to free himself. The other was worse off. She must have grabbed the edge of the ice, trying to push it back with her bare hands. As the ice spread, it froze her hands in place, leaving only her fingers protruding like tiny wrinkled toadstools. Her hair was locked in the ice, holding her head back.

The ice left barely enough room to crawl. Snow rolled onto her side against the wall and held her hands to her choker, using the still-warm mirrors to try to thaw her flesh.

Danielle was next through, followed by Roudette. Roudette crawled straight toward the closest goblin, her hammer scraping along the ice.

"No," Danielle said. "They're helpless."

"They would have killed and eaten you without a thought!"

"We came into their home." Danielle pushed herself between Roudette and the goblin.

Roudette stared at her, then turned to face Talia and Snow. "Is she always like this?"

"Pretty much," said Talia. "You get used to it eventually."

Roudette scooted to one side on her hands and knees, trying to circle past Danielle. "Those filthy creatures are of fairy blood! They—"

"Danielle's right," said Talia. "Leave them. Arathean

goblins are little more than animals. A bit like yourself in that regard. They're not working for Zestan. They barely even know how to speak."

Snow left them to their squabbling. She flexed her hands, gritting her teeth at the resultant pain that burned through her fingers. That pain meant she probably hadn't done any permanent damage. She crawled toward the center of the reservoir, stopping when the ice grew too thin to support her. A quick punch broke a hole through the ice, and she peered down into the water. The reservoir was surprisingly deep. The bottom shone like silver, reflecting the light from her choker.

It was also warm. Snow plunged her hands in, gasping as the water further thawed her fingers. Once she could feel her hands again, she slid into the water and swam toward the round shadow in the ceiling that marked the bottom of what she assumed to be the raikh's well. The magic of the reservoir swept the filth from her clothes, washing it in a single foul current toward one of the many openings in the walls. One of the sewer tunnels, no doubt.

She wished she had more time to study the magic. Public wells meant anyone could poison the raikh's water supply. The fairy magic not only cleansed the water, it probably purified any toxins. That would be a useful spell to learn, not to mention it would help her to understand how fairy magic worked in this land.

She held her breath and ducked beneath the surface, rinsing her face and hair. By the time she surfaced, the others were joining her in the water, leaving the squealing goblins trapped in the ice. Talia dove deep, shooting up a moment later like a mermaid to catch the stones at the base of the well. Her feet kicked as she pulled herself higher. A short time later, Snow could hear the rattle of metal from the top of the well.

"What's wrong?" Danielle asked.

Talia dropped out of the well, hitting the water with

hardly a splash. She surfaced and shoved her hair back from her face. "They've latched it. Most people don't bother, since the goblins aren't strong enough to climb up. It's probably a simple metal catch, but the lip of the well keeps me from reaching it."

Snow smiled and swam closer. This time, she didn't say a word about using magic to do what brute force couldn't. Judging from the annoyance in Talia's eyes, she didn't have to.

With Talia's help, she managed to pull herself up. Only the bottommost stones were damp. The rest were dry and easy to hold, save for where Talia had dripped against them when she climbed up. Even those were already beginning to dry. The Arathean air sucked the water from everything.

Snow rested her back against one side of the well, bracing her legs against the other. Her hands pressed flat behind her back. Straightening one leg, she pushed herself upward.

She soon had cramps in her feet and the backs of her legs as she made her way higher. She locked both legs and flexed her hands, trying to keep them from tightening as well. Talia made this sort of thing look easy.

The well was almost two stories high. Enough to make her nervous when she looked down, though the narrow confines meant she was unlikely to slip, and the water would break her fall in any event.

The cap atop the well was made of sculpted bronze in the shape of an overlapping sun and moon. Snow listened, but she heard nothing from the other side. Though if the cap was thick enough to muffle the sounds of sewer goblins, it would do the same for any noise within the mansion. She let her legs support her weight as she pushed against the cap, gently at first, then harder when it refused to budge.

Eventually, with her legs braced and both arms pushing the edge, she raised the cap slightly. It rose about the width of her little finger before catching. Not enough space to sneak a mirror through and examine the latch.

"Those other goblins won't stay away forever," Talia said.

Snow rested her head against the stone. So long as she wasn't trying to climb, this position was almost relaxing. She closed her eyes, then opened them again, willing her vision to focus. Given the choice between enchanting stone or metal, stone was slightly easier to work with. Neither would be pleasant, given how much she had already done today.

She grabbed her knife, then hesitated. She could age the stone, crumbling it to sand until the catch holding the cap in place loosened and slid free, but surely there was an easier spell, one that wouldn't add so much to her already throbbing skull.

A year ago, she would have cast the spell without a thought. She hated having to ration her power, to plan out how much magic she could perform before the pain overwhelmed her. But she had pushed too hard already, and the hand holding the knife shook, not from anticipation of the cut, but because she knew what would come next was worse.

"Damn it," she whispered. Pressing the blade to her hand, she forced herself to cut a thin line across her palm. She slammed her hand against the stone and muttered the incantation.

Nothing happened. Snow gritted her teeth and pressed harder until she felt the low warmth of fairy magic. The stones at the top were enchanted, just like the stones of the well and the reservoir below. She could punch through that extra layer of magic, but it would not be pleasant.

"What's wrong?" Danielle called.

"Proper spellcasting takes time," Snow said.

Talia's snort echoed clearly up the well. "When did you start worrying about propriety?"

Snow smiled despite her frustration. She touched the stone again, when a faint chirping sound on the other side startled her. She yanked her hands back.

"Wait," said Danielle. "Try to lift it now."

Snow did so. This time, the cap rose higher, revealing a round windowless cellar. A small brown and black bird with a tufted head stood on the edge of the well.

"Talia was getting impatient," Danielle explained. "I thought you might want help."

Snow said nothing. She reduced the light from her choker as she peered around the cellar. Once she was sure nobody was within, she braced herself and pushed the lid higher. It was surprisingly heavy, falling back with a loud thud. Snow froze, but heard nothing.

"I would have gotten it eventually," Snow called down. She climbed from the well, shooting an annoyed look at the bird. A metal rod the size of her little finger lay beside the bird, close to an iron loop anchored into the floor. "Oh, sure. It's easy to unlatch it from the outside."

The well itself was simply a hole in the stone floor. A bucket and rope sat to one side, the rope knotted to another bolt in the floor. Snow lowered the bucket to help the others climb out, then examined the room more closely.

The first thing she noticed was a low humming that reminded her of air playing over the mouth of a jug. The sound came from a round hole in the ceiling. Metal bars crisscrossed the hole, which was wider than the well and appeared to be a chimney of some sort.

The cellar was a small room with open doorways to either side. Heavy curtains had been tied back from the doors, allowing a strong breeze to pass through. The air chilled Snow's wet skin.

Clay jugs lined the walls. Most were painted in brown and orange designs, with images of animals both magical and mundane. Dust covered the floor, save for the paths from the well to the doorways.

Roudette emerged next, followed by Danielle. Danielle smiled when she spotted the bird.

"Thank you," she said. He fluffed his wings and flew into the air, disappearing into the hole in the ceiling.

"What is that thing?" Snow asked, pointing to the ceiling.

"Windcatcher," said Talia, pulling herself up onto the floor. "Remember the tall structure we saw outside? The wind flows past, sucking the air up through the tower and pulling cool air from the cellar throughout the mansion. The only downside is how easily a good thief can use them to sneak inside. Eventually people started building bars into the towers to keep out unwanted visitors."

Snow peeked up into the windcatcher, her pain momentarily forgotten. She had read of these structures but had never seen one. "There should be shutters at the top to control the effects of the wind."

"That's right." Talia coiled the rope and bucket onto the floor, then pulled the well cover back into place.

"So we made it to the cellar," Roudette said, looking around. "How do you intend to reach the gardens?"

Talia smiled at Roudette, her expression as wicked as Snow had ever seen it. She cut a length of rope from the bucket, tucking the ends away to hide them. She tied a quick loop in the end. "Where else would we take the newest addition to Rajil's menagerie?"

Wet wolf smelled a great deal like wet dog. Talia grimaced as she strode through the hallway, one hand clutching the rope tied around Roudette's neck. They passed the baths and several storerooms before being stopped by a young man in a sleeveless white tunic trimmed in red. He was carrying an enormous bundle of soiled clothes.

He jumped back at the sight of Roudette in her wolf form. "Who are you?"

"This beast is a gift for the raikh," Talia said. "Where can we find her?"

The man shifted his burden. "You're soaked. What happened?"

"Have *you* ever tried to bathe a wolf?" Talia demanded. "Believe me, the raikh would be most displeased if we delivered this animal smelling the way she did before."

Roudette turned her head, growling at Talia. The servant backed away, and Talia used the opening to drag Roudette another step toward the stairs. Roudette fought, and Talia had to grab the rope with both hands to keep her grip. Danielle grabbed the rope, adding her strength to Talia's. Roudette was putting up a good show. At least Talia hoped it was a show. "I've brought this animal a long way, and I'm eager to be rid of it. Where would the raikh be at this time of day?"

"Her private dining room," the man stammered, his eyes never leaving the black wolf.

"Thank you. And the garden?"

He gave hasty directions to both, and hurried past.

Following his instructions, Talia led Roudette toward the spiral stairs at the end of the hallway. A marble pillar rose through the center of the steps. Dozens of candles burned in small niches in the pillar, appearing perfectly normal except for the green tint of the flames that danced with the air's movement. As she climbed the steps, Talia could see that each candle was actually carved from white stone. More fairy magic.

Talia hurried past the first floor, heading for the gardens. She blinked as she passed the first of many narrow windows in the outer wall. The sun outside was surprisingly bright.

"What do you intend to do about Rajil?" Snow asked.

"There is only one punishment for a raikh who betrays her people and her city." It was a punishment rarely carried out. Every raikh took a vow, severing all familial ties and accepting the king or queen of Arathea as the head of his or her new family. Raikhs lived out their lives in the city, never stepping beyond its boundaries except by direct order of the king or queen. The people of the city became their children, and the raikh was expected to guard them as fiercely as any parent. But Talia had only to look at Snow's past to remember that not all parents put their children's welfare first. "We'll worry about her after we find Faziya."

At the top of the stairs, a doorway opened onto an open walkway. They were in one of the wings of the mansion. Talia could see another staircase at the end of the walkway, leading up to the gardens atop the central part of the building. Two guards stood on the front step, just far enough back to be shaded from the sun.

Unlike the guards outside, these wore formal armor of lacquered black breastplates. Their heads were shaved, even the eyebrows. Blue tattoos masked their eyes, giving the impression of feather masks.

"I've never seen tattoos like that," Snow whispered.

"Rajil is a fairy worshiper," Talia replied. "The wings are a symbol of the peri." Yet another sign where her true loyalty lay.

Both men watched closely as Talia pulled Roudette onto the walkway. They wore enormous scimitars at their sides, along with more practical war clubs.

Roudette tugged at the rope.

"Not yet." If Roudette truly wanted to break free, Talia wasn't strong enough to hold her. "This is a lousy place for a fight." Talia glanced over the stone railing. The fall wouldn't kill her, but it would certainly hurt. The grounds below were mostly empty. Most of the people should still be indoors, enjoying the cool shade and the breeze generated by the windcatcher.

One of the guards stepped out into the sunlight. "We weren't told of any new additions for the menagerie."

"The wolf is a gift from Father Uf'uyan and the fairy church," Talia said, continuing forward. "I was instructed—"

"I'm sorry, but nothing enters the gardens without permission from the raikh or her adviser." He gave a slight bow, appearing genuinely apologetic. "There are too many valuable creatures, and if that wolf hasn't been properly prepared, it could slaughter the raikh's other pets."

"Slaughter?" Talia stared at Roudette. "You think so? She looks so gentle."

"If you'll wait here," he said, "I can—"

"Go on." Talia dropped the rope. "Show them how gentle you are."

Roudette was on the first guard before his sword could clear its sheath. Talia followed close behind. She hopped onto the rail, arms outstretched for balance as she ran past Roudette. Then the second guard started to draw his weapon, and Talia leaped. Her shoulder hit him in the chest, knocking them both onto the steps.

Talia ducked a thrust of the guard's sword, then dodged a kick. She caught his foot in her arm and lifted. He fell again, his armor hitting the steps with a loud crack. Her own sword was at the inside of his thigh before he could recover.

"I don't want to kill you," Talia said. "You know how quickly you'll bleed to death if I cut you here?"

He set his sword on the step and raised his hands.

Talia risked a quick glance behind. "I said we don't want to kill them."

Roudette growled. Snow and Danielle were already pulling her back from the bleeding guard.

"Get their weapons." Talia waited, then led both men up the stairs at swordpoint. She readied her zaraq whip in her other hand, but there were no guards at the top of the stairs. Nor was there any gate or door to keep the animals from escaping. Only magic held the raikh's creatures in place.

The stairs might as well have led to another world. A fairy world, full of life and color. Fruit trees grew on two sides of the reflecting pool in the center of the garden. Familiar plants grew side by side with the exotic. Talia recognized several fairy species, including the pebble-skinned graniteberries growing along the wall and the long, silver-leafed elven pear trees bordering the stairs like a living doorway. The smell was overpowering, the sickly-sweet scent of the fruit mixing with the perfume of the flowers growing alongside paths of crushed green stone.

A white owl perched in the pear tree to her left. It cocked its head as Talia pushed the guards into the garden. Coyotes and jackals sunned themselves on stone benches. A desert cat batted lazily at a yellow fruit Talia didn't recognize. A brown snake as long as a man slid past a mouse, but neither animal paid the slightest attention to the other.

Talia pushed both guards against the wall, where they couldn't be seen from the stairs. The second guard was rather bloodied, but none of the wounds appeared deadly. Roudette had been toying with him. With a pointed glance at Roudette, Talia said, "I'd wait quietly if I were you."

She stepped away, footsteps crunching on the gravel path. "Faziya?" Several of the animals looked up at the sound of her voice, but she saw no recognition from any of them. "Snow, is there any way you can tell which one is Faziya?"

Snow studied a hawk that was bathing itself at the edge of the pool. "Their thoughts . . . there are no memories beyond the animal."

"What does that mean?" Talia asked.

Snow approached the hawk, one hand extended. It spread its wings, but it allowed her to touch the feathers of its neck. Snow jerked her fingers back. "This is more than shapechanging. Whoever this used to be, that person is gone."

Her words sucked the air from Talia's chest. She

shoved past Snow and crouched in front of the hawk, staring into its eyes. "Maybe some of the animals are natural. Maybe this one wasn't transformed."

"I can feel the curse running through his bones," Snow said. She bit her lip and turned to Danielle, as though she was asking for help. "I'm sorry."

Talia backed away. "Try the rabbit."

Danielle started toward her. "Talia—"

"No!" Talia spun, searching the bushes. Faziya was here, somewhere. "These are Rajil's prisoners. She could have killed them, but she didn't. What would she do if she needed to question one further? There has to be a way of reversing whatever was done."

"There probably is," Snow said slowly. "But this is fairy magic, stronger than anything I've seen."

"Deev magic?" Talia asked.

"Maybe." Snow shook her head. "Give me time alone with them, with Trittibar's help and access to my library, and I might—"

"We're in the middle of the raikh's mansion! The Wild Hunt returns tonight!"

"I know that!" Snow turned away, rubbing the back of her neck. "I can't do it. I'm sorry."

"Then we find Rajil." Talia pulled out her sword. "We do whatever it takes to make her restore Faziya." She was halfway to the steps when she heard shouts from below.

"I don't think finding Rajil will be a problem," Snow said.

Danielle readied her sword. "How many guards does your average raikh keep on hand?"

Talia smiled. "Let's find out."

Chapter 14

T ALIA MOVED TO THE SIDE OF THE STAIRS, hiding behind one of the pear trees. She calmed her breathing, listening as the footsteps slowed. She gripped a low branch and stepped around, kicking high enough to catch the first guard on the chin. He fell back, to be caught by his companions.

Talia swore. She counted six men in the lacquered armor of the raikh, as well as a creature of smoke and shadow. Men she could fight, but fairy magic was another matter. She jumped to the side, taking cover as a spear flew past.

"What's the plan?" Snow asked.

"I'm working on it." Talia could probably handle the guards, and Snow might be a match for Rajil's fairy adviser, but an open battle in the garden wouldn't help Faziya. Even if they won, the commotion would only attract more attention.

The next guard through carried a short spear in one hand and a northern-style club in the other. He raised the spear, but Talia made no move to attack. She jabbed her sword point down into the dirt and spread her hands.

The rest of the guards moved quickly to surround them. Roudette bared her teeth and growled.

"Wait!" Talia lunged to catch Roudette's rope, catch-

ing her in midleap. Talia was tugged off her feet, but she
managed to pull the wolf back. Before Roudette could
turn on her, Talia pushed herself to one knee and whispered, "Not yet."

The two men they had captured before gathered
weapons from Talia and her companions. Talia clenched
her jaw but waited as they disarmed her. It was a slow
process, and Rajil's men were thorough, taking even the
slender metal spike tucked through her hair. Two others
grabbed Roudette's rope, dragging the wolf away.

Talia and the others were herded into a tight circle
against the wall. The smoke shadow approached so
closely Talia could smell him, like burning leaves.

Only when he turned away did Rajil herself enter
the garden. She wore a gold robe that shone like satin,
held tight by a wide white belt. The silver buckle was
cast in the huma bird and tiger design of the royal crest.
A blue-green tourmaline mounted in the center marked
Rajil's status as ruler of Jahrasima. Her face was as Talia remembered, stern and narrow, the lips perpetually
frowning. She wore the same feathered mask tattoo as
her men.

Rajil studied them each in turn, keeping safely out of
reach behind her guards. Talia waited as Rajil's gaze lingered on her. Though Talia had seen Rajil before from a
distance, they had never met in person.

Rajil turned to examine the weapons her men had
taken. She picked up Danielle's sword, studying the
glass blade in the sun. "You're no ordinary thieves."

Talia straightened. "I think you know who I am,
Rajil."

The man of smoke moved closer, his movements almost eager. Rajil simply tossed the sword to the ground
and said, "Perhaps. Jhukha will learn the truth soon
enough."

"That he will." Whispering so softly she could barely
hear her own voice, Talia said, "Roudette, take Rajil."

Roudette had already shown her senses to be sharper than any human's. Roudette bounded forward, yanking her guards to the ground as though they weighed nothing at all.

Blue fire flashed from Jhukha's arms, racing over Roudette's body with no effect. As Talia had hoped, Roudette's cape protected her from fairy magic even in her wolf form. Rajil screamed as another guard was tossed aside like a doll, and then Roudette was atop her, jaws clamped around her throat.

The human guards hesitated. Not Jhukha. The fairy attacked again, loosing another wave of flame over Roudette. As before, his magic did nothing.

Talia used the guards' distraction to race toward their weapons. She dove and rolled, rising to her feet with Danielle's sword in one hand. The enchanted blade sliced through Jhukha's form. The path of the cut reformed as soon as the blade passed, but Jhukha drew back as though pained.

"If one of your men makes the slightest move, my wolf will tear out your throat," Talia said lightly.

"Stop!" Between Rajil's fear and the pressure of Roudette's jaws, the word was little more than a squeak.

"Watch that thing." Talia jabbed the sword at Jhukha. She trusted Rajil's human guards to obey. If any did try to attack, Talia was fast enough to deal with them. But who knew where the fairy's loyalties lay? To Rajil, she said, "You have a friend of mine here. I'd like her back."

Roudette loosened her grip ever so slightly.

Talia smiled. "She didn't have much of a breakfast, so she's hungry."

Blood dripped from small punctures in Rajil's neck, staining the collar of her robe. She ignored it, focusing her attention instead on Talia. "I do know you. I saw a painting once, as a child. Before Queen Lakhim ordered all such work destroyed. You look older, Princess Talia. Old and tired."

At the mention of Talia's name, Jhukha seemed to contract, his body growing smaller and darker until he appeared almost solid. Talia moved toward him, but before she could strike, the fairy burst into cloud, becoming no thicker than smoke from a campfire.

"Stop him!" Talia shouted, slashing through the smoke. Already Jhukha was flowing over the top of the wall.

Sunlight sliced into the fairy from Snow's mirrors, burning holes through the smoke, but it wasn't enough to stop him.

"Snow, you and Danielle watch the doorways." Talia knelt beside Rajil. "He can't save you. If I have to fight every guard in your mansion, I will."

Rajil sniffed. "He's not fetching help for me."

"Zestan," Talia guessed. Having heard Talia's name, he went to tell his mistress. "Can he travel by fairy ring?"

"He's not going anywhere," said Snow. She pulled a mirror from her choker and threw it after the departing fairy. The mirror shattered in mid-flight, turning to a stream of glittering dust which merged with the smoke. "If he tries, the mirror should scatter him across half of this world. He'll spend the next year putting himself back together."

Talia grabbed Rajil by the throat. "Release Faziya and tell us where to find Zestan-e-Jheg, and you may live to see another sunset."

"You'd ask me to betray Zestan?"

Talia fought the urge to strike her. "Have you seen Jahrasima today? Have you looked upon your people and the damage left by the Wild Hunt?"

"The Hunt came for you." Rajil sat up slowly, wide eyes watching Roudette and Talia both. "*You* led them here. Surrender yourself, and Jahrasima will be safe."

"Until the next time Zestan sends the Wild Hunt out on an errand." Talia handed the sword back to Danielle, mostly to avoid the temptation to use it. "Remember the oath you swore. To protect Jahrasima and its people with your blood. To pledge yourself to your city above tribe and family."

"That's exactly what I'm doing," Rajil snapped. "This city wouldn't exist without the help of the fairies. Where would we be if we had rejected their aid? Roaming the desert like Kha'iida savages. Squabbling over what little water we could find. Warring among ourselves, as we did for the hundred years you slept. They saved us from barbarism. Zestan will turn all Arathea into a jewel."

"By enslaving us?" Talia asked.

Rajil spread her arms. "Do I look like a slave to you?"

"You look like—"

Danielle coughed, and Talia caught herself. She didn't have time to fight with Rajil.

"The fairies wish to serve us," Rajil said, pouncing on the opening left by Talia's silence. "We are their penance. They will make this land a paradise."

"Tell that to the people mourning the loss of their homes and loved ones," Talia said softly. "Tell that to Queen Lakhim. You know Zestan means to kill her, right? Her and her grandsons both. Would you side with the fairies against your own ruler?"

"Asks the one who murdered Prince Jihab." Rajil spat.

Sparring with Rajil was a waste of time. "Zestan-e-Jheg is a deev."

For a heartbeat, she saw doubt in Rajil's eyes. "Impossible."

"Look at the power she wields. Look at the way she loosed the Wild Hunt on the Kha'iida and on your city."

"The Wild Hunt are a tool of God, sent to punish—"

"They will return tonight in force," Talia snapped. "They will tear this city apart to find me. You'll be the raikh of a dead, ruined city . . . assuming they leave you alive."

"Zestan wouldn't harm me."

"Which is more important to her, protecting a human or finding me? Your friend Jhukha didn't hesitate to abandon you." Talia leaned closer, lowering her voice. "Give me Faziya. Tell me where to find Zestan. In return, I promise to protect Jahrasima from the Wild Hunt."

"What are you doing?" Danielle asked.

"What she should have done." Talia nudged Rajil with her foot.

Rajil hesitated. "Zestan's influence was growing even before you awoke. Most of the fairy families in Arathea now pledge their loyalty to her, though few have ever seen her. It was only a year ago that she sent Jhukha to me." She glanced about. "This is his menagerie. His magic that binds the traitors into these forms. Even if I wished to help you, I couldn't restore them."

"All I need is for you to identify her," Talia said, trying not to think about that. "I'm looking for a Kha'iida woman. She would have come here roughly one month ago. She would have asked about the Wild Hunt, and about Zestan."

"The jackal," Rajil whispered. "I was sympathetic to her pleas, of course, but Jhukha—"

"I'm sure you had no choice," Talia said bitterly. "Just as you had no choice but to let Zestan attack your city." She turned, searching the garden until she spotted a white jackal standing beside a bush of oversized golden roses. Talia's chest tightened as she studied the jackal, trying to see Faziya in those blue eyes. The animal's oversized ears twitched as the jackal examined Talia in return.

"You're safe," Danielle whispered. "Please come to us."

Lean and long-legged, the jackal trotted toward them.

"She doesn't remember you," Rajil said.

"She will." Talia extended one hand toward the jackal. Toward Faziya. Slowly, Faziya stepped closer, taking a tentative sniff. Talia started to brush her fingertips over the fur, but Faziya jumped back in alarm.

Danielle continued speaking in soft, soothing tones.

"What about Zestan?" Talia asked, never taking her eyes from Faziya.

"Even if everything you say is true, I can't help you," said Rajil, her voice trembling. "Her messages come through Jhukha. She could be anywhere in Arathea." She brought her hands over her chest, closed her eyes, and began to pray.

Talia recognized the prayer, a plea for redemption and rebirth. Rajil expected to die here, at Talia's hand.

"You think your death will earn you a place in Heaven?" Talia asked. "That you might even be reborn as one of the 'Blessed Race' as a reward for your faith. For that you'd sacrifice your queen, your people, even your life? All to protect a deev."

"What would you have me do?" Rajil demanded. "If I'm right, Zestan is the salvation of Arathea. If you're right, if she is a deev and I betray her . . . no. Even if I knew where to find her, I couldn't tell you."

Talia's anger drained slowly. She turned to Snow. "Can you break whatever curse holds the animals here?"

"The curse tames them, but it doesn't trap them here," said Snow. "They could leave any time they choose. They simply lack the desire."

"Good." Talia retrieved her weapons.

As she tucked the last of her knives back into its sheath, Rajil spoke again. "If you truly want to protect Jahrasima, surrender yourself and your friends. If you flee, The Wild Hunt *will* return for you. Whatever destruction they bring will be weighed upon your soul, not my own."

"You've already sold yours to the fairies." Talia spat

on the ground, then turned to Danielle. "We'll need the animals' help in order to escape."

"They're too docile," Danielle said. As if to demonstrate, a lioness padded out from cluster of trees, flopped onto her side, and began to purr loudly enough Talia could hear it from halfway across the garden.

"My people know of your intrusion," Rajil said. "Even if you kill us all, you'll never escape this place."

Before Talia could respond, one of the guards stepped forward and bowed low. "I'll escort you. My name is Naheer el-Qudas. I've served the raikh for six years. Few here will question me."

"Traitor!" Whatever else Rajil might have said was lost in a frightened squeak as Roudette's teeth snapped the skin from the tip of her nose.

Talia studied the man who had spoken. He was older than the others, and the white scrollwork on his breastplate marked him as a higher-ranking soldier. She searched his face as he rose. A crooked nose and broken teeth showed he had fought his share of brawls, but she saw no sign of trickery. "Why would you help us?"

"My father's home was destroyed by the Wild Hunt. My mother was taken to the temple this morning. She may not survive." Naheer glanced at Rajil. "You offered to protect Jahrasima from the Hunt's return. Are you truly who you claim? Can you do what you promised?"

Talia inclined her head ever so slightly in return. "I am, and I will."

He bowed again, this time dropping to one knee. "Princess Talia, I will see you from this place myself."

For the first time since entering the raikh's mansion, Talia found herself at a loss. If Naheer's offer was genuine, and the rage on Rajil's face suggested it was, he had to know he had just accepted death. He would be executed before the sun set, yet he appeared far calmer than Talia felt.

Talia glanced at Danielle, but of course Danielle couldn't understand a word being spoken. Snow merely shrugged. "Thank you," Talia whispered. "We still need to secure Rajil and the others."

Another of the guards joined Naheer. "I will see that no one leaves this garden or cries for help until you're safely away from the mansion, Princess."

"As will I," said a third. The rest held back, though none of Rajil's guards appeared eager to take up arms and defend her.

"You can't," Talia said. "Rajil will—"

"Forgive me, Princess," said Naheer. "But our lives are yours now. Rajil has witnessed our choice. You can't scrape the memories from her mind."

"*I* can't, no." Without another word, Talia grabbed the back of Rajil's robe and hauled her to her feet. Talia's arm snaked around Rajil's throat. Her other hand gripped her wrist, and she pulled tight. Rajil struggled briefly, but Talia's hold cut off the blood to Rajil's head, and she soon slumped. Talia dropped Rajil to the ground and turned to Snow.

"And once again you turn to the sorceress for help." Snow grinned as she pressed a hand to Rajil's forehead. "I can probably block the memory for a few days. I'll try to make her sleep a while as well. What about the other guards?"

"We've fought together before," said Naheer. "Every man here took an oath to protect his fellows."

And not one had moved to stop Talia from knocking Rajil unconscious. Talia blinked hard. A lump in her throat kept her from speaking. Instead, she simply clasped Naheer's arm in her hand and squeezed.

He hesitated before returning the greeting, an old street gesture between brawlers. "Come, Your Highness," he said. "The sooner you leave this place, the safer you'll be."

*   *   *

The one called Naheer led them down the steps. Danielle didn't understand what had happened, but something in the garden had changed for Talia. Confidence and uncertainty warred on her face with no clear winner, but she appeared even more determined than before to lead them to safety.

Danielle spoke softly to Faziya, encouraging her with every step to keep her from fleeing back to the garden. Faziya was visibly trembling. Talia had tried twice to comfort her, but both times Faziya had shied away, hiding behind Danielle.

Between Naheer's calm presence and Roudette snarling at anyone who stared, they reached the back of the mansion unchallenged. The stables were built into the rear wings, with the back courtyard walled off to provide a small yard for the horses.

The inside of the stable smelled of dust, barley, and manure. Naheer shouted something to the boy mucking out one of the empty stalls. The boy set his pitchfork against the wall and hurried away.

Danielle approached the closest stall. She wasn't as comfortable on horseback as her friends, but she had learned enough to recognize a beautiful animal when she saw it. This was a gray mare, smaller than the horses back home, long-necked and muscular. Even in the confines of her stall, she held head and tail high, giving her a proud appearance.

Naheer was saddling a roan mare. The saddles were shorter and wider than Danielle was used to, with large saddlebags. The boy returned a short time later, carrying blankets and waterskins.

"What did Naheer say to him?" Danielle asked.

Snow grinned. "The boy is Naheer's nephew. He said to prepare the horses and that he'd box his ears if he loitered about to flirt with the girls inside."

"What will happen to him, once Rajil remembers?" Danielle asked.

Snow translated the question, as well as Naheer's response. "He is family. I will take him from this place tonight, and I will keep him safe." The obvious worry when he looked at his nephew gave the lie to his threat to beat the boy for any delay.

"Where do we go from here?" Danielle didn't know everything that had been said in the garden, but Snow had summarized Talia's exchange with Rajil. "We still don't know where to find Zestan."

"Faziya might." Talia threw a saddle onto a third horse. "We leave the city and do what we can to restore her, and we hope she learned more than we did."

Talia even sounded different. Her words were . . . not calmer, but more certain.

"What can I do?" asked Danielle.

"Keep Faziya calm." Talia yanked the second saddle tight and moved on to the gray mare.

"Uh-oh." Snow touched the empty spot on her choker where the mirror had been. "Our fairy friend is back."

Talia barked an order in Arathean. The boy paled and argued briefly with Naheer before fleeing. Naheer took a deep breath and grunted something to Talia.

"Ka hiran," Talia said softly. Then she kicked him in the face.

"Talia!" Danielle started forward, but Snow moved between them.

The blow knocked Naheer into one of the stone support pillars. He staggered forward, moving right into Talia's follow-up kick. Talia moved close, fist cocked back to strike, but Naheer raised his hands. He wiped blood from his mouth and muttered something in Arathean, then slumped to the floor. His eyes closed.

Talia grabbed the spear and club he carried, tucking the latter through her sash before mounting her horse.

"What did he say?" Danielle asked.

Snow grinned. "His exact words were, 'Nice kick, Princess.' He should be safe. His nephew will say we broke free and overpowered him." Snow climbed onto the roan. "We're out of time, Talia."

Already Danielle could hear shouts from within the mansion. She climbed onto the gray horse, then called for Faziya. After much urging and reassurance, Faziya allowed Talia to lift her up and pass her to Danielle. Danielle held Faziya with both hands, keeping her steady on the saddle and guiding the horse with her words. The horse shied away from Roudette, nickering in alarm.

"What about the gates?" Danielle asked.

"Stay behind me." Talia kicked her horse forward. "Snow, give me Father Uf'uyan and his friend."

Snow yanked the pouch from her belt and tossed it to Talia, who snatched it from the air.

"Can you reverse the spell on them?" Talia shouted as she urged her horse across the courtyard. An arrow thudded into the dirt. Three men rushed forward from the gates.

"Sure," said Snow.

"Do it!" Talia hurled the pouch through the air at the closest of the guards.

Danielle winced with sympathy as Uf'uyan and Yasar ripped through the pouch. They hadn't completely changed back to their natural forms when they crashed into the guards, but they had grown enough. Guards, priest, and naga lay groaning on the ground. Talia's horse leaped over them all. Talia jumped down, running to the gatehouse. Moments later the gate swung open.

"Now aren't you glad we spared them?" Danielle asked.

"Keep going," Talia yelled. Roudette had already bolted through the gate the instant it was wide enough. Snow followed, but Danielle lingered in the gate. In the yard, Talia stood facing the mansion, spear in one hand. She stepped to the side as another arrow buried itself in the ground. She raised her hands, as if challenging them to try again.

A shadow rose atop the wall at the edge of the garden. Jhukha.

Danielle narrowed her eyes. An instant later, an owl flew through the fairy's head. A falcon followed. Neither bird did any true harm, but the fairy stumbled, drawing his form back together where the animals had dispersed it.

Talia shouted and waved her spear. She dodged another arrow, then turned to run, leaping onto her horse and following Danielle onto the road.

"You want them to see you," Danielle said. "This was part of your plan."

"'Plan' might be an overstatement." Talia bent low as she urged her horse into the streets. The wind swallowed half her words as she passed Danielle and Snow. "The Wild Hunt wants me. If I simply disappear, they'll raze Jahrasima to find me. The best way to protect Jahrasima and the temple is to make sure Rajil knows I've left the city. What Rajil knows, Zestan knows."

"Dangerous," Danielle said, but she was smiling.

"That depends on how well Roudette's cape works."

Faziya was shaking in Danielle's lap. The jackal squirmed and peered back at the mansion.

"Stay with me," Danielle said. "A little longer and I promise you'll be safe."

Danielle bent over her horse, allowing Faziya to bury her head in the folds of her cape. Danielle did her best to keep up as the others raced through the streets. People and streets blurred past. The peal of bells made her jump. She urged the horses to greater speed, trusting Talia to know where she was going.

"Almost there," Talia shouted.

Up ahead, Danielle spotted a bridge similar to the one they had crossed when entering the city. Had it really been only a single day? Armed men moved to block their path.

"Keep going!" Talia brought one foot onto the saddle, then the other, until she crouched on the horse's back.

Raising her spear in one hand, she leaped from the horse and crashed into the guard on the right. Danielle called to Talia's horse, who stepped to the side, shouldering the other guard off of the bridge. Glowing jaan swarmed toward the splashing guard.

Roudette took care of a third. The mere sight of the charging wolf was enough to make him leap into the water.

That left only the guards on the far side. The horses galloped as fast as they could, but it wasn't going to be enough. Already the guards were raising lengths of chain to block off the end of the bridge. The chains were bolted to a large post on one side. Two men worked to secure them to a similar post on the opposite side, which would create a makeshift fence too high for the strongest horse to clear. Roudette pulled ahead, but she wouldn't be fast enough to stop them.

Danielle leaned forward, rubbing the mare's neck. "How do you feel about swimming, girl?" The water would make them easy targets, but it was the only way she could think of to get through.

A shortspear flew over her head, flying the full length of the bridge and splintering against the paving stones less than an arm's length from the guards. The guards dropped the chains and dove for cover.

That delay was enough. Roudette was on them before they could recover, and then Danielle and Snow were galloping past, leaving the stone bridge behind and tearing down the road.

Danielle turned, watching as Talia rode after. She had little trouble with the guards, catching up a short time later. She was twirling the club she had taken from Naheer.

"War club," she said. "A notch in the butt of the short-spear fits onto that hook on the club's handle, letting it double as a spearthrower." She smiled. "You'd be amazed at the range you can get."

For the first time since learning who had hired Roudette, Talia seemed like herself again. Danielle smiled to see it.

"Where to next?" asked Snow. "You know Zestan is going to be coming after us."

"Into the deep desert," said Talia, urging her horse forward. "There's an old Kha'iida saying. No prey is so dangerous as that which hunts you in return."

CHAPTER 15

T HEY PUSHED THE HORSES HARD AT FIRST,
putting Jahrasima as far behind them as possible. The
landscape changed quickly as they left the lake. Hills the
color of overbaked rolls stretched out ahead, dotted in
gray green scrub. Worn rock formations protruded from
the dirt like sun-bleached islands in a sea of sand.

The air was noticeably drier away from the lake. Talia
reached up to tighten her sheffeyah, her hands moving
automatically to pull the scarf over her mouth and nose,
then another wrap to protect her head and neck.

This was the real Arathea, deadly and beautiful and
unforgiving, yet she paid it little mind. Faziya had grown
even more skittish, shifting and squirming in Danielle's
lap. Talia kept remembering the way Faziya had shied
from her touch, back in Rajil's garden.

The thought crossed her mind that Rajil might have
lied, giving her some other poor soul. Was that why
Faziya didn't recognize her? The real Faziya might still
be trapped in Rajil's mansion, or worse. Talia twisted the
reins in her hand. Rajil was too much of a coward to
lie. Not with Roudette's jaws a hair's breadth from her
throat.

She slowed to a trot. "We need shelter. Rajil's people
will be tracking us. Lakhim's too, probably. If the queen

hasn't learned of our presence by now, she will soon enough."

Snow pulled her horse to a stop. "Where exactly are we going from here?"

"I hadn't planned that far," Talia admitted.

Danielle climbed down from her mare, then reached up to retrieve Faziya. "Let me see what I can find."

Faziya darted away once again as Talia jumped from her own horse and stretched. She tried not to take Faziya's fear personally. She failed, but she continued to try.

Dust coated her mouth and throat. She unpacked a waterskin from the saddlebag and took several long swallows before tossing it to Snow.

A ripping sound pulled her attention to Roudette, who was using her teeth to peel the wolfskin from her body. A long tear split the skin down the chest. Roudette growled and dug harder with her teeth, revealing a flash of red. Talia thought it was blood at first, before recognizing the other side of Roudette's cape.

Fingers poked through the pads of one paw. Roudette raised the paw to her mouth, using her teeth to rip the skin back, and soon her hand and arm were free. She grabbed the tear beneath her chin and pulled upward. She pushed the head higher, and her own face appeared through the gap in the neck.

Roudette gasped, and with that breath, the wolf appeared to collapse, becoming nothing but a skin once more. Still panting, Roudette pushed herself to her knees and reversed the cape. She shook out the worst of the dust before tying it back over her shoulders.

"You're going to melt in that thing," Snow said, throwing her the waterskin.

"So I've noticed." Roudette's lips twisted in what could charitably be considered a smile. "If I'm not wearing it, we lose the benefit of its magic. Your fairy friends will be on us before you can cast a single spell."

"Where did it come from?" Snow asked. "I've heard of animal skins enchanted to change the wearer's form, but the other powers—"

"You can thank the church for that." Roudette's eyes flashed. "The elders insisted that all children wear the red cape." She brushed her fingers over the runes embroidered along the edge. "Human magic was forbidden, much as it is here. The runes are fairy magic, designed to suppress any magical talent. After I took the wolfskin from my grandmother, I hired a witch to alter the runes on my own cape, turning the fairies' power outward. Combining the cape and the skin gave me the power I needed to fight them."

"Human and fairy magic combined into a single artifact," Snow said. Talia could see how badly she wanted to take Roudette's cape away for study, but she restrained herself.

Danielle had moved away, following a small brown lizard. The lizard vanished into a crack in the rocks, and Danielle laughed. "I'm sorry, but my friends and I need something larger."

"How long will it take to reverse Jhukha's curse and change her back?" Talia asked.

"That depends." Snow rubbed her hands, which were already beginning to pink from the sun.

Talia returned to the saddlebags, hoping Naheer had thought to pack proper desert wear. She soon dug out a brown linen robe and a matching head scarf. She tossed the former to Snow, then helped her with the scarf, tucking both ends in the back Kha'iida style so it covered all but the eyes.

"It won't be easy," Snow said. "I don't even know what Jhukha was, let alone what kind of power it might have."

"She was a Jinniyah," said Roudette. "Seducers of the soul. Rare, but powerful."

"She?" Snow repeated.

Roudette stared. "Jhukha was female. You didn't notice?"

"I've never seen one before." Snow rolled her eyes. "I saw a picture once, but it's hard to make out the anatomical details of a creature that's little more than a smudge of smoke and darkness."

"How long?" Talia repeated.

"Hours. Maybe days." Snow looked away. "Jinniyah have little power of their own. They're slaves, taking magic from their masters. The greater the magic, the stronger the master's control."

"If you're right about Zestan, that means Faziya was cursed by deev magic," Roudette said.

"You changed a priest into a mouse," Talia said. "If you can do that—"

"I could reshape Faziya's body." Snow grabbed the waterskin back from Roudette, pulled down her scarf, and took another drink. "You'd be left with a woman who has the mind and memories of a terrified jackal. Let me talk to Trittibar."

Talia walked away. She knew it was unfair to expect Snow to wave her hands and return Faziya to her, but it didn't matter.

"I think I might have found something," Danielle said, following a fox with oversized ears. The fox raced into the hills, then ran back to Danielle. "He wants me to follow."

"Go," said Talia. "Take Snow and Faziya. You've got food and water in your saddlebags. Once you find shelter, have Snow do what she can."

Danielle turned back. "What about you?"

Talia clasped her hands together. Her knuckles were white. "I've no intention of sitting around helpless in my own land."

"You're not helpless," Danielle said.

Talia pointed at Faziya. "I can't do anything for her. All I could do is watch and wait. I'm bad at waiting."

"I understand." Damn her, but she probably did, too. Danielle was like that.

"What are you going to do?"

Talia adjusted her sword. "Make sure Snow isn't interrupted."

"You should have killed Rajil." Sweat dripped down Roudette's face as she and Talia hiked through the hills. She had pushed back her hood and rolled her sleeves as high as they would go. The red cape was wool, made for a colder land. Combined with the wolfskin, she was afraid Snow White might have been right. She was sweating too much, and her body would dry up like a corpse soon if she wasn't careful.

She was tempted to return to her wolf form, which had only a thick coat of fur to worry about. But fur in the desert wasn't much of an improvement.

"I thought about it," Talia said.

"Zestan owns her, and that spell your witch cast won't hold forever."

"Sometimes there are better choices than killing everyone who gets in your way."

"Maybe," Roudette admitted. "I've found that killing is safest, though."

"If I killed Rajil, Jhukha would take control until Queen Lakhim named a new raikh." Talia reached the top of the hill and crouched low. "Rajil has her doubts, even if she refuses to admit them. You could see it in her eyes. Better a human coward in control than one of Zestan's fairies."

"It makes no difference." Roudette crawled up beside Talia. In the distance, she could make out a small band of men on horseback, following a pair of dogs. Mortal dogs, thankfully. "Humans ran my village, but they worshiped the fairies, just as Rajil does."

"Yet the Wild Hunt destroyed them anyway."

"The Hunt cares nothing for worship." Roudette

turned away from the approaching band, sitting with her back against the rock. "My father was a patriarch of the fairy church. From birth, my brother and I were raised to follow the Path. Only my grandmother turned away from fairy teachings."

She rarely thought about Grandmother these days. Of course, she hadn't spent this much time around other people since she was a child. "My grandmother had left the Path years before. She spent most of her time away, but one day I spotted smoke rising from her old cabin. I thought maybe she had come back for the festival of midsummer. My parents had warned us away from her, but the church instructed us to save those we love, to try to lead them back to salvation. So I snuck away with a basket of fairy cakes."

"Fairy cakes?" asked Talia.

"Muffins filled with red jam, to represent the blood of the sacrifice. Until I was five, I believed the Savior tasted like strawberries.

"I called out when I reached Grandmother's cabin, but there was no answer. I heard noises, so I snuck inside. The sounds were coming from the bedroom."

Talia shifted, studying the men below. "The wolf?"

"I thought it had eaten my grandmother and fallen asleep in the bed. I remember thinking how large her teeth were, bared even in sleep. Blood oozed from a cut in her side. The blankets were soaked. I started to sneak away, but she opened her eyes and looked at me. Her eyes were enormous, and I recognized them as Grandmother's. I stayed with her until nightfall, when the hunter came."

"The hunter from the story," said Talia. "He was part of the Wild Hunt?"

"The festival of midsummer was a time of prayer and confession, a time to cleanse ourselves of sin so that the Wild Hunt might look elsewhere for their prey. Grandmother knew better. She had spent years using the wolfskin to fight the Hunt, until at last she fell. She had been stabbed the night before. I don't know how she found the strength to return to her cabin. The hunter tracked her blood."

Roudette stroked the fur of the cape. "Grandmother couldn't speak, but she roused herself enough to drag me to a closet, hiding me before he entered. He cut the skin from her body while I watched, then pinned the skin to the floor with his spear. Fire exploded from the shaft. He left, expecting the flames to destroy Grandmother and the skin both."

She hadn't planned on telling Talia this, but after the past day, she thought it important for Talia to know, to see what was coming.

"Grandmother called to me." Roudette closed her eyes. She could smell the smoke, could see Grandmother's blood pooling on the floor. "She told me to take the wolfskin and save my family."

Talia's face hardened. "The hunter wasn't alone."

"The Hunt had spared our land for years. I had never heard the howling of their hounds except in stories, never seen their steeds save in pictures in church, but Grandmother knew. She had tracked the Hunt all her life, and when she realized their path would lead them to our village, she returned to try to protect us.

"I ran to the house, but the howling started before I was halfway there. I wanted to flee, but the touch of the wolfskin gave me strength. By the time I reached my village, little was left. Most of the Hunt were riding through the woods, chasing down the survivors. I ran into my house to find the same hunter who had killed my grandmother now standing before my parents. He murdered my mother while my father watched. He would have done the same to my little brother had I not donned the skin to stop him."

Roudette's hands were shaking. Strange, the power those memories still held over her. She dug her fingers into the wolf's fur until anger pushed the fear away. "The church taught that the Wild Hunt were minions of God, taking only the sinners from this world. For years I wondered what sins we had committed to draw the Hunt's fury. Only later did I begin to understand. I searched for meaning and motives from those who had neither. The Hunt has no purpose, no plan. They simply are."

Talia stared at the men below. "The Wild Hunt roams the entire world."

"Which means Zestan's power will do the same," Roudette agreed. "If she controls the Hunt, she can send them against anyone. For the moment she's content to conquer Arathea, but after that . . ."

Talia turned to retreat down the hill. "We'll cut a false path east, toward the Makras River. If we're lucky, we can divert them away long enough for us to disappear."

Roudette grinned. "I have a better idea. Those men have supplies, yes?"

"Nobody comes into the desert unprepared."

"We could use extra food and water, and I'm ready for another fight." Roudette unfastened her cape and flipped it about. She brought the hood over her head, letting the skin's magic seep into her skin. Pulling it tight would trigger the transformation, but she wasn't quite ready for that. She threw back her head and howled.

The sound faded quickly. Talia dropped flat, peering through thorny plants at the men below. "They're coming this way. You know, normally I prefer to have surprise on my side when I'm outnumbered five to one."

"Wait," Roudette said. A second howl made the men whirl, searching the hills for the source. A third followed, then two more. Roudette howled again, drawing on the skin's power to summon the wolves of the desert. "Who's outnumbered now?"

"One of Rajil's men will carry a horn," Talia said. "If he calls for help, or if even one of them get away—"

"You worry too much. We're all going to die someday." Roudette pulled the skin tight. As the wolf enveloped her, she added, "If it's today, you might as well go out fighting."

The cave the fox had found was hardly an ideal location for Snow's magic: low and cramped, full of sand and old spiderwebs. It had been full of old spiders too, until Snow used a quick spell to clear them out. She shivered, trying not to think about the parade of spiders and other creepy things that had poured from the shadows.

She would have given much for the comfort of her library, not to mention a good night's sleep.

"You can't restore her if you don't know what you're restoring her to," Trittibar said.

"I know that!" Snow scowled at the tiny image in her mirror. Trittibar's arm was bandaged against his body. His clothes were more subdued than normal, and his voice had lost some of its spirit, but he was doing his best to help. Unfortunately, there was only so much he could do from Lorindar. "When I use shapechanging magic, the subject's own memories help restore her to her natural form. Faziya has no memory of her former shape."

Snow turned the mirror so Trittibar could get a better view of Faziya, who lay curled in a furry ball near the back of the cave.

"We can argue for as long as you'd like," Trittibar said. "If you're right about Zestan, the kind of magic we're dealing with is far beyond anything I could counter, even when I was still able to draw upon the power of Fairytown." He stumbled only briefly. "Jinniyah aren't powerful enough for this kind of magic. Given what you've described, I'm sure she used Zestan's power to cast these curses."

"We already figured that out," Snow complained. "You're no help at all."

"Even if we knew how to break the spell, there's a

possibility neither one of us is strong enough to pull it off. Especially with your condition."

"I'm fine," Snow snapped. She clenched her jaw. Dropping the illusions on herself and Danielle had helped, but her head still throbbed from the spell she had cast into the jinniyah to prevent it from using a fairy ring. Not to mention the magic she had to maintain to keep anyone from scrying on them. Talia should be protected by Roudette's cape, but if anyone thought to search for Faziya, Snow wanted to be certain they found nothing. "There has to be another way."

"We're outmatched, Snow!" Trittibar pulled on his beard. When he spoke again, he sounded calmer. "Even with both of us at our best—"

"I know." Snow rubbed her eyes.

Outside the cave, Danielle called out, "They're back."

"Already?" How long had she and Trittibar been working? She muttered a farewell to Trittibar and returned the now vacant mirror to her choker. Faziya appeared content to sleep for the moment, barely cracking an eye as Snow crawled out of the cave.

The sun was dipping behind the hills. No wonder Snow's stomach had begun to complain.

Talia carried two large waterskins, one strapped over each shoulder. She wore a heavy pack as well. Sweat and dust caked a stripe across her eyes, though her forehead and the lower part of her face appeared clean. She must have pushed back her head scarf just a short time ago.

Roudette also carried water and supplies. Snow stared. Roudette appeared almost cheerful. She was even *whistling*.

"Where did these come from?" Danielle asked, stepping away from the horses.

"Courtesy of Jahrasima." Talia handed one to Danielle, who struggled with the unfamiliar skin. These waterskins were far larger than the bottles they had brought in their saddlebags. The bulging skin appeared to be made of goat hide, still covered in fur. The skin was stitched in a long, curved shape. When carried, it would fit around the ribs with the strap worn over the opposite shoulder. A small tube of ebony horn formed the mouthpiece.

Talia demonstrated with her remaining skin. Keeping the strap on her shoulder, she lifted the skin to the front of her body so the mouthpiece was on top. She used one hand to support the skin and the other to untie the mouthpiece. Pressure compressed the skin, shooting water into her mouth without spilling a drop. She swallowed and asked, "How is Faziya? Have you found a way to restore her?"

Snow took the waterskin from Danielle, drinking to give herself time to answer. The water was warm and faintly sour, but Snow gulped it down until Talia tugged the mouthpiece away.

"Don't drink too much at once," said Talia. "And make sure you don't completely empty the skins, or they'll go brittle and crack."

Snow stretched, arching her hands over her head and cracking her back. "Trittibar believes the spell was cast with an object. A wand or a piece of jewelry, something imbued with Zestan's magic."

"Meaning what?" Talia demanded.

"The safest way to break the spell would be to sneak into the mansion a second time and find whatever object Jhukha used when she cast the curse."

Talia stared. "They'll have figured out how we got in, and the guards will be on alert. Even if I go alone, it would be difficult—"

"You can't," said Snow. "You wouldn't know what to look for."

"So what do we do?" Talia removed the other waterskin and leaned it against the rocks.

"We can't go back. But there might be another way."

"I'm not going to like this, am I?"

Snow paced in a circle. She knew exactly how to proceed. She could see the spells she would need to cast. A circle to contain Faziya. A second spell to calm her. Back home, Snow would have brewed a potion to help her sleep. She had hoped Trittibar would have another option. "There are three known ways to break this sort of transformation. The first is to allow the spell to wear off on its own. Uf'uyan would have returned to his natural state within a day or two."

Talia nodded. "How long would Faziya—"

"Your curse lasted a hundred years." Snow glanced into the cave. "If this is deev magic, it could survive a thousand. The second way is built into the spell itself. You know the stories. The prince who's trapped as a frog is freed by a princess' kiss."

"We've got three princesses here," Talia said. "I could—"

Snow shook her head. "The kissing component is local to the lands around the Carifone Sea. Lorindar, Hilad, Najarin, and so on. Neither Trittibar nor myself have ever heard of it being used this far south. We can try, but I wouldn't expect it to work. Only the one who cast the spell knows the key to reversing it."

"Even if we could get our hands on Jhukha, I don't know how to make her talk," said Talia. "What's the third option?"

Snow turned away. "This sort of curse usually fades when the victim dies. As their life slips away, they shift back to their true form. Either the magic loses its grip as the victim's life fades, or else it's a deliberate piece of the spell, designed to give them a chance to speak their final words. Fairies like that kind of drama."

Talia's voice was hard. "You've spent too long in the sun."

"We don't have to kill her," said Snow. "The spell is broken in those final moments before death. That's the key. If we bring Faziya to that point, I could save her before—"

Strong hands grabbed Snow's shoulders, spinning her about. Talia squeezed Snow's arms. "Find another way."

"What do you think I've been doing?" Snow struck Talia's wrists, breaking her hold. She flexed her arms. Even through the desert robe, Talia's grip had been strong enough to leave bruises. "Without whatever tool Jhukha used—"

"Then we return to Jahrasima," Talia said.

Roudette chuckled. "We'll be sure to tell Faziya how you ran off to die for her. I'm sure she'll appreciate your courage. Or she would, if she weren't a jackal."

"I can save her," Snow insisted. "Remember when Beatrice was stabbed? The blade nicked her heart, but I—"

Talia whirled. "I remember that Beatrice is dying!"

"Enough." Danielle stepped between them.

Talia moved toward the horses. "I'll be back before morning."

"No, you won't," said Danielle. "Talia, stop."

"This isn't Lorindar, Princess," Talia snapped, climbing onto the horse. "Arathea is my land. You don't give the orders here."

Talia tugged the reins, kicking the horse in the side. The horse simply snorted. Talia tried again, then glared at Danielle.

"You may not listen to my orders, but they do," said Danielle. "If you rush back into Jahrasima, you'll be giving yourself to Zestan. It's your people who will suffer when she uses you against Lakhim. Your sons who will fall to the same curse that took your family."

Rarely had Snow seen such fury in Talia's eyes. "You heard what Snow's asking. What if it were Armand?" Her words were sharp as any blade. "What about Jakob? What would you do if I told you the only way to save your son was to drive your knife into his heart?"

"If I had to choose between trusting Snow's magic or losing him forever?" Danielle shook her head. "Faziya is your friend. She wouldn't want you to throw your life away like this."

"You don't know her," Talia said.

"None of us do." Danielle clucked her tongue, and the horse stepped closer. "But I know how you feel about her. I'm sorry, Talia. I can't let you go."

"She was the first . . ." Talia's voice grew even quieter. "You're not even sure this will work."

"It should," said Snow. "Fairy spells bind to life. The life of the fairy hill, the life of the victim . . . with that life cut off, the spells fail. It's why pixies lose their glow shortly after death. They—" She stopped herself. "If there were any other way . . ."

Slowly, Talia slid down from the horse. "Do it," she whispered.

Snow stood. "It will take me an hour or so to prepare the circle. Danielle, I'll need as many flat stones as you can find."

"Snow." Talia was crouched in front of the cave, staring into the darkness. "If she dies—"

"I know." If Faziya died, Talia would never forgive them. Snow took a long, slow breath, then pulled out her knife and began drawing a circle in the dirt.

CHAPTER 16

TALIA DID HER BEST TO STAY OUT OF THE
way as Snow laid stones around her circle, marking
a different rune on each one using blood from her finger. Danielle sat with Faziya, talking gently to keep her
calm and relaxed. Roudette had crawled off to sleep.
The cave made her snores sound twice as loud.

So far, Talia had watered and brushed the horses,
eaten some of their stolen rations without tasting them,
and inspected every one of her weapons twice. Stars
were beginning to appear in the sky. The air would cool
quickly with the sun gone. She spun around, intending to
retrieve blankets from the saddlebags.

Danielle's fingers stroked Faziya's neck. "The more
agitated you get, the harder it is to keep her calm."

"I'll go. I could hunt for—"

"Sit." She smiled. "It will be all right."

"Because things have been going so well for us thus
far." Talia scowled, but she sat beside Danielle. Faziya
growled and started to back away, but Danielle whispered to her, petting her fur and calming her until she
settled her head back down on Danielle's thigh. Faziya's
ears remained high, and her eyes never left Talia.

Danielle took Talia's hand. "It's all right," she said
again.

Talia wasn't sure if Danielle was speaking to her or to Faziya, but she allowed Danielle to guide her hand. Their fingers brushed the dusty fur on Faziya's neck. Faziya tensed but didn't pull away.

"I'll find the one who did this to you," Talia promised. Jhukha was only a servant. It was Zestan's magic that had cursed Faziya.

Snow removed her remaining mirrors from her choker and set them around the circle. When her neck was bare of glass, she touched the gold wires circling her neck. The wires pulled free, wrapping themselves around her index finger.

Snow avoided looking at Talia as she went to the saddlebag and pulled out a spare head scarf. Talia almost asked what it was for. She looked down at Faziya, imagining that scarf soaking up blood as Snow worked to save Faziya's life.

Snow folded the scarf and set it carefully on a stone. She raised her other hand, pursed her lips, and blew. Frost filled the circle.

"The cold will slow the bleeding," Snow said. "It should give me a little more time." She pulled out her knife.

"No." Talia allowed her hand to linger on Faziya's neck, feeling the quick, frightened breaths, the heat of her skin beneath the fur. "A sharper blade will make a cleaner cut, with less pain. Danielle, would you . . . ?"

Danielle stood and drew her sword. Faziya jumped to her feet and backed away.

"I should do it," Talia whispered. That blade was sharper than any razor. With luck, Faziya would hardly feel the cut. Talia made no move to take the sword.

"You don't have to," said Danielle.

"Yes, I do. You need to be able to speak to her, to keep her steady. Snow has to concentrate on her magic." Talia swallowed.

"Animals are built along the same principles as us,"

Snow said. "A cut to the throat will spill the most blood, but I'm afraid it would be too much, too fast. Try the leg, close to the shoulder. You'll hit—"

"I know." Talia thought about the mercenary who had taught her that move. She couldn't remember the man's name. He had been arrested less than a month after Talia met him, but he had shown her a number of knife tricks in that time. Block your opponent's knife hand with your forearm, opening up his arm. Slice your own blade up the inside of his biceps. It didn't take a deep cut to kill a man that way.

"Dogs' limbs are built differently," Snow said. "You'll need to cut closer to the front instead of the inside."

Talia took the sword. "I'm ready."

"Faziya?" Danielle crouched, one hand extended. "Please come with me."

Faziya's eyes were large, and she was panting, the tip of her tongue protruding from the right side of her mouth. Danielle stroked Faziya's back as she led her into the circle.

"Tell her not to move," Talia said. "Tell her I'm sorry."

"I will." Danielle knelt and began to whisper. Faziya was shivering, from either fear or the rapidly cooling night air.

Talia glanced at Snow, who nodded.

"You're doing the right thing." Roudette yawned as she crawled out of the cave, staring unabashedly. "Even if she dies, she dies human, free of their curse."

"She's not going to die," Snow insisted.

Talia tightened her grip on the hilt and stepped into the circle.

"Don't be afraid," Danielle said. Faziya glanced up at the sound of her voice.

Talia moved without thinking, taking advantage of Faziya's distraction the same as she would with an enemy. In a single motion, she thrust the sword and slid the blade along Faziya's leg.

Glass cut through skin and muscle, and she could feel the edge scraping bone. Even as Talia pulled back, she knew she had cut too deep. The sword was too sharp. She stumbled back, needing all of her will to keep from flinging it away.

Faziya snarled and snapped at Talia, then lunged at Snow, but she seemed unable to move beyond the circle. She kept her leg tight against her body and whimpered as blood spilled into the sand.

Talia stabbed the sword into the dirt and knelt at the edge of the circle. She forced herself to watch as more blood darkened the dirt. Faziya tried to lick the cut, but she couldn't reach it. She looked at Danielle and let out a low whine. Danielle had her hands clasped together, her lips moving silently.

All too quickly, Faziya grew lethargic. She retreated to the far side of the circle and curled up in the dirt.

"How much longer?" Talia whispered.

"Soon," said Snow. "As the life drains from her body, the curse loses its hold."

Talia couldn't remember the last time she had prayed. Losing everything and everyone she had ever known to a fairy curse had pretty much ended her faith in God and his prophets. But now she begged God to let this work.

Blood spread through the dirt around Faziya. She whined again, weaker this time, and Talia's heart constricted. "It's not working."

"It will," said Snow.

Faziya closed her eyes.

"Snow, stop this." Talia stepped toward the circle and froze. If she tried to move Faziya, she might only make things worse. "Help her."

"I know what I'm doing. The body can lose a great deal of blood and still survive."

Talia stepped around the circle. This time Faziya

lacked the energy to flee. Talia reached out, resting a hand on the warm fur of Faziya's neck. "Forgive me."

"Got you," Snow whispered.

Faziya's body twitched beneath Talia's hand. Her legs kicked out, and clumps of fur fell away to reveal skin the color of oiled olive wood. Her eyes snapped open, and her body began to grow.

Snow was already moving. She shoved Talia aside and rolled Faziya onto her back. She pressed one hand over the bloody cut on what was becoming an arm. More fur fell away. Faziya's next gasp sounded almost human.

"Press here, now!" Snow indicated a point above the cut, near Faziya's armpit.

Talia obeyed, squeezing hard. Snow whispered a spell, and the gold wire around her finger thinned like thread as it burrowed into the cut.

Talia brushed snarled black hair back from Faziya's eyes. Her face was cool to the touch.

"Too much blood," Snow muttered. "Press harder."

Talia tightened her grip, though Faziya cried out.

"Hold her still!"

"I'm trying," Talia said, grabbing Faziya's other shoulder and pressing her flat. "Faziya, it's me. It's Talia. I'm going to help you. Try not to fight."

"Sing to her," said Danielle.

Talia swallowed. One of her fairy blessings had been the gift of song. It was a gift she rarely used in front of anyone older than two. In a low voice, she began to sing an old ballad about an eastern prince and his Kha'iida lover.

The pain in Faziya's face eased slightly. "Talia?"

"I'm here," Talia said. "Don't move."

The years had changed Faziya. The lines of her face were deeper, hinting at the wrinkles that would one day mark her eyes and the corners of her mouth. Her hair was long and loose, framing her round face. Talia remembered it all, the dark brows, the tiny scar above her upper lip, the two small moles on the side of her chin.

"She's so pale," Talia whispered. Faziya's skin was damp with sweat.

Faziya tried to push herself up. "What happened to me?" Her voice was hoarse.

"You were taken to Rajil's menagerie," Talia said, holding her down. "Don't try to talk yet. Lie back and let my friend work."

Snow pulled her bloody hands away from the cut and grabbed one of her mirrors. She held it over Faziya's arm, and the glass turned red. Talia realized she was using it to look within the wound.

"Very slowly," Snow said, "ease up on the pressure."

Talia relaxed her grip on Faziya's arm. Blood oozed from the cut, but the flow was nothing like it had been before. Stitches of gold now sealed the edges of the wound.

Snow grabbed her scarf and wrapped it tightly around Faziya's arm. "Give her water. Not a lot at first. Don't make her cough."

Danielle hurried to fetch one of the smaller waterskins. She untied the cap and passed it to Talia.

Talia rested the mouthpiece of the skin on Faziya's chin, parting her lips and squeezing a small stream of water into her mouth. Some dripped down Faziya's cheeks, but she swallowed the rest.

"Will she be all right?" Talia whispered.

"She's alive." Snow rested a hand on Faziya's chest. "Her heart is beating awfully fast, and her breathing is shallow. She needs rest, time for her body to replenish the blood it lost."

"But she'll live."

"Maybe." Snow didn't look at her. "She'll need to be watched closely tonight. Move her into the cave and keep her warm. Try to keep her on her side, with the wound above the heart."

Talia slipped her arms beneath Faziya's body and lifted. Faziya groaned and nested her head against Talia's chest.

"Thank you," Talia whispered. Only then did she see all of the blood soaking the sand. Faziya's blood. Snow's clothes were covered in it, as were Talia's own. She steeled her voice. "The smell will carry. Anyone looking for us—"

"You think I didn't plan for this?" Snow clapped her hands, and blue fire leaped from her mirrors, filling the circle. There was no smoke and little heat, but when the fire died a moment later, the blood was gone. Only blackened earth remained.

Snow retrieved her mirrors and kicked dirt over the circle. "I'd do the same for us, but it wouldn't be healthy," she said. "You'll have to clean yourself the old-fashioned way."

"If we cover the cave mouth, it should help to block the scent," Roudette suggested.

Danielle had retrieved a blanket from their supplies. She wrapped it around Faziya, draping the ends over Talia's shoulders. "Will you need help getting her inside?"

Talia nodded gratefully. With Danielle's help, they finished bundling Faziya into the blanket. Talia laid Faziya on her side, then crawled into the cave. She reached out to take Faziya's head and arm, being careful not to disturb her injury. Danielle lifted Faziya's feet, and together they brought her inside.

Talia lay down behind Faziya, their bodies curled together.

Faziya shivered. Her skin was so cold. "Talia?"

"I'm here." Talia reached around, taking Faziya's hand.

Faziya mumbled something incomprehensible and drifted off. Talia closed her eyes, ignoring the muted conversation outside the cave as she listened to Faziya's breathing. Ever so gently, Talia kissed the back of Faziya's head. "You're safe."

*   *   *

Danielle woke to blackness. She sat up so quickly her head struck the top of the cave, a rather forceful reminder of where she was. Her vision flashed white, and she lay back, groaning and clutching her head.

"I'll try to remember to steal a hclmet for you next time," Talia said softly.

Danielle wiped tears from her eyes. She could feel blood on her scalp, and there would be a lump, but she didn't think she had done any permanent damage.

There was no way to tell how long she had slept. With the blanket stretched over the mouth of the cave, she might as well have been blind. Over Roudette's snores, Danielle could hear the howling that had awakened her, the cries stretching longer than those of any mortal hound. "The Wild Hunt?"

"They've been riding for a while now," Talia said. "So tar, Roudette's cape seems to be working."

"Faziya?" Danielle asked.

"She's woken up twice," Talia said. "She drank a little more water the second time. I don't think she understands where she is or what's happened."

"Should we wake Snow?"

"I already have. Four times." Talia sounded faintly embarrassed. "Snow says the best thing for Faziya is rest. We checked the bandages, and there's not much bleeding, which is a good sign."

"I'm glad." Danielle lay quietly for a while, uncertain whether to ask her next question. But the others were asleep, and there had been so few chances to talk privately with Talia. "What about Snow?"

"What about her?" The wariness of Talia's response suggested she knew perfectly well what Danielle was asking.

"I know how you feel about her."

"Whatever I might feel, Snow doesn't," Talia said curtly. "Her ... preferences aren't likely to change."

"Talia—"

"Don't." Talia sighed. "You think because I love Snow I'm incapable of loving anyone else?"

Danielle's face grew warm. "That's not it at all. I'm sorry, I meant—"

"You grew up locked in an attic, then married a prince. It's not your fault you have a simpler view of these things."

Slowly, Danielle smiled. "So you *do* love Faziya."

"I would have brought her to Lorindar with me if I could have. She wouldn't have been happy, though. She's a child of the sand, far more than I ever was. This is her home." Talia fell silent.

Danielle frowned. The howls from the desert had stopped. "The Hunt is gone."

"It will be dawn soon. Faziya needs rest, but Snow said she'll need food as well. Water will help, but it's not enough. Fresh meat is best to help her replenish the blood."

It took a moment to realize what Talia was asking from her. Danielle swallowed her instinctive refusal.

"Snow's useless when it comes to hunting," said Talia. "Roudette can't go out alone, thanks to Snow's spell. I'd do it myself, but I don't want—"

"I know." Danielle could hear the determination in Talia's voice. She doubted the Wild Hunt itself could drag her from Faziya's side right now. "I'm glad you found her again. I'll do what I can."

She crawled toward the cave entrance, being careful to keep her head low. She tugged the blanket aside, dislodging some of the rocks they had used to anchor it in place. "Faziya will be all right, Talia."

"She's not out of danger," said Talia. "The blood loss could kill her. The wound could turn septic. We can't stay here, but she's not strong enough to travel."

"I said she'll be all right."

"Yes, Your Highness." She could hear Talia's wry smile.

Danielle crawled out of the cave. She shivered in the morning air and carefully pulled the blanket back over the cave entrance to block the draft. She turned around and bit back a yelp. A wolf sat watching her from the rocks not ten paces away.

"You've been there the whole night?" Danielle asked. Now that she thought about it, Roudette had mentioned picking up a few friends while she and Talia were out yesterday. "I don't suppose you'd be willing to fetch something to eat?"

The wolf sniffed and turned away.

Danielle sighed. The simplest thing would be to call out, asking the animals to come to her. They would obey, trusting her right up until the moment she killed them. But she couldn't bring herself to betray that trust.

She searched the sky. To the east, a smudge of orange lined the horizon. Not a single cloud blocked the stars overhead. The moon had set for the night. Bats flitted about, invisible save when they passed in front of the fading stars.

There would be other predators too. Danielle closed her eyes, silently asking for help.

Before too long, she heard an answering cry. An owl swooped overhead, and Danielle could just make out the limp form of a jackrabbit dangling from its talons. It dropped the rabbit, which hit the rocks with a wet thump.

The wolf jumped at the sound, then turned to glare at Danielle.

"Don't blame me," Danielle said. She hurried over to retrieve the rabbit. "Was the big bad wolf frightened by a little bunny?"

The wolf hopped down, looking hopeful.

"Go get your own." Danielle chuckled as she pulled a knife from her belt. A few years earlier, the idea of sleeping with a weapon never would have crossed her mind. Thanks to Talia, she had done it last night without thinking.

"Watch over them, Mother," she prayed. "Talia's lost so much. Don't let her lose Faziya too."

With that, she sat down and began to butcher the rabbit.

Talia could hear Danielle outside, carrying on a quiet conversation with whatever vermin had come to keep her company.

Roudette stirred a short time later. She stretched, passed gas, and crawled out of the cave. Sunlight peeked past the blanket's edge, but still Faziya slept.

Talia reached out with one leg, kicking Snow in the hip until she groaned and slapped the foot away.

"Faziya's been sleeping a long time," Talia said.

"Lucky girl." Snow yawned and sat up. Her mirrors caught the sun from the entrance, adding to the light of the cave. With much of the gold wire from her choker being used to stitch Faziya's wound, Snow had reworked her choker into an armband around her right arm.

Snow reached over and pulled the blanket back from Faziya's shoulder. A splotch of dark blood marred the center of the bandage. Snow clucked her tongue as she peeled back the edge of the bandage to check the stitches. "She's oozing blood, but it's not bad. Go ahead and wake her up. Her body needs food and water."

Snow slipped out of the cave, leaving Talia and Faziya alone. Talia leaned her head close to Faziya's and whispered her name. When that didn't work, she kissed Faziya's cheek and tried again, more loudly this time.

Not a twitch. Talia fought fear. Doing her best imitation of Mother Khardija, Talia said, "Sister Faziya, wake up this instant. Your duties don't go away simply because you stayed out too late with your hoodlum friends!"

Faziya groaned and started to roll over. Talia held her shoulders, trying to keep her from moving her arm.

"Mother Khardija?" Faziya coughed, then gasped and grabbed her arm.

"I have you," Talia said. "Try to relax."

"Talia?" Faziya blinked and looked up at her. "How—" She coughed again. "What happened? Where—"

Talia kissed her. Gently at first, not wanting to aggravate her injury. Faziya wrapped her good arm around Talia's neck, returning the kiss with a hunger that reminded Talia of their first days together. All too soon, Faziya fell back, panting for breath.

"Don't try to move," Talia said, trying not to feel guilty. Even this small exertion might be too much for her.

"I used to pray that God would bring you back to me."

"God had nothing to do with it," Talia said.

Faziya pulled her down and kissed her again. When Talia broke away, Faziya smiled. "You taste like salt." Her lips pursed. "Though you smell like horse and blood."

"And you have jackal breath," Talia said.

Faziya frowned and looked down at herself. "I'm also naked."

"Yes, I noticed." Talia found herself wanting to laugh and cry at the same time. She did neither, instead doing her best to explain what had happened. She had only gotten halfway through the story when Faziya reached over to take Talia's hand in hers.

"Thank you for finding me," Faziya said.

Talia shifted against the rocks, allowing Faziya to rest against her head against Talia's chest. "How do you feel?"

Faziya shivered. "My arm feels like it's been smashed with a hammer."

"I'm sorry." Talia kissed the top of Faziya's head. "It was the only way."

"It worked."

Danielle coughed politely before crawling into the cave, carrying a skewer of meat and a waterskin, along with an extra robe and head scarf. She smiled when she saw them. "Snow said to make sure Faziya eats the liver and kidneys first. They're small, but they'll help with the blood loss."

"What's she saying?" Faziya asked. After Talia translated, Faziya frowned. "Her voice is familiar."

"Danielle helped to calm you when you were a jackal. When I—" She swallowed. "When we broke your curse."

"I remember," Faziya said. "It's hard. Like a dream from childhood. Please thank her for me." She pressed against Talia's body. "I remember being afraid. Terrified of everything." She broke off in another bout of coughing.

"That was the fairy spell." Talia helped her to sit up and take a drink. When Faziya had swallowed enough, Danielle passed her the meat.

Faziya chuckled. "Liver and kidneys first. Your friend is a good healer."

"I've given her plenty of practice," said Talia.

That earned another smile. Talia blinked and turned away, fighting tears that came out of nowhere. Danielle was already retreating into the sun, leaving them alone. "What were you thinking?" Talia whispered. "Leaving the temple, going to Rajil's mansion?"

"You would have done the same thing," Faziya said.

"You're not me."

"I know." Faziya swallowed. "Zestan-e-Jheg. She's—"

"Deev," Talia said. "Father Uf'uyan told us."

"I left my tribe years ago, but I'm still Kha'iida." The liver and kidneys were both gone, and she had moved on to the rest of the meat. Talia took her appetite as a hopeful sign. As Faziya chewed, she said, "My people swore an oath."

"You could have been killed."

"I went to Rajil the day of the new moon."

Talia nodded. Every raikh held open court with each

new moon. Faziya would have been one of hundreds, all petitioning to speak to Rajil or her adviser. "What did you plan to say? You can't simply march into the raikh's mansion and accuse her of conspiring with deev."

"*Now* you tell me." Faziya smiled. "I told her I was a fairy worshiper, and I wanted to serve Zestan. I hoped she would take me into her confidence. Instead, she brought me to Jhukha."

Talia's fists tightened. Once she had dealt with Zestan, she would return to Jahrasima to kill Jhukha herself. "You were always a lousy liar."

Faziya finished the meat and took another drink, then settled back down against Talia. Talia brushed the hair from her face. Faziya still felt cold. Talia pulled the blanket over them both.

"You *could* help me get dressed," Faziya pointed out.

Talia smiled. "I could."

"Mm." Faziya closed her eyes.

Talia's back was bruised from the rocks, and Faziya's weight was already starting to numb her right leg. Her shoulder was cramped, and her stomach growled. She hadn't thought to ask Danielle for any food for herself.

She couldn't recall the last time she had felt so content.

CHAPTER 17

DANIELLE WAS TALKING TO ARMAND and Jakob through the mirror on her bracelet when Talia and Faziya finally emerged from the cave. Danielle kissed the mirror and rose to greet them.

"Faziya wanted me to thank you," Talia said.

Faziya was pale and looked as though she would collapse without Talia's support. Her lips had no color, and she flinched against the sun. But she was alive. Danielle smiled. "You're welcome."

"About time you got up," Roudette said from the shade of the rocks. She bit into a strip of smoked goat meat, eating half in a single bite. Still chewing, she asked, "Did your friend tell us where we could find Zestan?"

"She doesn't know." Talia frowned and looked over at the horses, which were munching on a small, twisted tree. "What did you do with them last night?"

"I sent them away," said Danielle. "We hid the saddles and supplies. I told the horses to run and enjoy themselves and asked if they'd come back today to help us. Wild horses roaming the desert shouldn't draw attention, right?"

Talia led Faziya to a spot in the sand by the rocks. The way she held Faziya's arm reminded Danielle of a lord escorting his lady at a ball. The sun was still low, providing plenty of shade. Talia waited until Faziya was comfortable before turning to answer Roudette. "If Zestan is deev, then we'll need the help of those trained from birth to hunt and destroy the deev."

Roudette stood up and shook the sand from her cape. "You mean to find the Kha'iida? You realize that puts us back into the Wild Hunt's path. Having failed to catch us, Zestan will probably order them to resume hunting the Kha'iida."

"No doubt," said Talia.

Roudette bared her teeth. "When do we leave?"

Talia pointed east. "Faziya says her tribe should be at hai'ir tel this time of year."

"Hai'ir tel?" Danielle asked.

"The Valley of God's Tears," said Talia. "An oasis, about halfway between Jahrasima and the Makras River. Two days on horseback." She glanced at Faziya. "Possibly longer."

Snow pursed her lips. "I don't think it's a good idea for her to be on horseback so soon."

"Would you rather wait around until we run out of food and water?" asked Roudette. "Or until the Hunt finds us?"

Rarely had Danielle seen Talia so indecisive. Talia glanced at Faziya, whispering something in Arathean. Whatever Faziya said in response, it made Snow roll her eyes and walk away.

"She's as stubborn as Talia," Snow complained. "She insists she's well enough to travel."

"Healers make the worst patients, don't they?" Danielle teased, earning a mock glare from Snow. Danielle's face turned serious. "Waiting is too dangerous. I'll tell her mount to be as gentle as possible."

Talia nodded. "She can ride with me."

"Of course." Danielle helped gather the rest of their supplies into the saddlebags and packs, shifting as much weight as she could from Talia's horse to make up for carrying two riders.

Once everything was ready, Danielle sat down and tried to figure out what to do with the sheffeyah. She tried to remember how Talia had wrapped it for her the day before. She knew it wrapped three times, and the second loop protected the neck and lower part of the face, but she couldn't get it to stay in place.

Eventually, Talia took pity on her. "Don't start with the center of the scarf. Start midway between the center and the end, and wrap the long side." She moved to Snow, reaching out to help her next, but Snow shoved her hand away.

Roudette had already changed into her wolf form. Danielle checked the cave one last time to make sure they had left as little evidence of their camp as possible. Normally Talia would have done this, but she was understandably distracted.

Danielle watched Snow closely as they rode. Snow's scarf hid all but her eyes, making it difficult to read her mood, but it was clear something was bothering her. Normally she would have been joking with Talia or singing an obnoxious drinking song. The danger posed by Zestan and the Wild Hunt should have only made the songs more cheerfully obscene. Instead, Snow rode in silence. Fatigue at having used so much magic, or something more?

Roudette raced ahead of the others. She appeared to be testing the limits of Snow's binding spell, running until she stumbled, then waiting for the others to catch up. She repeated this time and again, each time getting about fifty paces before the curse stopped her. Once she even managed to scare up a lizard the size of Danielle's arm, which she gulped down as eagerly as Jakob did sweets.

Whereas Snow was uncharacteristically quiet, Talia

was almost chatty, commenting on various landmarks as they rode: hills of orange rock rippling like waves on the sea; an abandoned village, half-buried in the sand; a stone wall that stretched for more than a mile.

"Why build a wall in the middle of the desert?" Danielle asked.

"To hunt gazelle." Talia pointed into the distance. "A mile away, a second wall would have angled toward the first. The Kha'iida herded the animals into the narrowing walls, trapping them in a circular pen at the end. The animals could only escape by leaping over low spots in the walls, at which point they would fall into the pits on the outside. Some tribes still use them."

"I thought such traps were forbidden by Siqkhab," said Snow, speaking up for the first time since setting out that morning.

"They are," Talia said cheerfully. Snow didn't answer.

Enough of this. Danielle whispered to her horse and Snow's, asking them to slow down. When the others pulled ahead, she guided her mare closer to Snow. "What's wrong?"

"Aside from being stuck in the middle of Arathea, you mean?" Snow brushed her hands against her robe. "I feel like I'm carrying enough sand in my hair and clothes to start my own desert."

"You've been quiet ever since you cast that spell last night. Is that what's bothering you? You made the right choice. You saved Faziya's life."

"Maybe." Snow shrugged. "We'll have to see how she heals. Dragging her across the desert won't help matters."

"You don't like her, do you?"

"It's not that." Snow turned away, adjusting her sleeves to pull the cuffs down over her hands.

"Snow?"

Snow sighed. "It's not Faziya. It's *her*."

"Roudette?" Danielle asked.

"Talia. She's *different* here. She's been acting differently ever since we arrived. It's only gotten worse since we found Faziya."

"This is her home." Danielle paused. Despite fairies and humans both hunting for them, Talia was home. Whereas Snow was even farther from Allesandria than ever. A part of her had to envy Talia the chance to see her homeland once more.

"Look at her." Snow's sleeve flapped as she jabbed a hand at Talia and Faziya. "They're as bad as you and Armand used to be, back before you had Jakob and you turned boring."

"Boring?" Danielle stared, trying to gauge whether Snow was joking. "We're not—"

"The first night the two of you met, you danced until midnight. When was the last time you stayed awake that late? Between tending to Jakob, working with your tutors, and taking over Beatrice's responsibilities around the palace, how often do you and Armand exchange more than a tired peck on the cheek before crawling into bed?"

"You're trying to change the subject," Danielle said.

Narrowed eyes scowled at Danielle. "Between you huddling over that mirror, whispering to Armand and Jakob every time we stop, and Talia making out with Faziya all night long—"

"Really?" Danielle asked. "The whole night?"

Snow looked heavenward. "I exaggerate. You should know that by now." She sighed. "I'm not used to being the one without anything warm to press up against at night."

"You poor thing. A whole day in Arathea, and you haven't met anyone? I suppose you could always ask Roudette."

"Don't make me curse you."

Snow's tone was playful, but Danielle could hear something more beneath the words. "Don't tell me you're jealous."

Snow shook her head. "Not exactly. I know how Talia feels about me. For more than a year, I've wished I didn't. I know how to deal with a man who wants me, how to take one I want or get rid of one I don't, but with Talia, everything's different. She's my friend. I should be relieved she's found someone, for my sake and for hers."

"You're not relieved?" Danielle asked carefully.

"Oh, I am." Snow laughed. "But look at them. I miss that feeling. I haven't had that since Roland died. I would have married that man, you know. If my mother hadn't killed him."

"I'm sorry," Danielle said. Snow never really talked about the man her mother had hired to cut out her heart. Instead of killing her, Roland had fallen in love with Snow's beauty. He had brought a deer heart to Queen Rose in order to protect Snow's life, but eventually Rose discovered his deception and murdered him in front of Snow. "I never imagined you starting a family."

"Oh, gods, no!" Snow laughed again. "Marriage is one thing, but children? I've seen the trouble Jakob gets into. I'd have turned that boy into a frog long ago." She sighed. "It would be nice to feel love like that again, though."

"Give it time," Danielle said. "You can't force love."

"Speak for yourself." Snow withdrew her hands from her sleeves and waggled her fingers. Tiny sparks danced from her nails. "There are four popular recipes for love potions, and at least a dozen more obscure formulas. The most common last only a short time, but with the right ingredients—mermaid blood being one of the best—you can—"

"Just promise me you won't enchant any of the Kha'iida once we reach this oasis," Danielle said, laughing despite herself.

"I don't have the right equipment for potion making anyway," Snow said. Danielle could hear the smile in her voice. "Of course, there are *other* kinds of enchantments."

After three days, they were down to a single waterskin. Even with Talia slipping away each morning before Faziya awoke, gathering the dew that collected on the leaves, it would be a close thing whether they reached the Kha'iida in time. If Faziya was wrong about where her tribe should be this time of year . . . she tried not to think about that.

Each night Roudette's wolves kept watch over the group, and Talia kept watch over Faziya. Faziya still didn't use her left arm at all, keeping it bandaged tightly against her body. Snow had said little, beyond checking the wound twice each day. Faziya claimed she was starting to feel stronger, and the pain wasn't as bad.

Talia didn't believe her. She heard how Faziya groaned in her sleep. She saw the tightening of her body whenever the horse jostled her. Faziya needed better food and rest if she was going to recover.

Nighttime also brought the sounds of the Wild Hunt. The howls had been fainter last night, but Talia worried about what might await them at hai'ir tel. If Rajil knew which tribe Faziya belonged to . . . but few city-dwellers paid much attention to the Kha'iida tribes, save for those times the Kha'iida came to the edges of the cities to trade.

Shade and shelter were harder to come by now. They had left the rocky, scrub-dotted land behind, entering a stretch of what the Kha'iida called qa rablakh, the sea of sand. Last night they had ridden far later than Talia liked before finding a patch of hard sand between two dunes. Roudette had dug a pit while Talia had spread their robes and blankets to rig a crude tent. A layer of sand over the top had helped it to blend into the landscape, but she had spent the entire night on edge, trying to imagine how they would escape if the Hunt found them.

The desert stretched as far as she could see in all directions. Her horse's hooves sank into rippled sand with each step. For the past day, the only plants had been little more than bare sticks and thorny stumps poking through the sand. "How long until we reach the valley?"

Faziya inhaled. "We're getting close."

"How can you tell?" asked Talia.

"Can't you smell the water?" Faziya laughed. "You city-dwellers are so soft. So civilized. You wouldn't last a month in the desert."

"Says the woman who'd fall off her horse without help," Talia answered, keeping her arm wrapped around Faziya's waist. "I thought you desert barbarians were supposed to be tough."

Faziya leaned her head against Talia's shoulder. "Tough enough to put up with *you*."

Talia kissed her head, conceding the point. "What sort of welcome should we expect at hai'ir tel? You've never spoken about why you left."

Faziya tensed. "I'm not sure. Oath before family. Family before tribe. Tribe before country. Country before self. When I left, I put myself before the rest."

Snow glanced over. "Is she saying we might not be welcome? That would have been good to know three days ago."

"Oh, no," said Faziya. "*You* will be welcome. 'None may turn away a stranger in the desert.' You will be given water and shelter for three days."

"What about you?" Talia asked.

Faziya flicked her fingers, a dismissive motion that passed as a shrug. "If I'm fortunate, I'll be treated as a stranger."

The sound of hoofbeats changed, becoming more solid. The land sloped gradually upward here, and more plants had begun to appear. Talia spotted a bush with red-tipped buds that made her think of paintbrushes dipped in blood. A small lizard sunned himself on one of the branches.

"Beyond that hill," Faziya's hand tightened on Talia's leg.

"I just hope they can give us separate tents," Snow said. "If I have to listen to Roudette chasing rabbits in her sleep again, I'll go mad."

Roudette had already crested the hill up ahead. She trotted back down a short way and began to remove the wolfskin.

"Oath before family," Talia repeated, taking Faziya's hand in hers. "Whatever happened, you followed that rule. Zestan is deev. That's more important than anything else."

"If they believe us," Faziya said.

Talia tugged the reins with her free hand, guiding the horse uphill toward Roudette. "I'll make them believe."

By the time they reached the top of the hill, Roudette was human once more. She stood unmoving as the others joined her. "There's fairy scent, but it's old. The Wild Hunt probably passed through here a while back. Nothing recent."

Below them lay a wide, shallow valley. A pond stretched through the center, rimmed by trees and waist-high grass as green as any garden. A flock of sheep had spread through the valley to graze. Camels gathered near a second, smaller pond farther away. Black rectangular tents were laid out in parallel rows, facing east. Talia guessed there were at least a hundred. Horses were tied between many of the tents.

Talia unwrapped her scarf to show her face, leaving the top of her head covered. The air felt almost cool on her cheeks after so long riding. To the others, she said, "It's impolite to enter a stranger's home with your identity hidden."

She waited while Snow and Danielle did the same. Roudette pushed back her hood.

Several dogs broke away from the sheep and ran toward them, barking madly. Danielle closed her eyes, whispering until they calmed.

"Are you ready?" Talia asked.

"Does it matter?" Faziya forced a smile. "Whatever happens, thank you for saving me from Rajil's garden."

By the time they reached the base of the hill, a small crowd had gathered to greet them. The Kha'iida stared openly at the newcomers, paying as much attention to Faziya as they did the paler strangers. Talia heard Faziya's name whispered more than once.

Most of the Kha'iida wore two robes, a pale robe wrapped tight at the waist, and a second, looser one over the top. Sandals were common, though Talia saw several adults in boots. Many of the children were barefoot.

The men's robes were dark yellow, similar in color to the sand. The women's were darker in color, some decorated with embroidery and brocade. Men and women alike wore jewelry of silver and copper, mostly rings.

A man wearing an emerald belt stepped forward. Talia dismounted from her horse, then reached up to help Faziya.

"His name is Muhazil," Faziya whispered. "He leads the tribe."

Talia stepped forward to greet him. Muhazil's sun-baked skin was a deep brown, and his forehead furrowed as he looked from Talia to her companions. His hair was braided in plaits that trailed from his head scarf down his chest, and his beard was an equal mix of black and white.

"Peace to you and your family," Talia said, bowing at the waist.

Muhazil returned the bow. "And to yours. What brings massim this far into the desert?"

Massim, not the more derogatory *varahn*. Neither term was a complimentary one for city-dwellers, but at least he wasn't openly insulting them. "We ask for water to quench our thirst and shelter from the desert sun."

"I am Muhazil Yidab-ud-Ahra. You and your friends are welcome in my tent."

"Did he say his tent?" Snow leaned forward. "Is he asking us to—"

"No." Talia swatted Snow's shoulder without looking. "Thank you, Muhazil."

"Perhaps you would do us the pleasure of sharing your story?" he asked, the closest a Kha'iida would come to asking strangers why they had traveled so far from home.

"Is there a place you and I could talk privately?" Talia asked.

Muhazil turned and touched a finger to his lips. At this signal, a younger boy ran back toward the tents. "My grandson Lazhan will see to your friends' needs while we speak." He turned his back and walked away.

Talia fought a rush of anger. She had been too long in Lorindar, where turning your back was a sign of disdain rather than trust. To Danielle, she said, "You'll be safe here. Nobody tell them anything until I've had the chance to discuss things with Muhazil. Try to keep Roudette from snacking on their herd. Kha'iida hospitality only extends so far."

Faziya started to follow the others, but Talia caught her hand. "I need you with me."

"Muhazil won't like it," Faziya warned.

"I don't care. We need their help, and Muhazil needs to hear what you've learned."

Muhazil led them to a large tent near the center of the camp. The tents were spread far enough apart to allow individuals to pass between them without tripping over the lines, so long as they were careful. Talia kept one arm around Faziya's waist for support. Faziya was steadier than she had been three days ago, but a fall could still tear the stitches and start her bleeding again.

The front and back walls of most tents were tied open, allowing the air to circulate. Muhazil's tent was partitioned into two rooms, both of which were larger than Talia's chambers back home. Back in Lorindar, she corrected.

He brought them into the room on the left. Iron chimes hanging from the central pole rang softly as they entered. Overlapping rugs covered the ground, woven in intricate patterns of red, gold, and blue. Sleeping mats lined the edges of the tent. Each had been folded lengthwise and propped up to form low, makeshift couches.

Muhazil crouched at a small fire circle in the center of the room. He blew embers into flame, adding a small pile of tinder and what looked like dried dung.

Talia started to speak, but Faziya tugged her toward one of the mats, which was surprisingly firm. Like the tent, the mats were woven of goat wool, and each was decorated in a different pattern. This one was dyed in stripes of blue and purple. The bright colors of the Kha'iida camp were refreshing after her time in Jahrasima and the desert.

Talia waited impatiently as Muhazil prepared drinks. He dipped water from a basin into a small pot, which he set directly on the embers. He opened a small chest and pulled out a plain linen sack. The smell of coffee soon suffused the tent. Humming, he grabbed a handful of crushed beans and tossed them into the water.

Despite herself, Talia smiled. "I haven't tasted real coffee since I was a child. Even then, my parents wouldn't let me drink much."

"Why not?" Muhazil asked. "Coffee is good for the body and the spirit."

Talia smiled wryly. "They feared it would keep me from sleeping."

Faziya squeezed her hand. They waited in silence as Muhazil finished brewing the coffee. He poured for Talia first, handing her a porcelain cup lined with silver. She blew once and took a sip. The taste was more bitter than she remembered, but the saffron aftertaste drew a contented sigh from her lips.

Faziya's hand shook as she accepted her own cup. She took a small sip, then set the cup on the mat. "I'm sorry," she said. "I shouldn't drink much while my body is recovering."

"So says the Temple of the Hedge?" Muhazil asked.

Faziya straightened. "Yes."

Muhazil waved his hand as though brushing away an imagined insect, indicating that he had no interest in continuing the discussion. To Talia, he said, "You wished to speak alone."

"The Wild Hunt has plagued the Kha'iida in recent times," Talia said.

"They have pursued us for most of the past season," Muhazil admitted. "Two tribes have vanished. Three others have been broken and scattered. Fourteen survivors joined our own tribe a month ago. We've set out what protections we can to discourage the Hunt's return."

Five tribes destroyed. Talia took another sip of coffee, trying to match his composure. Inside, she was shaking. Five tribes meant hundreds, probably thousands of people. "Father Uf'uyan didn't say it had been so bad."

"The cities pay little attention to the desert these days," Muhazil said.

"A mistake that could destroy us all," answered Talia.

Muhazil leaned forward, setting his cup on the ground. "How so?"

"The Wild Hunt serves a fairy called Zestan-e-Jheg. We believe Zestan is deev."

"Impossible." Muhazil started to rise.

"If that were truly impossible, there would be no need for your oath." Talia looked out at the valley. "You've heard the sounds of the Wild Hunt these past nights. What lesser fairy has the power to command them?"

"You think we haven't considered the possibility?" Muhazil repeated the flicking motion. "The Kha'iida guard Arathea, following the paths of our forefathers to ensure that none of the gates have been opened. Our seers watch for any omen of the deev's return. When the attacks began, we increased our vigilance. No deev has escaped."

"That you know of. But why else would she target your people? Which tribe was the first to fall to the Hunt? Perhaps they had discovered evidence of Zestan's escape."

"We retraced their paths. There was no such evidence." Muhazil turned toward the right. To the south, she realized. Toward the mountains of the peri. "For generations we have told stories of the deev. Older children frighten their siblings with tales of deev who lurk in the shadows." A twist of his lips made Talia suspect he had been one of those younger siblings. "Tell me, have you *seen* this deev? Or are your fears based on nothing more than shadows and stories? Fairy magic is deceptive. Could it be this Zestan wishes you to believe she is deev, to spread fear throughout the cities?"

Faziya leaned forward. "I spent a month in Rajil's garden, cursed by Zestan's magic. Draw your knife. Let it taste the curse in my blood."

Muhazil frowned. "You are a guest here, child. Do not presume—"

"*I* presume." Talia stood. "You swore an oath to protect this land. So did my father, Hakim Malak-el-Dahshat. As princess of Arathea, I call on you to fulfill that oath."

Muhazil studied her a long time. "Talia Malak-el-Dahshat. For years we have heard rumors of your fate.

Please sit. I will listen to what you say, but I can promise nothing."

Slowly, Talia lowered herself to the ground. "Faziya faced the raikh of Jahrasima in her own mansion to try to help the Kha'iida."

Muhazil blinked. "Not the wisest strategy."

"Not at all," Talia agreed, earning a glare from Faziya. "My point remains. She *is* Kha'iida. She deserves your respect and your aid."

"Queen Lakhim has offered a reward for your return," Muhazil said.

Talia smiled. "Then I'm fortunate you too are Kha'iida, and would not betray the hospitality of a guest."

That earned a laugh. "Very well, Princess. I will indulge your fears." He reached into his robe and pulled out a small, bone-handled knife. The blade was a flat shard of crystal, vivid green and shaped as perfectly as Danielle's sword.

Faziya extended her hand, flinching only slightly as Muhazil cut her palm. He pressed the flat of the blade against her hand, coating the knife in her blood.

Talia clenched her fists. Every drop of blood weakened Faziya further. How much did the knife need?

Finally, Muhazil withdrew the knife. Talia ripped off her scarf and pressed it to Faziya's palm. Faziya was pale, but watched without blinking as Muhazil held the blade to the light.

He frowned and brought the knife closer. "Strange."

"Is the curse deev?" Talia asked.

"Were it deev, the blood would smoke at the touch of the crystal," Muhazil said. His tongue flicked out, tasting the blood. He winced and moved it away. "Blade and blood are hot. Almost hot enough to burn."

"Which means what?" Talia asked.

"I don't know." He held the knife in both hands. "There *is* magic here. More powerful than any mere fairy." He bowed to them both. "I will talk to our seer."

"If the curse is deev, will you help us to find the one responsible?" Talia asked.

"We are sworn to fight the deev," he said. "But whatever foe you face, this magic did not come from one of the cursed race. I'm sorry, Princess."

CHAPTER 18

TALIA SAT IN THE SHADE OF MUHAZIL'S tent, watching a young boy flee from his older brother. The younger child had flung off his robes and giggled madly as he raced toward the pond wearing nothing but his sandals. He splashed into the water, only to be scooped up by his brother.

Screams of delight changed to howls of protest, but the brother clearly had experience in these matters. He tossed the child into the air and caught him. A few more throws, and the boy was giggling once again.

The rugs in the tent softened the approaching footsteps. Faziya lowered herself gently, folding her legs beneath her. She handed Talia a bowl of bread and fresh olives. "Eat."

Talia popped an olive into her mouth. She spat the pit into her hand and returned it to the bowl, never taking her eyes from the scene below.

"I miss the desert sometimes," Faziya said. "The open air. Water untainted by fairy magic. The sounds of the animals at night. The city is so crowded, so full of strangers."

"Yet you've stayed in Jahrasima."

Faziya stared down at the pond. "When I was a child, I watched my mother die of the siphon sickness. Over the course of a single season, her body withered away until she weighed as little as a child. She was tormented by thirst, but her body emptied itself of fluids as quickly as she could drink. I stayed with her, bringing water and anything else I thought might help. Nothing did. She grew more and more tired, until one day she simply failed to awaken. I thought if we had taken her to the Temple of the Hedge, she might have survived."

Talia placed a hand on Faziya's back.

"There is no cure for the siphon sickness," Faziya said, her tone distant. "Having left the tribe, I was massim. A stranger. Many times during my first year at the temple I thought of setting out alone. There are tales of tribeless Kha'iida who wander the desert. But I discovered that even though I couldn't have saved my mother, there was joy and purpose in saving others."

"For a long time after I arrived in Lorindar, I used to sneak down to try to use Snow's magic mirror," Talia admitted. "Every night I'd try to make it show me Arathea, just so I could see my home again."

"Did it work?"

"No." Talia smiled. "I grew so frustrated I threatened to smash the damn thing with an ax. I might have done it if Snow hadn't caught me."

She turned to look at Snow and Danielle. With nothing to do while they waited for Muhazil and his seer, they had spent the afternoon helping with the animals. Danielle was helping, at any rate. Under her guidance, camels waited patiently to be milked. Snow was flirting with one of the shepherds, in between translating for Danielle. Snow's Arathean was painful to Talia's ear, but from the look on the shepherd's face, he found her accent charming.

Faziya leaned against her, head resting on Talia's shoulder. "She's beautiful, but isn't she a little old for you?"

Talia tensed and looked away, trying to make the movement a casual one. "Who do you mean?"

"Don't lie to me, my princess." Faziya kissed her neck. "I know that look."

Talia sighed, her face burning. "Snow is younger than me, actually. Her age . . . it's hard to explain. She and I aren't— She was the first real friend I made in Lorindar. The only friend, for a long time."

"But nothing more?" Faziya asked.

"No."

Faziya pulled away, appearing to weigh this information. "Good."

Talia smiled and returned her attention to Snow, giving up any pretense of subtlety. "Until last year, she thought I was simply too shy to talk about my liaisons with the men about the palace. Once she learned the truth . . . she's Allesandrian. Her people are less tolerant about such things."

"So was Arathea, in olden times." Faziya kissed her again. "Before the fairies led our society down the path of corruption and perversity." She pulled away, mischief in her eyes. "That *is* what people in other lands say about us, is it not?"

"Some of them," Talia admitted. Compared to the dalliances of the fairy race, human couplings were relatively boring.

"She doesn't like me, does she?" Faziya was watching Snow and Danielle. "Danielle is pleasant to everyone, and your wolf friend doesn't seem to care one way or the other, but Snow—"

"She's hurting." Snow would be furious if she knew Talia was talking to Faziya, but Faziya *was* a trained healer. Perhaps there was something she could do. "Her skull was fractured in a fight. Ever since, using too much magic has caused her tremendous pain. These past days have been difficult for her."

"That's dangerous," said Faziya. "Injuries to the head are unpredictable. The damage can lay hidden for years. There are medicines that might ease the pain, but I wouldn't suggest them. If she's anything like you, masking the pain would only lead her to push herself further, doing more damage in the long run."

"She would," Talia said. "But trying to get Snow to stop using magic is like trying to get you to leave the desert."

It was Faziya's turn to blush. "So what will you do now? Even if Muhazil decides my curse was cast by a deev, they clearly don't have any better idea than we do where to find Zestan."

Over the past several hours, Danielle, Snow, and even Roudette had come by to ask the same question. Talia gave Faziya the same answer she had given them. "I'm not sure."

"Liar." She smiled, but her eyes were sad. "You'd never be so calm if you didn't know what to do next. You're leaving, aren't you?"

She knew better than to try to lie to Faziya. "You heard what the Wild Hunt has done to your people. If Rajil is any example, the fairies already hold sway in the cities. I can't let Zestan take Arathea."

"I could come with you."

"You can barely walk!"

Faziya took Talia's arm, running her fingers up the sleeve until she touched the scar on Talia's forearm. "You make a habit of collecting scars and broken bones. You could use an extra healer. I could take some of the burden off of your friend Snow."

"Any healer would tell you to stay behind until you've healed."

"Will you make Snow remain as well? You've always tried to protect me, as though I were some fragile butterfly who would be crushed by the slightest weight." She stood and reached for the ties holding the tent flaps open. She glanced over her shoulder, her smile taking the edge from her words. "Maybe I should let you judge for yourself how recovered I am."

The front flap fell shut, and Talia's breathing quickened. "This is Muhazil's tent. Even if you were well, we shouldn't—"

"We're guests of the tribe," Faziya said. "His home is your home. To treat it otherwise would offend him."

Slowly, she reached out to loosen Talia's hair. Her fingers trailed down the sides of Talia's neck. Despite the heat, Talia shivered.

Faziya drew back, a playful expression on her face. "I might need help getting out of these robes, though."

"You're hurt." Talia swallowed, forcing herself not to reach out. "I shouldn't."

"I'm the healer. I'll judge what's best for my recovery." Faziya laughed. "I love the way your voice goes deeper when your passions are roused."

Talia was fighting a losing battle, and she knew it. Not that she particularly wanted to win. "You're certain you're strong enough?"

Faziya leaned close, her lips brushing Talia's as she whispered, "There's only one way to find out."

Roudette crossed the camp, ignoring the dogs that barked and followed at a distance. Only when one approached too closely did she turn to face it. She said nothing, simply staring into his eyes until he yelped and fled.

The rest continued to bark, albeit from a safe distance. When she reached Snow and Danielle, she said only, "Muhazil has emerged."

Muhazil and an older Kha'iida woman were already talking to Talia by the time Roudette and the others arrived.

Roudette sniffed the air and smirked as she entered the tent. Talia and Faziya had clearly put the afternoon to good use. She winked at Talia, who stiffened and pretended to ignore her.

"Your knife is hundreds of years old," Talia was saying to Muhazil. Her hair was loose and disheveled. Faziya lay sleeping on one of the mats behind her. "Its magic might have faded, or perhaps Zestan has found a way to mask her magic. The curse was cast by a Jinniyah, using Zestan's power. She might have tainted whatever magical tracks you're searching for."

Muhazil turned to the seer. "Turz?"

"Possibly," said Turz. She was an older woman who still looked strong enough to haul everything she owned halfway across the desert on her back without stopping to rest. Her black hair had the same reddish tinge Roudette had seen on some of the other Kha'iida women. "With the curse's power broken, it's hard to be certain. But I do not believe this spell was laid by a deev."

Muhazil held the knife in his hand. He had polished the blade, or perhaps that glassy finish was an effect of its magic. "The law is clear. Had you brought proof of the deev, every tribe would join behind you to hunt her down." He kissed the blade, then returned it to the sheath strapped over his heart.

Talia's fists tightened. "You can't—"

"Without proof, I can offer you only my own tribe," Muhazil continued.

Talia stared. "What?"

"If fighting this Zestan-e-Jheg will end the Wild Hunt's attacks on our people, we will give you whatever help we can." Muhazil smiled. "Have you any hints as to where she might be?"

"Not yet," Roudette said. "Remove this enchantment. When the Wild Hunt returns to the desert tonight, I will hunt them. They will give us Zestan."

"You're assuming they return to Zestan at the end of the night," Snow said. "The Wild Hunt vanishes with the coming of dawn. You can't track them beyond this world."

Roudette bared her teeth. "I said nothing of following them. They're weakest as dawn approaches. Let me pick off one of their number. I can drag him from the rest and force him to tell me what I need to know." She yanked back her collar, exposing the silver mark. "Take back your curse, and we will have our proof."

"While we wait here, trusting you to keep your word?" Talia asked. "I think not. Even if you manage to capture a hunter without getting yourself killed, I'm not about to release you into the desert without a leash."

Roudette shrugged. She had expected as much. With time, she might have been able to sway Danielle, but Talia was far too careful.

"What about Queen Lakhim?" Danielle asked. "If you were to work with her to find Zestan—"

"I killed her son," Talia said. "She would have me killed the moment I showed my face, both to avenge Jihab and to prevent me from being used against her. If Lakhim had the resources to find Zestan, she would have done so already."

Roudette stood, straightening her cape. "Lakhim might not be able to find Zestan, but Rajil will help."

"Rajil?" Talia repeated. "The same Rajil we robbed and humiliated?"

"Exactly." She turned toward Snow. "All the raikhs have scrying pools that allow them to receive commands from the queen. Can you use your mirrors to reach Rajil's pool?"

"That depends on what kind of protections they've raised, but I should be able to." Snow narrowed her eyes. "What exactly are we going to tell her?"

"Not we." Roudette smiled. "Me. Having captured Sleeping Beauty, I wish to negotiate directly with Zestan. My original contract was with Lakhim, but surely a great fairy can offer more than any human queen."

Talia glanced down, as if to assure herself that Faziya was still sleeping. Lowering her voice, she said, "Zestan will want proof. She won't even talk to you unless you have me."

"So we go together," said Roudette. "I deliver you to Zestan. In doing so, we lead the Kha'iida to Zestan's doorstep. The Kha'iida spread the word, and all Arathea turns against her. We should alert Lakhim as well, so that her people can reinforce the Kha'iida."

"What happens to you and Talia?" Danielle asked.

Roudette watched Talia closely. Talia knew what Roudette was proposing, and she knew the likely outcome.

"I won't let Zestan use me against Arathea," Talia said.

"Zestan could be anywhere," Snow protested. "By the time the Kha'iida catch up—"

"I know." Talia turned toward Muhazil. "Queen Lakhim owns an ebony stallion, a magical statue with the speed to travel anywhere in Arathea in the time it takes to speak its name. The horse could carry individual riders back and forth."

"How do you know this?" Muhazil asked.

Talia snorted. "She stole it from my family."

"There are Kha'iida camped less than a day's ride from the palace," said Muhazil. "Our knives bind us. I will have them send riders to Lakhim, urging her to come to hai'ir tel."

Roudette bared her teeth. "By the time they arrive, they might find Talia and myself toasting our victory over the deev. Imagine the stories they'd tell."

"More likely they'll find your corpses," said Snow. "It's not just Zestan you have to fight. Who knows what guardians she's gathered in addition to the Wild Hunt?"

"Can you think of another way to find Zestan?" Talia challenged them. Nobody responded.

"Tell me when you're ready to contact the raikh."
Roudette tapped her heart in salute, then left the tent.
The idea was planted; all that remained was for the others to work out the details.

This was the end of her path, then. At last she would
shed the wolfskin and complete her grandmother's
work. Soon Zestan and the Wild Hunt would be destroyed, and she would finally be able to rest.

Talia would have made a fine ruler. It was a shame
she would never have that chance.

It was decided that Snow should prepare her spells in
the seer's tent, which was already warded against detection. Kha'iida magic was new to her, and she spent far
too much time examining the tent itself, trying to figure
out how the wards were woven into the cloth.

As a point of pride, Snow was determined not to ask
Turz. She ran her fingers over the square panels of the
tent one by one. There were no runes, no patterns to
force the magic into a given form. It was as if Turz had
enchanted every individual strand and fiber.

She laughed when she finally figured it out. Turz
hadn't enchanted the tent. She had enchanted the *goat*,
probably moments before it had been shorn. The hair
from that goat had been blended and spun together with
nonmagical hair, so that every panel carried a trace of
magic. Such a spell couldn't be broken without destroying the entire tent.

With that mystery solved, Snow set to work. The others watched in silence as she used a makeshift quill to
inscribe tiny symbols on the largest of her mirrors. With
no proper ink, she had fetched a cup of cold coffee. The
watery symbols tended to run together, and they dried
quickly in the heat, but the enchantment remained, visible as thin lines of gold.

"You said before that every scrying pool was linked

back to Queen Lakhim's palace." Snow frowned and corrected one of the symbols. "What color is the rim of Lakhim's pool?"

"What does that matter?" Talia stood with Faziya in the open front of the tent. Faziya hadn't said a word since learning of their plans.

"Do you really want a lecture on the properties different materials have on spells of binding and protection, or the magical laws requiring such linked enchantments to be constructed of similar substances?" Snow gave her a wicked smile. "The principles of similarity have been around for at least six hundred years. A human sorcerer named Adgis of Millgason was the first to set them down in written form. He spent his life trying to quantify the exact degree of—"

"Gold, I think," said Talia. "I can't be certain. I didn't stay there for very long, and I had more important things to worry about than palace decor."

Snow grunted and added a new symbol to her mirror. "Paint, leaf, or solid gold?"

"How should I know?" Talia sighed. "Lakhim's too full of herself to settle for mere paint."

Snow returned to her preparations. Magical communication carried more risk than Talia or Danielle realized. An unguarded link could allow all manner of nastiness to attack those on either side. They had no idea how much magic Snow had cast into the mirrors they each wore in order to protect them from such attacks.

"Don't do this," said Faziya. She leaned against one of the tent poles for support. Her other hand held Talia's. "I saw the hedge once, before you awoke. It used to be traditional to make a pilgrimage to the hedge before taking our vows. Zestan would cast you back into that prison, and I would never—"

"I don't intend to give Zestan the chance," said Talia. "She'll believe I'm helpless, a prisoner to Roudette. I should be able to get close enough to strike."

"What then?" Faziya demanded. "Even if you some-how manage to slay a deev, you think Zestan's minions will simply surrender to you when she falls?"

"To *us*," Talia corrected. "Roudette has fought her share of fairies."

"Oh, forgive me. I forgot there would be *two* of you to face the Wild Hunt." Faziya made no attempt to hide her anger. "Your plan is foolproof, oh wise one."

Snow cleared her throat. "Could you argue quietly, please? Rajil's pool is well protected. I'm trying to break through without killing everyone in the tent."

"Sorry," Talia said gruffly.

Snow tried to concentrate on her mirror. The bick-ering didn't actually bother her. She and Talia had ar-gued almost every day since they first met, at least until recently. Until she saved Faziya. Now Faziya had taken Snow's place, whether it was the playful banter over meals or fighting over whether or not Faziya could ac-company them to face Zestan.

Snow touched a flat packet on her belt. The leather pouch held four sharpened steel snowflakes Talia had commissioned for her several years ago.

She should be happy for Talia, the way Danielle clearly was. They could be facing a deev before the night was out. Why should it bother her if Talia had a quick fling before the battle? Especially considering the odds against any of them surviving that battle. Hadn't Snow herself been flirting with that shepherd—what was his name again?—only hours before?

"Do you trust Roudette?" Danielle asked softly.

"No." Talia smiled. "But she wants Zestan and the Hunt destroyed as badly as any of us."

Snow jabbed her quill into the coffee and finished her spell. She rubbed her eyes, then studied the inscrip-tions. "I think I've established a bond. We should be able to— Uh-oh."

"What's wrong?" Danielle asked.

Snow dropped the mirror and jumped away as a gout of flame shot up from the glass, scorching the roof of the tent. "I think they noticed me. We should probably get outside."

They obeyed with alacrity. The flame showed no sign of stopping. It had already burned through the top of the tent. Most of Turz's protective magic was meant to guard against attacks from outside. That magic did little against an attack from within. Snow stepped back, peeking up from outside to see how high the flames rose.

It could have been worse. The tower of fire was barely taller than the trees by the pond. The Kha'iida were running toward her, many carrying buckets and bowls of water. Not that water would be of any help against this fire.

"So you want to play?" Snow muttered as she removed a second mirror from her armband. Turning her face away from the heat, she advanced slowly toward the flame. She flipped the mirror so the reflective side faced downward. "Fine. Let's play."

She darted forward, dropping the mirror onto the flames. It clinked onto the top of the other mirror, sandwiching the flames between them. For a moment, fire burst from between the mirrors, spreading out in all directions. An instant later, the fire died and black smoke began to fill the tent.

Talia shoved her to the ground. Before Snow could protest, Talia grabbed a bucket and poured water onto the flames that flickered on the bottom of Snow's robe. Others hurried past to extinguish the rest of Turz's tent.

"I'm sorry about that," Snow said.

Turz walked through her tent, inspecting the damage. The fire had done little to the walls, but the panel overhead had a blackened hole the size of a dinner platter. "How did you stop the attack?"

Snow wiped sweat from her face, checking to make sure she still had her eyebrows. "I didn't. I reflected it." She frowned at the two mirrors. "There's a decent chance we just set Rajil's mansion on fire."

Children ran toward the tent, only to be dragged back by the older Kha'iida. The dogs were in a frenzy, riling the rest of the animals. Danielle hurried away to help get them under control.

Roudette chuckled as she studied the tent. "So it's fair to say we should have their attention?"

"I should say so. One way or another, they're listening now." Snow started to reach for the mirrors. "Everyone else might want to stand back."

"You're sure they won't send more fire through?" Roudette asked.

"Nope," said Snow. "But that was a powerful spell. I don't *think* they could do it again so soon."

"How comforting." Roudette nodded for her to go ahead.

Snow removed the top mirror. The glass was cool to the touch, showing no sign of damage. She returned it to her armband and stepped aside, allowing Roudette to take her place.

Roudette picked up the remaining mirror. "I would speak to the raikh of Jahrasima."

Snow closed her eyes, extending her vision to the mirror in Roudette's hand. She could see Roudette staring down at her. The hairs on Snow's arms and neck rose as a second presence stepped into view within the mirror. Snow found herself looking both at Roudette and at the jinniyah's shadow from the raikh's palace. The ceiling over the raikh's scrying pool was blackened from the flames.

It was Rajil herself who spoke, though she was hidden from view. "Whoever you are, you shall suffer for—"

"I have Princess Talia," Roudette interrupted.

"Give me proof." Undisguised eagerness dripped from Rajil's words.

Roudette reached over to grab Talia by the throat.

Caught off guard, Talia slammed a fist into the outside of Roudette's elbow. Roudette grunted and tightened her hold. Snow was readying a spell when Talia relaxed, allowing herself to be dragged in front of the mirror.

"I've a very generous offer from Queen Lakhim for this one," Roudette said. "I've been told your fairy friends can pay more, but if not, I'll be on my way."

Snow watched as the jinniyah stepped aside, making way for Rajil. Hatred filled Rajil's gaze as she studied Talia. One hand touched her throat, no doubt remembering Talia's arm clamping around her neck. Rajil's gaze moved to Roudette. "I know you."

Snow tensed. Roudette had been in her wolf shape the entire time they were in the mansion. If Rajil had somehow recognized Roudette and realized she was working with Talia, this plan was useless. But Rajil merely smiled. "How did the Lady of the Red Hood find the power to control my scrying pool?"

"I didn't," Roudette said easily. "That was done by one of Talia's friends, a witch from Lorindar."

"Talia's *friend* helped you?" Rajil asked.

"Not at first." Roudette bared her teeth. "They had another friend. By the time I shattered both of her knees, the witch agreed to do whatever I asked."

Few things rattled Snow these days, but Roudette's casual smile as she lied about torturing Danielle made her shudder. Something in Roudette's eyes suggested she would have no qualms about doing exactly what she said if the situation required it.

"What is it you want?" Rajil asked.

"Zestan controls the Wild Hunt. I want her word as a fairy that the Hunt will never again enter Morova."

Snow frowned. That hadn't been part of the discussion.

Rajil didn't even blink. "How will we find you?"

Roudette grabbed Snow's robe, hauling her in front of the glass. "The witch will lead you."

"The mirror," Snow said, doing her best to sound broken and resentful. "There's a bond connecting it to your pool. Any halfway competent wizard can follow that thread."

Rajil smiled, hunger plain on her face as she stared at Talia. "I will pass your request to Zestan. Perhaps she'll be kind enough to give Talia's friends to me in payment. They would make fine additions to my garden."

Roudette brought the mirror to her face, so close her breath clouded the glass. "You have until sunrise. I know Zestan wants Talia alive. Betray me, and I'll kill her myself. I'll claim my bounty from Lakhim, and you can explain your failure to Zestan."

With a thought, Snow darkened the mirror. She tugged free of Roudette's grip and massaged her eyes, trying to ease the headache. She still needed to cast yet another enchantment that would allow the others to follow Talia and Roudette. "We're safe. They can't hear us unless I let them."

"We will follow you as quickly as we can," said Muhazil. "The Wild Hunt has plagued my people for too long. I am in your debt."

"Yes, you are." Talia slashed a hand through the air, cutting him off. This was a side of Talia that Snow had rarely seen. She held her head high, articulating every syllable. She was shorter than Muhazil, but her posture made it seem as though she was looking down at him. "In payment of that debt, you will welcome Faziya back into your tribe. This shall be her home for as long as she chooses."

Muhazil glanced at Faziya, who had gone still at Talia's words. "She left of her own free will. She walked away from her heritage, from her—"

"Do we have a bargain?" Talia asked.

Muhazil bowed, one hand to his chest. "We do indeed, Princess." He turned to shoo the crowd away. When the others had left, he said, "If Zestan is indeed deev, you know there is little chance you will survive. The strength of a deev can split mountains. Their temper shakes the earth itself. Their skin is like rock, their—"

"Their flatulence slays entire herds," said Talia. "Yes, I know. I learned about the deev before your grandfather was born."

Muhazil burst into laughter. "So you did." He glanced to the south. "I hope you are wrong about Zestan, Princess. For your sake, and for Arathea's."

CHAPTER 19

"YOU'RE STAYING HERE." Talia's tone left no room for argument. Naturally, Danielle argued anyway.

"You're taking Snow, but you'd leave me behind?"

"I'd leave Snow too if I could." Talia and Danielle stood at the edge of the pond, where Talia had been filling a small skin. Even knowing the fairies were coming for her, the habits of the desert were too strongly ingrained for her to set out without water.

She should have known the conversation would follow this path. She should have just punched Danielle out the moment she started talking about coming along. Though there was still time to correct that mistake. "Without Snow's magic, we've no way of leading Turz to Zestan. Or so she claims."

"So I'm to stay behind, among strangers who can't even understand my language, while my two best friends go off—"

"Yes." Talia grabbed Danielle's shoulders. "You have a son who needs you. *Lorindar* needs you. What would Beatrice say if she knew what you were trying to do?"

"I've already talked to Queen Bea," Danielle said evenly. "I spoke with Armand and Jakob as well." She pointed to the pouch at Talia's belt. "Snow is in there already, I assume?"

Talia reluctantly loosened the pouch, allowing Snow to peek out. Snow made a cute mouse, with sandy fur and a long, tufted tail.

"What happens to her if something goes wrong?" Danielle asked.

"We all know what we're walking into." Talia pulled Danielle into a quick, awkward hug, being careful not to squish Snow between them. She had been friends with Danielle for almost two years, but she still wasn't entirely comfortable with the hugging. "I'm sorry. I know how hard it is to be left behind. You and Snow never should have been drawn into this. Don't ask me to risk your life too."

"I'm not asking." Danielle returned the hug, then pulled away. "If you're killed, Snow will be trapped. She can't use magic to change herself back without risking discovery. But nobody would notice an owl or hawk swooping down to snatch a mouse. Or two mice. I can get her out, if things go wrong. Leave me behind, and you condemn Snow to die with you."

It was the one argument that could sway Talia's mind, and Danielle delivered it as coolly as a master swordsman dispatching a foe. She was as bad as Queen Bea. "You stay hidden. Do nothing unless you need to save yourself and Snow. If I fall, you leave me. No rescue. No mad attempt to summon a gazelle herd against the Wild Hunt. You call your hawk and you flee. Get out of Arathea. Promise me, Danielle."

"I promise."

Talia sighed. "Snow, we need one more spell." A short time later, she was setting off toward the edge of camp, a second mouse squirming in her pouch. Briefly, she considered tying the pouch shut and leaving them both behind. They would be better off, though they'd never forgive her. But if Snow was telling the truth, Talia needed her. And if Danielle could save Snow . . .

"Damn you both," she muttered.

Up ahead, Faziya stood talking to Roudette. As Talia neared, Roudette tossed her a length of rope.

"Have Faziya bind your wrists. Don't take long." Roudette was already walking away. "Zestan's fairies should be on their way. We want to be away from the valley so we don't bring them down upon the Kha'iida."

Talia handed the rope to Faziya. "You're not coming, so don't ask."

"I know." Faziya took her hand. Her skin was still too cool, especially now that the sun had begun to set, spreading shadow over the valley. "Even if by some miracle you get close enough to strike, the deev are all but impossible to kill. Their skin is impenetrable, save by magic."

Talia reached into her robe and pulled out one of Roudette's knives. "Pure iron."

"That's not enough," Faziya protested. "Iron is little more than a nuisance to one such as Zestan. It won't even scratch the skin."

"So we aim for a target with no skin to protect it." Talia flipped the knife, catching it by the tip of the blade. A flick of her wrist sent it spinning through the air, sticking in the stump of a small shrub no more than three fingers thick. "Do you remember when I first learned to throw a knife? I spent weeks practicing until I could plant a blade in a target the size of a man's eye from seven paces."

"I remember," said Faziya. "You killed that poor fig tree, you know."

"Mother Khardija made that very clear as she was spelling out my punishment." Talia walked over to retrieve the knife.

"So you'll kill Zestan. And then the Wild Hunt will take you away from me."

Talia flicked her fingers. "Who knows? Maybe with Zestan gone, whatever hold she has over them will dissolve, and they'll simply move on."

"You don't believe that."

Talia said nothing. Faziya would only see through the lie.

"Are you coming or not?" Roudette shouted.

Talia tucked the knife away and extended her hands. "What will you do now?"

"I'm not sure." Faziya's eyes shone, but Kha'iida were taught early not to cry. The body's water was too precious to waste on tears. She looped the rope around Talia's wrists. "I spoke to my father."

"Your father is still alive? You never said—"

"Until Muhazil rescinded my banishment, he couldn't even acknowledge me as his daughter." Faziya stepped close, her good arm snaking around Talia's waist. "Thank you for that."

Talia closed her eyes, indulging herself just one moment longer. Then Roudette shouted again, and the moment passed. She waited for Faziya to finish tying the rope, then tested her bonds. They were tight, but she should be able to slip free.

"Wait," Faziya said. "Do you remember what you told me at the docks five years ago?"

Some memories were so clear she could have painted them. "You made me promise to return. Faziya, I can't—"

"I know." Faziya stepped around to kiss her. "Give me the lie."

Talia brushed her fingertips over Faziya's face. "I promise."

Without another word, Faziya turned away. Talia started to say more but caught herself. This wasn't Lorindar, and farewells were for strangers.

Talia did her best to maneuver the waterskin with her bound hands. Roudette had also tied a loop of rope around Talia's neck, no doubt in part to repay her for leashing Roudette back at the mansion. The rope was tight enough to make swallowing uncomfortable, but she managed to take a drink, then handed the skin back to Roudette.

"We'd make faster time if we'd taken the horses," Talia said.

Roudette gulped down most of the remaining water. Even in the night air, she was sweating beneath her hood. "Horses don't like me."

"Do you even remember what it was like to be human?" Talia asked.

"Yes." Roudette shouldered the waterskin and increased her pace. They had no destination. The only goal was to get as far from the Kha'iida camp as possible. "That's why I chose to be more."

"You chose to be a killer. How many people have you murdered?"

"This month?" Roudette glanced at Talia. "I kill fairies. I'd expect you to understand."

"You kill anyone, for the right price." Talia raised her arms. "I have the scar from your attempt on Queen Beatrice."

Roudette smiled. "A glorious fight that was."

"You would have murdered a good woman."

"What did you do after my attempt on Beatrice?" Roudette didn't wait for an answer. "You strengthened your magical protections. You set more guards to watch the walls. You prepared yourselves. *That* is my service. I made you stronger. You would spend your time trying to defend the weak, to help them feel safe in a world poised to devour them. I remind the weak to protect themselves."

"Is that what your grandmother wanted when she gave you that skin?" Talia asked.

"Grandmother thought like you and your friends," Roudette said, turning away. "She fought to protect us. As a result, my people lay down like sheep to be butchered by the Wild Hunt. Just as yours will."

"We'll see." Talia flexed her hands, testing the ropes again to see how easily she could escape and reach her weapons, both the iron knife she would use against Zestan and the second, smaller one she had hidden in her robe in case she failed. If her first blade failed to kill Zestan, the second would ensure Talia couldn't be used against Arathea. The fairy curse wouldn't work if Talia was dead.

The first sign of the fairies was a distant light, like an oversized yellow firefly—a will-o'-the-wisp. As the light grew closer, Talia realized several of the creatures were flying together.

"Don't stare," Roudette warned. "They'll entrance you if you look too long."

The will-o'-the-wisps streaked over the desert, zipping about like animated torch flames. They moved in total silence, splitting into two groups and circling Talia and Roudette.

Roudette growled and swung a fist at one that flew too close. Another bobbed around Talia's head. Will-o'-the-wisps were barely intelligent, about as smart as an average dog. This one seemed to have decided Talia was less dangerous than her companion, and was carefully keeping Talia between itself and Roudette.

With a smile, Talia snapped a kick that sent it flying backward. Roudette chuckled as it crashed into the sand, light flickering. Slowly, it rose back into the air.

The will-o'-the-wisps kept a safe distance after that.

Talia flexed her foot. The impact had covered her sandal in glowing yellow powder, as fine as pollen. She dragged her foot through the sand, rubbing off the worst of it.

The hounds were next, their howls carrying over the desert, making it sound as though they closed in from all sides.

Roudette tightened her grip on the rope running to Talia's neck. With her right hand, she drew a double-edged iron knife so long and thick it was practically a sword.

"We've made no bargain yet." Roudette rested the edge of the knife against Talia's throat. "They may try to take you by force. Whatever happens, stay calm."

Talia fought to keep from moving. Snow's curse wouldn't allow Roudette to kill her, no matter how she might threaten. "Calm? Even if this works—even if we kill Zestan and lead the Kha'iida to her lair to destroy her minions—we're unlikely to see another sunrise."

"You agreed to the plan," Roudette pointed out.

"That doesn't mean I have to like it."

Roudette laughed softly. "I chose my path when I donned the wolf. Grandmother's death showed me where that path would ultimately lead. I was too young to stop the Hunt then. You've given me another chance, and for that I thank you."

Roudette dragged Talia in front of her as the first of the hunters came into view. Not that Talia would be of much use as a shield. Fairy archers were said to be able to shoot the stinger from a wasp. But any impact would knock Roudette back, dragging her knife across Talia's throat.

The hunters rode through the sky upon a path of smoke and embers that appeared before them, vanishing after their passage. The riders themselves shone like moonlight. The rumble of the horses' hooves sounded like distant thunder. Talia realized she was pressing against Roudette, her body instinctively retreating from the approaching hunters.

"Few have witnessed the approach of the Wild Hunt and survived to tell of it," Roudette said.

"How comforting." Talia sniffed. Roudette's breath was foul, smelling of blood and raw goat. "I told you to leave the animals alone!"

"The Kha'iida won't miss just one."

Talia counted eight riders, only a small part of the

Wild Hunt. She couldn't imagine what it would be like to watch the full Hunt thundering through the sky.

Their garb was an eclectic mix. One man wore a helm fashioned from the skull of a young dragon. Another was naked from the waist up, his body painted in swirls of red. A third wore fur-lined garments and heavy boots.

The lead rider raised a twisted horn to his lips. Talia heard nothing, but the hunters reacted instantly, spreading out to encircle their prey. The hounds filled in the gaps between the horses.

"Say nothing," Roudette whispered. To the hunters, she shouted, "I will bargain with Zestan-e-Jheg, and her alone."

The lead rider nudged his horse forward. White hair streamed behind him like a cape. He said nothing. Thinking back to the hunter at the temple, Talia wondered if they could speak at all. Will-o'-the-wisps bobbed behind him, as if peeking over his shoulders.

Roudette dug her knife into Talia's throat, and the rider stopped. A drop of blood tickled Talia's neck. She hadn't even felt the blade break the skin.

"Your word as a fairy," said Roudette. "You will deliver us safely to Zestan. Should we fail to reach an accord, you will return us to this spot and leave us in peace for one night. Those are my terms. Reject them, and I'll spill her blood right here."

"The riders are human," Talia whispered. "Not bound by fairy oaths."

"Their humanity died long ago. They are the Wild Hunt."

The hunter tilted his head in assent.

Roudette sheathed her weapon. "Don't try to run, Princess," she said. "The dogs would bring you down before you took your second step, and believe me, these are not gentle creatures."

Talia made a show of pushing back as Roudette dragged her toward the hunter. A backhanded blow sent Talia sprawling. "Consider that repayment for the cut you gave me in Lorindar," Roudette said, touching the scab on her face.

Talia pushed herself to her feet, tasting blood. She spat, and then the rider was reaching down to seize the front of her robe. He hauled her onto the horse behind him. Even if she had wanted to escape, the hunter's grip was steel. Talia hastily adjusted her robe and pouch to protect Snow and Danielle from being crushed.

The hunter's body was warmer than she had expected, almost feverish. He gestured, and the bare-chested hunter rode forward, reaching for Roudette.

"I ride with my prey," Roudette said, still holding the end of Talia's leash. The other hunter backed away, and Roudette climbed up behind Talia.

The horse took a quick step forward, off-balance from the weight of three people. Talia spat again. If Snow's mirrors failed, maybe her blood would help the Kha'iida trackers find this spot.

The leader blew his horn once more. Though it made no sound, this time Talia was close enough to feel the air grow warm, as though an invisible fire burned within the horn. As one, the Wild Hunt brought their horses about, and then they were off. The air shimmered and tore before them. Hooves pounded a smoldering trail through the air. Sweat soon dampened Talia's robe.

The hounds barked and yowled as they ran alongside their masters. There was no wind, even as the hills of Arathea rushed past. The landscape shimmered as though she looked upon the desert through a curtain of moonlight. As far as she could tell, they traveled northeast, toward the Makras River.

Rock and sand changed to grassy marshes, which gave way to the wide, slow-moving waters of the Makras. Such a distance would have taken two days for a mortal rider. The Hunt crossed the Makras without slowing, each horse clearing the river in a single leap.

They veered north, cutting through the marshlands as they followed the river. Eventually the Hunt slowed. Up ahead, marshes changed to a broad, open plain of sand and cracked earth. A chill crawled down Talia's back, despite the heat of the hunter. "I know this place."

"It looks like an old lakebed."

Talia turned back toward the river. "The lake was drained while I slept. The family of Prince Qussan spent thirty years and their entire fortune to do it. They diverted the Makras more than a mile upstream, damming off any tributaries that tried to feed into the lake. They hoped that by robbing this place of water, they might kill the hedge that had taken Qussan."

According to the histories she had learned at the temple, this had been about ten years after Talia was cursed. With the palace engulfed by the hedge, many in the city had already fled. As the water dried, the rest soon left, leaving only the Sisters of the Hedge behind.

The ruins of the old city stood on the far side of the lake. Drifts of sand covered the roads. Beyond, she could make out the silhouette of a castle.

Talia forced herself to breathe. "This was my home."

The original Temple of the Hedge sat empty a short distance from the palace. The palace where she had grown up was in better shape than the crumbling city. Perhaps the hedge had preserved it as well. One of the windcatchers still stood, though the other had fallen and ripped a gash in the wall of the western wing. Patches of vines covered the ground, struggling to survive, though most appeared brittle and broken.

A lone figure waited outside the palace. Talia's mouth went dry, and she brought her hands to her chest, feeling the reassuring weight of the knives in her robe. As the Hunt brought her closer, she relaxed. This wasn't Zestan. It appeared to be a swamp troll, tall and broad, with skin like a rotting log and hair the color of algae.

Roudette jumped down, dragging Talia after. "I come to bargain with Zestan!"

The troll lumbered forward. Her face was so warty Talia could barely make out her eyes. It was as though she wore a mask made from toadskins. Her clothes were crocodile skin the color of old tobacco, and she carried a staff of twisted driftwood.

Roudette's knife found Talia's neck. The troll slowed. Her nostrils flapped open as she sniffed the air. She moved closer, until her toes almost touched Talia's. The troll inhaled so sharply that wisps of Talia's hair disappeared up her nose. Yellow eyes narrowed. A serpentine tongue darted between her lips, touching the side of Talia's neck.

Talia twisted away, but the troll was done. She stepped back, both hands on her staff.

"Are you satisfied?" Roudette demanded. "This is Princess Talia Malak-el Dahshat. Where is Zestan?"

"You'll understand if Zestan prefers not to meet with a known killer of fairies," the troll said.

At the sound of the troll's voice, something deep inside Talia recoiled. Her breathing quickened, and only Roudette's unbreakable grip kept Talia from lunging forward and stabbing her knife into the troll's chest. "Who are you?" she whispered.

The troll's smile exposed huge yellow teeth. "You know who I am. A part of you remembers. My name is Naghesh. I saved your life, long ago."

Talia stared, trying to understand her reaction. She would have sworn she had never seen Naghesh, yet some part of her recognized the troll. Recognized and hated her.

"You were a sickly thing then," Naghesh went on. "Your brothers and sister were healthy enough, but not you. Small and weak, born almost a month before your time. Your parents feared for your life, so they summoned the fairies of Arathea, begging us to transform you from a sniveling runt into the princess they truly desired."

She circled Talia and Roudette, the end of her staff grinding into the sand with each step.

"You were there," said Talia. "You were one of the fairies who did this to me."

Naghesh dipped her head. "I was the last. The one who saved you from my sister's curse of death."

Talia stomped her right heel onto the arch of Roudette's foot and bent forward. Roudette was strong, but Talia was faster. She tossed Roudette over her hip. Even as Roudette slammed onto the ground, Talia was yanking the knife from Roudette's hand. She leaped at Naghesh.

The driftwood staff in Naghesh's hands writhed to life, striking Talia's arm like a snake. The knife fell into the dirt. A second blow numbed Talia's shoulder. "You have no secrets from me, child," said Naghesh. "My magic flows in your blood."

Talia yanked her hands free of the ropes. She slid her foot into the sand and kicked the knife into the air, snatching it with her left hand. Magic or no, she doubted the troll was fast enough to dodge a thrown blade.

Roudette crashed into her from behind, knocking them both to the ground. Her hand seized Talia's wrist, squeezing until the bone threatened to snap.

"You can't," Roudette said.

Talia fought to keep the knife. She jabbed her fingers at Roudette's eyes, then kicked behind her at Naghesh. Roudette blocked and returned the blow, striking Talia in the head hard enough to make her vision flash.

Roudette's eyes widened, and she fell back. Her hands ripped her shirt, exposing the mark Snow had left on her shoulder. She grabbed the mark with both hands.

Talia rolled over, raising the knife to throw when a silver arrow buried itself in the sand between them. Three of the hunters sat with bows drawn.

"Twitch and they'll pin you to the earth," Naghesh said, stepping around Talia. "I know your gifts, child. You're not fast enough."

Dropping the knife was one of the hardest things Talia had ever done. "I *will* kill you for what you did to my family."

"Perhaps." Naghesh reached out to dig a claw into Roudette's shoulder. "This resembles a fairy mark. Don't tell me humans are trying to steal our magic."

Roudette's body arched and she fell back, whimpering through clenched teeth as Snow's curse took effect, boiling the blood in her body. Furious as Talia was at Roudette's betrayal, she had no desire to see her tortured to death by such magic.

Naghesh pressed the end of her staff to Roudette's shoulder. Roudette collapsed, gasping. Even in the moonlight, Talia could see that her shoulder was red and blistered. Red streaks webbed the back of her hand.

"There we go," said Naghesh. "Nothing Zestan's magic can't cure. You're in Zestan's debt now, Red Hood. Not that I imagine that will mean anything to you."

Roudette pushed herself to her hands and knees. "I did as I said I would, Naghesh. I delivered Sleeping Beauty to you."

"And you shall have the reward you were promised."

Talia faced Roudette, her own blood going cold as she realized the truth. "You were never working for Lakhim. You work for Zestan."

Roudette said nothing.

"I should have killed you the moment we arrived in Arathea."

"Yes, you should have." Roudette stood and walked over to reclaim her knife. "Remember that lesson when you awaken in another hundred years."

CHAPTER 20

ROUDETTE SWALLOWED, TRYING TO suppress the wolf's eagerness. She held Talia's rope at the knot, her knuckles pressing the back of Talia's neck. Knife ready in her other hand, she marched Talia forward.

The air stank of fairy magic. The hunters kept their distance, blocking off any escape but otherwise paying little mind to Roudette and Talia. Naghesh walked ahead, confident as a queen.

Roudette knew Talia was waiting for the right moment to break free and attack. Roudette would be her first target. Talia would fight, hoping either to kill Roudette for her betrayal or else to force Roudette to kill her in return, robbing Zestan of her prize. She tightened her grip on the rope, keeping Talia off-balance the best she could.

Roudette wasn't sure who would win such a fight, not with her body burned from within. The pain had been worst in her shoulder, but the fire had spread quickly through her body. Pain continued to burst through her chest with every heartbeat, making her feel as though she had been stabbed. Naghesh had ended the curse, but she couldn't reverse the damage it had already done.

As she neared the palace, she could make out the

destruction left by the hedge. Stone blocks the size of wagons lay cracked, strangled by dead vines. An entire tower had collapsed to the west. A lone windcatcher hummed in the breeze, shutters long since broken away. Fallen masonry lay half buried in the sand.

Pain stabbed Roudette's foot as though she had trodden on shards of glass. She tugged Talia back. "What is that?"

A line of stone cut through the dirt in front of them. It appeared to be the ruins of a wall, crumbled save for the very foundation. Though only one or two stones high, the line extended unbroken in both directions, circling the palace.

"A simple boundary wall," said Naghesh, stepping over the stone. "Fairy magic, to keep out the unwanted. You have my word it will not harm you."

Roudette shoved Talia forward, letting her cross first to make sure nothing happened. There were too many things that might not fall under the exact meaning of "harm." She hoped her cape would protect her.

Talia appeared unharmed. Roudette braced herself and stepped over the wall. She grimaced as pain coursed through her. Thanks to the cape, her body reacted to fairy magic the same way some fairies reacted to iron. The pain was soon forgotten, however, as she looked around.

Within the bounds of this wall lay another world, a fairy world. The moon had tripled in size, the light transforming the sand to silver dust. The ruins of the palace had changed as well, as if a giant spider had wrapped a web of green crystal over the walls and towers that remained.

Roudette tightened her grip on Talia as a small army poured forth from the closest tower. The stench of death identified them not as fairy guardians, but as the spirits of the dead. Here within the bounds of the fairy wall, these men appeared as real as Roudette or Talia, as if the moonlight gave them form and solidity.

They stood in the garments they had worn in life, silken sashes and carefully tooled leather, golden rings and jeweled crowns. Most carried ornately decorated weapons, swords encrusted with enough gemstones to feed half a city.

"They're princes," Talia whispered. "These are the men who died trying to reach me. The hedge killed them all."

"Killed them and kept them, from the look of it." Kept them until Zestan arrived to use them as her protectors. There had to be more than a hundred ghosts filling the open land in front of the palace. Roudette spotted one with a gray beard hanging to the middle of his chest. Beside him stood a boy who couldn't have been more than five years of age. His parents had probably hoped his smaller size would allow him to slip through the hedge where larger men had failed.

"I never realized there were so many," said Talia. Her breath caught, and she pulled toward a middle-aged man in a long blue jacket. Bloodless holes in his chest showed how he had died. "Prince Amabar. He was my cousin. Amabar, it's Talia."

Amabar didn't move. None of them seemed to recognize the prize they had died trying to reach.

Talia dropped to her knees. She appeared to be praying, but Roudette could hear her whispering to Snow and Danielle. "Be sure to warn the Kha'iida what they face here."

"Where is Zestan?" Roudette demanded.

"She waits inside," said Naghesh, indicating the palace with one hand. She pulled a necklace from her shirt, a pendant of green crystal the size of her thumb. "She sees and hears all that happens here."

Roudette folded her arms into her cape. "Fulfill your bargain. Summon the rest of the Wild Hunt."

"The Hunt obeys Zestan," Naghesh said. "You have her word they will trouble your land no more."

"And when Zestan falls?" Roudette shook her head. She felt like a child again, fighting to keep her voice from shaking. She was so close. "Let them all witness. Let the Wild Hunt itself pledge to obey."

The Wild Hunt appeared without signal or sound. Each hunter seemed to carry a shard of the moon within himself, adding to the light until it was bright as day. Their mounts crowded together between the fairy wall and a depression in the earth that might have once been a decorative stream circling the palace.

Roudette's fingers dug into a small pocket sewn into the hem of her cape. She carefully pulled out a small barbed weight, concealing it in her sweat-slick palm.

Naghesh spread her arms. "Zestan-e-Jheg swears to you that the Wild Hunt will never again trouble Morova. In exchange, you will hand Talia Malak-el-Dahshat into my keeping."

With her other hand, Roudette hauled Talia to her feet. "Your word as a fairy that Zestan waits within those walls, that she hears and affirms this bargain?"

"You have my word," said Naghesh.

Over a hundred years old, the lead weight was sharp as the day it was cast, all but untouched by age. Teardrop shaped, with tiny spurs curving up around the central point, it still showed the bloodstains from the last time its barbs had pierced Talia's skin. Roudette could feel the magic of the fairy poison clinging to the metal, heating her palm. If she held it for too long, her skin would begin to blister.

According to the stories, Talia's curse had affected everyone within the palace. Every animal had fallen, even the flies had dropped from the air, asleep. That curse had stood for one hundred years, unbreakable by blade or magic.

Roudette doubted her cape would be strong enough to protect her from such power. For a hundred years Aratheans had tried to penetrate the hedge and lift the curse of Sleeping Beauty. Even artifacts from the war between peri and deev had failed. But perhaps she would have a few extra moments before she joined Talia and the others in sleep. Time enough to ram her knife through Naghesh's throat. She owed Talia that much.

And then she would finally rest and, with her, the Wild Hunt. The Kha'iida would arrive to find the hedge reborn, their enemies trapped. With one strike, Roudette would protect the world from the Hunt for the next hundred years.

The Kha'iida would remember. They would pass the story to their children and their grandchildren, how the Wild Hunt attacked their people, and how Red Hood and Sleeping Beauty worked together to capture the Hunt and their master. They would remember, and they would be waiting. When the hedge began to fall, they would find the Wild Hunt still sleeping. Queen Lakhim's son had murdered Talia's family in their sleep. The Kha'iida would do the same to the Hunt and to Zestan as well, ridding the world of their evil.

This was Roudette's purpose. Her life. Queen Lakhim's gold had gone to find the tip of the zaraq whip. From there she had bargained with Zestan and the Duchess. The fairy sprite was to bring her here, where she could trigger the curse and end it all. Charlotte had fought the sprite, and Snow had broken free of the fairy ring, but Roudette's path had led her back.

Talia would understand. She might even thank Roudette for saving Arathea. She yanked Talia's rope, hauling her close and keeping her between herself and the hunters.

Talia didn't resist. Instead, she lunged back, her head smashing into Roudette's nose. Roudette lost her grip on the rope. Instantly Talia was spinning away, hands swinging up to sweep Roudette's arms aside.

"You tense before you strike," Talia said, kicking

Roudette in the chest. "Like a wolf preparing to charge. It's a bad habit for an assassin."

Talia snatched a knife from Roudette's sheath. Roudette lunged again, but Talia was too damned quick. The knife slashed Roudette's forearm. The zaraq weight fell to the sand. Roudette reached for it, and Talia slammed the pommel of the knife into Roudette's throat. It was a blow that could have killed even the Lady of the Red Hood if she hadn't seen it coming. She twisted, taking the impact on the side of the neck instead. It was still enough to send her staggering back.

"That's enough!" Talia pressed the knife against her own throat. She was smiling, though Roudette could smell her fear. "It's my turn to bargain. Where's Zestan?"

Talia's foot nudged the weight. Her gaze flicked downward, just long enough to identify it. Even that was almost enough time for the Hunt to strike. Two hunters leaped from their mounts, swords appearing in their hands as if by magic.

"I wouldn't," Talia said, turning to face them. "You're fast enough to kill me, sure. Fast enough to disarm me before I use this? I think not."

"What do you want, Princess?" Naghesh's amusement grated. Roudette would have loved the chance to carve that fairy arrogance from her warty face.

Talia ignored her, speaking instead to Roudette. "That's a zaraq weight," she said, her voice soft. "That style hasn't been used in a hundred years."

"She meant to curse you again," said Naghesh. "To curse us all."

Talia's anger was so strong Roudette could feel it from here, but there was something deeper there: understanding. Roudette wouldn't have expected forgiveness, nor would she have accepted it, but she had known Talia would understand. In the face of her failure, she was surprised at the comfort that brought.

"It's not too late," said Roudette, hoping Talia would understand. Talia could grab the weight, close her fist around the barbs, and trigger the curse.

"I'm afraid it is," said Naghesh. "My dear Talia. Even as a babe, your spirit held such fire. Almost fey, the way it burned. It's one of the reasons our curse worked so well."

Talia's eyes narrowed.

"Roudette's plan might have worked," the troll continued. "The poison still clings to the metal. Zestan would have paid nicely for that little trinket. Instead, I've spent several years working to duplicate the poison."

"It was hidden in Lakhim's palace," Roudette said, trying to keep Naghesh's attention. "They were trying to develop a potion to reverse the effects, to protect themselves." Lakhim believed it was the fairies who had broken into her home and stolen the weight.

"You could have earned the favor of the most powerful fairy in Arathea," Naghesh said.

"Not interested." What was Talia waiting for? Her arm was tense, her hand trembling, but she didn't move.

Naghesh's smile grew, exposing teeth like slabs of cracked ivory. "My magic flows through her limbs with every heartbeat. Limbs which obey my will, not hers."

She stepped forward to retrieve the zaraq weight. To Talia, she said "You're mine, child. As you've always been."

Talia's eyes found Roudette, pleading. Roudette gathered herself, calling on the wolf's strength. She was too weak to fight Naghesh, but it would only take a single rush to reach Talia and shove the knife home.

An arrow slammed into Roudette's thigh, burying itself to the fletching. A second struck her side. She crashed into Talia's legs, knocking them both to the ground.

"Don't kill her," Naghesh shouted.

The knife had fallen away, out of reach. Roudette tried one last time, pulling herself along the ground toward Talia's throat.

Naghesh's staff cracked against the back of Roudette's head, and she collapsed atop Talia. The hands of the Wild Hunt burned as they pulled her away.

"Take them both inside. Once we've learned the extent of Roudette's betrayal, you may have her."

Had she been stronger, Roudette might have felt dread at those words. Better a thousand deaths than to be made one of the Wild Hunt. But she had nothing left for dread. She had no thought for anything but her failure—and for the pouch she had torn from Talia's belt.

As the hunters dragged her through the broken remains of the palace wall, she dropped the pouch into the rubble.

Her last thought was that maybe she would be lucky enough to bleed to death before the Hunt took her, and then everything went white.

Snow pushed her nose out of the pouch, whiskers twitching nervously.

What's happening?

Strange to hear Danielle's voice in her mind. This must be what animals heard when Danielle spoke to them. Snow wasn't sure what to make of it, though she found herself strangely pleased that her shapeshifting magic worked well enough for her to hear Danielle's gift. It would have been far more convenient, however, if Snow had been able to respond in kind.

Two hunters were dragging Roudette into the palace. Snow couldn't tell whether she was dead or simply unconscious. The ghosts remained, though they had faded until they appeared little more than man-shaped mist. Naghesh and Talia were walking this way.

Snow squeezed out of the pouch and crawled into the

darkness between the fallen stones. Danielle followed a moment later. They waited in the shadows, watching as Naghesh entered the palace.

Naghesh stopped to pick up the pouch. She turned it over, frowned, and tucked it into her belt.

Talia followed without any sign of resistance. Snow had never been able to sense Talia's fairy curse, though she knew some fairies were able to do so. But now the tingle of magic was so strong it penetrated her skin, making her very bones itch. If that weren't enough, when she looked at Talia's shadow in the moonlight, she saw Naghesh's form outlined in the darkness. Talia was completely in Naghesh's power.

How long before the Kha'iida find us? Danielle asked.

Turz should already know their location, but it would take time for the Kha'iida to reach Lakhim. It would take longer still for Lakhim to gather enough men to attack, no matter how fast her magic horse was. They couldn't afford to wait. Snow shook her head, exaggerating the motion the best she could as a mouse.

I promised Talia we'd stay hidden, that I'd get you out of here.

Snow sat back on her hind legs. If Danielle tried to call a bird to take them away from here, Snow was going to bite her on the tail.

I think she even believed me. Danielle began making her way along the rubble of the wall, into the palace. *She's getting far too trusting.*

A long marble walkway led into the palace, though most of the stones were cracked and uneven. It appeared as though a colonnade had once bordered the walk. Broken columns edged the path like rotted stumps, and fallen pillars of jade-flecked stone provided cover as Snow and Danielle ran toward the palace.

The stairs leading to the main entrance were broken and sunken. Statues of old Arathean kings guarded the doorway. Dead vines clung to the stone, obscuring the statues' features. Inside was a wide hallway, curving away on either side. Moonlight shone through high, circular windows, as well as through gaps where the ceiling had collapsed.

Snow's ears twitched. She could hear footsteps to the right, walking away from them. They were taking Roudette and Talia into one of the wings of the palace.

Sand covered the hallway. Broken tiles littered the floor near the walls where old mosaics had crumbled away, leaving only the occasional blotch of color. Cool, pungent air wafted over her.

She felt the ghosts before she saw them. Three princes guarded the doorway up ahead. Snow froze, eyes wide. As a mouse, her heart was beating so quickly it felt like a bumblebee buzzing in her chest.

Will they care about a couple of mice? Danielle asked.

Mice weren't built to shrug. Snow crept forward.

She made no sound, but one of the princes glanced down as she approached. A short spear appeared in his hands. Snow wasn't certain what a ghost's weapon might do to a living creature, but Zestan wouldn't have used them if they were ineffective.

The prince strode toward her. Snow backed away, but he kept coming. The other two watched, but they didn't leave the doorway.

Snow fled. She slowed only long enough to make sure Danielle was with her.

A grand spiral staircase was built into the inner wall of the hall, descending to the lower level of the palace. Snow jumped through the railing, letting out a shrill cheep as she plummeted a short distance to the steps below. A short distance for a human being. As a mouse, the impact was enough to leave her stunned, even with the layer of sand cushioning her landing.

The sight of the ghost at the railing was enough to

clear her mind. She and Danielle jumped down the stairs and ran into the darkness below.

The air was colder here. This would have been mostly storage and extra sleeping quarters for use during the hot summers. The walls were in better condition, though Snow could see cracks where vines and roots had broken through.

Snow led Danielle through the corridor, following the faint smell of water. She checked one doorway, then another, until she found what she was looking for: a narrow archway leading down another set of stairs.

A quick spell provided just enough light to keep from falling. These steps went at least two stories deep before reaching the ground. Once there, Snow eliminated her light and set to work restoring herself and Danielle to their natural shapes.

Her body began to shift, bones creaking into new positions, muscle stretching and re-forming. Snow stayed on her hands and knees, clenching her body until the worst had passed. Between the change and the pain of casting the spell, she felt like she would—

"Oh, no." She managed two steps before vomiting. When she could move again, she pushed herself upright and leaned against the wall for support. She wiped her mouth on her sleeve.

"You're getting better," Danielle whispered. "That wasn't nearly as painful as the last time you cast that spell on me."

Snow smiled and unstrapped the small waterskin she had brought with her. "More importantly, I figured out how to transform us without leaving our belongings behind." She rinsed and spat.

Silver light filled the top of the stairs. The prince peered down, spotting them despite the darkness.

Snow took another drink, then began weaving a web of magic within it. Her eyes watered as she worked her spell. She was used to the pain, but the vomiting was new. How much more could she push before her body couldn't take it?

"What are you doing?"

Snow waved her to silence. The ghost was halfway down the stairs. He wore heavy armor, though the steel plates of his mail obviously hadn't protected him from the hedge. Snow wondered how far he had gotten before the thorns pierced his armor.

He was close enough now for his light to illuminate Snow and Danielle. Danielle held her sword ready, and the prince raised his spear in response.

"Snow?" Danielle whispered.

"Almost ready." Snow forced her attention back to the waterskin. Jaw clenched, she wove the final threads of the spell.

"Snow!"

Snow tossed the skin forward. The prince swung his spear as if to knock it away. Instead, the spear vanished from his hand.

The ghost tried to back away, but a trail of light bound him to the mouth of the skin. Even as water dribbled from the skin, it pulled the ghost inexorably back. Snow climbed onto the stairs and picked up the skin, filling it with her own magic and drawing the ghost inside. Moments later, Snow and Danielle were alone in the darkness.

"What did you do?" Danielle asked.

"Soul jar." Snow folded the waterskin's mouth shut and tied it tight. "Want a wet ghost?" She set the skin carefully on the floor beside the steps. "It won't last for long. A few days if I'm lucky. I didn't have time to do a proper job."

She waited, but no more ghosts followed. She sat back on the steps and called sunlight from her mirrors, illuminating a broad cavern with a vaulted ceiling. Pillars stretched in endless rows, disappearing into the darkness. Toward the center, the floor changed from dirt to black glass.

"Is that water?" Danielle asked. "Where are we?"

Snow closed her eyes, then opened them again, willing her doubled vision to merge. It didn't help. She stepped down and walked toward the water. "This is the cistern. There should be a hole somewhere overhead that they used to bring up the water."

The floor sloped like a shallow bowl. When they reached the water, it came no higher than Snow's ankles at the deepest point. The fact that any water at all remained after a hundred years was impressive. Snow suspected she would find magical protections worked into the pillars if she looked for them.

Instead, she used the water to wash her face and dampen her hair, slicking it back from her head. "There are too many ghosts." She didn't look at Danielle. "I'm not strong enough to get us past them all, not to mention the Wild Hunt."

"It's all right," Danielle said. "Talia wouldn't want you to kill yourself trying to save her."

"I didn't say we weren't going to save her." Snow sat down, resting her feet in the water. "We're just going to have to be clever about it."

Chapter 21

SNOW BRUSHED HER FINGERS OVER HER
mirror and waited until Ambassador Trittibar became visible. He appeared to be on the northern wall, staring out at the ocean. "What are you moping about?"

Trittibar jumped. He spun around, searching until he spotted the small mirror hidden in the crenellations of the northwest tower. "Snow?"

Snow beamed. "Did you miss us?"

He stepped closer and folded his arms. "Do Theodore and Beatrice know about all of your mirrors?"

"You're looking better." His arm was bandaged, and his skin was pale. Tonight he was dressed even more garishly than usual, a sure sign of his improving health. That yellow and green shirt was more suited to a jester than to an ambassador. A former ambassador, rather. "If you have any ideas for banishing the Wild Hunt or controlling an army of ghosts, I'd love to hear them."

"Ghosts too?" Trittibar stared. "You've been gone less than a week! I've found no answers for you regarding the Hunt, and now—"

"It's not my fault!"

"It never is."

"Trittibar, they have Talia." Quickly as she could,

she told him what had happened since arriving at the palace.

"The hedge was formed to hold its prey," Trittibar said, playing with his beard as he thought. "If its magic was strong enough, it might have trapped these men even after death. Killing the hedge could weaken its hold over them."

"The hedge is all but dead," said Snow. "Nothing remains but dry, broken vines. The hedge might have held them, but Zestan controls them now." She stopped. "Ghosts are ... *simple*. They're caricatures of who they were in life."

"What does that mean?" Danielle asked.

Snow kissed the mirror. "Thank you, Trittibar! Go tell Beatrice what's happening." She slapped the mirror back onto her armband and started making her way back to the wall. She brightened her light, searching until she found a pipe built into the base of the wall. "The ghosts are princes of Arathea. They died trying to reach Sleeping Beauty. What do you think will happen if they realize she's returned?"

Danielle stared. "I'm not sure."

"Neither am I." Snow dropped to the ground and peered into the pipe. It looked wide enough, though she could see where roots had cracked through the clay, and she wouldn't be surprised to find spiders and other crawly things inside. Maybe Danielle should go first. "But whatever hold Zestan has over them, they *died* for Talia. I say we find out whether that's strong enough to beat even deev magic."

Danielle dropped to the ground and crawled into the pipe. "Where are we going?"

"This place is built in the old Arathean style," Snow said as she followed. "The public gardens would have been behind the palace, but the royal family would also have a private garden in the center of the palace, complete with a pool. If I'm right, this pipe fed that pool."

Snow allowed Danielle to move ahead, then stopped to massage her skull. The throbbing had made its way to the front of her head, behind her eyes, and it would only get worse from here. She envied Trittibar his ability to tap into the power of the fairy hill at Fairytown. Or she had before that ability had been severed.

Human magic came from the one who wielded it, and it always exacted a price. Snow's mother used to sleep for days at a time after working particularly powerful magic, even with her mirror to help her.

Snow had always been able to ignore the warning signs. She cast spells almost as easily as a fairy. She might sneak an extra nap from time to time, and often she ate enough for two in order to regain her strength. But that was before the accident.

The pain wasn't the true problem. Pain could be ignored, at least for a while. The danger was what could follow the pain. Sooner or later she would push too hard. If she was lucky, the effort would leave her unconscious and exhausted. If not . . .

She pushed such thoughts aside. Magic wasn't a game for those expecting a long, peaceful life.

Snow sniffed the air. She couldn't see the end of the pipe, but she could smell flowers on the far side. She slowed. "Deev prefer the underground."

"What?"

Nothing could survive here without magic. The hedge had sucked the life from the land. Why would a deev waste magic on flowers? She twisted her head, looking back toward the cistern. The whole thing was one big cave, yet she had seen no sign of habitation. The sand on the steps had been undisturbed. "I'm not sure. This doesn't feel right."

She crawled on, extinguishing the light from her mirrors as they neared the end of the pipe. Metal bars blocked the end, but the pipe was so old and cracked that Danielle was able to yank them loose.

"Another ghost." Danielle handed her own waterskin to Snow.

Snow did her best to repeat the spell she had used before. It took longer this time, and she turned away to keep Danielle from noticing the pain. Not that it helped.

"You need to rest."

"Sure." Snow wiped her face. "You think Zestan will agree to wait until we've napped to use Talia against Lakhim?" She finished the soul jar and shoved it back to Danielle. "Throw this at the ghost."

Danielle did so, then crawled out into the moonlight. "I think it worked."

Snow followed, finding herself in a broad, circular pool, long since dried. Old tiles clung to the sides. The edges of the pool were flat and broad, designed to be used as benches. Snow picked up the dribbling waterskin and tied it shut.

"This is beautiful," Danielle said.

"Yes." Snow frowned as she looked around. "And that's bad."

No mortal had ever possessed a garden like this. Pink-leaved trees bordered meandering paths of green moss. Lavender buds hung from the branches like strings of tiny bells. Deep blue flowers rose like sweet-scented stalagmites to meet them. This place made Rajil's garden look like a patch of weeds beside the road.

The walls of the garden rose several stories all around them, the balconies curtained in flowers that reminded her of roses with blossoms the size of a man's head. Arched walkways passed overhead, a web of vines stretched between them.

Petals and fallen leaves blanketed the ground. Blue-green moss sank beneath her feet as she walked to pick up a leaf. She rubbed it between her fingers. The leaf left a golden residue on her skin. "This makes no sense."

She wiped her hand on her robe, then sat on the edge of the pool and grabbed a mirror. She waited impatiently for Trittibar to respond.

His voice sounded distant. He was in the royal library, with several books laid out on the table in front of him. "Theodore is talking to Lakhim. I know you're in a hurry, but you have to give me time to—"

"I think Zestan-e-Jheg is a peri."

Silence. Snow watched Trittibar set aside the book he had been reading. He approached the mirror, which was hidden in the back of a sconce near the door. "I don't understand."

"Look through the mirror." Snow turned slowly, giving him a good view of the garden. "Remember Volume Three of *Penkleflop's Histories*? 'Round him grew blossoms of every shape and color. Pleasing perfumes eased his troubles. Here the peri gathered to anoint their champion.'"

"Lots of fairies have gardens," Trittibar said. "The fairy queen—"

"The fairy queen isn't deev. The deev preferred the darkness of their caves. But the peri *needed* their gardens. 'They took neither food nor drink, subsisting only on the sweet scents of the world.' We know Zestan is powerful enough to command the Wild Hunt. When the Kha'iida studied the curse Zestan laid on Faziya, they couldn't identify it. It wasn't deev magic, but something similar. It was peri, not deev."

"Why would a peri take Talia?" Danielle asked. "I thought they were the ones who protected Arathea."

The howling seemed to come from nowhere, making Snow jump. She squinted at the mirror, trying to make out the windows behind Trittibar. Was there an orange tint to the glass?

"What's happening?" Trittibar asked.

"It's dawn there, isn't it?" Dawn in Arathea came later than in Lorindar. About one hour later. The Wild

Hunt ended their ride each night an hour before dawn, and it sounded like the rest were coming home.

Two hunters brought Roudette to what had once been the palace library. Most of the contents had been looted or destroyed long ago, judging from the sand and dust covering the empty stone shelves. What books remained were torn and damaged, though the desert air had pre-served them better than Roudette would have expected. Broken statues lay on the floor, as if they too had fallen asleep when Talia's curse struck.

Roudette was dropped roughly against the wall. The impact jarred the arrows in her body, making her cry out. She tried to stand, to fight and force them to kill her, but the hunters had already vanished, and her leg wouldn't support her weight anyway.

Naghesh gestured, and Talia followed her into the li-brary. "Remove her weapons."

Without a sound, Talia bent over Roudette and began stripping her of her hammer and knives. Roudette held her breath, waiting for Talia to reach for the dagger on Roudette's left hip. As Talia's fingers closed around the handle, Roudette grabbed Talia's hand. She twisted the knife toward Talia's chest.

Talia snapped a light kick against the arrow in Rou-dette's ribs. Roudette howled and fell, clutching her side.

"She retains the reflexes I gave her," Naghesh said as Talia finished disarming Roudette. "The only difference is that now those reflexes serve me."

"You?" The voice came from the doorway.

"Us," Naghesh said quickly. "She serves us. Serves you, I mean."

"Zestan-e-Jheg?" Roudette guessed.

"Welcome, Roudette." Shadows clung to Zestan's body, obscuring all detail.

Roudette had spent her life hunting fairies and learning their ways. She might not have memorized every detail the way Snow White had, but she knew fairykind better than most. The deev were supposed to be horned monsters, twisted creatures of such ugliness and evil that mortals fled in despair. Creatures who tortured their victims or crushed them with their bare hands.

Zestan moved with such grace as to make Talia appear clumsy, and her voice was song. "What are you?" Roudette demanded.

The shadows snapped outward, then fell away.

Zestan was taller than any human, with pearl skin. Elongated ears poked through ebony hair. A green jewel hung from a silver chain around her neck, similar to the one Naghesh wore. She was dressed in a violet tunic that clung to her form, a body that seemed neither male nor female. From Zestan's back stretched brown-feathered wings, so broad they would have struck the walls if fully extended.

She—he?—was beautiful. Too beautiful. Her face was too perfect, her body without a single flaw. She seemed less a living, breathing thing than an artist's masterpiece come to life.

Zestan's smile held genuine warmth. "I've plans for you as well, Roudette. The Wild Hunt—"

Roudette grabbed the arrow in her side. "I'll kill myself before I let you turn me into one of them."

"Go ahead." Zestan's smile never changed. "Dead or alive makes no difference to the Hunt, but that's not what I meant. The Wild Hunt was created by lesser fairies, and they are flawed. Limited to the darkness, burdened by the remnants of their humanity. Soon they will no longer be of use to me. I would make you the first of a new hunt. A band formed by peri magic. *Angels*, perfect and without limits."

"So the stories were wrong," said Roudette. "It wasn't the deev who meant to conquer and destroy this world. It was you."

"Oh, no. The deev are evil, brutish things. Strong and cruel. Like yourself, in many ways."

Roudette caught herself relaxing, lured by the gentleness of Zestan's voice. She twisted the arrow, using the pain to help her focus.

"We protected this land," Zestan said. "We saved the people from the deev. We fought and we died, all in the hopes that the people would grow and redeem themselves, and in doing so earn redemption for us as well."

"You sound like a preacher." The words were the same ones her father had spoken, but never had his voice carried such sorrow and pain.

"We were cast out of Heaven for our cowardice." Zestan's wings shivered. "Banished to this world for failing to fight in the uprising, and sentenced to watch over and protect your race until we earned forgiveness. Only then would we be welcomed back home."

Roudette had heard variations of this lie from the fairy church ever since she was a child. "You actually believe this?"

"Not anymore." Zestan was no longer smiling, and her words chilled Roudette. "*We saved this world.* Do you know how many of our kind died against the deev? How many of us were tortured and maimed, imprisoned in cages and left to wither into nothingness? We gave you freedom."

"I thought it was humans who fought the deev," Roudette said.

"Girded with *our* power." Zestan's wings snapped out, then slowly settled behind her like a feathered cape. "All these years we've tried to guide you, until one by one we fell into despair and retreated to our mountains to sleep. I've tried to rouse them, but the loss of hope casts a curse as potent as the one that struck Sleeping Beauty. They choose to sleep until humanity finds peace or until this world comes to an end. Would you care to wager which will come first?"

"You're alone?" Roudette tried to keep the hope from her voice. A single peri couldn't fight all of Arathea. Once the people learned the truth, they might still destroy her.

"I'm tired." Zestan spoke plainly, the weight of her desolation striking Roudette like a blow. "We will never return home. If paradise is forbidden to us, then I will remake this land into paradise."

She took the zaraq weight from Naghesh and examined it. "For a year Naghesh and I worked to duplicate this poison."

"Why?" Roudette asked, genuinely curious. "You're peri. I thought you could wave your hand and crush this entire palace to dust. Why go to such lengths?"

"I could destroy Lakhim and all who serve her," Zestan said, "but it would turn this nation against me. Better to let them believe a deev has escaped and loosed this chaos on the world. When the time comes, I will break Talia's curse myself. Her story will end the way it always should have ended. Talia will return to lead Arathea."

"Under your control," Roudette said, looking to Naghesh.

"An elegant plan, don't you think?" said Naghesh. "We don't even need to waste an assassin this time. Once we send Talia into the palace, I'll force her to poison herself and trigger the curse."

"War would have come eventually," said Zestan. "Fairies against humans. How many would have died on both sides? All fairykind watched what happened in Lorindar, how the humans forced my descendants into their treaty, imprisoning them in the middle of their island. The spread of the fairy church, the original curse against Talia and her family, these are only a few of the steps we've taken to prevent such a thing from ever happening again, but it's not enough."

Her eyes were so wide, shining like black pearls. "My

kin may have turned away from this world, but I will not. There will be no war. There will be only paradise, and you will be a part of it."

Zestan actually believed what she was saying. Believed it and wanted Roudette to believe as well. Roudette had seen it many times growing up. Her father had been like that. So convinced of his own righteousness he thought simply pronouncing those beliefs to the world would be enough to persuade all who listened.

"The people will fight you," Roudette said. "There will always be wolves."

"The wolves shall bow down before the angels," Zestan responded. "If they refuse, the angels will destroy them."

Roudette closed her eyes. She had never won an argument with her father, either.

CHAPTER 22

THE WILD HUNT CLOSED IN FROM ALL SIDES of the garden. Danielle thought about fleeing back through the pipe, but the hunters would only catch them. There were so many, bodies pressed together until she couldn't see the walls beyond. So Danielle waited, sword held ready.

"I could summon the dwarves," Snow offered.

"Not yet." Danielle doubted Snow had the strength to call up her demonic helpers. Even if she could, Danielle wasn't convinced they would be strong enough to fight the Wild Hunt.

She was surprised to see women among the hunters. Though fewer in number, their appearance varied as much as the men's. One wore hide armor trimmed in brown fur, while another rode bare-chested, carrying only an enormous wooden spear. A third wore a long Hiladi hunting jacket, broad-shouldered and trimmed in copper.

Danielle lowered her weapon. "I would speak with you." She searched them all, trying to identify a leader. Did anyone from the original Hunt still survive?

"What are you doing?" Snow whispered.

"Do you remember what Mother Khardija said at the temple?" she asked. "That the Hunt sometimes spares those with the courage to face them?"

"I remember it's a stupid thing to risk your life on," Snow said. "I never should have translated that for you."

Danielle managed a smile.

A man garbed in green rode forward. A golden horn hung at his side, and he carried a simple wooden longbow. His horse was a sooty chestnut, as though black ash had been sprinkled over the animal's back and sides. Both horse and rider studied Danielle, though neither one so much as breathed.

She sheathed her sword and stepped forward, drawing on all of her training to present herself as calm and unafraid. "How long have you been this way?"

They stared. For a moment, Danielle feared the Wild Hunt, like everyone else in this country, simply didn't understand her language.

"How long since you were truly alive and free?" she asked. She could make rats understand her. Surely she could do the same with the Wild Hunt. "How long?"

The hunter's bald scalp wrinkled ever so slightly. "We've no memories of our lives before."

Danielle smiled. Despite everything, she found herself ridiculously pleased to hear her own tongue. The Wild Hunt knew no boundaries, and from what Snow said, they were in many ways a single creature. If one of their number spoke a language, they would all know it.

She could feel Snow pressing closer, her back to Danielle's as the rest of the Hunt moved inward. Their glow had faded with the rising sun, but Danielle could still see the moonlight shining from his skin.

"Zestan promised you freedom," Danielle guessed. "That's how she controls you. Night has passed, but you remain."

"She has given us the freedom of the moon," the hunter said. "To carry its light. Soon we will once again ride when and where we choose."

"Where you choose?" Danielle repeated. "You ride

where Zestan sends you, doing her bidding. Instead of being bound to the darkness, you would be slaves to a fairy master, hunting her prey."

He lowered his bow. "You offer us a better bargain? You wouldn't be the first to beg for your lives."

"Not to beg. To give you a choice." Danielle stepped closer, trying to reach past the fairy curse and speak to whatever trace of mortality remained. "You weren't always like this. You used to be free to roam the world. Wild and unfettered, serving no one. Now you run and fight and die at Zestan's whim."

"If you get the chance, ask where they came from," Snow said eagerly. "Scholars have spent centuries trying to trace the origin of the Wild Hunt, but nobody knows for certain. If you could learn which country they—"

Danielle glared, and she fell silent. "You wear the shapes you had in life. Some part of you remembers that life."

"Those days are past." The huntsman nocked an arrow, each movement slow and deliberate. "The man I used to be is long forgotten from this world. All that remains is the consequence of his foolish pride."

"That's not true," Danielle said. "The pride also remains. I see it when I look into your eyes. You could regain that pride again. Run free, answering to neither man nor fairy. Tall and free and proud."

"You have courage, though your words cannot change what we are," the hunter said. "Perhaps Zestan will allow you to join us."

Danielle blinked. "I'm sorry, but what makes you think I was talking to you?"

The hunter hesitated, confusion crinkling his brow.

Remember and be free! Danielle stepped forward, reaching toward the horse and silently urging with all of her strength. *Go!*

The horse turned and leaped away, nearly spilling the rider. Horse and hunter alike vanished into flaming shadow. The rest of the Hunt followed, disappearing into the moonlight.

Snow whistled. "Zestan is going to be so mad at you."

Danielle wiped her palms on her clothes. Her heart drummed in her chest. "Is the Wild Hunt known for holding grudges?"

"I'll strengthen the wards when we get home," Snow promised.

"We still have to get past the ghosts."

Snow was shaking her head. "They're gone too."

"How?" Danielle spun.

Snow pointed toward the walls. "I'm not sure. I can feel a handful scattered throughout the palace, but I think Zestan sent the rest into the desert. She might have noticed our reinforcements gathering."

In which case everyone Muhazil and Lakhim sent to help would be riding into an ambush. Danielle grabbed Snow's hand and pulled her through the garden.

Roudette was dying.

If not for the magic of her cape, she might have already succumbed, but there were limits even to the cape's strength. Blood stuck her shirt to her skin. The arrow in her side scraped her ribs with every breath. The sounds of her body filled her ears: the pounding of her blood, the gritted gasps, the muffled cries of pain. Zestan and Naghesh were distant presences, their voices rising and falling like the waves of the ocean.

This whole place stank of death and fairies. Roudette could smell them all. Zestan's ghost slaves. The Wild Hunt, little better than ghosts themselves. And Roudette herself, soon to follow her grandmother.

Roudette clenched her jaws as Naghesh rolled her over. The troll's thick fingers pushed Roudette's hair out of her face, tracing the lines of her face. "'Twas a potent curse that created the Wild Hunt. It will take time to prepare her."

"We may not have as much time as we expected."

Zestan's wings snapped out, startling Roudette into alertness. Zestan circled Talia. "Your little army is not unexpected. I sent my ghosts to patrol the desert the moment Naghesh captured you. But you found a way to sneak your friends into the palace, haven't you? Who among them has the strength to banish my hunters? Was it the witch? She must be powerful indeed."

"How?" Roudette croaked. No magic known to man could turn away the Wild Hunt, and the hunters feared nothing, not even death. Roudette had spent her life fighting the fey, striking the Wild Hunt when they crossed paths. Never had she accomplished anything save to kill the occasional hunter. Yet if Zestan was telling the truth, Snow and Danielle had sent the entire Hunt away. Roudette had underestimated them.

"Prepare a fairy ring," said Zestan. "I don't know what they've done, but we may need to use Sleeping Beauty sooner than planned."

With that the peri swept from the room, shadows peeling from the wall to cloak her in darkness. Naghesh dragged Roudette into the center of the library. She kicked an old table aside, clearing space for her fairy ring. She set her staff against the wall and picked up a book. Half the yellowed pages fell like leaves. With a touch of her finger, she set the book alight and held it as green fire enveloped the pages.

"That should work." She dropped the book and stamped out the flames, then began collecting others, laying them out in a circle. She had only set out half of the ring when she straightened, her warty face compressing into a scowl. "Who's there?"

Roudette spotted them at the same time as Naghesh: two lizards the color of sand, about the length of her arm, crawling along the wall.

"How kind of Zestan to send me a snack." Naghesh reached for one, but a spark leaped from the lizard to her fingertips. She jumped back, sucking her fingers.

The lizards dropped to the ground, bodies shifting and growing. "Why do trolls always try to eat us?" Snow asked as the scales of her face melted away. "Are we really that tasty?"

Danielle drew her sword and attacked in a single motion, slicing upward and nearly catching Naghesh's chin with her blade.

"You're the ones, eh?" Naghesh lunged for her staff, but Danielle was faster, swinging her sword against the staff hard enough to crack the wood. A steel snowflake sank into Naghesh's shoulder.

She grunted and pulled the snowflake loose. Dark blood dripped down her arm. "Very well, then," she muttered.

Roudette tried to warn them, but she couldn't form the words. Talia attacked Snow from behind, unleashing a flurry of punches too fast for Roudette to follow. Roudette doubted Snow even knew what had happened. Talia backed away, allowing Snow to slump to the ground.

"Talia, it's us," Danielle said.

"Magnificent, isn't she?" Naghesh asked, stepping back to allow Talia to reach Danielle. "As close to fairy as any human has ever come."

Danielle kept her sword pointed at Talia, who circled to one side.

Roudette closed her eyes. *Grandmother give me strength.* She reached around her leg. The tip of the hunter's arrow was sticky with Roudette's blood. She tried to pull it free, but it refused to move. That left only one option.

She unfastened her cape and yanked it over the arrow in her side. Every movement left her dizzy with pain, but she managed to pull it around so the fur faced outward. She grabbed the edges and tugged the cape tight, trying to trigger its magic.

She reached up to draw the hood over her head, and her body began to change. She screamed as her bones ground against the wood of the hunter's arrows.

Naghesh hauled her upright and ripped the cape away in the middle of her transformation. The pain nearly made her pass out as her body slipped back into its normal shape.

Naghesh tore the cape free, wrenching the arrow in Roudette's side. "Zestan wanted to keep this. Me, I think we'd be better off dropping it into the deepest ocean." She bundled the cape into a ball and tossed it aside, out of Roudette's reach. She dropped Roudette to the ground.

Behind her, Talia had slipped past Danielle's guard. Danielle's sword clinked as it hit the floor. Danielle did her best to evade Talia, backing away and trying to keep tables and shelves between herself and Talia. Without her weapon, she wouldn't last long.

Roudette clutched the arrow in her leg. She hadn't completed the change to wolf form, but it had been enough. As her body shrank and shifted, it had bent the arrows with it. Without the wolf's strength, they probably would have just torn through her body. Thanks to her grandmother's gift, she had felt one of the arrows snap within her.

Roudette slid the point and shaft free. Naghesh had turned her attention back to Talia, and why not? Roudette was all but dead, and Naghesh had taken away her cape. What possible threat could she pose?

With a feral smile, Roudette slammed the broken arrow into the back of Naghesh's knee. The troll screamed and swung a fist the size of a tree stump, but Roudette fell back, allowing the blow to pass over her head.

"Kill her!" Naghesh shouted.

Talia obeyed at once, turning away from Danielle and walking toward Roudette. Talia had picked up Danielle's sword, but she didn't bother to use it. In Roudette's current state, even a crippled child could have beaten her.

Talia pressed a heel against Roudette's throat. A good choice. A single kick would finish Roudette off, or she could just bear down, letting her weight crush Roudette's windpipe.

Roudette saw a blur of red, and Danielle crashed into Talia, knocking them both to the ground. Danielle clung hard, wrapping Roudette's cape around Talia's body.

Talia's struggles stopped. She rose slowly, one hand holding the cape in place, the other grasping Danielle's sword.

Naghesh limped back a step. "Kill them both."

Talia pulled the cape over her other shoulder, brushing her hand over the runes on the hem. "I watched them carry the bodies of my family onto the funeral barge," Talia said softly. "My parents. My brothers and sister. Everyone I had ever known. Dead, because of your curse."

"We made you what you are today." Naghesh's staff was cracked, but Roudette could smell the power still contained in the wood. It grew into a gold-pointed spear, which Naghesh jabbed at Talia. "We made you great. Just as we will make Arathea great under your rule, Princess. As it was meant to be."

Talia walked forward. Naghesh jabbed her spear. Talia turned sideways and snatched the shaft. A swing of Danielle's sword splintered the spear.

Naghesh's eyes widened. She tried a spell, and the air rippled around Talia, but once again Roudette's cape protected her from the troll's magic.

Naghesh attacked again, swinging a fist the size of a club. Talia caught the blow on her forearm and rammed Danielle's sword through Naghesh's stomach. She tossed the troll against the wall. Her next swing cut Naghesh's head from her body.

Roudette smiled. Naghesh had been dead the moment Talia donned the cape. With the strength of the wolf combined with Talia's speed and grace, few things in this world could stop her.

She wondered whether her family waited for her to

join them. Despite everything, a part of her wanted to cling to the lessons of her childhood. To believe that the souls of her grandmother, her parents, and her brother all lived on, that their deaths had been simply another step on their eternal journey. It would be especially good to see Jaun, to finally be able to ask his forgiveness for failing to save him.

A lifetime ago, Roudette's grandmother had given the wolfskin to her, hoping Roudette could succeed where she herself had failed. Roudette lay back and closed her eyes. "Good hunting, Talia."

The cape was heavier than Talia had expected, particularly the hood, which was lined with the flattened features of the wolf's head.

She had felt the cape's power the instant Danielle wrapped it around her body. Naghesh's magic had been like the clamor of a thousand voices all crying out, filling her mind until she could hear nothing else, until only the voices were real. The cape had brought silence, silence and relief so great she could have wept.

Talia stared at the troll's headless body. She had killed Naghesh with hardly a thought. "I could get used to this cape."

She only wished the fight hadn't been so quick. Naghesh deserved to suffer for what she had done.

"Are you all right?" Danielle asked.

"The cape blocked Naghesh's magic. Thank you." Talia turned away from Naghesh. Danielle's face was bloody, one eye swollen. "What happened—" She frowned. "I did that to you."

"*Naghesh* did this." Danielle crouched over Snow, helping her to sit up. Snow didn't appear as badly battered, but her eyes were shut. She groaned and tried to push Danielle's hand away.

"Snow?" Talia dropped the sword and knelt beside them. "What did I do to her?"

"Not you. Snow pushed herself too hard," Danielle said.

"Nonsense," Snow mumbled. "I pushed just the right amount."

"I'm sorry." Talia scooped Snow into her arms. Her weight was nothing. "Where's Zestan?"

"Probably summoning the Wild Hunt back to the palace." Danielle retrieved her sword and checked the door. Though she sounded calm, Talia could smell her nervousness. Another side effect of the cape, no doubt. "I sent the Hunt away, but it won't last long."

"She knows about the Kha'iida." Talia frowned, trying to remember. Everything since Naghesh took control of her body was like a dream. Or what she remembered dreams to have been like, at any rate. It had been so long. "We have to get out of this room."

"The ghosts." Snow's eyes twitched, never focusing on any one point. "You have to take them from her."

Talia stared down at her. "I've committed thievery plenty of times, but I've never stolen a ghost."

"You can steal these." Snow leaned her head against Talia's shoulder. "You have to reach the Kha'iida. Warn them that Zestan knows. Wait for the proper moment, then turn the ghosts against the Wild Hunt."

"First I get you out of here," Talia said.

"No time." Snow closed her eyes. "The Wild Hunt is already on their way."

Talia swore and headed for the doorway. "Danielle, get Snow somewhere safe and stay hidden."

"Safe?" Danielle arched an eyebrow. "Where exactly—"

"Zestan doesn't care about you. She wants me." Talia set Snow down, steadying her until she regained her balance. She slipped Snow's knife from its sheath. While not as powerful as Danielle's sword, that dagger had power of its own, and Talia suspected she would need all the help she could get. "May I?"

"Will you let me buy that dragon?"

Talia grinned and swapped Snow's knife with one of her own.

"What about Roudette?" Danielle asked.

Talia glanced back. Roudette appeared smaller without her cape. Smaller and older, scarred from a lifetime of fighting. "Tell the Kha'iida to take her to the desert. Lay her out with her weapons in her hands, her eyes open to the sky to help her spirit find its way."

"She killed so many people."

"So have I."

"Not like this. Not for money, or for pleasure."

"I could have." Talia pulled the hood over her head. "I know what it's like to lose everything and everyone you ever knew. The temple took me in. Faziya taught me to feel joy again. And then Queen Bea found me. Roudette . . . she had no one."

"She looks almost peaceful," Danielle said.

Talia took Danielle's sword in one hand, Roudette's hammer in the other. "That's because she knew what I intend to do to Zestan."

CHAPTER 23

TALIA TORE THROUGH THE PALACE. Zestan had left the occasional ghost behind, but Talia dodged past them before they could strike. This wasn't like Snow's magic, transforming only the shape of her body. Roudette's cape joined her to the wolf, merging two spirits into one and combining Talia's mind with the instincts of the wolf.

Wind rushed through her fur. She could hear Zestan's summons, calling to the Wild Hunt. She could smell the fairy magic permeating the place that had once been Talia's home. She felt the ghosts before she saw them, their mere presence causing her hackles to rise.

Faster than any horse she crossed the courtyard. She leaped through the broken gates and sprinted into the desert. The sun had risen, warming her body as she crossed the dry lakebed. Dead vines cracked beneath her paws.

She could hear the howls behind her now. Whatever Danielle had done to send the Wild Hunt away, it wasn't enough to hold them against Zestan's call.

A part of her wanted to turn and fight, to face the enemy the wolfskin had been created to kill. Instead, she ran faster, wind roaring in her ears. She felt almost as if she were flying over the desert.

She scented them the moment she crested the first

hill, smelling of sweat and old leather. Lakhim's men gathered with the Kha'iida, more than a hundred strong. Talia growled deep in her chest at the sight of the white-and-green livery of Queen Lakhim.

As she watched, a streak of black resolved into a stallion carrying three more Kha'iida warriors. The men leaped from the horse's back to join their fellows. Talia's growl grew louder. The ebony stallion belonged to *her* family, not Lakhim's.

The stallion vanished. The rest of the men were turning toward the palace. They could hear the howls of the Hunt as well.

Talia sat and dug her teeth into the skin, tugging and biting until she found the seam running down her chest. One of the Kha'iida had already spotted her. By the time she removed the skin, she was surrounded. She settled the cape around her shoulders and stood.

One of Lakhim's people rushed her, thrusting a sword at her chest. Talia slapped the flat of the blade and back-handed him to the ground. "Zestan knows you're here. We attack now."

"Talia?" Muhazil's lips pressed together as he took in the cape. "What?"

"Zestan summoned the Hunt. You can hear—" She stopped to sniff the air. "Faziya?"

"She insisted on coming," said Muhazil. "I've ordered her to stay out of the fighting, but she said she could help to heal the wounded."

"And you allowed it?" Talia took a step, but caught herself. She wanted to grab Muhazil, to throw him to the ground and break him. "*She's* wounded."

"She's Kha'iida," he said, a rueful smile on his face.

Talia drew Danielle's sword in one hand, Roudette's hammer in the other, trying not to think about that. There was no time to send Faziya away. The only way to protect her now was to make sure the Wild Hunt never reached these hills. "Prepare your men."

The Wild Hunt rode a path of smoke and moonlight as
they thundered across the desert. Zestan's magic cloaked
each one in night and moonlight, giving them freedom to
ride beneath the morning sun.

Zestan would be watching, as would her ghosts. Talia licked her lips, which were cracked and dry from the
desert air. If Snow was wrong, this would be a short-
lived battle. As the warriors formed ranks behind her,
she raised her sword and shouted, "I am Talia Malak-el-
Dahshat." Could the ghosts even hear her? "You came
to this palace to save me."

The words tasted like tainted meat. To *save* her? They
had come to claim her as a trophy, to steal her family's
power. They were little better than Zestan, thieves who
meant to take Arathea from its rightful rulers.

"Protect me now!" she yelled. "From the Wild Hunt.
From Zestan. Protect me and those who fight beside
me! Protect Arathea!"

Prince Amabar was the first to cross the low wall surrounding the palace. His movements were uncertain as
he strode into the sunlight. Talia could hear the warriors muttering to themselves as the ghost prince strode
forward.

Talia swore. The Wild Hunt would be upon them in
moments, and she had only a single ghost who looked
too lost to fight. She called again, with no better luck
than before. "Snow, you said the ghosts would follow
me."

"If we're to attack, we should do it before the Hunt
reaches the hills," said Muhazil.

"If we attack now, they'll slaughter you all." Talia
scowled at the lone ghost below. "Zestan has an army
of the dead waiting beyond that wall. If they join us, we
might have a chance against the Hunt."

A middle-aged man wearing the green and gold sash
of a raqeem, or field commander, approached from the
other side. This would be the leader of Lakhim's forces,

then. "*Now* is the time to strike, before the Wild Hunt has time to prepare."

"These aren't bandits and thieves," Talia snapped. "The Wild Hunt will slaughter you all. Now shut up and let me do this."

The raqeem's hand went to his sword. "I take no orders from murderers. You are no princess here."

"She risked her life trying to protect Arathea." Muhazil raised his sword. To Talia, he said, "The Hunt will not wait. Summon your ghosts if you can." He slashed the blade through the air and ran. The rest of the Kha'iida followed, shouting as they charged the Wild Hunt.

The raqeem ordered his own men to follow, though Talia noticed he allowed the Kha'iida to keep the lead. The Wild Hunt hit hard, trampling through the Kha'iida and coming about for a second charge. Hounds attacked as the hunters spread out to surround the group. Their weapons lashed out, and humans began to fall. Even the best mortal fighters wouldn't last long against the mounted fairy warriors of the Hunt.

Talia turned her attention back to the palace and Prince Amabar, the only one to respond to her call. The only one to remember her.

She bowed her head, thinking of her mother. Beautiful and proud, her every gesture slow and confident. Her mother had lived in the shadow of her husband, but no one who looked upon her ever questioned the strength and power she carried, even if that power was rarely used.

Her mother wouldn't have raised her sword like a common soldier. She was queen of Arathea, and when she spoke, her word was law.

Talia lowered her weapons and walked toward the palace, doing her best to ignore the battle below. "My bloodline runs back to the very founding of this land. Obey me, or forsake the honor of your families' names. The Wild Hunt threatens your nation. They threaten your rightful princess." Another ghost joined Amabar, then a third. "You are princes of Arathea, children of the desert, and your home is under attack. Defend it!"

The dead surged from the palace, Amabar in the lead. Lakhim's troops had already hit the Hunt from behind, forcing them to widen their ring, and now the ghosts struck from the opposite flank. Hounds and hunters turned against the ghosts, who fought back in spectral silence.

Talia was halfway down the hill before she knew she was moving. Each step was longer than the last, until she felt as though she flew over the desert like the huma bird of old. The wolf's eagerness left no room for fear or hesitation. She raised her weapons, laughing as she reached the Hunt. She jumped over a fallen Kha'iida and swung at the closest hunter.

He parried the first blow. His horse reared, hooves kicking at Talia's skull.

Danielle's sword cut the leg from the horse. It fell, and Talia finished off the rider with Roudette's hammer. She leaped to intercept the next hunter. There was no thought. No strategy. Allies were nothing more than obstacles blocking her path to the next enemy. Only when the ground itself shook did she pause in her rampage.

Injured men cried out in pain. Many lost their balance as the trembling grew more violent.

Talia blinked and backed toward the edge of the fighting. She wiped her face on her shoulder. The Wild Hunt had been hurt, but for every hunter who fell, three humans lay unmoving in the sand. The ghosts continued to fight, but their numbers had diminished as well.

The hunters retreated toward the palace. Talia started to follow, but one of the Kha'iida caught her arm from behind. Talia recognized Muhazil by smell. Muhazil clutched a wound in his side, but he still stood. His eyes were wide, and he stared at her as though looking upon a monster. "You fight like the deevslayers of old."

Talia pointed toward the palace where Zestan stood atop the central wall, an angel shadowed in darkness. The air around her rippled, as though burned by her mere presence.

"Enough!"

The ghosts continued to harry the Wild Hunt, but they vanished as they passed over the fairy wall. The humans stood frozen by the power of Zestan's voice.

Talia swallowed. More than half the men who had attacked the Hunt lay dead or dying, and she didn't see a single warrior who had escaped injury. Looking back, she saw archers standing ready atop the hill. These would be late arrivals to the battle, brought by Lakhim's ebony horse.

Zestan raised her hands. "Bring me the one called Sleeping Beauty, and I will be merciful."

Muhazil touched his chest. "That is no deev."

"No," said Talia. Sweat soaked her robes and stung her eyes. She was breathing hard, from excitement and eagerness as much as fatigue.

"A peri." His face slackened into an expression of awe.

"A peri who turned the Wild Hunt against the Kha'iida," Talia reminded him.

Another Kha'iida stepped forward. "The peri were said to sit at the right hand of God. If she demands the princess, perhaps we should—"

"You're welcome to try." Talia raised her sword and smiled.

Thunder echoed through the desert, so close it was as if the sky itself had cracked overhead. The air grew still, and Talia's skin tingled. A burned-metal smell made her wrinkle her nose.

"Peri magic," breathed Muhazil.

In the distance to the right, the sand began to swirl, growing higher as Talia watched. Soon a pillar of whirling sand danced toward them.

The warriors whispered among themselves. Talia could smell their fear, like sweat and piss. A second whirlwind joined the first, then a third. All around them, the desert reached up, raising towers of sand that seemed to pierce the sky itself. They writhed like living things, bending and bowing as they crept closer, swallowing all in their path. Entire hills were torn to nothingness faster than Talia could see.

Talia raised her sword. She ignored the whirlwinds, concentrating only on the Wild Hunt arrayed behind the fairy wall, waiting. "Help me pierce their lines. If I can reach Zestan—"

He stabbed his weapon into the sand and stepped close, gripping her arm. "Princess, your ghosts are beaten. Our people cannot survive another battle with the Hunt."

"You don't have to survive! Just get me through. I won't let her take Arathea." She stopped herself. Muhazil was right. All she wanted was to fight until either she or Zestan lay dead. She couldn't even distinguish the wolf's anger from her own anymore.

"If you flee, your cape's magic might allow you to escape," Muhazil said. "The speed of the wolf—"

"I've been running and hiding since I awoke." Talia touched her throat. All that held the cape in place was a thick tie of folded velvet. "Zestan wasn't afraid of me," she whispered, frowning. "Or of Roudette. But she worked to turn the rest of Arathea against you. She sent the Wild Hunt to attack your tribes. We thought it was because she was a deev . . . Muhazil, I need your knife."

His face tightened. He knew which knife Talia meant. "That weapon has been passed down for more than fifty generations."

"*Why* does Zestan fear the Kha'iida?" Talia handed him the glass sword without waiting for an answer. "This sword belongs to my friend Danielle. It's as precious to her as your knife is to you. Please see that she receives it back." Unspoken was the assumption that any of them would survive.

Muhazil reached into his robe. Talia moved so her body would block Zestan's view as she took the crystal knife from his hand. She tucked it away, then drew Snow's knife.

Talia flipped open the mirror at the crossguard. "I hope you can hear me," she whispered. "I need your help."

"I offer you one final chance," Zestan shouted. Flames the color of blood grew within the whirlwinds. Smoke darkened the sky overhead.

"Dammit, Snow, wake up or we're all dead."

"Stop yelling at me." Snow's voice was strained. "What's happening out there? It sounds like thunder."

"You don't want to know. Are you strong enough for one more spell?" If Talia hadn't already known how drained Snow was, the lack of an indignant response would have told her. "If I had any other ideas, I wouldn't ask."

Snow gave a weak laugh. "You see? All that fighting, and you still turn to me and my magic in the end."

Talia held her cape shut as she approached the palace. The hood blocked her vision to either side, shutting out the burning whirlwinds of peri magic that threatened the others. That threatened Faziya. She stopped herself from turning back. Why hadn't Faziya had the sense to stay behind? If Talia failed—

If that happened, at least she wouldn't be around long enough to wallow in guilt or grief.

The Wild Hunt waited to escort her inside. Many were still mounted, mostly those in older armor. Talia wondered if there was any truth to the rumor that the original hunters would be destroyed if they ever dismounted. She fought the urge to drag one from his horse and find out.

Instead, she stopped at the doorway to the palace, reaching out to touch one of the old statues. The stone was rough, cracked and pitted from age. As a child, she had named the statues Qazella and Anil, "Big Nose" and "Ugly." Her father had *not* been pleased when he overheard those nicknames.

Talia followed the hunters up the staircase. She and her brothers used to compete with one another to see who could jump from the highest step. She smiled again, remembering the day those games had come to an end. She had been seven years old. It was the first time she learned her fairy gifts couldn't protect her from her own stupidity. Her broken leg had eventually healed. More important to young Talia, none of her brothers had dared to match her final leap.

The edges of the steps had crumbled with age. She glanced down into what had once been the great hall. Her father's hunting trophies used to decorate those walls. How many times had she and her brothers and sister snuck down to sit in their parents' thrones? She could hear her sister's voice, a perfect imitation of their mother, addressing the imaginary crowds.

There was no door at the top of the stairway. Nor were there guards, at least none Talia could see. Zestan stood on the wall, staring at the people below.

"I can't let them leave after seeing me," Zestan said. "But I will keep my word. In exchange for your surrender, I will spare their lives."

"That's your mercy?" Talia stepped forward, but two hunters cut her off. "What will you do, transform them into animals with no memories of who they were?"

"They will be safe, with neither fear nor worry. How many of your kind can say the same?"

Talia turned to look out at the sandstorms Zestan had raised. Despite their fury, the air here was still and silent, as if she had passed into another world when she entered the palace. "I suppose I should thank you."

"Indeed?" Zestan spread her wings.

"If not for you, I never would have found Naghesh." Had Talia's smile been any more wolfish, she would have grown fangs.

Zestan brushed a hand through the air. "Naghesh served her purpose. The poison is prepared. I can control you myself if I must, once we destroy that cape."

"I'm through being controlled," Talia said.

Zestan laughed, a sound so empty of joy she might as well have been weeping. "You plan to steal my victory by killing yourself?" She pointed to the hunters. "Fairy magic is stronger than death. Your suicide would delay matters, but a changeling raised on your blood would serve just as well. I've grown weary of waiting, though."

The hunters reacted as one, seizing Talia's arms and wrenching her hands out of her cape. She grunted in pain as her arms were bent back.

Zestan studied the crystal knife in Talia's right hand. "We created these blades. Did you think I wouldn't feel its presence?"

Talia reversed her hold on the knife and stabbed the tip into the hunter's wrist. There was no blood. She stabbed deeper, but the fingers gripping her arm merely clamped tighter. The hunter twisted. Even with the wolf's strength, she couldn't escape that hold. Her bones would snap before much longer. She tried one last time, shoving the knife as deep as she could.

The hunter's other hand closed over hers. He yanked the knife from her grip and shoved her to the ground.

"You have so much in common with the Lady of the Red Hood," Zestan said. "Such hatred. It killed her in the end."

Talia flexed her hand. The fingers were numb, and bloody blisters showed where the hunter had squeezed her wrist. She hugged the wrist close to her body, beneath the cape. "Hate was all the Hunt left her. It kept her alive. It gave her purpose."

Zestan took the knife from the hunter. Her smile disappeared. "What is this?" She raised the knife, and Snow's illusion fell away, revealing simple steel. The mirror at the crossguard was still exposed.

Talia's right hand shot out from the cape, throwing Muhazil's knife. At this distance, not even Zestan was fast enough to stop the blade from sinking into her chest. Zestan staggered, one hand coming up to touch the hilt.

The hunters grabbed her from either side, but she stepped back, ramming her elbows into their stomachs. The blows didn't do much, but the hunters bent over enough for her to reach up and catch the throat of the hunter to her right. She spun, slamming him into his companion.

They recovered quickly, but even as the rest of the Hunt moved toward her, the moonlight started to fade from their bodies. Talia ducked one attack, blocked a spear thrust with her forearm, and then they were gone.

Talia stood, rubbing her arm. Zestan's other spells were dying along with her. One by one, the towers of sand collapsed, sending clouds of dust out until they obscured everything below. Talia coughed as the sand billowed over the palace wall.

"Thank you, Snow," she whispered. Bending down, she yanked the knife from Zestan's chest. White cracks spiderwebbed the blade. As she straightened, pebbles of crystal fell away until only a single broken shard remained, jutting from the hilt. Muhazil would not be happy. She picked up Snow's knife as well, tucking it through her belt.

"I would have made Arathea great." Zestan shivered. "Just as we made you great. If not for us—" Her body tightened, wings stiffening beneath her.

"My parents trusted the fairies who spoke such words. Who offered to save me, to make me better than human." Talia bent down, grabbing Zestan's tunic in both hands. The peri was lighter than Talia expected. "Khardija. Faziya. Beatrice. Snow and Danielle. *They* made me who I am today. You just make me angry."

With those words, she threw Zestan's body from the wall, then went to scarch for her friends.

Chapter 24

"**S**NOW?" TALIA MADE HER WAY THROUGH empty hallways and abandoned rooms. The stables were a putrid mess of mud and decaying grass. A single whiff told her this must be where Naghesh had slept. She could smell traces of fairy magic, and she spied a handful of tiny animated wisps of wind and water cowering on the far side of the stables. None were strong enough to be a threat. "Danielle?"

The palace swallowed her shouts. She hurried through the garden, where Zestan's flowers had already begun to wilt in the sun.

"Talia!" Danielle's voice came from the northern wing.

Talia found them at the base of the broken windcatcher. Snow was leaning against Danielle for support, but they were both alive. Talia hurried to take Snow's other arm.

"I'm all right," Snow protested. "I can walk."

"I know," said Danielle. "You walked right into the wall, remember?"

Snow flushed. "I didn't think you saw that."

"What happened?" asked Talia. "Are you—"

"What happened is you yelling at me through my mirror," Snow complained, "demanding an illusion with no time to prepare." She squinted at the sky. "The moon is gone. I assume that means Zestan is dead?"

"Your magic worked," said Talia. "Thank you."

"Of course it worked." Snow stumbled over a half-buried stone. The collapse of Zestan's whirlwinds had dumped several dunes worth of sand. "Did you have to get sand all over everything when you killed her? I've never felt this gritty in my life."

Outside, the survivors had split into two groups. Many of the Kha'iida were gathered around Zestan's body, singing a deep, somber melody that reminded Talia of a mourning chant. She recognized neither the tune nor the language. Farther away, people worked to treat the injured. Talia searched until she spied Faziya.

"I think I'd like to go home now," Snow said.

Talia smiled and helped Danielle lower Snow to the ground, settling her in the shade against the wall. When she straightened, Muhazil was coming toward her. He carried Danielle's sword.

"A magnificent weapon," he said, offering it to Danielle.

Talia translated, and Danielle bowed as she took back her sword. "How do you say thank you?"

"Kuhran," said Talia. Danielle repeated the word.

Talia turned to watch as the Kha'iida took turns kneeling before Zestan's body. One by one, they each used their knives to cut off a lock of hair, which they set in the sand beside the peri.

"She meant to enslave you all," Talia said.

"I know." Muhazil touched the short hank of hair at his neck. "The peri founded the Kha'iida tribes. They protected us from the deev. We grieve for what she was, not what she became."

"You barbarians have some strange customs." Talia handed him the remains of the crystal knife. "I'm sorry. I didn't realize—"

He dismissed her apology with a flick of his hand.

"Each blade was meant to be used but once. Only by re-leasing all of their power can they overcome the strength of a deev." His voice softened. "Or a peri."

"What of the other peri?" Talia asked.

"We will send riders to the mountains," said Muhazil. "There are ancient roads leading to the green peaks, hidden to all but a handful of our people. Our seers will awaken the peri and tell them of Zestan's betrayal."

She could feel the wolf urging her to fight, to follow the Kha'iida back to the mountains and kill every last peri, to make certain they never again threatened Arathea. As far as she knew, the peri had never spread beyond the borders of this land. Destroying them here would end their threat forever. "If they're asleep, maybe you're better off leaving them that way. Zestan might not be the only one who's tired of waiting for redemption. Better still, if they're asleep, that means they're vulnerable . . ."

"Just as you and your family were?" Muhazil asked.

For a moment, Talia imagined she could see the hedge surrounding her, could hear the shouts of the sisters as they ran toward her. She exhaled slowly, pushing the memory from her mind. "You're right," she said softly. "Zestan's crimes are her own. I apologize."

"Should the deev ever return, we will need the peri again." He glanced at Zestan. "I admit, I'd prefer if they stayed in their mountains until that day comes."

Talia would have said more, but Faziya was hurrying toward her. Muhazil smiled and left without another word.

"You're mad," Talia said as she wrapped her arms around Faziya, lifting her into the air. "Your bandages are still spotted with blood, and you ride into the middle of battle?"

"Me? You attacked the Wild Hunt! You fought a peri!"

"I won, didn't I?" Talia kissed her.

Faziya returned the kiss with enthusiasm before pulling away. "Your hand. What happened?"

"I'll live." Talia took her arm. "Could you please look at Snow? She—"

Faziya was already moving. She crouched and held her palm in front of Snow's mouth, checking her breathing. Snow shoved the hand aside. Faziya made a scolding noise and felt Snow's cheeks, then her forehead.

"I'm just tired," Snow protested.

"You're cold. Your breathing is quick and shallow, and your pupils are too large." Faziya gently ran her fingers through Snow's hair. "This hard lump. This is where you injured your head?"

"I'll be fine as soon as I get some sleep." Snow covered her eyes with one hand. "Arathea is too bright."

"You need food and water to restore your strength," Faziya insisted. She pinched the back of Snow's hand. "You haven't been drinking enough. Your body needs more water in the desert." She turned away to shout at one of the other Kha'iida, telling him to bring a waterskin. To Snow, she added, "You know it's dangerous to sleep after an injury to the head."

"This isn't a new injury," Snow said. "It's more than a year old—"

"But never fully healed," Faziya countered. "You've aggravated it. You need rest, but not sleep."

Danielle leaned close to Talia. "Which one do you think will win?"

"I thought you couldn't understand Arathean," Talia said.

"No, but I know Snow's tone." Danielle glanced past Talia, and her smile vanished.

Talia turned to see more of Lakhim's soldiers approaching. A growl built in the back of her throat. The ebony horse must have continued to bring Lakhim's men. They now outnumbered the Kha'iida nearly two to one, and the newcomers were fresh and ready for battle. "Stay here."

Talia strode to meet them. She was unsurprised when Danielle followed.

The raqeem walked at the head of his men. His sash of rank was knotted around a gash in his thigh. He kept his hands open, away from his weapons. Little comfort, given that his men held spears and swords ready.

"Talia," said the raqeem. "Our orders are to bring you back to Queen Lakhim." He at least had the decency to sound apologetic.

Talia spread her arms and smiled. "Be my guest."

"Wait!" Muhazil moved to stand beside her. "This is Talia Malak-el-Dahshat. She risked her life to protect this land. She probably saved Lakhim's life."

"She murdered Prince Jihab," said the raqeem. "Whatever else she might have done, she must answer for that death."

Those Kha'iida who could fight were spreading out behind Talia, readying their weapons.

Talia still carried her own knives, but she didn't bother to draw them. Even with one hand injured, she could spring forward and break the raqeem's neck before anyone else reacted. She *wanted* to fight. Numbers made no difference. These men served Lakhim, the woman who had sentenced Talia to death. Whose family had taken everything Talia ever knew. Her nation, her heritage, even her children.

Zestan had been right. Arathea *would* follow Sleeping Beauty. Just as Rajil's guards had turned against their raikh to help Talia. Just as the Kha'iida gathered behind her now. One fight at a time, she could take Arathea back.

"What do you want?" asked Danielle. She hadn't even drawn her sword.

Talia's rage broke. If she fought, Danielle would be

caught in the middle. Faziya and Snow were farther back, but all it would take was a single clumsy shot with a bow to kill them both. Snow would try to fight, and who knew what would happen if she continued to push herself to use more magic.

Roudette had spent her life fighting. Talia didn't want to follow that same path.

Danielle must have read the answer in Talia's face. She stepped forward, putting a hand on Talia's shoulder. "Go with them."

"I can't—"

"Do you trust me?"

Talia glared. Danielle's smile was highly inappropriate for one standing between angry warriors.

"These soldiers are men of Arathea too," Danielle said. "Your people. I've watched you this past week, Talia. I know you don't want to fight them."

"I don't want to have my head cut off, either," Talia snapped.

"I won't let that happen."

The wolf's rage was building, urging Talia to attack. She pushed it back. "You've been spending too much time with Beatrice."

Danielle's smile grew.

Talia turned around, looking past the Kha'iida to Snow and Faziya. Danielle was right, damn her. To the raqeem, she said, "I'll go with you."

Muhazil started to protest, but Talia cut him off. "Your people have more important duties than to protect me."

She watched as two soldiers ran to fetch the ebony horse. The raqeem climbed onto the horse's bare back. Talia followed, watching Danielle closely. Danielle said nothing. She simply waited, lips twitching.

A second soldier mounted behind Talia. The raqeem kicked his heels into the horse's sides and shouted, "To the queen!"

Nothing happened. The raqeem kicked again and repeated his command, slightly flustered.

This time the horse did respond, but rather than vanishing into the wind, it trotted at a leisurely pace toward Danielle. She smiled and reached up to stroke the horse's head. "Talia, would you please translate for me?"

Talia looked at Danielle, then at the horse. Slowly, she too began to smile.

"Tell this man to stop yelling at his horse. Otherwise, I'll ask it to ride out to the middle of the ocean. I know *you* can swim."

Talia repeated Danielle's words. The ebony horse couldn't actually cross the ocean, but she doubted the raqeem would know that.

The raqeem straightened. "Who are you?"

"That makes no difference," said Danielle. "What matters is I've told your horse who Talia is. He knows his true master."

Talia pursed her lips. "I don't know what you're planning, but even if we steal the horse, Lakhim will never stop—"

"I've never stolen a thing in my life," Danielle protested. "Despite what my stepsisters used to say."

The raqeem reached for his sword. The ebony horse turned his head. A single red-jeweled eye flashed in the sun. Slowly, the raqeem removed his hand.

"Talia and I will speak to your queen," Danielle said.

He didn't move. Talia could have tossed him from the horse, but she restrained herself. "You were ordered to bring us to Lakhim. I give you my word we will go to her. Not to fight but to talk."

He twisted about, studying her for a moment, then climbed down from the horse. He barked an order at the other soldier, who followed.

"I assume the horse knows where to find Queen Lakhim?" Danielle asked.

"The palace," said the raqeem. "She returned home

as soon as she received word of Zestan's death." He glanced at the spot where Zestan had fallen.

Danielle climbed up behind Talia.

"Wait," said Faziya. She moved slowly, doing her best to hide her weakness. She stepped past both groups of warriors until she reached the horse. There, she looked up at Talia and said only, "Return to me."

Talia's throat knotted. "I will."

Faziya walked away without another word. Danielle whispered a command, and the desert vanished.

There was no wind. No sense of movement. Nothing but cold and darkness, lasting only long enough for Talia to wonder what might happen to one who jumped free before arriving at her destination.

Shouts erupted all around them as the horse trotted to a halt. Talia didn't bother to hide her smirk. "You told it to bring us to the throne room?"

Danielle shrugged. "I said to take us to Lakhim. Be thankful she wasn't using the privy."

Neither Talia nor Danielle moved as guards surrounded the horse. Queen Lakhim sat in the single throne in front of an abstract painting of the sun, as though she were the source of all light. Talia gritted her teeth. Her family had never stooped to such drama.

Burgundy carpeting covered the floors, woven with intricate geometric designs in gold and silver thread, now marred by large hoofprints. The pillars were trimmed in gold leaf, as were the arches supporting the high vaulted ceiling. Each section of the ceiling had been painted with an image of Lakhim's family.

Talia tensed as she spotted the portrait of Prince Jihab. The artist had painted him in front of the accursed hedge, sword gleaming in the sun as he prepared to cut his way into the palace.

Danielle touched Talia's arm and pointed to the right of the throne, where two children stood in the shadows.

Talia's nails dug into her fists. She could have passed her sons on the street and never would have recognized them, but who else could they be, dressed in the gold-and-green robes of nobility, their faces all but identical. They had their father's deep set eyes and angular jaw, but their faces were narrower, reminding Talia of her own brothers. Their hair was cut short, dark bangs swirling flat against their brows. She had no idea which twin was which.

"Talia." Lakhim spat the name as though it were a curse. The years as queen had taken their toll. Her hair was grayer, her face more wrinkled than Talia remembered. She stood with a slight hunch, making her appear shorter. She wore a golden circlet, the crown of the haishak, the regent for the princes.

The twins stared at Talia, fear and confusion plain on their young faces. They hadn't recognized Talia, but it was clear they knew her name.

Danielle jumped from the horse. "Lakhim, I am Danielle Whiteshore of Lorindar. I've come to discuss an end to your vendetta against Princess Talia."

Lakhim stared at Danielle, her expression stone. "This woman murdered my son."

Lakhim's speech was heavily accented, but she spoke the language of Lorindar well enough for Danielle to understand. Danielle met her glare without flinching. "And your assassin murdered my people. Her actions resulted in the death of my stepsister."

"Roudette was sent to retrieve a killer and a threat to Arathea." Lakhim glanced at Talia. "Apparently she failed."

"Shall we debate whose was the first sin, Lakhim?" Danielle strode forward. If Talia hadn't known her, she never would have seen how nervous Danielle was. Her tutelage under Queen Beatrice had paid off. "What of Talia's family, preserved with her behind the hedge?

Whose hand slit their throats as they slept, killing even the smallest child?"

Lakhim rose. "You dare—"

"Zestan is dead," Danielle said. "As is your assassin. Arathea has already jeopardized its friendship with Lorindar by sending a killer to our land. Would you sever that relationship altogether for the sake of vengeance?"

The queen clasped her hands together, changing tactics. "Lorindar is a beautiful nation, but a small one."

"True," said Danielle. "But Lorindar does not stand alone. Alynn and Francon of Lyskar recently found themselves in our debt. Not to mention our close ties to the undine."

Lakhim waved her men back a step. "You would enter my home and threaten my land? What makes you think I won't have you both killed for this intrusion?"

Talia brushed a hand over her cape. "What makes you think your men would survive such an attempt?"

"You won't." Danielle glanced at Talia, the warning obviously meant for her as well as Lakhim. Danielle raised her wrist, tapping the mirrored bracelet. "Not while my husband listens through this glass."

Lakhim studied them both. Talia could almost hear her calculating the odds. Finally, she brought her hands together and said, "So long as Talia lives, she is a threat to Arathea."

"Rescind the sentence on Talia." Danielle turned around, and for the first time her composure cracked. She mouthed the words *I'm sorry* before raising her head to say, "In exchange, Talia will renounce her claim to the throne of Arathea."

"No." Talia had expected something like this, but the whisper slipped out before she could stop herself.

"My son is dead. You would ask me to let his murderer go free?" Lakhim glanced at the princes. "You are

a mother yourself, Danielle. Could you forgive the one
who took your child away?"

"Will war bring him back?" Danielle countered.
"Will more death change what happened?" She stepped
forward, shedding her formal court manners. "I can't
imagine the grief you feel to this day. I have nightmares
about losing Jakob. But think of Arathea. Talia is a threat
because there are many who would follow her. Kill her,
and her fame only grows. But none can rally to a banner
that Talia herself refuses."

Lakhim turned to face Talia, formally acknowledging
her for the first time. "What do you say to this?" She
spat the words, not bothering to hide her hatred.

Talia couldn't answer. Her family had ruled Arathea
longer than any line in memory. What would her ancestors think if she were to hand everything over to the
very family who had plundered her home and stolen the
throne? Arathea should be hers, even if it took a lifetime to wrest it from Lakhim's power. It was Talia who
should sit on that throne.

"What do you want?" Danielle asked, just as she had
before.

Talia closed her eyes, thinking of Lorindar. Of rainy
mornings and bland food. Of Prince Jakob demanding
one more song from "Aunt Tala." Of Beatrice, and everything she had done for Talia over the years. Of Snow's
smile, her laughter that could fill a room.

She could kill Lakhim and escape. With her gifts and
Roudette's cape, none here could stop her. She could
take the crown . . . and she would spend the rest of her
days fighting to keep it. Warring against Lakhim's allies,
not to mention those fairies who had given their loyalty
to Zestan. "I accept the terms."

"Very well." Lakhim's eyes narrowed in triumph.
"Let us—"

"Under one condition." Talia stepped forward until
she stood as close to Lakhim as family. "While you were

busy hunting me and sending your assassin to Lorindar, Zestan spread her spies throughout the fairy church. She corrupted the raikhs and attacked the Kha'iida. Allow something like this to happen again, and I will return to Arathea to do what you can't and protect my people."

Talia spoke her final words more softly still, forcing Lakhim to lean forward to hear. "And should you or yours *ever* threaten me again, the last thing you see will be your blood spilling from your body, mixing with the red of my cape."

CHAPTER 25

TALIA AND DANIELLE FOLLOWED LAKHIM to her scrying pool, a small pond lined in mother-of-pearl deep in the heart of the palace. The room was circular, as was traditional, but instead of a garden, Lakhim had decorated the room as garishly as the rest. Statues filled the room, along with tapestries and carpeting in colors so bright they could have been fairy-made. There they waited while Lakhim summoned her mage, a human, gray-haired and heavyset.

"I thought Siqlah prohibited human magic?" Talia asked.

"*I* rule Arathea." The words were as sharp as any blade, rousing the wolf in Talia. "The church protests, but I remember what the fairies did. Do you?"

Talia snorted. "Is your pet mage the one who warned you of Zestan's plan?"

"No." Lakhim hesitated. "It was a priest of the fairy church, a naga, who first came to me. Zestan's influence was strong, but there are still those who believe in their duty to 'protect' us." She straightened. "I expect these coming years will see a schism within the church. I mean to encourage that split."

"Good." Turning the church against itself would weaken their power. "And the Kha'iida?"

Lakhim flicked her fingers. "They think themselves above my law. That they're above those of us who live in the cities. Let them solve their own problems."

Only Danielle's presence stopped Talia from punching the Queen of Arathea in the face. "The Kha'iida are the reason you still have your crown." She bared her teeth. "Their people have a term for those too ill-mannered to appreciate such a gift."

"My patience grows thin," Lakhim warned.

"And your words grow tiresome. If you had the courage to act, you'd have done so already."

After that, she waited in silence as the mage contacted the raikhs of Arathea, until the rulers of every city waited to hear Talia acknowledge Lakhim as queen.

The ritual was ancient, unchanged for more than a thousand years. Talia repeated them in a flat tone, barely hearing her own voice. Her eyes were fixed on the carpeting at her feet. Though the water came all the way to the gold lip at the edge of the pool, not a drop spilled onto the rich blue-and-purple carpet.

And then it was over. Given how many generations Talia's family had spent uniting Arathea under their rule, it took surprisingly little time for her to lose it all.

Talia stepped forward, peering into the water. She saw nothing but her own reflection, but she knew the raikhs were watching. She smiled. "Hello, Rajil. Don't think I've forgotten about you and your fairy friend."

The water rippled and went still.

"You are a commoner now," Lakhim said, clearly relishing her victory. "I'll thank you to cease your threats against my raikhs."

Talia shrugged. "Rajil plotted with Zestan against you. Maybe fortune will turn in my favor, and the two of you will end up killing each other."

Lakhim sighed. "Rajil is not the only one to choose Zestan over her own kind."

"Perhaps," said Talia. "But Rajil is the one who enslaved a friend of mine."

"I will deal with the raikhs." Lakhim started to say more, and then her eyes widened. "Mutal, no!"

Talia could already hear the boy's bare feet hitting the carpet as he ran through the room. She spun, and the blade that would have struck her back caught instead on her cape. Talia slapped his forearm, and the knife flew across the room. He cried out and backed away, clutching his arm. Talia stepped after him.

"Talia!" Danielle's voice was sharp as Talia had ever heard it. Talia stopped, doing her best to slow her breathing. Her fists unclenched, and she gradually allowed herself to relax. She looked past Mutal to his brother, who was hiding in the doorway.

The mage grabbed Mutal, pulling him close. Stopping him from trying to attack her again, or protecting him from Talia? Lakhim clapped her hands, and both twins jumped.

"Away, both of you." Lakhim's voice cracked like a whip. "Get yourselves to your room and stay there until I decide what to do with two princes who would stab a woman in the back."

"Wait." Talia checked her side. The knife hadn't even pierced the cape. She swallowed and took a step toward Mutal. "You know who I am."

"You killed our father." His voice was high-pitched, with only the faintest quaver.

"Yes."

From the doorway, Mahatal said, "Grandmother told us you meant to kill our family and take our crown. She named you a liar, no better than the deev."

Talia glanced at Lakhim, who raised her chin and returned Talia's gaze. "You should learn you can't always trust the gossip of old women."

"Why did you kill him?" Mutal demanded.

Talia closed her eyes, searching for answers that would

make sense to a child of eight. No matter what she told them of their father, of the slaughter of her own family, it wouldn't change the emptiness. It wouldn't heal their grief for a man they had never known. "Ask me again when you are both men," she said at last. "I will tell you the truth, if you choose to hear it."

"*Your* truth." Mahatal spat. "You're a filthy, lying—"

Mutal punched his brother on the arm. "Shut up! I want to know."

"*You* shut up," Mahatal shot back, but fell silent when Mutal raised his fist.

Talia's vision blurred. She turned away, fighting back memories of her brothers squabbling in exactly the same tone. Taking a deep breath, Talia slid her hands into the sleeves of her robe and pulled out two knives.

Lakhim clapped her hands again, and guards appeared in the doorway, weapons drawn. They must have been waiting just outside. Lakhim didn't trust Talia any more than Talia trusted her.

Talia knelt, flipping both knives so she held them by the blades. She extended the first to Mutal. "Your strike was slow and clumsy. When you attack, hold the blade flat to slide between the ribs." She spun the knife and demonstrated against an imaginary foe. "At your height, the kidneys are a good target. The inside of the thigh is also good. A cut there can sever the artery."

Mutal glanced at his grandmother, waiting for her approval before accepting the knife with his left hand. His fingers tightened around the hilt. He chewed his lower lip and looked up at Talia.

Talia's mouth quirked. "Try it, and I'll throw you into that pool."

Danielle snorted.

"What is it?" Talia asked.

"I may not understand the language, but I know that tone." Danielle smiled. "Who says you wouldn't have made a good mother?"

Talia pushed that thought from her mind as she turned to Mahatal, offering him the second knife. "Don't let fear stop you. When your brother attacks, your enemy's attention will be on him. Use that distraction to strike. Twist the blade when you pull back, to break the suction and create a larger wound."

Mahatal ignored the knife. "Is that how you murdered my father?"

Talia stood, returning the knife to its sheath. She couldn't blame him for hating her. To the twins, their father had no doubt been the prince of the stories, the hero who rescued Sleeping Beauty from the hedge, only to be betrayed by the very princess he had saved.

"Why do you stand there?" Mahatal shouted to the guards. "She killed my father!"

"Mahatal, stop this," said Lakhim.

He grabbed the mage's arm. "Ullam, if you ever loved my father, you'll strike her down with your magic."

"*Enough.*" Lakhim's thin fingers snatched Mahatal's wrist. She dragged him through the doorway, passing him to one of the guards. "See that they remain in their room until I arrive."

Mahatal stormed off, but Mutal turned back to Talia, turning the knife over in his hands. "You aren't how I imagined you." With those words, he followed his brother.

Talia stared after them, her stomach churning.

"Mahatal is a passionate child." Lakhim stepped around to block the doorway, her message clear. Talia's time with the twins was over. "Mutal's temper is cold, but Mahatal's burns like fairy fire."

"Like their uncles," Talia said, deliberately reminding Lakhim whose children these were. Lakhim's face turned dark.

The scent of the boys' nervous sweat hung in the air long after they had left. Talia inhaled deeply, then turned away from the queen. "I'm ready."

Ullam and a half dozen guards escorted them back through the palace.

"You haven't lost your family's heritage, you know," Danielle said softly. "You simply passed that heritage to your sons. Your bloodline will still rule Arathea once Lakhim is gone."

Talia sighed. "I should thank you for what you did today. Ever since I fled Arathea, I've been waiting for Lakhim to find me. Watching the shadows and hoping when the day came that no one else would be caught up in the bloodshed." She turned away. "I should thank you, but I can't. Not yet."

"I know," said Danielle.

No more words were necessary. Talia glanced back only once, then did her best to push this place from her mind. Snow and Faziya were waiting, and she was ready to go back to Lorindar.

To go *home*.

Snow tugged her head scarf forward, trying to shade her eyes. Talia and Danielle seemed to be taking their sweet time. She had spied through Danielle's bracelet long enough to make sure nothing had gone wrong, but the longer she split her vision, the worse her head pounded.

Instead, she busied herself studying the remnants of Zestan's magic. The troll's fairy servants had already vanished, but Zestan's remained, bits of wind and flame and moonlight given the illusion of life. It was one of the latter Snow watched now, a glimmer of moonlight the size of a large coin that danced along the sand.

The ghosts were gone. The Kha'iida believed they had escaped into the desert, but Snow disagreed. The princes had died searching for Talia. Having found her at last, there was nothing left to hold them in this world.

Snow was more worried about the Wild Hunt. Without Zestan to command them, who knew what they would do. They *might* return to their old ways, their end-less journey across this world. They might not even re-member Danielle and Snow, or if they did, they might not care. All Snow knew was that she would be talking to Trittibar and Father Isaac the instant she returned home, and she didn't intend to rest until the wards around the palace had been strengthened.

If that failed . . . Zestan had controlled the Wild Hunt using the promise of moonlight. Anything fairy magic could accomplish, human magic could duplicate. She reached out with her mind, and the flicker of moonlight vanished. She looked into the mirrors on her armband, where a tiny moonbeam now danced.

Oh, yes. If the Wild Hunt returned, Snow would be ready. She couldn't wait to get home and share what she had learned with Trittibar. Ever since arriving in Arathea, she had wondered how fairy magic could function without a hill. Zestan's body had given her the clue she needed. The peri acted as her own fairy hill. Perhaps she had absorbed the magic from the crys-tal mountains, or perhaps peri were natural sources of power.

That was how the fire sprite had been able to create a fairy ring within the walls of Whiteshore Palace. Zestan must have imbued it with her own magic.

She considered trying to catch the rest of Zestan's servants, but trapping even a single glint of moonlight had been enough to make her eyes water. She sat down and rested her head against the wall until the pain eased. She would be fine as soon as she had a chance to rest, preferably in a real bed, with real food and drink.

Shouts alerted her to Talia's return. The black horse trotted lazily through the sand. The raqeem was the first to approach them. He and Talia spoke too softly for Snow to hear, but when he turned around, his relief was obvious.

He raised his voice. "Talia Malak-el-Dahshat has

renounced her claim to the throne of Arathea. In exchange, the queen has generously agreed to spare Talia's life."

Talia raised her eyebrows. "Something like that, yes." She jumped down, holding Roudette's cape bundled beneath her arm.

"The ebony horse will take us to the coast," Danielle said. "Captain Hephyra and the *Phillipa* are waiting for us."

"What are you going to do with that?" Snow asked, indicating the cape.

"Lock it away." Talia rubbed her arms. "When I wore it, the only thing I wanted was to fight. I didn't care who."

"Oh." Snow blinked, feigning confusion. "So it didn't really affect you, then?"

"Hush." Talia exchanged a look with Danielle. "I could have killed my own son. My next blow would have snapped his spine."

Danielle smiled and reached out to take the cape. "Find me a mother who hasn't wanted to strike her child at one time or another. What matters is you stopped."

Both Snow and Talia turned to stare. "You're joking," said Snow. "Princess Danielle Whiteshore, the most foolishly forgiving woman in all Lorindar?"

"Do you remember last month when Jakob stole my glass slippers?" Danielle asked, still smiling. "He refused to give them back, screaming loudly enough he woke Beatrice. He tossed one down the stairs. Then he smashed the other against my knuckles when I tried to take it away. I was ready to lock him in the dungeon."

"Talia!" Faziya hurried toward them, her robe bloody from tending the injured. Snow and Danielle might as well have turned invisible. Talia stepped past them both, wrapping her arms around Faziya.

Danielle took Snow's arm and tugged her away. "Come on."

Snow didn't fight her. She did, however, cast a small spell to allow her to listen in.

"So you're to leave again?" Faziya was asking.

"Lakhim suggested it would be best for all involved if I were to leave Arathea as soon as possible," Talia said.

"I had hoped . . . I thought with you having killed Zestan—"

Snow could imagine Talia's sad smile. "That only makes things worse. Sleeping Beauty, Protector of Arathea. I might have given up the throne, but she'll always fear me." Talia hesitated, then blurted out, "You could come to Lorindar with us."

Snow stumbled. Danielle caught her arm. "Are you all right?"

"A little dizzy," said Snow. "It will pass. Have you spoken with Armand yet?"

Warmth suffused Danielle's face. She touched two fingers to her bracelet. "I've told him we'll be returning home soon."

Snow nodded absently, still listening to Talia and Faziya. Faziya was inspecting Talia's hand, chiding her for not wrapping it. Snow snorted. *She* could have taken care of Talia's hand if Faziya hadn't come running.

She almost walked into Danielle, who had stepped around in front of Snow. "What's wrong?"

"Stop eavesdropping on your friend," Danielle said.

Snow stuck out her tongue.

"She's not going to leave you, you know."

"What do you mean?"

"The two of you have been uncomfortable with one another ever since you learned of Talia's feelings for you." Danielle gave a mock-scowl. "I'm getting a little tired of it."

Snow matched her pose. "Oh, really?"

"You're not upset because she's attracted to you. You're scared that's all there is. That if she finds someone else, she won't need you anymore."

"That's ridiculous," Snow said, keeping her voice light. "Who else is going to save her hide the next time she gets herself into more trouble than she can fight?"

Danielle simply folded her arms.

"Do you know why happily ever after is a lie?" Snow asked. "Because life is change. When it was just Talia and me working for Queen Bea, I loved it. Then you came along. That turned out to be a good change."

"I'm glad," said Danielle.

"Talia and I weren't sure about you at first, but you turned out all right." She winked. "Now Beatrice is dying. You're going to be busier around the palace. Talia . . . I don't know what she'll do. Did you know Captain Hephyra invited Talia to turn pirate with her?"

"She didn't!"

Snow grinned. "Talia told me about it earlier this year. The point is, people move on."

"Is that what you see when you watch them?" Danielle asked. "Talia moving on?"

"I see her finally loosening up and having some fun. About damn time, too." Snow touched her mirror. "Don't worry about me, Princess. I have plenty to keep me occupied when we get home. Have you seen Reynald, the new smith? The way that man handles his hammer . . ."

Danielle laughed and took her hand, tugging her back toward the palace. "What happened to Zestan's body?"

"Muhazil and the Kha'iida brought it into the garden. He means to carry the body back to the mountains. I guess a fallen god is still a god."

They stopped at the entrance to the palace, and Snow looked back to where Talia and Faziya stood with their fingers interlaced. Talia turned, as if she could sense someone watching. Her smile faltered slightly when she spotted Snow.

Snow winked, ignoring the churning in her stomach. With a touch of her hand, she ended her spell, giving them their privacy.

*   *   *

"I can't," Faziya said softly. "I wouldn't know how to survive anywhere else. The desert is in my blood, Talia."

"I learned to survive in Lorindar," Talia said, knowing it was futile.

"Of course you did." Faziya laughed. "You're a city-dwelling massim. We barbarians are a different breed. Living in the temple was difficult enough." She pulled Talia close, bodies pressing together in a way that would have been highly improper in Lorindar. "But it might be nice to visit for a while, to see your home and spend time with you without having to worry about fairy hunters chasing us down."

Talia's heart was a snarl of emotion. She pushed the worst aside. She knew Faziya would never be happy anywhere else. She could dwell on that fact, or she could enjoy the time they had. Faziya would come with her. It was enough for today. That she would return to Arathea was something to face at a later time. "Remember one thing. If anyone offers you black pudding, say no."

Faziya laughed again, a sound of pure joy. "Talia, could you do something for me?"

Talia pulled her close. "Anything."

"In all your time at the temple, you never spoke of your family." Faziya kissed her lightly on the side of the neck. "You never even speak the names of your brothers or sister."

"No, I suppose not." She gave a halfhearted shrug. "It was easier that way, trying not to remember."

"I'd like to know."

Talia looked past her to the ruins of her home. "My sister was Janilwa. She looked like our mother, far more than I ever did. Taqib was my oldest brother. He loved horses more than anything in the world. Yasan was next, and he was more trouble than the rest of us combined. Fahni was the youngest. He—" Her throat knotted, and she turned her face away. "I'm sorry."

Once upon a time...

A broken mirror. A stolen child.
A final mission to try to stop an enemy they
never dreamed they would face.

When a spell gone wrong shatters Snow White's
enchanted mirror, a demon escapes into the
world. The demon's magic distorts the vision of
all it touches, showing them only ugliness and
hate. It is a power which turns even friends and
lovers into mortal foes, one which will threaten
humans and fairies alike.

And the first to fall under the demon's power
is the princess Snow White.

Danielle, Talia, and Snow return in

The Snow Queen's Shadow
by Jim C. Hines

Coming Summer 2011

"Do we look like we need to be rescued?"

DAW 156

"When you're ready," Faziya whispered.

Talia closed her eyes. "I'd like that."

Faziya kissed her again, then pulled away. "It was kind of Queen Lakhim to let you borrow the ebony horse to reach your ship."

Talia's lip twitched. "Yes. 'Borrow.'"

Faziya chuckled and hugged her again. When they finally broke apart, Talia kissed her and nudged her toward the palace. "I'll join you in a moment."

She waited for Faziya to leave, then turned in a slow circle. Eight years ago she had awakened here and made her way through the hedge to find everything she knew gone.

Zestan's sandstorms had buried the last traces of the hedge. The lakebed was a rippled plain of sand, and the gold hills stretched out beyond. She breathed in the air, smiling at the lush, sweet scent.

She felt . . . *free.*

Once upon a time...

Cinderella, whose real name is Danielle
Whiteshore, did marry Prince Armand.
And their wedding was a dream come true.

But not long after the "happily ever after,"
Danielle is attacked by her stepsister Charlotte,
who suddenly has all sorts of magic to call upon.
And though Talia the martial arts master—
otherwise known as Sleeping Beauty—
comes to the rescue, Charlotte gets away.

That's when Danielle discovers a number of disturb-
ing facts: Armand has been kidnapped; Danielle is
pregnant; and the Queen has her own Secret Service
that consists of Talia and Snow (White, of course).
Snow is an expert at mirror magic and heavy-duty
flirting. Can the princesses track down Armand and
rescue him from the clutches of some of
Fantasyland's most nefarious villains?

The Stepsister Scheme
by Jim C. Hines
978-0-7564-0532-8

"Do we look like we need to be rescued?"

DAW 130

There is an old story...

...you might have heard it—about a young mermaid, the daughter of a king, who saved the life of a human prince and fell in love.

So innocent was her love, so pure her devotion, that she would pay any price for the chance to be with her prince. She gave up her voice, her family, and the sea, and became human. But the prince had fallen in love with another woman.

The tales say the little mermaid sacrificed her own life so that her beloved prince could find happiness with his bride.

The tales lie.

Danielle, Talia, and Snow from
The Stepsister Scheme return in

The Mermaid's Madness
by Jim C. Hines
978-0-7564-0583-0

"Do we look like we need to be rescued?"

DAW 109

Jim Hines
The Jig the Goblin series

"Clever satire… Reminiscent of Terry Pratchett and
Robert Asprin at their best."
—*Romantic Times*

"If you've always kinda rooted for the little guy, even
maybe had a bit of a place in your heart for Gollum,
rather than the Boromirs and Gandalfs of the world,
pick up Goblin Quest."
—*The SF Site*

"This exciting adult fairy tale is filled with adventure
and action, but the keys to the fantasy are Jig and the
belief that the mythological creatures are real in the
realm of Jim C. Hines."
—*Midwest Book Review*

"A rollicking ride, enjoyable from beginning to end…
Jim Hines has just become one of my must-read
authors." —Julie E. Czerneda

GOBLIN QUEST	978-07564-0400-0
GOBLIN HERO	978-07564-0442-0
GOBLIN WAR	978-07564-0493-2

To Order Call: 1-800 788-6262
www.dawbooks.com

Seanan McGuire

The October Daye Novels

"...will surely appeal to readers who enjoy my books, or those of Patrica Briggs." —*Charlaine Harris*

"Well researched, sharply told, highly atmospheric and as brutal as any pulp detective tale, this promising start to a new urban fantasy series is sure to appeal to fans of Jim Butcher or Kim Harrison."—*Publishers Weekly*

ROSEMARY AND RUE
978-0-7564-0571-7

A LOCAL HABITATION
978-0-7564-0596-0

AN ARTIFICIAL NIGHT
978-0-7564-0626-4

(Available September 2010)

To Order Call: 1-800-788-6262
www.dawbooks.com

DAW 142